"I'm always thrilled by seeing a new author press the boundaries of the conventions of fantasy. Chris Evans does just that—taking the broad sword and sorcery archetypes and placing them squarely in a new and exciting environment."

—R. A. Salvatore

"An outstanding military fantasy series unlike any since Glen Cook's beloved Black Company series."

—*Library Journal*

Critical acclaim for Chris Evans's epic fantasy series

ASHES OF A BLACK FROST

BOOK THREE OF THE IRON ELVES

"Evans ably continues the saga of the determined and driven Iron Elves and their valiant leader in this gritty follow-up. . . . Heroic action that keeps fans coming back."

—*Publishers Weekly*

"Mixes magic and early 19th-century warfare and showcases intriguingly memorable characters. Fans of Glen Cook's Black Company novels, Naomi Novik's Temeraire series, and James Barclay's Chronicles of the Raven will appreciate this well-detailed and intensely told story."

—*Library Journal*

"Fast-paced, action-filled . . . with characters from fairy tales to nightmares who all play their roles beautifully, especially the enigmatic Konowa Swift Dragon."

Reviews

They might be doomed, damned, and buggered for all eternity, but that didn't mean they couldn't sparkle like a diamond in the sun and grin like a skull in the moonlight on their way to oblivion.

Praise for

THE LIGHT OF BURNING SHADOWS
BOOK TWO OF THE IRON ELVES

"Evans evokes the era of Napoleon with muskets and slashing swords while neatly mixing in military fantasy, swords and sorcery, and a great deal of success; readers will no doubt end up desperate for the next volume."

—*Publishers Weekly* (starred review)

"A gutsy fantasy set in a world of imperial greed and magical plotting, with an eye for the ordinary soldier's plight that would have done Kipling proud."

—Karen Traviss, #1 *New York Times* bestselling author

A DARKNESS FORGED IN FIRE
BOOK ONE OF THE IRON ELVES
A *Library Journal* Best Book of 2008

"A masterful debut—if J.R.R. Tolkien and Bernard Cornwell had a literary love child, this would be it."

—Karen Traviss, #1 *New York Times* bestselling author

"Strong storytelling, a compelling cast of heroes and villains, and a keen knowledge of military tactics of the Napoleonic era . . . A splendid read for both fans of science fiction and fantasy military adventure. Highly recommended."

—*Library Journal* (starred review)

Also by Chris Evans

A DARKNESS FORGED IN FIRE
(Book One of The Iron Elves)

THE LIGHT OF BURNING SHADOWS
(Book Two of The Iron Elves)

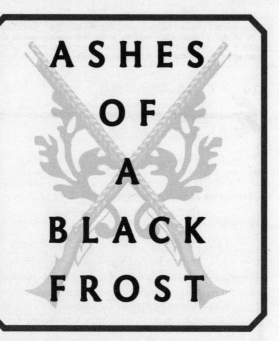

ASHES
OF
A
BLACK
FROST

BOOK THREE OF THE IRON ELVES

Chris Evans

POCKET BOOKS

NEW YORK   LONDON   TORONTO   SYDNEY   NEW DELHI

Pocket Books
A Division of Simon & Schuster, Inc.
1230 Avenue of the Americas
New York, NY 10020

This book is a work of fiction. Names, characters, places, and incidents either are products of the author's imagination or are used fictitiously. Any resemblance to actual events or locales or persons, living or dead, is entirely coincidental.

Copyright © 2011 by Chris Evans

Map by Michael Bechthold

First Pocket Books paperback edition October 2012

POCKET and colophon are registered trademarks of Simon & Schuster, Inc.

For information about special discounts for bulk purchases, please contact Simon & Schuster Special Sales at 1-866-506-1949 or business@simonandschuster.com.

The Simon & Schuster Speakers Bureau can bring authors to your live event. For more information or to book an event contact the Simon & Schuster Speakers Bureau at 1-866-248-3049 or visit our website at www.simonspeakers.com.

Manufactured in the United States of America

10   9   8   7   6   5   4   3   2   1

ISBN 978-1-4391-8067-9
ISBN 978-1-4391-8068-6 (ebook)

To the shooting star who lit up my sky
and helped me find my way.
Thank you.

We giving all gained all.
Neither lament us nor praise.
Only in all things recall,
It is Fear, not Death that slays.
—Rudyard Kipling, "Epitaphs of the War"

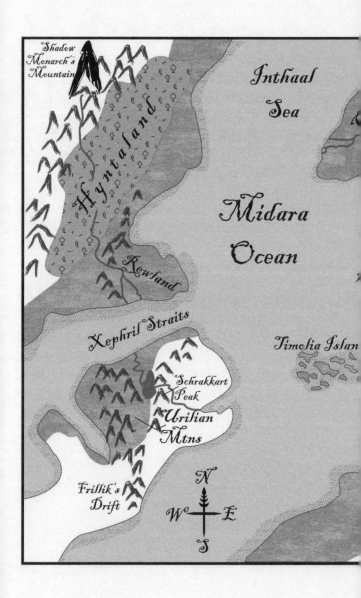

Shadow
Monarch's
Mountain

Inthaal
Sea

Hyntasand

Midara
Ocean

Rewsand

Xephris Straits

Timolia Islan

Schrakkart
Peak

Urilian
Mtns

Frillik's
Drift

N
W   E
S

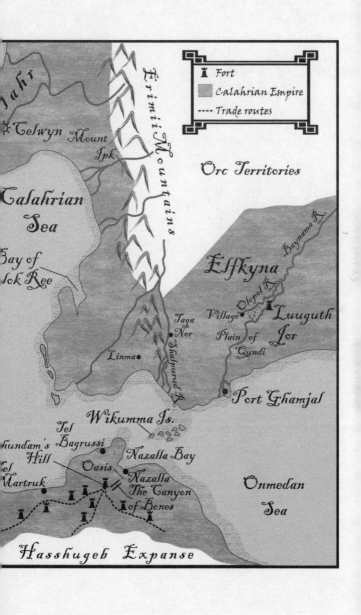

Mrs. Yimt Arkhorn
4th Level, Blue Granite Quarry
Yussel County
Calahr

It is with deepest regret that I must inform you that your husband, Regimental Sergeant Major Yimt Arkhorn (per battlefield promotion) of the Iron Elves Regiment commanded by His Majesty, the Prince of Calahr, is reported missing and presumed dead. Though his body has not been recovered, this letter will serve as right and proper legal claim in all matters from the date of reception of this notice that the aforementioned soldier is struck from the rolls of the Imperial Army and considered deceased. As his immediate kin, you are hereby entitled to compensation to be paid by the state per the Fallen Soldier Act as decreed by Her Majesty the Queen. This includes a widow's pension in the amount of 1/3 of your husband's pay plus an additional 1/10 per living child until the child has reached the age of sixteen, been incarcerated, institutionalized, died, or joined the Imperial Army or Navy. Additional compensation may accrue dependent on whether your husband is awarded any posthumous medals.

Major Konowa Swift Dragon
Signed by Major Konowa Swift Dragon on behalf of H.R.H. The Prince of Calahr

P.S.: Please forgive the rather formal wording of the notice. Having known your husband for only a ~~short~~ brief period of time I feel certain that he would think this letter far too premature. Alas, I wasn't there when he fell and so there is little I can tell you about the circumstances. I hope in time we will know more, and I assure you that I will let you know. What I can tell you is your husband was one of the toughest, bravest, mule-headed bastards I have ever had the pleasure to lead in battle. He destroyed a lot of the enemy and saved a lot of lives. You have every right to be proud of him.

I am so very sorry for your loss.

Yours sincerely,
Major Konowa Swift Dragon

ONE

The night sky deepened, stripped bare in the growing cold. Stars burst forth like silent musket volleys, pricking the heavens with rosettes of white light. On the desert floor below, remnants of lives littered the sand in all directions. Broken bodies draped limply over rocks. Ash piles marked the deaths, though not the final resting places, of many more. Bones jutted from the sand at angles—not odd angles, though, for that would suggest that there were ways bones could protrude that made sense—and the eyes of those still living stared and saw nothing.

Or did their best not to.

Major Konowa Swift Dragon, second-in-command of the Calahrian Empire's Iron Elves, stood among the carnage. His six-foot-tall frame loomed above the fallen like the last tree in a dying forest. Red-rimmed eyes and cracked and bleeding lips stained with black powder offered the only contrast in a face coated in gray soot. The ferocity of the battle marked his uniform, too. The once vibrant silver green of the cloth was now mottled in blood, dirt, black powder, and bits of gore. Ripped and burned sections of uniform exposed strips of bare brown flesh streaked with grime.

He didn't know how long he'd been standing there. He realized he wasn't sure what time it was, or even what day. Battle did that, winnowing away everything until all that was left was a furiously burning spark that ignited only one of two actions—kill, or flee and be killed. But battles didn't last forever, at least, not in the physical realm. Konowa felt his warrior veneer slip a little as time reasserted itself. The toxic high of battle that sustained and drove him when he shouldn't have been able to swing his saber one more time began to subside. Visions of the grotesque, the obscene, and the heartbreaking began leaching into tissue and memory, staining his very character and thoughts so deeply that no lifetime of drink and repression would erase them.

The wind snatched at the loose strands of his long black hair tied in the back in a regulation queue. A storm front was moving in.

With his left hand he absently pushed the hairs out of his eyes and behind his ear. His fingers paused as they traced the shorn ear tip. He'd been marked as a chosen one by the Shadow Monarch, his ear tip frost-blackened in the womb. He was one of the first so marked to remain with the tribe, albeit minus part of an ear. So fearful were the elves of the Hyntaland of the Shadow Monarch's touch that they chose to abandon babies born with the disfigurement to their deaths in the wild rather than raise them. In this way the Shadow Monarch gained Her children, collecting the babes and raising them as Her own. In time, they grew to be as twisted and dark as the Silver Wolf Oak at the center of Her mountain forest.

Neither their fate nor Konowa's was one any elf should have to bear, but no one had asked if they accepted the burden. A thin, cold pain gripped his chest where the black acorn, the source of the Iron Elves eternal existence, rested against his chest. It was a reminder that the power of the frost fire and the curse of a hellish life after death had been a burden of his own choosing.

His hand reached up to adjust his shako, the distinctive tall black hat with its winged appendages, and realized it had fallen off. He looked down and spied it a few feet away. He walked over slowly, ignoring the wet sounds beneath his boots, bent down, and picked it up. When he tipped it right side up to place it on his head, a silver locket fell out and landed in the sand. *It's not my shako*, he realized.

After looking inside to see if anything else was there, he put the shako on his head and crouched down to where the locket lay half-buried in the sand. He grasped it gingerly between finger and thumb as if he were plucking a rose and trying not to get jabbed by a thorn. The metal was cool to the touch and Konowa realized that it wasn't silver at all, but simple pewter. It was oval in shape and no more than an inch tall, and a small post at one end was broken where a chain would have fastened, no doubt explaining why the soldier had chosen to keep it under his shako for safekeeping.

Konowa stood back up, cringing as his left knee spasmed and threatened to collapse. He closed his fist and pounded it against the joint, and the spasm shuddered to a halt. When he opened his hand again, he saw that the locket had popped open. He brought his right hand up to open the locket all the way and stopped in surprise. He was still holding his saber.

A sliver of his reflection stared back at him from the polished steel. He twisted the blade slowly, letting it catch the starlight. Shadows slid across his face, arcing from nose to eye socket, concealing and revealing eyes that had seen more than they ever should.

Still, they did not blink.

He lowered the blade and sheathed it one handed in a single, fluid motion. Releasing his grip on the pommel sent blood flowing back into his fingers with a fiery sting. He flexed them a few times, then pried the locket completely open. The hinge broke and the two halves lay flat in his palm. The right half contained a small lock of blond hair tied with a thin, purple thread. The left bore an inscription of just four words—*Come back to me.*

Konowa's hands fell to his sides, the pieces of locket tumbling to the sand. Noises he hadn't realized were there filled his ears. The soft *ting-ting* of cooling musket barrels; the gulping down of brackish water by throats parched and raw from inhaling smoke and shouting; and a single, ragged scream from someone dying. All of it slid in deep between the ear and the brain like a sliver that would never work free.

Come back to me.

It was a plea, an admonition, a desperate hope from a wife. Everything was implied—love, trust, need, desire—but nothing would be fulfilled.

Nearby, a quill began scratching across a piece of paper. The sound carried to Konowa in thin, clear tones. He felt the rhythm of the point as it curved and sliced its path. He turned, letting something more than his hearing guide him. Her Majesty's Scribe, Rallie Synjyn, sat on a rock among the bodies, a scroll unfurled across her lap. Her black cloak blended with the darkness as if the night itself was part of her. The feather barbs of her quill fluttered as the wind and her writing picked up speed.

Konowa watched, mesmerized. From this distance he couldn't see what she was writing, yet he imagined he saw every word. The quill rose above the page, moved over, and plunged back down. He saw the story unfold back in the world they'd left behind.

This desert of wasted lives and damaged souls was a battle won, the sharp end of imperial power applied. On maps in headquarters far away, the red-rimmed limits of the empire would surge outward as another pin was pushed in place. Bottles would be uncorked and talk of promotions—discreet of course, lest one be seen as too eager—would creep into conversation. Through the news sheets and crier services, the citizens of the Calahrian Empire would learn of the Iron Elves' latest feat of arms and rejoice at their triumph over the Shadow Monarch's minions and the ancient desert power of Kaman Rhal's dragon. Evil was thwarted once again and the power of a new Star was delivered unto the people, courtesy of the benevolent Empire. The cost—fifty-four soldiers dead, wounded, and missing, and a couple hundred native warriors lost against untold hundreds of the enemy—would seem satisfactorily grim and proportionate.

Sergeant Yimt Arkhorn and most of his squad. Missing . . .

. . . his mother, Chayii Red Owl; his father, Jurwan Leaf Talker; Tyul Mountain Spring; and Jir, his bengar companion. Missing . . .

Visyna . . .

These names, these people, would mean little to someone back home, except for a very few for whom these names would be everything. No doubt the masses would show appropriate concern at the frittering away of valuable resources in such a far-flung place. Konowa suspected they would be satisfied that the losses suffered offered the requisite sense of drama and the all-important Imperial motif of the few overcoming the many. No one, not even an empire, wants to be viewed as a bully.

Konowa knew celebrations would ensue, albeit without the guests of honor that had made it possible. Still, it was everyone's patriotic duty to hoist a pint, shout brave slogans, and remind all those within earshot that if not for "this bum knee" or "a wife and six young children to feed" they, too, would be over there, instead of quartered safe in here. Smiles would abound as revelers congratulated one another, winking as they nodded their heads and said with gruff pride, "Damn right, we showed them, eh?" If a twinge of embarrassment caught in their throats as they pronounced "we," it would be quickly washed away with the next round of drinks.

For now, however, the "we" were confined to a few small acres of ravaged land so far from home that home seemed more like a fevered dream than something real. There was no backslapping, no loud shouts of martial prowess or Imperial superiority. Quiet sobs of those trying to understand that the "we" were now fewer were studiously ignored by those fighting to keep it together. The tenets of diplomatic doctrine and the flush of Imperial pride found no purchase here. Later, perhaps,

Konowa thought, they would see themselves as victors. For now, it was enough to struggle to comprehend that they were survivors.

The wind worried the edges of Rallie's scroll. Konowa shivered. Rallie paused, her quill frozen above the paper. She looked up, pushing the hood of her black cloak back on her head. Gray, frizzy hair framed her face, hard-earned wisdom etched into every crease. The end of the cigar clenched between her teeth glowed fiery orange as she inhaled. Her eyes found his.

She was weeping.

A moment later her face disappeared in a veil of smoke. The drop of ink at the tip of the quill trembled. A chill breeze set the downy barbs thrumming. The drop fell, splattering onto the page.

It began to snow.

Konowa blinked. Flakes fell and skittered along the sand and the bodies lying there. A few snowflakes found the gap between his neck and the collar of his uniform, sending tiny rivulets of water down his back as they melted. He took a breath, his whole body shuddering as he let it out.

It was snowing.

Snowing in the middle of the bloody desert.

The laugh that escaped his lips startled him. He gritted his teeth, but more laughter rose up, spilling out in ragged gasps. His breath exploded in chalky sprays in the cooling night air. Soldiers lifted their heads to turn and stare. He couldn't stop. His ribs ached and his lungs seared as they struggled for air, yet the laughter only grew.

He stood surrounded by death. The very smell of it permeated him so deeply he could no longer tell where it ended and he began. So many gone, condemned to a living hell of service after death—and here he was, laughing. He doubled over and braced his hands against his knees, but the laughter would not die. The natural order, always a buzzing, confused noise on the edge of his understanding, coursed around him as if storm-tossed by the approaching blizzard. He didn't even bother to make sense of it. He didn't need to. He stood up straight, gasping for air, with tears running down his face. He was still laughing, but now finally under control.

He was alive, and he was an elf. Maybe not an elf like the others, but then who said he had to be? What mattered was what he felt. A dawning, as yet barely grasped and understood determination, began to fill him. It flooded into the spaces left empty by the losses he'd suffered. It calmed, though it did not quench, the pain and agony he'd been using as fuel. This was something different, something quieter, yet stronger because of it. He knew now in a way he hadn't before that the fallen did not die in vain. The missing would be found, no matter what their fate. And the Blood Oath of the Iron Elves would be broken.

He had no words for it, and doubted he could explain it even if he did. This went beyond anything he could say. All his life he'd known anger. It burned him, but he'd come to enjoy that pain. He was never more alive than when he was screaming at the top of his lungs and charging headlong at the enemy. Now . . . now he saw the first steps on a new path, one that saw beyond the horizon of battle.

He took in a few deep breaths, letting the laughter subside. So be it. There was always a price to pay, and his would be higher than most. He would pay it a thousand times over to end what the Shadow Monarch had started. He wasn't going to be a pawn any longer. Not for Her, not for the Empire, and not for his anger. He rolled his shoulders and stood straighter. His body relaxed as muscles unknotted. He felt . . . taller, stronger, more alive than he had in a long time. In another place he might have even felt happy, but the carnage around him ensured that that emotion remained distant. If there was any joy at all to be found, it was in this: Before he took his last breath, he would end Her.

Konowa became aware that silence had fallen around him. The sound of Rallie's quill on paper had ceased. He glanced up. The stars had vanished, the sky muddled with thickening clouds.

"It appears to be snowing, Major," Rallie said, as gruff and matter-of-fact as ever. Konowa was relieved to hear she had stopped crying. He couldn't handle that, not right now.

He shook his head and snow cascaded down from his shako. *This wasn't good.* Konowa had never been to the desert before and had no inkling of the annual levels of rain or other weather events that might occur within the Hasshugeb Expanse. Still, he was certain that before tonight, the chances of snow blanketing this typically sunbaked landscape had been specifically "none." And before his arrival, the chances of snow falling in this desert wasteland would have remained none, probably for eternity. But of course, those damn stars were changing all that.

Konowa turned his gaze to the north. The Shadow Monarch's forest blocked his view. He should have found comfort in the fact that the malevolent trees and the many foul creatures that roamed within their thrashing embrace were retreating, pushed back by the power unleashed by the fallen Blue Star, the Jewel of the Desert. Having transformed into a towering tree, it rose high above the valley floor, the blue fire of its energy blazing from deep within branch and leaf, wreathing every shadow in cobalt. He wanted to find solace in the knowledge that here, as in Elfkyna, the power of the Stars was greater than that of the Shadow Monarch, but he couldn't.

One of the reasons stood a few yards away, watching.

Konowa risked a glance at Private Alwyn Renwar. The soldier, if that's what he still was, had not moved since his transformation. Once a meek and trembling lad barely able to hold a musket steady, jumping at his own shadow . . . now in command of the shades of the dead.

In another time and another place, Private Renwar's lone battle against a long-dead dragon magically reanimated from the skeletal remains of donor bodies would have earned him the highest medal of valor and a hero's funeral. No one should have survived the destruction of that monster. But Renwar had, his body a fused bonfire between the competing magics of Rhal's dragon and the Shadow Monarch's oath. Perhaps his intent had been to die, but like Konowa, a sense of service had compelled him to make a far more difficult choice.

I don't know whether to pity him or hate him.

"You might try talking to him," Rallie said. "He's lost a lot this night. We all have."

Konowa shivered and didn't bother to lie to himself that it was because of the snow. Rallie's uncanny ability to know, or at least sense, what he was thinking always left him feeling unsettled. He took a steadying breath and turned to face her. "I know, but he made a deal with Her," he said. "He made a deal with the Shadow Monarch and became Her Emissary. He defeated the dragon because She gave him the power to do so."

Rallie shook her head, her frizzy gray hair obscuring her eyes. Her quill remained poised above the paper. Konowa noticed that despite the falling snow, not a single flake fell on the scroll laid out before her. "You're stating the facts, but not the truth of them. He is *Their* Emissary, not Hers. He speaks for the dead now."

Konowa waved away the distinction with a hand. "Hers, theirs, the difference is moot. He forsook the regiment. He had a duty to fight against Her, not grow stronger by joining Her."

"Major, don't you see, he followed your example," Rallie said, brushing snow from her hair. "He sacrificed his well-being and that of this regiment for something greater."

"The oath remains, Rallie. Those killed still become shades doomed to do Her bidding. Every day Her power over them grows. What is it you think he's accomplished?"

Rallie shook her head from within her hood. "You're wrong, Major. She no longer holds sway over them as She did before. It might seem small, but it is important to note. She might think She's gained an ally in Private Renwar, but I think She's miscalculated, and not for the last time."

Konowa's retort stayed behind his teeth. It was easy to convince yourself that your enemy always knew what it was doing, that every setback you encountered was a

clever trap laid by design. Konowa grudgingly considered that maybe Rallie was right. Maybe the Shadow
Monarch underestimated Alwyn. Twice now She had
failed to acquire a newly returned Star, first at the battle
of Luuguth Jor in Elfkyna, and now in the Canyon of
Bones in the Hasshugeb Expanse. In each case the returning Star, a vessel of natural magic attuned to the
land from which it had originated, was free to transform,
becoming a towering tree coursing with power. They
were guardians in much the same way the Wolf Oaks of
his homeland stood watch over the natural order, bridg-
ing the gap between the heavens and the earth.

"Perhaps, but I don't trust this," he said, waving his
hand vaguely to take in the devastation around them. A
gust of wind blew snow in his face. "The Stars of
Knowledge and Power are returning, and that appears
to be positive, if you don't take into account the growing likelihood that the Empire will be torn apart from
the inside. Every colony and native people see this as
their chance to be free. Who will have the power then?
The Queen in Celwyn, presiding over an ever-dwindling
realm, or the Shadow Monarch on Her mountain? Last
time I checked, the ruling monarch of Calahr couldn't
do this."

Rallie waved her quill in the air. Snowflakes swirled
around it as if deliberately trying to avoid it. "Which
begs the question, why are we still here and not
moving?"

The sigh was past Konowa's lips before he could
stop himself. "Prince Tykkin is still searching through
what's left of Rhal's library." He wasn't sorry the library
had been destroyed in the fighting. The Prince's quest
to find the fabled lost library and bring back to Calahr

all its purported treasure of knowledge accumulated over the ages had seemed more like a boy's adventure than anything else. Perhaps it was Konowa's lack of sentimentality, but a dusty tome on ancient mathematics or spells paled in comparison to the pressing needs of the here and now.

He looked over at her. "I thought you would be there with him." It wasn't meant as a slight. Konowa genuinely assumed Rallie would be interested in ancient artifacts. A spark of self-preservation saved him from saying *ancient* out loud, but as he looked at her pursed lips he suddenly wished he were somewhere, anywhere, else.

"What I'm looking for isn't there," Rallie said, her tone as gruff and kind as ever. She blew the hair from her eyes with a smoky puff from her cigar.

Konowa held her stare for a moment. "Dare I ask what that is?"

Rallie shrugged. "I'm not entirely certain myself. It's more than annoying, I assure you." Her face brightened and the quill stabbed the air. "But I will know it when I find it."

"Won't we all," Konowa said, turning again to look north. A wall of churning snow crawled ever closer. He reflexively hunched his shoulders and stamped his boots in the sand. "It's time we were going." Steel buttressed his voice. He saw his immediate future and it was crystal clear, despite the darkness.

"Visyna was—*is* the one with the knack for weaving the weather. My abilities work along other lines," she said, chuckling at the pun. "Putting aside the fact that you still have to pry His Highness out of the library, how do you think we're going to make it through all that?"

Konowa started to reach for his musket, then instead brought his left hand to rest against his thigh. The fingers of his right hand closed around the pommel of his saber. Black frost sparkled on the hand guard.

"I'm going to have a little chat with the shades' new leader," he said, louder than he'd intended. Soldiers turned to look. The wind piled drifts of snow and sand against his boots as the blue light of the Star tree pulsed faster. He fixed his gaze on Private Renwar and started walking.

Renwar remained where he stood, his head tilted to one side as his completely gray eyes stared without blinking, and without emotion. Black frost limned his wooden leg, a magically rendered replacement after his real leg was lost in the Battle of Luuguth Jor. The blue light of the Star tree shattered and refracted through the wind-driven snow, strobing the air with images that vanished and reappeared.

Shades of the dead materialized around Renwar. They didn't occupy space as much as create a black emptiness in the air, which they temporarily filled while crossing into this world from the one in which they now existed. Looking directly at them was difficult, and not just because of the emotional shock of recognizing the faces of friends and comrades. It physically hurt Konowa to stare at them for any length of time, as if his vision were being drawn into their world, a place where no living being could survive. Pain flowed out from them like a tide, and it was growing stronger.

Konowa narrowed his focus to Renwar. The soldier's gray eyes gave nothing away.

Unbidden, and without orders, the Iron Elves began to form up behind Konowa, falling into step as he marched across the battlefield. They numbered little more than a hundred now, their ranks decimated by claw, fang, arrow, and magics no soldier should ever have to face. Yet they had, and they would again before this was over. Konowa would understand if they loathed him. It was his doing that had bound them to the regiment for eternity. He hated himself for it, but like them, he was a soldier, and together they would see this through to the end. It wasn't particularly elegant or even noble, but it was what a soldier did. And so they marched with him, stride for stride. They could hate him a thousand times over, but they would follow where he led, and for that he loved them all.

They were the Iron Elves.

His Iron Elves.

Konowa kept walking. The knuckles of his right hand lost all color as frost fire sparkled along the entire length of his scabbard. All eyes, living and dead, were on him as he led what was left of the regiment across the sand. With each step, the black acorn against his chest grew colder.

Behind the regiment, the fine, sharp stitch of quill on paper resumed. A legend was being woven into the fabric of history. The late-evening cries of thousands of celebrating patrons in pubs around the Empire would no doubt repeat with full-throated joy what Rallie Synjyn penned this night.

Anyone brave enough to look over Rallie's shoulder, however, would have seen that her quill was not flowing in a smooth left to right path across the page, but instead tracing the same shape repeatedly on one small section of the paper. There, the shape finally clarified and revealed itself as the ink glittered and flickered in the blue light of the Star.

It was the image of a black acorn wreathed in flame with two words in ancient elvish script emblazoned within it.

Æri Mokali:
Into the Fire.

TWO

The new forest of *sarka har* was starving. The Shadow Monarch's blood trees drove their roots into the cold sand of the Hasshugeb Expanse and found little to feed on. They flung their branches in ever-widening arcs trying to trap anything unlucky enough to stray near. Spawned by the Shadow Monarch's frost-burnt Silver Wolf Oak, these twisted saplings craved the heavy, bitter ores found deep in the distant mountains of the Hyntaland. Here, however, in this wide-open plain of dunes and disintegrating rock, there was barely enough to keep them alive. They took what they could from anything living, but there were not enough humans in this sparsely populated land to satisfy their hunger. Rakkes and dark elves roamed between their trunks and would have been easy hunting, but Her Emissary had forbidden such feeding, and they had no choice but to obey its order.

They needed other prey.

A hint of metal tantalized them to the south. They

had no idea it was called Suhundam's Hill, or that elves from Her land now lived there, only that they sensed the great upthrust of rock in the desert floor through vibrations received in their roots. The rock and what lived there promised them ore and blood and something else. There was a darkness there that spoke to them in a language they understood, but how to get to it? The power of the returned Star, the Jewel of the Desert, kept them at bay, hemming them in along the northern coast of the Expanse.

As their need grew, so did their frenzy. Again and again, the *sarka har* flung their roots forward in an effort to seek purchase in the freezing sand and move south. All the while, more *sarka har* sprang forth from the ground behind the tree line that marked the edge of the Shadow Monarch's influence and the beginning of the land now under the protection of the returned Star. Black, gnarled roots stabbed again and again like clawing fingers into the crust of snow over the desert floor in an effort to get to the rock. They scrabbled at the ground in desperation. Trunks shattered and roots snapped and sheared off in the growing violence, but no matter how hard they tried, they could go no further south.

Rakkes and dark elves began to fall to the flailing limbs. A limb skewered a rakke in the chest, the beast's howl of pain cut short as it was torn apart by others joining the feast. A dark elf tilted its head, staring with unblinking eyes at a sight it knew should not be. It continued to stare even after a branch scythed its head off and sent it tumbling to the frozen earth.

When no blast of frost fire struck down the trees, more began to search for food. The screaming didn't last long. When the last of the Shadow Monarch's creatures had been slaughtered within the forest, the *sarka har* thrashed the air in search of more. Their appetite was whet; now they needed to sate it.

Unable to move forward because of the power of the Star, the *sarka har* did what they knew best. The ground was soft here, not like the mountain of Her realm.

The digging would be easy.

Roots burrowed down through the sand, no longer questing for food, but for power. They found fault lines and hairline cracks in the deep bedrock and worked their way in, prying deeper into the darkness. The ground above shook. Cracks opened up in the desert floor, swallowing dozens of *sarka har* into its black depths. Yet Her forest was relentless, pushing its roots ever deeper. When it seemed that their search would be fruitless, a lone *sarka har* found disturbed rock in a channel running from the surface. Its roots wormed into the passage and followed it down. Whenever the passage had been dug, it had been filled in again millennia ago. Nothing had been down this far in a very long time.

Other *sarka har* followed, and soon the passage was filled with writhing, pulsing roots. Only the Shadow Monarch's Silver Wolf Oak had plunged its roots this deep before. The *sarka har* knew only instinct, and instinct told them there was great power down here.

Sand crackled underfoot as Konowa came to a halt five yards away from Private Renwar. Only then did he realize he hadn't given the regiment the order to halt. He half-expected to see them march right past him, but they came to a smooth stop two yards behind him. Konowa didn't need to turn around to see it; he heard it as every right boot slammed down at exactly the same time.

Konowa forced himself to release his grip on his saber. He casually adjusted the hem of his jacket while taking care to look directly at Private Renwar. *I'll be damned if I'll speak first*, he thought.

Silence cocooned the tableau. Snow swirled everywhere, piling in drifts a foot high, but in the space around Private Renwar not a single snowflake fell.

Konowa forced himself to look past Renwar to the shades of the dead. He squinted as if looking into the sun. Their anguish was growing stronger with every passing day. It flowed out from them with an intensity that caught Konowa in its glare and wouldn't let go.

He easily recognized Regimental Sergeant Major Lorian sitting astride the warhorse Zwindarra, the pair of them felled at the battle of Luuguth Jor. Konowa hadn't considered before now that the horse obviously hadn't taken the oath, but Lorian had talked about the bond between a cavalryman and his horse. Tragically, the bond must have been strong enough to carry over into death, dooming the horse to a fate it had no hope of understanding. And there was one-eyed Private Meri Fwynd, the patch still covering his lost eye. Their forms shimmered as if black flames made up their bodies. Konowa couldn't shake the feeling that he was peering into the abyss. Each shade appeared darker at its core, as if a bottomless pit now replaced each dead man's soul. Konowa shuddered at the thought and banished it from his mind. He took a moment to acknowledge each dead face, fearing to see the dwarf among them, but no shade of the salty sergeant appeared. Konowa wished he could feel relieved, but he suspected the white fire of Kaman Rhal had taken Yimt. Private Kester Harkon's shade never rejoined the regiment, and it seemed Sergeant Arkhorn's now shared his fate. Maybe, Konowa allowed, it was a blessing. At least those two weren't condemned to suffer in eternal service.

Konowa ignored the coursing flood of pent-up energy inside him and pushed the frost fire back down. He wouldn't be ruled by emotions. He knew that with all eyes on him, he had to keep his composure. He was an officer in the Calahrian Army, and standing before him was a private in his regiment. If they were buried in snow a mile deep, he would wait for Renwar to salute.

Private Alwyn Renwar continued to stand and stare. His gray eyes appeared depthless and cast his face in a deathly pallor, but the power that resided behind them was unmistakable. Konowa would have shivered if his body had been any warmer.

Somewhere behind Konowa, a ramrod began to slide out of its brass rings. The sound of metal on metal rang like crystal. A soldier was preparing to load a shot.

Renwar's eyes never flickered, but Konowa felt the communication between the private and the shades. Though it didn't seem possible, the air turned colder and every lungful stung as if filled with tiny razors.

Movement to Konowa's left drew both his and Renwar's gaze. Rallie stood off to the side, her quill in one hand and a large scroll of paper in the other. At first Konowa thought she was scratching her head, then realized it was a gesture aimed at Renwar. The private looked back to Konowa. Slowly, as if trying to remember something from a very distant past, he stood to attention and raised his right hand in salute. It wasn't parade-ground sharp, but for here and now it was enough.

More surprisingly and definitely unnerving, the shades followed suit.

Konowa didn't fool himself that the dead saw him as their leader anymore, but they were clearly following the lead of Renwar, and he was still a living member of the regiment Konowa commanded—the Prince notwithstanding.

Konowa waited three beats, enjoying the building tension because now it was his to control, then returned the salute. The air warmed as a collective sigh passed among the soldiers.

"Right," Konowa said, taking his time to exude a calm he didn't feel. "Private Renwar, I'll need you and the lads there to form up and follow me. We're heading due north for the coast." He raised his voice and shifted weight from one boot to another in a studied act of nonchalance. "These Stars are going to keep dropping from here to hell. I don't know about the rest of you, but I don't plan on spending the rest of my life, living or dead, tracking them down one by one. It's time we took this fight to its home, and that's the Shadow Monarch's mountain."

The cheer that greeted this pronouncement was hardly boisterous, but it had a flinty edge to it that filled Konowa with hope. The regiment was still with him . . . or at least those living were.

"You ask a lot," Private Renwar said in his new role as spokesman of the shades. He spoke quietly and carefully, sounding more like the young soldier Konowa knew. Konowa chose to view it as a positive sign even if the response wasn't. He decided to bull ahead.

"I'm not asking, Private, but even if I were, I'm not asking any more of you than I am of myself or the rest of the regiment," Konowa said, taking a couple of steps to turn around and take in the assembled troops. They were no longer the shiny rascals of the Elfkynan campaign. The marching, the fighting, and above all the oath, were taking a fearsome toll. The once tall winged shakos now had a crumpled, weathered look about them. Many wings had shed so many feathers that it was more accurate to describe their headgear as plucked. The original velvety sheen of their Calahrian silver-green jackets was faded, ripped, patched, bloodied, and loose-fitting. Konowa dared look in their eyes, fearing the worst and feeling his heart swell when they met his gaze. There was strength there yet. They were grouped tightly together, shoulder to shoulder, each holding his musket in both hands. Many had attached their bayonet though no bare metal showed signs of frost fire. *Good*, Konowa thought, *good*.

"Every last man here, and Rallie, too, knows this has to end, and it can only end one way, and in one place. That means heading north and setting sail for the Hyntaland. Every hour we stand here is an hour She grows stronger and our mission becomes that much more difficult."

Renwar stared, his eyes revealing nothing of his thoughts. The shades around him, however, began to fade. Konowa felt the unnatural cold of the oath and Her power falling away, to be replaced by the biting wind driving sand and snow before it. Finally, Private Renwar spoke.

"She knows this and will be waiting. She is . . . not pleased. Her Emissary yet lives and marshals Her forces," he said, his gray eyes straying briefly to where Her forest lay in wait beyond the snow.

Konowa silently cursed. Viceroys were clearly proving to be the bane of his existence. The last two appointed to oversee the Protectorate of Greater Elfkyna had turned out to be in league with the Shadow Monarch, each acting in succession as Her Emissary. Konowa had killed the first, which had set the entire chain of events in motion leading to here and now. Private Renwar had dispatched the second, but they weren't done with that foul thing yet. Former viceroy Faltinald Gwyn was nothing if not determined . . . and as a twisted puppet in the Shadow Monarch's hands, he had become manically so.

Konowa allowed himself a little bravado. "Not pleased? I should think so. In fact, I imagine She'll be furious, and maybe a little frightened, too. When the Iron Elves come calling, it doesn't go unnoticed." A few grunts of approval from the troops reached Konowa's ears. They all knew that what he was proposing was tantamount to suicide with only the slimmest chance of survival, but it would be a death on their terms, fighting for something they believed was right. In the life of a soldier, bound by a dark oath or not, that was no small thing.

"As for Her Emissary," Konowa said, his upper lip curling of its own volition into a sneer, "you seem more than capable of handling it. You flung the creature miles!" More soldiers added their voice to the cheers this time. It *had* been a spectacular sight.

The shades of the dead and their leader did not

raise their voices in support. "I did what I had to do. What you ask now is less . . . clear. The oath is different now. Those who perish answer to me, not Her. They now have a voice. *My* voice. Why should those who have gone beyond this life continue the struggle? It won't bring them back. It won't bring Yimt back."

The dwarf's name caught Konowa off guard. For the first time, Konowa fully saw Private Alwyn Renwar for who he was and not as an emissary of the dead before him. "We don't know what happened to him. I can see that he's not among the shades and you should know that no one found his body. He's the toughest bugger in this army. If anyone is a survivor, it's Sergeant Arkhorn."

"I felt him fall, then nothing more," Alwyn said.

Konowa sensed morale crumbling as the regiment pondered the loss of the dwarf, and he spoke quickly to rally what spirit in the troops remained. "Arkhorn's been busted in rank more times in his career than there are one-eyed newts stumbling around a witch's garden, and he's climbed right back up the ranks again every time. I'm not about to count him out yet and neither should you. But whatever the case, I know damn well he'd be placing one very large boot up each and every one of your backsides if he thought for a moment any of you were going to give up, and that includes the Darkly Departed." Konowa looked around and let a grin creep across his face. "I don't know how, but I'm sure he'd find a way to kick a shadow. And with good reason. As long as the Shadow Monarch lives the oath will never be broken. We're tied to Her and She to us. But remember this: Her power, however dark and unwise its origins, is ours to use as well. And that's what we're going to do. Our dead aren't at rest, and Her *sarka har* and rakkes and every other abomination She can pull out of the depths haven't gone away. This only ends one way, and that's when the Shadow Monarch and Her forest are destroyed."

Konowa caught motion out of the corner of his eye and turned. A small group of six soldiers accompanying Prince Tykkin and Viceroy Alstonfar were marching toward them from the direction of the library. The Prince led the way, though his gait suggested a man leaving the pub after a few stiff drinks.

The group came to a stop right between Konowa and the Iron Elves on one side and Private Renwar and the shades of the dead on the other. The Prince looked down at his boots, shuffling them like a child. He sighed and shrugged his shoulders, all the while muttering to himself "It's gone, it's all gone." The smell of smoke wafted off the Prince and the knees of his trousers were black with soot. He'd been down in the burned-out library sifting through the debris since the battle ended. Konowa realized with some surprise that he sympathized with the Prince. Both had come here looking for something—Konowa his lost elves, the Prince the Lost Library of Kaman Rhal—and both had come away empty-handed.

Viceroy Alstonfar shambled to a halt beside the Prince and attempted a smile at Konowa from behind a huge pile of scrolls clutched tightly against his substantial stomach. *Perhaps not entirely empty-handed,* Konowa thought, marveling at the load carried by the Viceroy. More scrolls, bronze canisters, and thin wooden boxes bulged from canvas sacks hung from both shoulders. As Alstonfar bent over to catch his breath, Konowa spied an overfilled pack with even more items on his back.

The Prince turned, and catching Konowa off guard as much as anyone else, motioned to a couple of soldiers to help the diplomat. The Viceroy stood up gratefully and nodded his thanks as the weight of the sacks was taken from him. Despite the cold, the Viceroy's face was red from exertion and beaded in sweat. His pastel blue Calahrian Diplomatic Corps uniform, designed to exemplify and project the peaceful intentions of the Empire during stressful negotiations, now suggested much darker intentions. Konowa tried to imagine the reaction of a foreign ambassador if forced to sit across from the now sooty, sweaty, and bloodstained Viceroy and decided this new look would be very effective during peace talks. Small burns from black powder speckled the front of his coat, indicating that at some point in the battle the Viceroy had actually fired a musket. The once glittering array of silver-plated buttons showed gaps in their ranks and those that remained had lost much of their luster. His scabbard, however, was firmly tied to his belt and the hilt of his saber had clearly been polished since the battle ended. Konowa knew without checking that the blade was clean, too. Alstonfar might appear to the world like a wobbly piece of fat ripe for the first bayonet to split him open and spill his guts on the sand, but there was gristle under there, somewhere deep. The coming march across the sand might help reveal more of it.

The soldiers stood to attention as best they could. Konowa looked at Renwar, wondering what the soldier would do. Never once taking his eyes off Konowa, he, too, stood to attention. The sharp bite in the air lost some of its tooth. The shades of the dead then faded until Konowa couldn't tell a shadow from a swirling patch of snow. *Go back to your darkness and stay there until you're really needed.*

Konowa saluted and Prince Tykkin returned it without fanfare and absently waved the men to stand at ease as he brought his hand back down. Konowa expected him to begin speaking, or possibly yelling, but instead the Prince began to fiddle with his uniform, worrying at a dangling piece of embroidered cord hanging from his lapel. He then reached up to straighten a cockeyed epaulette on his shoulder, slowly spinning in a complete circle like a dog chasing its tail. As he did so every soldier couldn't help but see the left sleeve of his jacket. A large tear ran from the cuff up to the outside of the elbow, revealing a blood-soaked bandage underneath. The Prince—future ruler of the Calahrian Empire— had been in battle, and not on the periphery.

Konowa fought a battle within himself between disgust and admiration and was pleased that admiration won. The Prince, however reluctantly and by sheer misadventure, was becoming a leader of men. The gilded popinjay who grew up on a diet of privilege and arrogance had run stride for stride with the regiment and had not flinched as the Iron Elves smashed into the enemy. Not having taken part in the Blood Oath, there was no afterlife waiting for the Prince, however horrific that life might be. His death in battle would be finite and forever. Leading the men, Konowa knew, was no more than what the Prince should have done, yet he couldn't banish the grudging respect with which he now viewed the future king. Konowa was convinced the Prince was still a royal prick of the first order, but the man wasn't a coward, and that counted for a lot.

"So," the Prince said, looking around at the assembled soldiers. He seemed to struggle for what to say, opening and closing his mouth a few times as he searched for the words. His gaze fell on Alwyn, but if he was startled by the private's appearance he showed no sign of it. Spying Rallie, he dipped his head in acknowledgment and stood up a little straighter as she dutifully poised her quill above her scroll.

"So," the Prince began again, his voice stronger this time. "I should like to congratulate you all on a battle well fought. Due to your exceptional efforts another Star of power has been returned to its land and its people. Our enemies, both ancient and new, have been crushed and sent scurrying for cover." The Prince pointedly chose to ignore the forest on the horizon marking the limits of their victory. Here and now in this exact place though, the Empire was triumphant.

Instead of filling his lungs and lustily carrying the speech to a roaring climax as he usually did, the Prince grew quiet, his shoulders sagging again as he finished. "Most wonderful and worthy . . . yes, a feat of special significance. In fact, one that no doubt will go down in the annals of history and mark this moment as an auspicious one for this modern age . . ." he said, his voice trailing off. He caught Rallie's eye as if pleading with her to make it so.

Stupid, silly bugger getting that bent out of shape over a bloody library, Konowa thought. He did genuinely feel sorry for the man, but there was a limit. They still had a war to fight. And win. *Someone's going to have to have a talk with him,* Konowa realized, knowing deep down that the task would fall to him.

Without looking around, the Prince started to walk

away, but caught the toe of one of his boots on a sack that Viceroy Alstonfar had been carrying. He stopped and stared down at the spilled scrolls, nudging at them with his boot tip. Rallie's quill bit hard into the paper with a sharp ripping sound, drawing the Prince's attention back to the moment. He raised his head and jutted out his chin. "And of course we discovered the long-lost Library of Kaman Rhal and all its treasures."

Several soldiers looked to Konowa for guidance, their eyebrows rising along with their shoulders in a clear sign they were unsure if they should cheer. Konowa sighed and slid his saber from its scabbard and lifted it high into the air feeling half the fool and glad the night would hide the grimace of embarrassment on his face. "Three cheers for His Majesty! Three cheers for our glorious victory won this night! Three cheers for the return of the Jewel of the Desert and the finding of a great treasure!"

Still catching his breath, Viceroy Alstonfar struggled to stand straight and lifted his saber into the night sky, almost launching it out of his hand in his enthusiasm. The Prince looked genuinely surprised, and began dabbing at the corner of his eyes. Muskets rose, too, their bayonets flashing in the falling snow. Despite himself, Konowa found his voice growing louder with each cheer.

They *had* defeated the Shadow Monarch and Kaman Rahl's dragon this night. They *had* returned another Star to its rightful people. And though he didn't give two hoots of a lice-infested owl about it, they *had* found a pile of books and other ancient knickknacks buried in the sand.

Given all that, a foreign feeling now gripped Konowa,

one that seemed at odds with the current situation. The fate of Visyna, his parents, and even Arkhorn and his squad remained to be determined, and he was no closer to reuniting with the original Iron Elves. None of that was very happy news, yet the strange emotion that now filled him only grew stronger. He continued to ponder its full meaning long after the cheers had died down and Color Sergeant, now acting Regimental Sergeant Major, Aguom, began bellowing at the troops to fall in and prepare to march. As the regiment gathered up its weapons and equipment in preparation for setting out, Konowa looked up to the snow-filled sky and shook his head.

"It's called hope, Major," Rallie said as she walked past, turning her head toward him so that her words carried on the wind. "Now that you've found it, finding everyone else doesn't seem so impossible, does it?"

Konowa didn't bother to look at her. He didn't have to. Rallie would know that for the briefest of moments, a true and genuine smile graced his upturned face.

THREE

The roots of the *sarka har* stretched to the breaking point in their hunt for power. They were so deep below the desert now without finding anything that the trees above were beginning to wither and die. Without a new source of power to feed them Her forest in this land would soon cease to exist. There was no choice but to go deeper. The passage of disturbed rock they had followed was their last resort. Something had to be at the end of it.

Something was.

A root brushed up against a leathery-smooth object. The root began snaking its way around the oddity, slowly encircling it without disturbing it. Anything found at this depth required caution. More roots followed, branching out and finding other, similar objects. When nothing happened, they wrapped their roots around the exteriors of the strange things.

It became apparent at once that these weren't rocks. These objects were unlike any others they had encountered before. Their surfaces were hard, but not brittle. They were round, but with one end larger than the other, creating a slightly distorted oval shape. What was most curious, however, was that these objects were hollow, but not empty. Each one was large enough to hold a fully grown elf . . . or something else of that size.

The roots plunged their tips into the objects, smashing through the thin walls. They had no idea what they'd found, but in the bottom of each object lay a pool of congealed, brownish ichor. As debris fell inside, it landed in the liquid, swirling up greasy strains of darker material that gave off a familiar, bitter tang.

Yes. This was what Her forest needed. *This* was ancient power.

The *sarka har* couldn't know it, but they had come across eggs, potential life that had been long abandoned and left to rot and die deep underground by the last of an ancient race of creatures that had once ruled this world. Even if they had known it would have made no difference.

Their desperate search for sustenance had been rewarded.

Roots drilled into the ichor and began pumping it up to the dying trees above.

The changes were immediate and terrifying.

The few *sarka har* with roots directly in the new-found power grew taller. Branches that were once thin and brittle now flushed with the liquefied remains of long-dead embryos as the brown ichor flowed into them. As they grew supple they began twisting and rubbing against each to slough off their old bark. In its place, a new protective armor of dull black scales emerged. Leaves sprang forth like arrows fired from a bow, their needle points eight inches long and dripping with a glistening red fluid that resembled blood. As one, the leaves unfurled, revealing a variety of differently shaped leaves, each one translucent in the light of the falling snow. The veins in the leaves filled with the bloodlike fluid and the leaves began to change colors, rapidly shifting from green to brown to red and more as they swayed in the wind.

But it wasn't just energy the *sarka har* had found. These were simple creatures, their sole purpose the survival and perpetuation of Her realm. Each was but a dark, stunted, and twisted offshoot of the Shadow Monarch's great Silver Wolf Oak. Now, however, those feeding from the dead eggs experienced an unexpected side effect. No longer were they simply creatures of pure instinct. A crude kind of intelligence began to permeate the *sarka har* along with something far more sinister—they began to think for themselves.

Crude, stark thoughts crawled through their heartwood, worming into every branch and leaf. Images of a time long forgotten imprinted themselves in every fiber. It had been a brutal world, one of even greater peril and death than this one. Every thought struck the *sarka har* like bolts of lightning. They shook and quaked as this new consciousness permeated them.

They had to move. To remain still and stay here in this barren wasteland was to die. These *sarka har* were not going to let that happen.

Now thirteen feet tall and towering above their brethren, the newly transformed *sarka har* spread out their branches, seeing by touch and tasting the air with their leaves. They understood how different they were from the others. They understood they were anchored in place by a root system driven deep into the ground, and so they tore themselves free from the soil, severing their roots when the last of the ichor had been drained. Pain was not new to them, but understanding it was. It filled them with a whole new concept: anger.

They ignored the thrashing fury of the *sarka har* around them that could not change, and focused on their own growing awareness. In order to move, they could not stay as they were. More pain would be required.

Much more.

They twisted the remaining shards of roots into two distinct shapes. The first wound itself into a corkscrew shape that drilled back into the ground, anchoring the tree in place. The second took the form of a massive claw, and began crawling inch by inch in the opposite direction. The *sarka har* groaned as the tension built on its trunk. Cracks began to appear in their new bark that quickly spread to the wood beneath. The more the claw crawled the bigger the cracks grew until the night was shattered by explosive ripping and splintering.

These *sarka har* now had legs.

Pulling the twisted root back out of the ground, they took their first awkward steps across the line of power drawn by the Jewel of the Desert. Sparks flew as they crossed the line. Flame crackled but then died. This new land was inhospitable, the soil filled with the power of the Star, but they remained on its surface, and were not struck down by it.

Each step was a stumbling, broken motion that threatened to topple the trees over, but they soon learned to swing their branches to act as a counterbalance. The *sarka har* had learned to walk.

As they walked, they began to transform further. In order to better move across the snow-covered desert, the *sarka har* altered their form to something more suited for traveling upright over distances. Their trunks split further, lengthening the two pieces they were using as legs while their branches twisted together to form two rudimentary arms.

Two *sarka har*, however, took a different, more difficult form, finding a template long lost in the power of the ichor. Their transformation was much more painful and time-consuming. Branches tore and trunks shattered as the two *sarka har* remade themselves. Ichor spilled on the snow and steamed as it burned. Leaves spun away in the wind, but more sprouted. Larger. Stronger. They didn't grow tall, but they grew long, extending themselves along the ground. It was a strange and horrifying sensation for a tree to fall toward the earth, but as more of the transformation took hold, they saw the power in this new stance. When the transformation was complete the other *sarka har* were gone, their trail in the snow already erased by the wind. It mattered little. These *sarka har* had discovered a new means by which to travel, and they knew where their brethren were heading.

Deep in the heartwood of every transformed tree lived a surging intelligence adapting itself to its new-found form after laying dormant for centuries untold. There was little for it to find beyond basic needs in the *sarka har* except for one, pure thing—a hatred of elves. In fact, it was a distorted echo of an emotion so ingrained in the Shadow Monarch's Silver Wolf Oak that its acorns spread the poison of this feeling. The emotion of Her Silver Wolf Oak was a confused maelstrom

of fury and love aimed at a single elf. As a result, the
forest sprouted from its acorns reproduced this hatred
in every *sarka har*. These new *sarka har* felt the hatred
burning deep inside them, and while they little understood it, they were driven by it all the same. And unlike
the *sarka har* who had not transformed, these trees could
do more than lie in wait. They could move, and they
could hunt. Their leaves tasted elf in the air. They
weren't far.

Without knowing its name, its history, or even what
it was, the transformed *sarka har* began to close in on a
single point in the Hasshugeb Expanse.

Suhundam's Hill.

To march is to grind the body slowly with a torturer's
attention to detail. Granules too small to see find that
perfect place between flesh and strap, rubbing skin until
it blisters, weeps, and tears, staining shirts and filling
boots with an oozing, red-tinted mud. Muscle and
sinew explore pain so searing that the onset of stabbing
needle pricks of numbness comes as a welcome relief.
Shoulders erupt in burning cauldrons of agony that
ache long after pack straps have been pried off, while
wild thoughts of amputation race through the mind
with every footfall.

At his most cynical, Konowa even wondered if it
was all diabolically planned to be this way. Soldiers have
very little to say about marching that's relatable in mixed
company. And when no officer or sergeant is around,
their comments usually start by spitting in disgust, and
for good reason. The prospect of battle, no matter how

terrifying, grows in the mind of the soldier to be a kind of salvation from all the damned marching.

Konowa pushed away those thoughts and scanned the inhospitable wasteland curtained with snow. That in itself was worrying enough. What only yesterday had been a broiling pan of bleached sand and wind-frayed rock was now an unnatural tundra, cold and unforgiving. That the Iron Elves were about to march straight into the teeth of it was of less concern than what lay on the other side. Every man knew that the Shadow Monarch and Her creatures would be at the end of this journey. This march would have to be several types of hell for that prospect to look good.

Konowa did his best to buoy their spirits. "Just a short jaunt to the coast, lads. Not exactly a walk in the park, but we'll make it." Soldiers nodded, mostly because he looked at them, but hopefully because some actually believed him.

"Remember, the Prince brought a whole fleet with us when we landed," Konowa said. "Admittedly, the navy types are a bit soggy, but they'll be there for us when we need them." *I hope.*

Konowa gave up on his pep talk and wandered among the men. Every soldier was busy examining the contents of his pack, lifting it and judging the weight, knowing every ounce carried would become ten pounds of pain in a few hours. Contents were dumped out and reexamined on the snow as soldiers thought long and hard about what to keep and what to discard.

"You might find your stomach will wish you'd kept those," Konowa said, stopping by one soldier who was kneeling in the snow, busily dumping out the hard-as-rock biscuits given to them from the HMS *Black Spike*'s stores. *Feygan . . . Feyran . . .* Konowa tried, but couldn't remember the man's name, if he ever knew it. This soldier was scrawny and his uniform so dusty and torn that he looked more like a beggar sifting through a rubbish heap.

"My stomach don't have a death wish, but if yours does you're welcome to them," the soldier said, then looked up and realized who he was addressing. He jumped to his feet and saluted. Eyes still wild from battle stared back at Konowa from a gaunt, sunburnt face smeared with black powder. Konowa recognized the look, knowing his own visage was just as startling. He returned the salute and motioned for the soldier to continue with his packing.

"You're right; they are an acquired taste. Still, if you dunk them in a mug of arr they almost become edible."

The soldier's face took on a puzzled look. He reached up and brushed a greasy lock of blond hair off his forehead. "Well, sir, if that means poison then I agree with you there. I tried feeding one to a rat on the ship and the little bugger took one sniff and hightailed it in the other direction."

Konowa could smell the soldier from here and suspected the rat hadn't reacted entirely to the biscuit. None of them, save the Prince perhaps, were too fresh at this point. "Smart rat. How are you set for cartridges?"

At this, the soldier brightened. "Chockablock full there, Major. These heathen warriors use a ball just a smidge smaller than ours. They might rattle a bit coming out the barrel, but we've been grabbing up as much as we can carry. I'd wager our muskets will still be true enough to a hundred yards give or take."

Cartridges weren't the only thing the Iron Elves were stripping from the dead Hasshugeb warriors littering the sand around them. In addition to jewels and coins quietly pocketed, belts, robes, daggers, and goat-hide water skins were quickly becoming part of the regiment's dress. Konowa marveled that the Prince had nothing to say on the subject—a far cry from the parade-ground dress he had demanded just a few short months ago. That strange sensation of hope stirred in Konowa again. *If the Prince could learn, who knew what else was possible?*

"Very well," Konowa said. He paused, a question forming that he wasn't sure how to ask, or even if he should. He knew most officers and certainly the Prince wouldn't inquire of a soldier how he was doing. Soldiers do what they're told. For the most part Konowa accepted it as the way it had to be. He also believed, however, that a soldier fights better when he understands the situation, at least as far as he's able to grasp it. And that meant officers needed to understand things, too, most especially the hearts and minds of the troops.

Konowa realized the soldier was staring at him so he simply said: "How are you holding up?"

The soldier pointed to his chest. "Me, sir? Better than most," he said, waving in the direction of the battlefield. "I'm still here, got all me parts, no extra holes, and I'm looking forward to moving out."

Konowa strained to hear a trace of sarcasm, but couldn't detect a note. "Eager to get at the Shadow Monarch are you?"

The soldier shrugged his shoulders. "You could say that, sir. Way me and the lads see it, when we climb the elf witch's mountain and kick Her down the other side, well, we'll be good and done with the oath. With that taken care of, I've been thinking I might take me back pay, retire from this here army, and take on a new job, one with a little less danger if you take my meaning."

Konowa did. "Clerking in a shop perhaps, or driving a milk wagon?"

The soldier's eyes grew wide and he shook his head vigorously. "Lordy no, sir. I was thinking about joining the navy. Except for these biscuits, the sea air felt good somewhere deep inside me, you know? A man can *breathe* out there."

Thoughts of the ocean for Konowa brought about the immediate opposite reaction. "I suppose everything qualifies as a job with less danger when compared to our current activities." Konowa hunched his shoulders as a blast of wind drove more snow down his back, where it melted and trickled down his spine. The chill made thoughts of the ocean a little too real for him. "Can you swim?"

"Not as such," the soldier said, a shy smile stealing across his face, "but I *float* like a champion. I figure that's close enough."

"Could be, but try to bunk near some cork, just in case. Carry on, Private," Konowa said. He saluted as he took a step to walk on, then stopped and turned back. "Feylan."

The soldier's smile grew. "Aye, aye, Major!"

Konowa enjoyed the rest of his time moving among the troops. Wherever he went, they nodded or gave a thumbs-up. A few even grinned. Despite the horrors they'd faced and the losses they'd suffered, these men were not broken. He felt a small yet rousing speech coming on when an icy blast threw snow in his face and brought him back to reality. It reminded him that despite the black acorn connecting him to a cold magic, he still needed to stay warm. Konowa began to search for a dead warrior still clothed, but wherever he looked, the bodies were already stripped bare. He spied the Prince in conversation with Rallie and deliberately angled away from them. He had all he could handle right now with the coming march.

The determined form of Viceroy Alstonfar heading straight for him, however, begged to differ.

"Viceroy," Konowa said, nodding his head in greeting as the man rolled to a stop. He was swaddled from head to toe in robes from at least five different Hasshugeb warriors. "Think you'll be warm enough?"

The Viceroy beamed a smile that suggested he'd missed the sarcasm completely. "You'd think my few extra pounds would keep me warm, but all they're really good for is lowering people's estimation of me when we meet."

Konowa inwardly cringed. This man before him was an accomplished diplomat with obvious intelligence between his ears who had shown real courage on the field of battle. Before Konowa could form an apology the Viceroy carried on.

"I find it works in my favor more times than not, although not as well as I'd like when it comes to the fairer sex. And please, call me Pimmer." His smile, thankfully, did not leer at the mention of women, but the conversation was heading in a direction Konowa didn't want to follow.

"Are you ready?" Konowa asked, wondering how the man could ride a camel wearing so many robes. "We should get moving as soon as possible. With a bit of luck, we can break through what trees remain and reach the coast at Tel Bagrussi in two days." Konowa saw the expectant look and relented. The man had earned it. "Pimmer."

Pimmer's eyes misted and Konowa worried for a moment that he might actually tear up, but another cold gust of wind took care of that. "Ah, yes, Tel Bagrussi. Quite a little cesspool. I've only been there once and I can assure you it's not for the faint of heart or those with a sense of smell. They ferment a fish there that attracts a beetle that lays its eggs in the rotting flesh, which then hatch as larvae to consume the putrid mess. Now here's where it gets interesting. They then take the larvae and grind them into a pulp which—"

Konowa raised a hand to ward off any more. "I don't imagine we'll be there for long. We just need to signal the fleet and jump aboard."

"Quite true, quite true, but alas, we won't be going to Tel Bagrussi."

"Pardon?"

"It's too close to Nazalla, I'm afraid. The citizenry there will be filled to overflowing with anti-Imperial fervor. It was a close run thing getting out of the city. Trying to get back in would be tantamount to storming a castle at this point. The Jewel of the Desert has returned, Major. Our time here, and by that I mean the Calahrian Empire, appears to be coming to a close. Oh, don't look so surprised—there will be some in the royal court and more on the Imperial General Staff who will try to hang on to every far-flung piece of land like this, but I fear it's a losing proposition. And even if that weren't the case, we are faced with the immediate problem of no longer being able to travel under the auspices of the Suljak."

Konowa sneered at the name. Both spiritual and political leader of the far-flung Hasshugeb tribes, the Suljak had played a dangerous game in invoking what he
had thought was the ancient magic of Kaman Rhal.
What he called forth instead was an abomination. The
feeling of absolute stunned terror Konowa had just experienced when he'd come face to skeletal face with that
dragon of bones still lingered.

Pimmer shuffled closer to Konowa. "I'm afraid the
poor man has suffered quite a setback in the eyes of his
people. Not that I'd wager on such a thing, but after his
dalliance with Rhal's dragon it's only a matter of time
before he's taken out to a nice patch of desert and diced
into small bits."

Konowa felt no pity for the man. "He caused a lot
of needless deaths."

"I don't disagree," the Viceroy said, "but his demise
will create turmoil among the tribes as each puts forth a
new leader to claim his place. Couple that with the return
of the Jewel of the Desert, which is viewed as a powerful
symbol of native self-determination in these lands, and
you have all the ingredients for a full-scale revolt."

"That really isn't our problem anymore," Konowa
said, emphasizing each word. "We have to get to the
coast." He felt his newfound sense of hope wavering in
the face of this new reality.

"You are right, Major, and we will. There is a trading route that runs parallel with the coast to the west of
here. It has the added benefit of having several fortifica-
tions guarding it, which should provide us with some
lodging and provisions as we proceed. After no more
than two or three days' march, we'll be able to turn
north and be in Tel Martruk a day after that."

"To the west?" Konowa asked, turning to look in that direction. Snow and darkness worked against his elven vision and revealed nothing.

"Toward Suhundam's Hill, as a matter of fact," Pimmer said, his voice dropping slightly. "The place where your elves are stationed. For all we know they could still be there even now, although with Her forest . . ."

It was a thought Konowa had refused to explore, but now he could no longer avoid it. What if he found his elves dead? For all he knew they had been slaughtered and spitted on *sarka har* all across the desert. He started to curse, then caught himself. He should have found a way to go there first, but that damn Star had changed things. Only a few months ago the idea of the Stars was little more than long-held myth. Konowa wished desperately for those days.

"And the Prince approves of this plan?"

Pimmer looked over to Rallie and the Prince before turning back and motioning for Konowa to come closer still. "The Prince is in a rather delicate state at the moment. The loss of virtually the entire collection of the library has had a devastating effect on him. Defeating the Shadow Monarch's forces, destroying Kaman Rhal's dragon, and ensuring the safe return of a Star of power would be more than enough for most men, but his Highness, despite all the bluster, is not a warrior at heart. Not like his father and definitely not like *you*. I did my best and managed to grab up some truly remarkable documents and a few other priceless trinkets that are . . . invaluable, to the peoples of the world of course." At this he paused and looked down at the ground. "Still just odds and ends though. I'm afraid most of what was in the library is now gone forever."

"Good riddance," Konowa said, knowing it would upset the Viceroy and not caring. "Searching for treasures, no matter what form they take, makes men do stupid things."

If the Viceroy was insulted he didn't show it. He looked up at Konowa with genuine hurt on his face. "Knowledge is worth preserving."

"So are lives."

Faces of those Konowa held dear immediately sprung to mind, and he had to swallow hard before trusting himself to continue. "In any event, the library is gone and the Prince will have to get over his disappointment." He paused to let the building anger subside. Pimmer wasn't the Prince. "About this caravan route to the west that will take us to Suhundam's Hill. You're certain about our path?"

At this, Pimmer lowered his voice again, making Konowa strain to hear him over the wind. "As certain as can be in these uncertain times. We'll have Her forest to the north, and it's difficult to say how the tribes further to the west will react should we come in contact with any of them. But one factor above all others makes me believe this is the way to go."

"And what is that?" Konowa asked.

"Miss Synjyn agrees with me."

Konowa reached out a hand and placed it firmly on the Viceroy's arm. The cloth was soft and thicker than Konowa had realized. Frost fire began to sparkle along the fabric and he removed his hand before he hurt the man. A wind gust picked that moment to drive a flurry of snow in his face. They were in for a long, cold march. "Then it sounds like we have a little more walking in the snow to do than I thought. Tell me, Pimmer, I seem to have missed out on the procurement of foul weather clothing. How much for one of your robes?"

FOUR

The world appeared washed-out and blurry through Alwyn's open eyes.

Everything he had known was fading, as if the colors that made life vibrant and fresh now feared to be near him. Even his memories were taking on a patina of gray, diluting the emotions he once associated with them and gave them meaning. He knew that before long the very concepts of laughter, compassion, even love, would be lost to him.

He would fight it, but he wasn't sure how long he could resist.

Alwyn closed his eyes, but his vision didn't darken. Even with his eyes closed he saw the world, but now as a vast sea swirling and frothing with energy. Major Swift Dragon stood speaking with Viceroy Alstonfar twenty yards away. He saw them clearly; the elf and the man shone like two torches against black velvet. Alstonfar showed as a warm, soft blend of oranges and yellows. The major's aura was a twisted mess of greens and reds surrounding a metallic black core, a source of energy and power to be directed and used.

Threads of pulsing force connected everything, and all Alwyn had to do was reach out and pluck one and claim the power for himself.

He understood the Shadow Monarch better now. The pull of the energy surrounding him was seductive. His right hand began to rise as anticipation coursed through his body. He could use his life force, direct it to better purpose. He could make things right again.

Alwyn forced his eyes open, fighting back a scream as he did so. Dizziness threatened to topple him. He brought his already raised hand up to his head and squeezed his temples. The pressure felt good, and he shifted his weight to his wooden leg, testing his balance. Pain flared in the stump of his leg and frost fire sparkled briefly wherever the thin wooden branches of the artificial limb touched his flesh. A wave of cold spread throughout the stump in response, and the pain melted away as his flesh went numb. The magic that had once infused the wooden leg was dying, overwhelmed by the growing power of the oath inside him. Already Alwyn could see new black shoots sprouting from dead branches in the leg.

Before much longer the leg, like the rest of him, would belong to Her.

Snow gathered on the sand around him and he looked up into the sky. A scouring wind was driving the snow at an increasingly sharp angle as it moved in from the coast. Carried on the wind was the unmistakable smell of Her presence. He shook his head and turned to Yimt only to stop and catch his breath.

Yimt was gone.

Thoughts of the dwarf burst through the darkening vistas of his mind and he desperately clung to them, finding strength in the memories of his lost friend.

"Kill him."

Alwyn looked up as the shade of Regimental Sergeant Major Lorian, astride the warhorse Zwindarra, materialized beside him in the gusting snow. Laced with pain, Lorian's words were more plea than command. Alwyn returned his gaze to follow Major Swift Dragon as he resumed walking among the troops. The Blood Oath that bound the dead to the regiment and Her lived through the major. Killing him, however, would not break it, but it would satisfy an all-consuming need for revenge. *"Kill him,"* Lorian said again, his voice a cold echo inside Alwyn's head.

Lorian's anguish washed over him in ethereal waves flooding between this world and the next. Alwyn fought for balance again as more shades materialized, their suffering adding to the surging eddies of vengeance that threatened to carry him along until their desire was his.

Alwyn alone would have yielded to their cries, but he was no longer just Private Renwar. He was more. He had assumed the role of leading the shades of the dead, giving voice to their anguish and their anger. In doing so, he held a power the shades did not. Unlike them, he remained part of both worlds—their allegiance, however confused and harrowing, was his to lead. He hadn't wanted that, but he had bargained with the Shadow Monarch in his dream, freeing the shades from Her grasp while condemning himself in the process. His task was simple—ensure that Konowa arrived safely to Her mountain. Too late he realized that it had been no bargain at all. Alwyn had hoped that in freeing them he would ease their pain, but the brilliance of Her plan was in its very simplicity. The dead were now bound to Alwyn, and he was bound to Her, and so the Blood Oath was not diminished. Through it all, the shades' suffering grew.

"No, he must live," Alwyn replied, focusing his thoughts on the shades. These were former comrades, men who had risked their lives for something greater and deserved better than the existence they now endured. All that stood between them and immortal service was Alwyn's force of will, and he knew he couldn't hold out forever. Either the Shadow Monarch died, or they were all doomed.

"He caused this," Lorian's shade said as voices of the dead around it howled in agreement.

"No. *She* caused this," Alwyn shot back, concentrating his strength and adding power to his voice. "He is as much a victim as we are." *As is She*, he thought to himself. It was Her love for the dying sapling that had driven Her to extreme lengths to save it. That one, desperate act now drove them all to find a way to end it, and Her.

Shrieking in protest, the shades drifted back into darkness. They could not defy their Emissary. Their agony reverberated in the air for several seconds.

Alwyn shuddered. Time was against them. Even now they watched the major and he felt their need to destroy him.

It was becoming his need, too.

It seemed right. Before long he would know it was right, and then all would be lost.

"Prepare to march!"

It took a moment for Alwyn to recognize the

command referred to him as well. No living soldiers came near him, and Alwyn understood. He also knew that if Yimt were still alive, the dwarf would be cajoling him to snap out of it and get a wiggle on. The thought almost brought a smile to his face. Marshaling his thoughts and focusing on the humanity that yet remained inside him, Private Alwyn Renwar of the Calahrian Empire's Iron Elves shouldered his musket, and without waiting for further orders or looking behind him, began to walk to the west.

From high on a broken rock face overlooking the battlefield, a pair of milky-white eyes followed the procession of human meat marching behind a limping figure.

Even from this distance, the rakke could sense Her mark on the one leading the men. It was similar, but not identical, to the mark carried by Her Emissary, and it was much stronger than the aura that filled the air around the column of men.

Every instinct was on fire, urging it to charge down there and tear into all that wet flesh, to feast until its stomach was full. Drool glistened off the rakke's fangs. Its eyes narrowed to slits as it calculated the fastest path down the rocks that wouldn't set it tumbling through the air to its death. The way was difficult, but not impossible. Ignoring the snow falling on its raised hackles, it began to shiver, not with cold, but anticipation.

The rakke leaned forward until it was almost tipping over the edge. Its muscles throbbed with tension as its nostrils flared, drawing in the frigid air and filling its lungs in preparation to charge. It caught the scent of the meat below and almost howled in joy. The procession of men and animals acted like chains with hooks dug deep into its flesh, pulling it closer. It leaned a little more, feeling its body start to fall forward. It would have allowed itself to keep falling, knowing it would then be forced to leap and begin its run, but a thin suggestion of caution slipped through the red haze of wanton hunger, tempering its rapacious needs. It caught itself and leaned back, snapping its jaws in frustration. Reluctantly, it searched the procession with greater care. The rakke could see only the living, but the storm-driven snow alternately revealed them, then hid them from view, giving the column a spectral appearance in the night. The rakke knew to be afraid of the shadow ones. It was difficult to be sure if the shades were there or not, and so it eased itself away from the edge.

Settling back down among the rocks, it turned its head and growled in anger at the glow of the blue tree now dominating the landscape. Everything about the tree was wrong. Instead of offering a wet, dark place to hide in like Her forest, this tree shone light everywhere. It felt to the rakke as if the radiance was worming its way into its skull, slowly killing it with its light. It knew in the most primitive way that the tree was trying to send it back to the nothingness that the Shadow Monarch had rescued it from. The rakke longed for Her power to return here and cleanse the land of this new terrible light. The rakke's desperation to move away from the tree increased, but it would wait and watch until the enemy left. Only then would it abandon its perch and report back to Her dark elves.

Gnashing its teeth and ripping at the rocks with its claws, it stayed in place. It would endure the agony of the blue light and go hungry. Soon enough, it would be able to hunt again, and when it did, its prey would know true agony before it died.

The rakke was so consumed with rage that it didn't notice the shadow that suddenly appeared behind it. A soft, gurgling sound like that of water in a mountain brook was swept away by the wind before it reached the rakke's ears, denying it a final opportunity to escape. A single spark of dull green blossomed into a teeming mass of phosphorescing globules from deep within the shadow. They clustered into a roiling ball as they surged up a black throat and into a gaping maw.

A sudden shift in the wind brought the scent of something sweetly caustic and distantly familiar to the rakke's nostrils. Its bowels turned to ice water as a fear it had long forgotten shut down its ability to think. Primal instinct took over. It bared its fangs and hurtled its body to the left as it unleashed its claws to slash at the horror behind it.

The rakke was a blur, swinging its massive arm out in a wide arc. The explosive force of its move would have torn plate armor like parchment, but its claw met only air. Without the weight of flesh and blood to slow the momentum of its swing, the rakke overrotated and pitched backward toward the rock-strewn desert floor far below. Instinctively, the rakke pushed its legs out to brace itself, but found only open air behind it and began to topple over the edge. It flung out its right hand to grab on to anything, but by now its body was too far away from the rock face and already beginning to accelerate.

The rakke accepted its impending death on the rocks below with relief. Anything was better than falling prey to the green death stalking it.

The swirling green mass spit forth from the shadow, hitting the rakke in the chest even as it fell.

The green globs separated on impact. Each uncurled, revealing tiny legs and a sharp beak shiny with acid. A hissing sound enveloped the rakke as the tiny creatures released their toxin and began to burrow into its flesh.

The rakke screamed as it tumbled through empty space, savagely ripping at its flesh wherever the minute invaders touched it. Arterial spurts of blood arced through the air as it dug its claws deep into its own rib cage. Howling in agony, it began pulling itself apart in a desperate attempt to get at the burrowing green creatures. Its heart pumped furiously as they crawled ever deeper, burning voraciously through sinew and bone.

The rakke was dead before what was left of its body hit the desert floor with a squelching thud, scattering the pieces in a wide, wet crescent.

FIVE

Konowa looked up at the canyon as they marched past. *Were those rocks falling?* The wind howled and whatever it was got lost in a swath of snow that blocked his view, muffling all sound more than a few feet away. He considered pushing his senses outward using the power of the black acorn, but as he felt no urgent warning from the frost fire, the effort didn't seem worth it. Stomping his boots hard enough in the snow to make the soles of his feet sting, he kept marching, hoping that eventually the process would warm him up.

I miss the heat of Elfkyna, he realized, shocked that he could ever think that. The whole time he'd lived in that accursed place he'd wanted to be anywhere else, but now that he was, Elfkyna didn't seem all that bad. He reached up and knocked some snow off the wings of his shako. *Snow in the desert.* He no longer felt like laughing about it, but cursing would waste too much energy. He settled for sighing, and tried to look ahead to where Private Renwar marched at the head of the column.

Tiny orange lights bobbed in the gloom. He knew he was seeing the burning ends of cigarettes cupped in soldiers' hands so that the palm of the hand protected the lit end as they marched. Smoking on the march was prohibited, but Konowa wasn't about to say anything. They deserved every bit of comfort they could find, and if an enemy could see the glow of cigarettes, it was already close enough to see them.

He could just make out an area of darkness with no telltale orange lights, and realized that would be Private Renwar. He squinted and saw the dimmest of outlines of the limping soldier. He walked a good ten yards in front of the column, alone and yet not alone.

With Renwar out front, it meant the Darkly Departed would be, too. It was a thought that provided Konowa with less comfort than it had just a day before. It wasn't jealousy, he told himself, but a growing concern over where Renwar's loyalties lay. The understanding between Konowa and Renwar was fragile at best, and Konowa knew it couldn't last. The private was bound to Her now in a deeper way than even Konowa, and that could only lead to a very dark end. Killing the first Viceroy had been a clear and necessary duty. What remorse he felt for doing it focused solely on the terribly unfair banishment and disgrace his act had brought down on the original Iron Elves. To kill Private Renwar though would be something else entirely . . . but he knew that time might soon be upon him.

Konowa's footsteps broke through the building layer of snow and crunched in the frozen sand beneath, momentarily throwing him off balance. Regaining his footing, he pulled the robe from Pimmer a little closer around his shoulders and leaned into the wind. The cloth was surprisingly good at keeping out the wind, yet wasn't burdensomely heavy. Konowa still marveled at how little he had had to trade in exchange for the garment. The Viceroy had simply asked that Konowa dine with him once they reached the small fortress at Suhundam's Hill. Konowa had readily agreed, though it was no real barter at all. Still, Pimmer's beaming smile and his training in the Diplomatic Corps where negotiations came as naturally as breathing made Konowa wonder if there was perhaps more to the trade than he realized.

A new flurry of snow snapped Konowa's attention back to the here and now. The snow was falling in ever-thickening sheets, so that for most of the time Konowa found himself marching alone. He did enjoy the peace and quiet it afforded him, but as second-in-command, he knew he couldn't indulge in such luxury for long. Someone had to lead, and the Prince was still in no condition to do so. Slapping the hilt of his saber in annoyance, Konowa halted and turned to look back over the column.

He could just see the shapes of the Viceroy and the Prince atop their camels. Konowa had been offered one of the beasts, but the Prince didn't insist and Konowa happily volunteered the camel as a pack animal instead. Marching in snow was a frigid version of hell, but it was still preferable to riding along on one of those monsters.

Konowa hunched his shoulders against the wind as the column marched past. It wasn't a happy sight. Soldiers and animals alike walked with a slow, plodding gait, heads bent low against the elements. There was no singing, no laughing, barely any talking at all. Few even noticed Konowa as they marched past, and fewer still bothered to acknowledge him with a salute or a half-hearted wave. It occurred to Konowa that in his Hasshugeb robe in the dark, he probably didn't look all that different from any other Iron Elf in the regiment. He hoped that was the case, choosing not to dwell on less charitable ideas.

The camels carrying the Prince and the Viceroy ambled past. Neither man turned to look at him. Konowa made no move to draw their attention. Before long he would have to confront the Prince and snap him out of his sulk, but for now he actually preferred the future king silent and moping. It certainly kept him out of Konowa's way and let him get on with the business at hand.

A motley assortment of bullocks and camels plodded past towing the naval contingent's battery of three cannon. Despite the wind and his damaged hearing, Konowa was convinced he heard a good deal of cursing going on. He'd made it clear the guns would travel with them despite having exhausted their supply of ammunition. Pimmer assured him the forts along the trade route they were following were well supplied with gunpowder, among other items that could, in a pinch, be shoved down the barrel of a cannon and fired. The idea of traipsing across a snow-covered desert with no ammunition was clearly not what the naval gunners had signed up for, but it was their lot and they could deal with it.

Behind them and still marching in bare feet were the twenty-three surviving volunteers of the 3rd Spears. Whether it was stubbornness, pride, or a genuine imperviousness to cold, the soldiers from the Timolia

Islands refused all offers of footwear or even rags to wrap their feet. Placing these fearsome warriors directly behind the grumbling artillery gunners had been a deliberate move on Konowa's part. The gunners could grouse all they wanted, but with the 3rd Spears behind them, they would keep the guns moving.

As the 3rd Spears marched past, Konowa squinted to catch sight of the rear guard. He knew they were a squad of scared and unhappy soldiers, but just like the naval gunners, they had to accept it. Konowa had seen the terror and anger in their eyes when he assigned them the task, but there was no other choice. The rear of the column had to be protected, and whoever got that duty knew it was filled with risk. What he had promised them, however, was that they wouldn't have to shoulder the burden alone. Two other squads were picked to take turns bringing up the rear. Konowa knew it wasn't time yet to make the change, but he could at least fall back and march along with them for a bit and perhaps pick up their spirits.

As the backs of the Timolian soldiers disappeared in the swirling snow, Konowa stepped out onto the trampled path and waited for the squad to appear. They should be just a few yards behind.

As the seconds stretched into a minute, Konowa grew increasingly worried. The rear guard should have been directly behind the 3rd Spears. He drew his saber, conscious of the fact that he was now completely alone.

"One of these days your impulses are going to get you in trouble," he muttered to himself. He reasoned that it was likely already too late, but hoped the trouble was something he could handle.

Realizing his current position was the worst possible

one he could be in, he started walking backward while keeping his eyes peeled for the rear guard. "C'mon, lads, be okay," he said, gripping the pommel of his saber tight.

He shivered in the cold, only realizing a few moments later that it wasn't the weather, but the black acorn against his chest.

A soldier appeared out of the snow twenty yards away.

"Over here," Konowa hissed, waving his saber in the air then crouching down as he looked around for the danger. The soldier stumbled as if severely wounded. Konowa could barely make out his form in the snow and couldn't tell how badly he'd been hurt. His first instinct was to rush forward to help the man, but the stab of ice against his chest was growing colder. The enemy was closing in.

The smart thing, the proper thing, for Konowa to do was to turn and run back to the end of the column. It was foolhardy to risk his life for one soldier when the entire regiment needed his leadership. Konowa was already running toward the soldier before he'd made up his mind that the smart thing and the right thing weren't always the same.

The soldier stumbled again and went down on one knee. The acorn blazed with freezing intensity, causing Konowa to gasp with pain. Ignoring it, he jogged the last few feet to reach the fallen soldier and help him up.

"How badly are you hu—" Konowa started to ask before his ability to form words left him.

The "soldier" climbed back to its feet on two gnarled chunks of roots. The . . . tree, Konowa's mind finally registered, had taken the rough form of a soldier.

Its branches were bent and twisted at impossible angles to form a pair of large shoulders, from which two arms hung. Long, sharp thorns for fingers twitched and snapped at the end of each arm. Its head was a thicket of leaves and thorns crafted into something that in the dark and the snow had looked convincingly like a soldier wearing a shako. But as disturbing as it was to see a tree take on human form, it was the bark that froze Konowa's gaze. It was dragon scale. He was sure of it. The scale had shaped itself to look like a uniform.

How or why he didn't know and likely never would, but somehow the *sarka har* had changed.

Luckily, Konowa's instincts were still working even as his mind pondered the impossibility before him.

Konowa started to backpedal even as he brought his saber up in front of him and slashed at the tree. The stroke missed, which threw his balance off. His boots slipped and he fell backward to land hard on his back. Snow flew in the air hiding the abomination from sight.

Konowa rolled to his right, burying his face in the snow in the process. He felt the thump of a heavy root slam down on the ground just inches from where he had been. He continued rolling several more times before finally scrambling to his feet, one hand pushing his shako back down on his head as the other held his saber at the ready. He shook his head and blinked the snow from his eyes.

There were five of the walking *sarka har* now. Each one looked like a child's idea of a soldier. Everything was there, but all of it was distorted. In the light of day, their disguise would fool no one, but in these conditions they were more than good enough to get close to a potential victim.

"I'm not dead yet!" Konowa shouted, mad at himself that he even considered himself lost. He'd been in tough scraps before, where the odds were stacked so high against him he couldn't see over the enemy's chips and still he'd prevailed. These were still *sarka har*, and he had the frost fire at his command.

"This is why I *HATE TREES!*" Konowa bellowed, charging forward, the blade of his saber wreathed in black flame.

The closest tree had no time to parry as Konowa's blade slashed down across the midsection of its trunk.

Black ice crystals exploded as blade met trunk. Konowa's entire right arm erupted in burning pain like he'd been stabbed with a thousand needles. He stumbled backward, barely managing to hold on to his saber. The tree he'd struck was engulfed in frost fire, but whereas normal *sarka har* quickly burned to ash, the dragon-scale bark seemed to be shielding it from the worst of the flame.

"And Visyna wonders what I have against the bloody forest," he said to himself, flexing his arm to get feeling back into it. He caught motion out of the corner of his eye and more of the transformed *sarka har* appeared out of the snow. They marched along the path left by the column, ignoring Konowa just as the soldiers had before. He had to get out of here and warn them.

That's when he remembered he had more than the frost fire to call on.

"Renwar! Get the Darkly Departed off their arses and cut down these damn trees!" He turned while keeping an eye on the burning *sarka har* and its four companions. There was no sign of the shades of the dead.

"That wasn't a request—it was an order!" he

shouted into the wind. The black flame on the tree he attacked guttered and went out. Singed leaves fell from its head and it continued to stumble, but it started to come toward him again as the other four fanned out to cut off any chance of escape.

Konowa turned and started to run, but in the deep snow he knew at once he wouldn't get far. The *sarka har* would catch him exhausted and that would be that.

He turned to face his fate.

The dawning realization that he was looking at the very real possibility of being killed by a bunch of walking trees brought a snarl of a smile to his lips. His whole life he'd loathed the forest with a passion that bordered and sometimes crossed the line of sanity. It never occurred to him until now that the forest might just feel the same way about him.

He was charging at the trees before his battle cry pierced the air.

"Timber, you bloody pieces of lumber! *Timber!*"

SIX

A pack of fifteen rakkes clustered around the mangled remains of one of their brethren. Despite the blowing wind, the tang of fresh blood hung in the air above the corpse. Normally, the rakkes would have welcomed the chance at fresh meat even when it was the body of one of their own, but not this time. Green insects crawled over and through the rakke's flesh even as the falling snow buried the body from sight. A primal fear of the green death kept the rakkes at bay.

Four gray blurs drifted through the snow, coming to a silent stop a few yards behind the rakkes. The pulsing, rhythmic blue light of the Star tree slowed momentarily like an ocean wave retreating down a beach as four dark elves appeared from out of the gloom.

Even amidst the cobalt-tinged darkness and swirling snow it was clear that nothing about these elves was natural. The points of their left ear tips absorbed what light there was, making them blacker even than the surrounding night. Every joint and limb appeared angular, sheared, and incomplete as if sheets of stone as thin as parchment had been wrapped around bundles of metal stakes. For clothing, they wore only ore-saturated leaves secured with steel-colored vines, revealing far more than they covered. If the elves felt the bite of the cold, they gave no indication.

Each elf held a long bow the color of rusted iron in its hands. Drawstrings thrummed as they were drawn to their full pull, the limbs of the bows arching back to create grotesque smiles with tongues of thin, black arrows. At this distance, the arrows would pass through the back of a rakke's skull and continue on through with enough force to embed themselves in another victim.

Bony fingers flexed and creaked as they curled tighter around the vine-wrapped grips of the bows. Wet, black eyes stared at the assembled rakkes calculating distance and trajectory. With no eyelids, the orbs shone like polished granite, and with as much warmth. The elves would not miss. They waited only for the command.

Her Emissary materialized behind the elves. Or rather it attempted to. Parts of it were simply missing, lost forever when that damnable Iron Elf soldier had summoned a vortex of magic and blown it to pieces. It knew pain now as it had never before, and the experience was transcendent. Twice in the life of the creature formerly known as Viceroy Faltinald Gwyn it had served powerful rulers—always in the pursuit of more power—and each time it had suffered greatly. Now, as every shredded fiber of its flesh and soul screamed in agony, it called on the power so horribly earned to rebuild itself one more time. It focused its energies on a dark, fathomless core—the black acorn planted into its heart by the Shadow Monarch.

It was rewarded with nothing. The acorn had shattered when the soldier had attacked—all that remained of the Shadow Monarch's gift were cracked and broken shards. Her Emissary's form mirrored that of the acorn, as did its mind. In its insanity it was finally free, but still the Shadow Monarch's will filled its thoughts, commanding it to destroy the rakkes.

"Kill them. They grow too wild and will destroy everything in their path. My lost children must be allowed to return to me alive," said the voice in what remained of Her Emissary's head. It understood. The pact She made with the soldier that turned him into an emissary of the dead meant Her power over the fallen was diminished. She needed the Iron Elves brought to Her alive.

A crease of a smile cracked across its frost-burned face. If Her dark elves looked like mannequins created in an iron foundry, then Her Emissary was the wretched slag that remained. Redoubling its efforts, it coalesced enough of itself from the ether to create a form roughly human in shape. It drew what little power remained from Her gift, but found a new and more plentiful supply in something far stronger—rage. This was an endless well of power it could call its own.

It stumbled forward, growing stronger with each step. At that moment the wind shifted and the rakkes noticed the terrible being behind them. The elves pulled back on the bowstrings a little more, waiting only for Her Emissary to relay Her command.

It never came. Instead, as Her Emissary found a rasping, hissing voice barely capable of speech, it only needed to utter one word.

"Die!" A ragged scythe of ice formed in the air in front of Her Emissary. It reached out and grabbed it, swinging it in a wicked arc faster than the eye could follow. For a moment nothing happened, then as one the four elves crumpled to the ground, their heads falling away from their bodies. Fingers no longer restrained by life released the bowstrings and the arrows flew true, still aimed at the rakkes. The creature knew it had the strength to stop the arrows in midflight, but it did not. Six of the rakkes fell. Those remaining stood rooted to the ground.

"Build your strength," the creature commanded. *"Soon you hunt for fresher game."*

The rakkes roared their pleasure and fell on the bodies, both rakke and elf. The remnants of the acorn in the creature's chest flared with frost fire, but it extinguished them with its madness.

The Shadow Monarch no longer pulled its strings.

High above on the canyon wall and undetected by those below, something stirred. A pair of eyes studied the scene on the desert floor through the falling snow. The figure remained deep in shadow as it watched the rakkes tear into the bodies of the dark elves first and then their own kindred. The rakke it had slaughtered earlier was untouched. Stupid, rudimentary creatures that they were, they knew enough to avoid that.

And here, off to the side and cloaked in shifting darkness, a violently misshapen thing directed the rakkes.

Interesting.

Killing one rakke had been satisfying. Killing this pack and its new leader would be . . . enjoyable.

From deep within a black throat, a green glow came to life. Stalking this prey would be more difficult than the first kill, but not impossible. The green insects began to multiply, responding to subtle signals that a new quarry was at hand. But just as quickly, the signals then weakened. The rakkes were moving off, carrying what meat they could as they began to track west.

The watching shadow had no choice but to move into the open to begin tracking the rakkes, who no doubt had picked up the trail of the Iron Elves.

A group of six rakkes detached themselves from the rocks along the ridgeline where they had been hiding and spread out in a rough U-shaped pack. Claw tips extended and fangs began to glisten with drool as they set out after the shadowy figure.

The hunter was now the hunted.

"Major, get the hell out of the way!"

Konowa was so intent on his last charge that the shouted warning went unheeded. He was still several feet from the nearest *sarka har* when it blew apart in a red-orange explosion. Thousands of black scales cartwheeled through the air followed by flaming splinters. Konowa's shako was blown off his head and he skidded to a halt, his arms thrown across his face. Only the flaring of the frost fire into a frigid wall in front of him saved him from being cut to ribbons.

"That's new," he gasped, equally impressed by the exploding tree and the frost fire's reaction to it.

A familiar ringing in his ears told him musket fire had sounded a moment before the tree was destroyed. The remaining trees seemed oblivious to the fate of their brethren and continued to close in on Konowa.

"Major, over here!"

Konowa spun around. Several more soldiers had appeared out of the snowy night. He kept his saber at the ready, unwilling to be tricked again by a shadowy form seen in the distance. The soldiers advanced—Konowa relaxed as he recognized them as his rear guard.

"What in the bloody hell are those things?" Konowa asked when the soldiers came to a stop.

"We were hoping you'd know," one of the soldiers said. Konowa recognized him as the young private planning on joining the navy.

"What's your name again, son?" Konowa asked.

"Feylan, sir, Private Bawton Feylan."

"Well, Private Bawton Feylan, all I know for sure is never trust a damned tree."

As a group, they began to fall back, walking backward to keep the trees in sight the whole time. Six soldiers knelt in the snow and fired their muskets at another *sarka har*. Huge chunks of bark and wood tore from the trunk in great flashes of flame. One massive arm cracked and fell away, but unlike the tree before, this *sarka har* remained intact. The remaining five soldiers walked a few more paces, halted, and having reloaded their muskets, took aim and fired at the wounded tree. This time it blew apart.

"Why do they explode like that?" Konowa asked, resheathing his saber and unslinging his own musket. He banged snow out of the muzzle and unwrapped the leather covering that kept the fire lock dry.

"Haven't the foggiest, sir, they just do," Feylan said. If he was scared he was doing a fine job of hiding it. "It's like they're filled with gunpowder or something. Hit them with a few musket balls and you can hurt them, but it takes at least five or six all at once to light 'em up."

"A little more dragon than you bargained for, eh?" Konowa shouted at the trees, ramming home a charge in his musket and preparing to fire.

Instead of advancing, the remaining *sarka har* converged on the spot where the last tree was destroyed. They unsnaked their branches and began picking up pieces of bark, applying it to their trunks.

"That's brilliant, that is," Konowa said, spitting in the snow. "Not only have the buggers learned to walk, now they've figured out how to protect themselves." He was tempted to add "what's next?" but the question became moot as the trees began grabbing burning pieces of wood and crushing them into flaming spheres. As the spheres grew, the ends of their branches caught fire and began to burn. The night turned an ugly orange as each *sarka har* held up its two arms, now transformed into massive torches.

"Well that wasn't too bright now, was it?" Konowa shouted at the trees. "You've gone and set yourselves on fire, you dumb bastards. Guess you missed the lesson about fire and wood."

The private looked up from reloading his musket and screamed, "Take cover!"

"I don't see—" was all Konowa managed before the private tackled him to the snow.

Konowa looked up from the snowbank Feylan had dumped him into to see the *sarka har* bend backward as if being pummeled by a hurricane, then whip forward. The ends of their arms splintered and tore from the rest of their bodies to fly toward the soldiers. Konowa stared in total amazement as burning cannonballs of wood hurtled toward him. *Did every tree have it out for him?* He slammed his head back down and buried it deep into the snow as he tried to burrow to the center of the earth. Searing heat passed over his back, and a moment later the ground reared up and punched him, knocking the breath from his lungs.

Explosions sounded all around him, accompanied by screams.

"Is anyone hurt?" Konowa shouted, spitting out snow as he finally dared to lift his head again. Large black scorch marks dotted the snow for twenty yards in every direction. Flames still burned in several of them.

"Grostril caught one full in the chest. Nothing left of him but his musket," a soldier said, his voice trembling. "He was right beside me . . ."

Konowa tried to picture Private Grostril, but he realized he no more knew who the soldier was than he did the one who had carried the locket in his shako that he had found back at the canyon. It hurt him, both that he had lost another man under his command, and that he didn't even have a face he could call up in his memory to honor his falling.

"Major, they're still coming at us!"

Konowa got up to his knees and pointed his musket at the *sarka har*. Sure enough, they had resumed their awkward march forward, smoke streaming from the burned ends of their branches. It was time to get the rear guard out of here.

"Listen up. We're going to keep falling back in an orderly fashion. Stay together and hold your fire. These damn trees are walking powder kegs! We'll fall back fifty yards, then we'll hold and wait for them to close in on us. When they do, we'll all shoot at the furthest tree. That should punch through the extra scales or bark or whatever the hell it is."

The soldiers didn't need a second invitation. The ten remaining men got up and scrambled through the snow. Konowa made sure they were all moving, then followed after them. He was sweating freely and almost ripped the Hasshugeb robe off, but the sight of all the snow persuaded him he'd best keep it. He counted out fifty yards in his head then called a halt. The soldiers turned and formed a single line shoulder to shoulder. Without waiting for the order, they took a knee, a few having to yank their robes out of the way. Each man brought his musket up to his shoulder and waited for Konowa's command to fire.

"Remember, lads, they're just trees," Konowa said, walking behind each soldier and patting him on the shoulder. "They might have learned a few tricks, but we're a damn sight smarter than any walking piece of wood."

"I see one!" a soldier shouted, swinging his musket in the direction of a *sarka har* emerging from the snow.

"Steady, and watch where you point a loaded musket. Remember your drill, lads. We'll wait until the others show themselves, then we aim for the last one. If they want to try that flaming fireball trick again, they'll have to backtrack, and by then we'll be gone."

Three more trees appeared, each moving forward in a stilted, creaking gait. Konowa shuddered, but quickly stamped his boots in the snow to regain control. He waited another minute, but no more trees showed themselves. "Okay, we'll take out the one on the far left."

As one, the soldiers leveled their muskets at the *sarka har*. Konowa brought his own musket up to his shoulder and sighted down the barrel.

"Ready . . . fire!"

Eleven muskets crackled to life. White-orange flame lit the night as sparks flew from the barrels. All eleven musket balls hit the trunk of the *sarka har* at almost the same instant. The double layer of black dragon-scale bark proved no match for the lead balls. The heartwood splintered, filling the air with a mist of brown ichor. A flickering flame on a piece of bark ignited the mist and the tree went up like a bomb.

Konowa dropped down beside the soldiers as flaming pieces of the tree, trailing an oily, foul-smelling smoke, flew over his head.

"Go back to where you came from, you stupid buggers!" Private Feylan yelled, slinging his musket and picking up a still burning length of branch and snapping it in half before quickly slapping his hands in the snow to cool them. The surviving *sarka har* ignored his taunt and went about the same procedure as before, stumbling back toward the flaming wreckage and adding more dragon scale bark to their trunks before gathering up burning chunks of wood.

"Nicely put," Konowa said, tapping the private on the shoulder and motioning for him to fall back. "Now it's time for us to advance in the other direction and get the hell out of here. We've got to warn the column there are more of the damn things coming after them."

"I sent three of the men after the column as soon as we realized we were in trouble," Feylan said.

Brave and thinks on his feet. Konowa was impressed. "If they stay clear of those things, they should hook up with the column before long. Good work."

Konowa risked a quick glance over at Private Feylan and was pleased to see the young private's face only had the barest of smiles on it. *Proud, but professional.* It made Konowa wonder how Feylan landed in the Iron Elves, but he'd have to ask him that another time. For now he focused his attention on the trees.

Their branches began to blaze as they caught fire again, but with each backward step the falling snow and the dark masked them until they disappeared completely. Konowa stopped for a moment and stared at the night. It all seemed like a terrible nightmare. Of course, it was—it was just that they were awake.

"Everything okay, Major?" Feylan asked.

"What?" Konowa said, making a show of removing his shako and wiping his brow with his sleeve before putting the hat back in place. "Just had to slow down for a second to cool off. All this running around gets me a little hot."

Silence greeted this, and Konowa remembered they had just lost a friend. He wanted to ask them to describe Grostril, hoping something would trigger a memory, but he realized that would only make them feel worse.

"Look, lads, just keep doing what you're doing and we'll be fine. Grostril was unlucky. Keep your heads on your shoulders, stay sharp, hold your fire, shout out if you see anything, and you'll have better luck."

They continued to backtrack through the snow. What had started as a neat line soon collapsed into a tight ball with muskets covering all points of the compass. Konowa had seen it before in battle. Soldiers would seek the comfort of having a comrade nearby and orderly lines began to mesh into ungainly herds. It was dangerous to be grouped so close together like that, especially when the *sarka har* could hurl flaming chunks of exploding wood, but the morale boost it gave the men was worth the risk, so Konowa said nothing.

"I would have thought the Darkly Departed would have showed up at some point," Feylan said. It sounded rhetorical, but Konowa knew all the soldiers were wondering the same thing, and so was he. *Why hadn't the dead appeared when they needed them?*

"Could be they're busy elsewhere," Konowa said, hoping the regiment wasn't currently under attack. "Or maybe they finally got some leave."

No one laughed this time, and Konowa didn't blame them. He opted to change the subject. He slowed his pace a little and motioned for Feylan to walk with him as the other soldiers continued moving in a tight cluster.

"Damn impressive the way you've organized the men. What happened to your corporal?"

"A branch took his head clean off," Feylan said, his voice surprisingly calm for such a statement.

Konowa cringed, recalling he'd just told the men to keep their heads on their shoulders.

Now Feylan's voice did catch, but he covered it with a cough. "When we first saw the trees, we thought they were soldiers, too, and he started to cuss them out for getting lost. He walked right up to one. After that I sort of just took over, but any of them could have done it. Guess I just piped up first."

Konowa knew better. Leaders stepped forward in times of danger. "You did more than that."

They walked on in silence. Konowa became aware of his boots crunching through the ice crust forming on the snow. He strained his ears in hopes of hearing the approach of the 3rd Spears coming back to their aid, but of course they'd have to fight their way through the other *sarka har* that were now somewhere between the end of the column and the rear guard.

I failed them. The thought struck Konowa particularly hard. If the rear guard hadn't moved off the path to save him, they would have stayed in position to slow down the *sarka har* and warn the 3rd Spears. Because of him the entire column was at risk. It all came down to the three soldiers Feylan had sent forward to warn the others. If they didn't make it, the *sarka har* would catch them completely unaware.

"I think I hear something," a soldier said.

The group shuffled to a stop. Konowa doubted any of them were breathing, himself included, as they focused all their energy on the night around them. Konowa didn't bother pushing his senses. The acorn was a constant cold pain against his chest now, which, when added with the numbing cold of the weather, was making it increasingly difficult to tell one from the other.

After a minute of listening to nothing, Konowa was about to order them to move when a piece of wood creaked somewhere in the dark.

"There, did you hear it?" the soldier asked. "It's one of them *sarka har*, and it's close."

"Shhhhh," Konowa said, waving at the soldier to be

quiet. Konowa turned his head to one side and closed his eyes. He heard the creaking sound again, but couldn't get a location on it. *Damn these ears.* Realizing it was pointless, he opened his eyes and looked at the soldiers around him. They had all turned and were staring in the direction the column had taken.

"Off the road, now," Konowa hissed, using his musket to direct the men. They moved quickly, pushing through the deeper snow until they were fifteen yards away. He turned and dropped to one knee, wrapping the leather sling of his musket around his left forearm, grounding the weapon on his thigh to keep it out of the snow. The men formed up beside him to his left, following his lead. Konowa kept his eyes on the road as he addressed them.

"We'll hit the *sarka har* as soon as they appear. That should draw them this way. While they pick up the bark and get ready to throw more fire, we'll swing around and run like hell to catch up with the regiment."

The sound of creaking wood grew closer. Someone coughed, followed by a thump as another soldier whacked the offender.

Konowa rolled his head to work a crick out of his neck and forced his breathing to slow. "I'll call out the tree to aim at and then we fire on my command. We'll reload once, I'll designate another tree, fire again, then take off. If any of you get separated from the group, stay on the road and keep running. They're slow and stupid. You're faster and not as stupid."

There was no telling if the soldiers laughed because the sound of wood grinding and knocking against itself rose in pitch to drown out even the wind.

"Bloody hell," Feylan said, "that sounds like twenty of them charging."

"Ready . . ." Konowa said, bringing the butt of his musket tight against his shoulder and resting his cheek against the stock. The smooth coolness of the wood felt comforting against his skin.

Somewhere down the line a soldier began to sob.

"Remember the boys that aren't here anymore. Remember . . . Grostril," Konowa said, thinking of so many others they had lost. "This is our chance to avenge a lot of wrongs."

The groan of wood being pushed to its limit filled the night. Konowa shifted his knee in the snow and sighted down the barrel of his musket. His world constricted to a small patch of snow-covered road fifteen yards away. All his anger and frustration poured out of him and focused on that place. The Shadow Monarch Herself wouldn't survive if She showed up now.

"As soon as the first one appears I'll call it, then we fire."

No sooner had Konowa spoken the words than a shadow burst out of the darkness and entered the killing ground.

SEVEN

The shadow grew in size, filling the area on the road directly in front of Konowa's musket.

"Ready . . . Aim . . ." He hesitated before uttering the final command. The acorn against his chest was no longer cold. Konowa lifted his cheek from the stock and looked closer.

"Hold your fire! Hold your fire! It's Rallie!"

Her Majesty's Scribe appeared out of the dark in a swirl of snow. As it settled, her wagon and the team of camels pulling it became visible, making the sound of the creaking wood clear. She pulled on the reins and brought the camels to a halt. The beasts brayed and spit and shook their heads, clearly agitated. With the reins still bunched in her hands, Rallie stood up and looked at Konowa.

"Bit of a cold night for a walk. I thought you fellows might enjoy a lift."

Konowa turned to the soldiers beside him to make sure they had lowered their muskets. It had been that close.

"On your feet," Konowa said, relief making it difficult for him to keep his voice from shaking. "Get in the back and stay alert."

They ran toward the wagon like a drowning man reaching for a lifeline, and Konowa realized that was pretty much the truth. He walked up to the front by Rallie, ignoring the camels, then turned to make sure all his men were aboard.

A set of large yellow teeth flashed out from the darkness and made a grab for Konowa's right shoulder.

Konowa shouted and flung himself out of the way, punching wildly and missing. He landed hard on his back and his musket fell from his hand. He fumbled madly for his saber, which was now tangled up in his robe. His shako popped off his head as if the wings on it were giving it flight in the storm-driven wind. The blast of icy air on his scalp cleared his senses.

It dawned on him as he frantically fought to get the blade free that the black acorn hadn't flared. He sensed several sets of eyes staring at him and he looked up.

"Come now, Major, the darling thing meant no harm," Rallie said from six feet above him. Her four camels hitched in pairs in front of the wagon stared at him in direct contradiction. She sat back down on the wooden bench and teased out the bundle of leather reins in her hands.

"I beg to differ," Konowa muttered, scooting back another few feet until he was well out of reach of the less-than-darling thing's teeth and hooves. Only then did he risk climbing to his feet, scooping up his musket first and then his shako. He placed it back on his head, all while keeping a wary eye on the camels. He heard a snicker and snapped his head around to look at the back of the wagon. Ten heads looking over the side of the wagon vanished in an instant.

Rallie's reins snapped and the camels reluctantly turned away from him and began lumbering forward. Konowa let them pass, then jumped up onto the wagon to sit beside her. He set his musket between his legs and turned to look behind him. The soldiers were huddling together to stay warm in between bundles of supplies and what appeared to be at least some of the Viceroy's things. They had their muskets pointed outward though and were scanning the darkness. None of them risked looking at Konowa, but a couple of them gripped their muskets tighter and leaned forward to indicate their dedication. Konowa growled, but he knew he didn't blame them. He would have laughed, too, if it hadn't been him on the wrong end of an angry camel.

"The *sarka har* can walk," Konowa said, turning back to face the front, "and throw fire. Oh, and they explode now, too."

Rallie sawed on the reins and the camels turned to the left, stomping through the deeper snow until they had turned the wagon around and were heading on the road in the same direction as the column. "Rather nifty, that," Rallie said, her voice revealing more than a trace of fascination. "It seems they found some dragon eggs, Major. Lucky for us a brood nest only held no more than fifteen."

"Dragon eggs . . . Is the regiment okay? Did those trees attack?"

"The regiment continues much as it did before, although I must say the degree of overall jumpiness has risen sharply. Three members of the rear guard made it back in time to warn us and with the 3rd Spears leading the way, they dispatched another six of the *sarka har*. It was a remarkable sight, but I guess I don't have to tell you that."

"No, I have a pretty good idea what that looks like," Konowa said. "And the Darkly Departed?"

"Stellar service, as always. Private Renwar made sure of it. Why?"

"We could have used their help," Konowa muttered.

"Ah," Rallie said, leaving it at that.

"But dragon eggs? How did they find any out here?" Konowa asked, choosing to change the subject. "I don't recall hearing about dragons in these parts for centuries."

Rallie didn't answer right away. When she did, she chose her words carefully. "Do you think me . . . mysterious, Major?"

"You're a woman," Konowa blurted out before he could stop himself. "I find your entire species mysterious."

Rallie chuckled. "Oh what I wouldn't give to see you appointed to the diplomatic corps one day. But truly, do I seem different?"

The heat generated from his close encounters was rapidly dissipating and Konowa shivered, pulling his robe closer around him. "If you're asking if I think you know a lot more than you let on, yes. Do I think you have your reasons for that, yes. Do I care, not really. You've more than earned my respect and gratitude. I have no doubt that if there was something I needed to know, and you knew it, you'd tell me."

"Why, Major, you've made an old woman blush,"

she said, and by the timbre of her voice, he could tell she wasn't joking.

"Why do you ask?" Konowa said. "You've never seemed too concerned about what anyone thought about you before now."

Rallie stared ahead, her cloak billowing as the wind picked up. "I can accept the aches and pains of old age, but losing one's memory wasn't part of the bargain."

Konowa sensed a shift in her mood to something darker. "What are you talking about? You're as sharp as a box of tacks."

Rallie nodded, but kept looking straight ahead. "It used to be two boxes," she said. "I'm old, Major, older than you think, in fact, older than I think I think."

It was tempting to ask her if she'd been drinking, but Konowa knew better. "We are going to make it through this, you know," he said at last, hoping it was the right thing to say.

This time Rallie did turn and look at him. Her eyes were misty, but there was a smile on her lips. "That, Major, was the perfect thing to say."

They rode on in silence with only the creaking of the wagon and the wind disturbing the night. Konowa fidgeted on the wooden bench. He was still keyed up from the battle. His thoughts were a mess. What was up with Rallie? He hoped it was just the cold and the dark. She'd always been a rock; the idea that even she could crack wasn't something he'd considered. And what of Renwar? He wanted to rail at the soldier for abandoning them to the *sarka har*, but was it malice on his part, or sound judgment? A rear guard was often sacrificed in order to give warning to the rest of the column. Konowa tried to convince himself that's what had happened, and failed. He shook his head and tried to think of something else.

"It's cold," he said, blowing on his hands before tucking them into the folds of his robe. A sudden thought popped into his head. "Will your creatures survive weather like this? All the ones you let go back at the canyon?"

Rallie turned and looked to the north before turning back. "Dandy and Wobbly are survivors. I've every expectation of seeing them again. The sreexes should be all right if they stayed together as a flock, but in this wind it's difficult to say. Alas, it's my brindos I fear for. A bit delicate, if you want to know the truth. I fear I coddled them, but they are such adorable animals, so how could I not?"

Konowa remembered the brindos as vicious-looking, armor-plated beasts that would just as soon trample you, but he kept it to himself. Rallie had even named one of them Baby. "If they had any sense, they would have headed south and away from this," he said, looking around at the snowstorm. "I hear there's nothing but grassland to the far south once you get through the desert."

"I do hope you're right, Major," Rallie said, her voice uncharacteristically quiet. "They deserve a better fate than to perish here."

"Don't we all," Konowa replied.

The wind blew between them piling up a drift of snow on the wooden bench. Konowa absently pulled a hand out of his robes and brushed at the snow and began tracing out stick figures.

"I believe she's alive," Rallie said.

Konowa looked up from the snow. *Visyna*.

His heart didn't beat faster as much as it beat stronger, deeper, at the thought of her. He'd done his best not to think about her, focusing instead on the task at hand. The regiment came first. It had to. The lives, and the souls, of each and every soldier depended on him. Who knew what horrors would jump out of the darkness next? Still, if Private Feylan could see a future beyond this, maybe he could, too.

Images of burning trees and exhilarating fear still raced through him, but thinking about Visyna brought memories of her power. He stared out at nothing as he remembered how she infuriated him in the quiet way she held her hurt, aggravated when she raged back at him, and cut when her eyes judged him and found him wanting. But when she smiled . . . He realized he was grinning and brought his hand up to his mouth to cough.

"Do you sense something?" he asked.

Rallie stared at him for several seconds before responding. "Not exactly, but nonetheless I believe it to be true. I certainly hope it to be the case, and hope is a power unto itself. It should not be taken lightly."

"And the others?" Konowa asked, thinking of his parents, his soldiers, and his four-legged friend, Jir.

"I don't know," Rallie said. "I thought it best to get them out of the way when I sealed them in one of the tunnels. Perhaps I made a mistake in sending them that way, but at the time it seemed the proper thing to do."

Konowa reached out and patted Rallie's arm. As soon as he did it he tensed, expecting frost fire or something worse to happen, but nothing did. "You did what you thought was best. That's all we can ever do. I'm sure they'll appear again."

The chuckle from Rallie caught Konowa off guard.

"I said something amusing?" Konowa asked.

Rallie snapped the reins and the camels brayed in response. "My dear Major, I do believe you're starting to get the gist of this hope thing after all."

A single transformed *sarka har* continued to trudge after the column, its pace slowed by the increased weight of several layers of dragon-scale bark. Snow and ice started to accumulate in its branches, weighing it down further. It paused and shook itself, keeping the form of a soldier though it wasn't sure what that was. It knew, however, that this shape would allow it to continue moving, and that need burned brighter than all others.

It sensed a vibration in the wind. It stopped and raised its branches, opening its leaves to better feel the disturbance. Two objects were approaching it at great speed. It saw no reason to defend itself, however. These were more *sarka har*. It lowered its branches and began trudging forward again, aware that the objects were now only yards away and closing fast.

Thick branches grabbed the *sarka har* on either side and lifted it high into the night sky. In its short, violent life the *sarka har* had never been out of touch with the earth. If it had had a mouth, it would have screamed. Then the other two *sarka har* let go. The tree plummeted to the earth, twisting and turning end over end as it fell. It smacked into the ground with a thunderous crack. Its trunk snapped in two, its branches broke and thick, brown ichor leaked from a thousand fractures.

The two *sarka har* landed and approached the fallen tree, tucking in their wooden wings as they did so.

Unlike their brethren, these *sarka har* had transformed into the shape of the dragons the eggs had meant to hatch. Instead of many small leaves they had grown green-brown skins that stretched between branches forming large wings. They had no heads, but where a jaw would be a branch jutted out lined with ten-inch thorns as thick as an elf's wrist.

Looming over the dying tree, each took turns slashing down with their spiked branch, tearing the stricken *sarka har* to bits. They grabbed its trunk and pulled, ripping it in half, and then half again. With each cut and tear more of the brown ichor flowed. As it pooled, the two trees moved to stand in it, absorbing the liquid through the remnants of their root system.

As they drank, they grew stronger. The scalelike bark covering their trunks thickened and took on a metallic sheen. More thorns sprouted along the leading edge of their wings.

When all the ichor had been absorbed, the two *sarka har* unfurled their wings and flapped them a few times. With each up and down movement their pace grew faster and more powerful. With a final pump the two trees leaped into the air and disappeared into the night heading due west.

"Are we there yet?" Private Scolfelton Erinmoss asked. Scolly wasn't bright, but what he lacked in intelligence he made up for in perseverance. "It's just that it seems that we should be there by now, shouldn't we?"

No one answered, leaving the question to chase the darkness beyond the light of their lanterns until it could no longer be heard. Boots scuffed over a thin skiff of sand on the tunnel floor in a mindless rhythm, filling the air with a rasping pulse.

The elves led by Private Kritton marched in front and behind the small band of human soldiers with Visyna. Though there was barely room to walk two abreast, Chayii Red Owl stayed at Visyna's side. Visyna opened and closed her mouth a couple of times to speak, but each time words failed her. Chayii's jaw continually clenched and unclenched and sweat beaded on her brow.

"Soon?" Scolly asked again.

Visyna cocked her head to the side then caught herself. She had instinctively listened for Yimt to bellow another anatomically unlikely occurrence involving a unicorn's spleen, Scolly's mother in the moonlight, and quite improbably something to do with cabbage. The realization that Yimt wouldn't be answering added to the darkness.

"No, Scolly, not yet," Visyna said, a tightness in her chest catching her breath. Visions of the dwarf falling to the floor in the library refused to go away. Anger was still in the future. Right now it was all she could do to put one foot in front of the other. She had no idea where they were going or how long they'd been walking. She was beyond tired to the point of feeling lightheaded with weakness. She shook the grit from her sandals as she walked, wishing she owned a pair of boots. Her thin cotton leggings and blouse were not designed for a desert environment.

Visyna recognized the beginnings of a downward spiral and tried to find something positive to think about. The caustic feel of the ancient magic in the library was gone, but even then she had little energy left to try and pull power from the air around them. And even if she could, what then? They were heavily outnumbered, the soldiers were stripped of their weapons, and the tunnel was narrow and stretched on far beyond her sight. A fight in here would be a bloody mess with little chance of succeeding. Maybe, she wondered, they were already dead. Kritton couldn't let them live, could he?

A low, rumbling snarl raised the hairs on the back of her neck. She turned and saw Jir limping behind her, his wounded shoulder causing him significant pain. She reached back with one hand and the bengar came close enough to let her fingers brush the top of his head. It surprised her that Jir should be so docile. She'd expected the elves to kill the beast out of hand, but in his wounded state the bengar appeared helpless. For reasons she couldn't comprehend, Jir had been allowed to follow them, and he seemed to understand the arrangement and made no outward signs of aggression. It was as if the bengar understood that this wasn't the right time to seek revenge.

A tongue like bark licked her hand and she pulled it back in surprise. She looked back at Jir, who returned her stare with an intelligence she had never seen before.

"I regret having to invade another creature's mind, but it was necessary to keep him calm, and alive," Chayii whispered between her teeth.

Visyna turned to look at her. "You're controlling him?"

"In a manner of speaking. I have connected with him, drawing out much of his rage and need to hunt," she said.

"What does it feel like?"

Chayii turned to look at her. Visyna tried to move away and put her shoulder into the tunnel wall. Raw, savage violence flashed in the elf's eyes. Chayii's lip curled into a snarl and the muscles in her neck rippled with suppressed energy. She rotated her head slowly, easing her shoulders down.

"I have never partaken of the flesh of another animal in my entire life," Chayii said, "but it is all I can do not to rip out the hearts of these elves and feel their blood trickle down my throat." As she said it her hands flexed as if she were extending claws.

Visyna hoped the horror that suddenly welled up inside her didn't show on her face. She looked around quickly to see if any of the elves had overheard, but no outcry arose. Perhaps, like Konowa, these elves had lost much of their hearing from constant exposure to musket and cannon fire. She knew her own hearing had suffered since deciding to accompany the Iron Elves.

"Do you have a plan on when to release Jir and we can escape?" She opted not to voice her growing concern that they would likely share Yimt's fate at the hands of Kritton before much longer.

Chayii shook her head. "I am doing what I can to control Jir. It is up to you, my child, to figure out what we do next."

The hope of a moment before dimmed, but did not die. *She's right*, Visyna realized. Thoughts of being little more than a damsel in distress brought blood rushing to her cheeks. *I can do this.* She brought her hands in front of her and gently began to weave the air. There was power here she could use. She lowered her hands and began to think. Even elves can't march forever. They would have to stop sometime to rest. When they did she would have to be ready.

"Are we there yet?"

This time Visyna smiled. "Soon, Scolly, soon."

EIGHT

Trailing the unknown shadow among the rocks, the rakkes moved cautiously at first. The green death was instinctively terrifying, but it was more than seeing one of their own kind eaten alive by it. Buried deep in their primal core lay a memory that any other sentient creature would have understood to be a nightmare. They couldn't fight the green death, only flee from it, and that went against their very nature.

They didn't understand why they were here, or even how. Each retained the memory of its death centuries ago—drowning, falling, burning, beheaded—horrors a rakke could understand. But to be here in this time and place, and faced with a death they couldn't tear with claws or rip apart with fangs added to their distress. They knew, however, that the thing that set the green death free could be torn. It would bleed, and so they trailed it, desperate to feed on its flesh while equally terrified that their own flesh would be devoured before they got the chance. A high wind drove between hairline fractures in the rocks issuing forth a razor shriek that dominated all other sound. Stone and sand tumbled as claws sought purchase on rocks slick with ice and snow as the rakkes picked up their pace, growing bolder with each passing minute they went undetected. They were many and it was alone and unaware it was being hunted.

The shadow continued on, moving from cover to cover, but having to expose itself more to the open in order to keep up with the rakkes on the desert floor below. Each sighting amidst the wind-driven snow spurred the rakkes on. They were closing in. Soon, they would feed.

A heavy gust of wind kicked up a mix of snow and sand, momentarily blocking the shadow from the rakkes' view. When it had passed the shadow was gone. Surprised, the rakkes lurched forward, forgetting their caution of before and now only focused on picking up the trail of their prey before it could slip away in the night. They bounded over rocks in blind pursuit, howling and yelping to each other as they worked themselves up into a killing frenzy. Long-extinct red-throated screams ripped through the air, seeking to flush out their quarry.

It worked.

The rakkes scrambled up and over a twenty-foot-high pinnacle of granite and descended into a shallow valley in front of another chunk of granite where the shadow stood waiting for them.

It was smaller than they had imagined; its hunchbacked body balanced on just two thick, short legs. Two ragged wings sprouted from its head and its face was covered in a thick matt of wind-blown fur, but its eyes were visible and without a glimmer of mercy. The green glow of impending death, however, came not from its mouth, which now smiled revealing gleaming metal teeth, but from the long black metal pipe with a wide-mouthed nozzle the demon held in its hands. Only now did the rakkes see the copper-wound hose that hung from the back of the pipe and curled up behind the demon to attach to the brass tank strapped to its back.

"You should have stayed extinct, you stupid buggers," Yimt said, squeezing the trigger on the weapon.

Three things happened at once. The heel of Yimt's left boot slipped on a piece of ice and his leg shot out in front of him dropping him straight down onto his backside. Instead of hitting all six of the rakkes the arc of the green phosphorescent insects shooting out of the weapon's metal nozzle only covered the two on the far right, their howls of fear and pain drowned out by the frenzied glee of the four remaining rakkes now lunging forward.

"Damn it, damn it, damn it!" Yimt shouted, struggling to climb to his feet before the rakkes could reach him. He clutched his chest, his hand covering a torn hole in his uniform. He stood up and swayed under the weight of the weapon on his back. Realizing it was too late to run he squeezed the trigger again, moving the nozzle side to side to spray the oncoming rakkes. Nothing came out. Elevating his cursing to greater heights he shrugged his shoulders out of the straps holding the tank to his back and heaved the entire weapon at the charging rakkes now scrambling up the other side of the crevice toward him.

The brass tank hit a rakke in the head with a satisfying clang and the hose of the metal barrel got caught up in the legs of the one behind causing all four rakkes to stumble and go down in a tangle of limbs. Not waiting to see if the tank had burst open, Yimt rolled over and crawled on his hands and knees up and over the rock he was on and rolled down the slope on the other side until a pile of rock debris stopped him.

He sat up with both arms crossed over his rib cage and let out a growl of pain. The sound of yammering rakkes clawing at the rock just on the other side of where he sat got him to his feet, though the effort had him spitting blood. He searched around in the dim light looking for a weapon and a place to hide, but the first rakke had already crested the top of the rock above him. The creature's howl vibrated off the rock around them and Yimt lost his footing again, going down to one knee.

The other rakkes appeared a moment later and then all four began to make their way down the slope toward him. Yimt took a quick look behind him, but the desert floor was still hundreds of feet below and the slope far too sheer for him to climb down. Turning back to the rakkes, he picked up a large rock in each hand and started calculating the odds. Two rocks, four rakkes.

Yimt blinked and wiped snow and sweat from his eyes and looked again. Two more figures stood atop the rock. It was difficult to make them out through the snow, but the wind died down just as they began to descend. He had time to see a drawn sword in the hand of one and a bow and arrow held by the other. A new gust of wind blew up and just before they were lost in the falling snow Yimt saw something far worse. Pointed ears.

"Nuns in butter," he muttered, twisting the heels of his boots into the gravel in hopes of better footing on the slippery rock. "Rakkes I can deal with, but dark elves, too?" *Fine*, he decided, he'd have to make sure he kept an eye on the elf with the bow. If the twisted beastie decided to hang back and shoot he'd have little chance. *Think, you daft dwarf, think.*

He'd have to take out the elf with the bow first and then turn his attention to the rakkes, who were much closer. Hopefully, if the snow kept blowing he'd have enough cover that he could take on his attackers one at a time. It was a long shot, but it was all he had. He cocked back his left arm ready to hurl the first rock when he noticed black frost burning on its surface.

"Well I'll be a newt in a pot," he said, stopping in mid-throw. He focused on the rock and concentrated. Black flames rose two inches high along its surface. The roar of a rakke startled him as it reared up just feet away. Saliva flew from its open maw as its curving yellow fangs lunged for his throat.

With no time to look for the elf with the bow Yimt threw the rock. It smashed into the rakke's face, breaking one of the upper fangs clean in two. The creature screamed in agony, but not from the broken tooth. Frost fire from the rock covered its face, washing it in flickering black flames. The oath magic took hold quickly, devouring the rakke before his eyes. First its black fur disappeared, revealing a gray, leathery hide that quickly eroded, revealing muscle and sinew that fell away in ribbons until only the silently screaming skull of the beast remained, before it, too, was consumed by the black frost.

Oblivious to the other rakke's fate or simply too maddened to care, another of the creatures leaped over the rapidly disintegrating remains and caught Yimt full in the ribs with a clenched paw. White sparks exploded behind Yimt's eyes as the other rock grew heavy in his hand and slipped from his fingers. He flew backward, landing in a crumpled heap on the edge of the ridge line with his head hanging over the precipice. His shako flew from his head to twirl like a top all the way to the desert floor.

Gasping for breath and clutching his side Yimt forced himself to his elbows and then his knees. He reached out with his right hand and patted the dirt looking for another rock to throw. A dark figure loomed over him and he looked up to see a rakke standing a foot away. Its mouth was a gaping jigsaw of sharp fangs. Yimt wondered why it hadn't already lunged at him when he noticed it was cradling one of its paws. It was clearly shattered.

"You daft . . . silly . . . bugger," he said, forcing the words out between breaths.

The rakke tilted its head in obvious pain and confusion.

"Punching a dwarf in the ribs that's spent his whole life chewing crute is like taking a swing at a boulder. It's the rock spice you bloody nitwit!" Yimt shouted, though the effort almost blacked him out. "It seeps into our teeth *and* bones. Makes them denser than you. Hell, not even a musket ball can make it through these things. And I should know."

The rakke roared and threw back its head in preparation to pounce. Its head went back, and back, and then kept on going, rolling across its right shoulder and then tumbling down its arm and onto the gravel where it landed face up. Blood spurted from its neck as the body remained perfectly still.

"What the hell?" Yimt said, his hand finally locating a rock. He gripped it as hard as he could, feeling the frost fire take hold. His eyes, however, remained fixed on the headless rakke standing in front of him. Then as if the strings holding it up had been cut, the body collapsed straight down. It didn't flop or spasm. Standing behind it, shrouded in swirling snow, was the elf with a now bloody sword. Looking past it, Yimt saw the crumpled bodies of the other two rakkes.

"Much obliged to you, but you ain't taking me alive," Yimt said, picking up the rock and bringing his arm all the way back. He saw the other elf appear out of the corner of his eye. Its bowstring was pulled fully back and an arrow pointed straight at him. The frost fire blazed like a star in his hand as he brought his arm forward to throw the rock at the elf holding the sword. The second elf released the bowstring setting the arrow to flight.

This, Yimt thought, *is going to hur—*

NINE

Konowa sat up straight on the wagon's wooden bench and reached for his chest. The black acorn flared then grew quiet again. He grabbed up his musket and peered out into the night. There was nothing to see but snow and rocks and sand. Now back with the column and relatively safe he should have been able to relax, but it wasn't working. *I'm getting jumpy,* he decided, sitting back against the bench. He looked over at Rallie, who continued to stare straight ahead, giving no indication she had noticed, though he knew damn well she had.

Better safe than dead, he consoled himself, resting his chin on his chest and pulling his shoulders up as far as he could. The cold was seeping into him, making him jumpy. He crossed his arms and, tucking his hands into the folds of his Hasshugeb robe, eased back further on the bench. With a scarf fashioned from a piece of a burlap sack wound around his face and his shako pulled low over his forehead only his eyes remained visible. Guilt gnawed at him in his cocoon, knowing the majority of the regiment marched in the foul weather while he rode in relative warmth. An icy gust found a chink in his fabric armor jolting him upright. He adjusted the robe before slipping back down into a semi-reclined position. For now, he could live with the guilt.

He wasn't sure when he'd slept last. If they had any hope at all of getting out of the Expanse and to the coast he'd need to be sharp. It was a rationalization and he knew it, but he dealt with it by knowing the rear guard led by the very able Private Feylan rode along with him in the back of Rallie's wagon. It was a well-deserved luxury and they had earned it.

Lest he be seen as playing favorites, he had also given the regiment permission to dip into the last sack of arr beans. There was no hot arr to be had on the move, but the soldiers popped the beans into their mouths and sucked on the bitter juice. Just the memory of the vile taste filled Konowa's mouth with saliva. Each bean was like a shot of lightning. He'd once marched five days straight on nothing but water and a handful of arr. Of course, he'd started seeing orcs riding flying unicorns by the end, but he'd survived, and so would the Iron Elves.

He wriggled around, trying and failing to get comfortable. Muscles ached with memories of battle he was doing his damnedest to forget. He carefully rolled his right shoulder and quickly stopped as the motion gave fuel to the burning coal of pain lodged deep in the socket. His old friend the Duke of Rakestraw called it saber shoulder and said it happened a lot in the cavalry.

Konowa wondered what Jaal was up to. *Hopefully something far less desperate than this.* The wagon tilted as its right-side wheels found a rut and Konowa slammed against the wooden slat that acted as an armrest. The pain in his shoulder flared, bringing his attention back to the here and now. *Why couldn't the damn cold of the oath deal with that?* he wondered.

The wagon righted itself and the ride went back to being simply bone jarring. He peered into the sky. He tried to calculate the time and gave up immediately when he realized he wasn't entirely sure what day it was let alone the hour. Already his sense of time was stretching and twisting. The driving snow dulled everything, turning the world before him into a gray-tinged blur. Not long ago such a storm would have been enough to foul his mood and send him questing deep into himself, asking why him and what the hell was going on. Now he saw the way forward and would not be deviated to either side. The Iron Elves were headed for the Shadow Monarch's mountain and one way or another, the oath would be broken. That was the why and the what of it.

A sudden gust of wind tore a brief window in the screen of snow. The column appeared, stretching out ahead of them like a black snake, its body a series of curves as the soldiers marched. A moment later it was gone again, lost in the swirling snow. Konowa considered finding Viceroy Alstonfar—Pimmer—he corrected himself, and asking him again if he was certain the regiment was heading in the right direction. Private Renwar appeared to know, but just how sane the soldier was Konowa couldn't say. Still, Konowa told himself, Pimmer would no doubt sound the alarm if they strayed off course. His faith in the diplomat continued to grow. Besides, to check with Pimmer would mean leaving the wagon seat just when he thought he was finding a position offering the least amount of pain.

And the last time Konowa had set off by himself had not exactly gone as planned.

The regiment, Konowa concluded as he let his back sag a little more, was unerringly headed for the fort on top of Suhundam's Hill. They would arrive at the foot of the hill in the next few hours . . . probably. What he hoped to find there remained a mystery to him.

The wind changed direction and Konowa picked up voices in the dark. He realized they were coming from the soldiers riding in the wagon bed behind him. A laugh drifted to him and the urge to turn and join in the conversation pulled at him hard, but he instinctively knew this was a time when soldiers needed to be alone, free to piss and moan and laugh about life, the fairer sex, food, officers, and the general state of the world from their vantage point. Konowa forced himself to stay where he was. He did, however, turn his head slightly so that he could catch a bit more of what was being said.

". . . you grease it up nice and thick, see, and that keeps it from sticking when it gets hot. Now if you're baking a rye bread you might want to consider a flat stone instead of a metal pan. Personally, I like to let the dough rise . . ."

Konowa smiled. A world of monsters surrounded them and their main concern was food. His own stomach gurgled and the taste of a warm loaf of fresh bread pushed all other thoughts out of his head. His fingers twitched as he remembered tearing pieces of a still hot loaf into chunks as steam rose from the soft bread within. His mother always had a wooden bowl of fresh honey for dipping, but only if he promised to eat a handful of berries and nuts as well. It was a bargain he was always happy to make. Maybe one day he'd have that chance again.

". . . with the damn recipes. I could gnaw the knobby bits off a camel at this point, so leave off would you? Now here's what you want to be puttin' your minds to. Where's our treasure then, eh?"

Ahh, a soldier with a bit of the pirate in him. Konowa wondered where this would go. Just a few scant hours ago all of them were a hairsbreadth from dying at the hands of infernal trees, and now they were talking about loot.

"Are you on about that again? The library burned, didn't it? Mostly rubbish was left, scrolls and papers and such which the fire didn't touch. The Viceroy grabbed those up and he's welcome to them is how I see it."

"But not all of it burned, did it?" the first soldier said. Konowa tried to place the voice but he couldn't. He realized the only soldier he knew by name out of the rear guard was Feylan. He'd have to learn the others. They all deserved a commendation.

"Think about this," the soldier continued. "We sail across the ocean jumping onto island after island to gut every last rakke and dark elf we find, yeah? We're all gonna get medals for it, too, right?"

Another soldier interrupted. "Me mum'll be right proud of me coming home with a medal or two on my jacket." Konowa recognized the voice. Definitely Private Feylan.

"She'd be a damn sight prouder if you had a small chest of coins tucked under your arm is all I'm saying."

More voices chimed in. Talk of riches clearly captured their imaginations.

"Duhlik says there was more in the library than

we're bein' told. He says he knows for a fact that there's fifty pounds of gold coins in small bags that made it out of the library."

"Who's Duhlik then and how many arrows did he take to the brain?"

Laughter greeted this, but the soldier talking about the gold coins would not be deterred.

"Duhlik, short fellow, about yea high, kind of weedy in the face. He's the one what got the sister who goes bald every time she's in a motherly way."

"That ain't Duhlik, that's Wistofer, and it ain't his sister, it's his wife. Saints and rabid owls, man, can't you tell them apart by now?"

"Look, it doesn't matter who said it, right? What matters is that it's true. We're marching along here as thin as paupers and the Prince and the major have packed away a fortune in gold coins. Why do you think we're lugging those cannons around with no shot for them? They stuffed the coins down the barrels see."

"I don't think Major Swift Dragon would do that," Feylan said.

Konowa nodded silently in agreement, but he did admire the other soldier's view on his general level of craftiness. Hiding valuables down a cannon barrel wasn't a bad idea at all, at least until you had to use it.

"He's an officer, ain't he? They're every one of them thieves of a sort. You know what it costs to be an officer? Lots, that's what. You gotta buy extra uniforms for fancy balls and such, mess hall fees, rounds of drinks, nice shiny swords, a horse more times than not, and at least one mistress on the side in addition to a wife and kids. All adds up."

"That may be true," Private Feylan said, "but the major's not like that."

You just made corporal, my son, Konowa decided.

"He's an elf, and they're kinda peculiar when it comes to money," Feylan continued. "Not too keen on minted coins. Now, if it was something natural like diamonds or rubies on the other hand, he'd be stuffin' them down his pants and under his shako to be sure."

And back to private you go.

The first soldier tried to get them back on point. "What I'm saying is, there's treasure to be found out here. That library was just one spot, but there have to be others. Think about it. We're going to this fort, right, and it sits on a hill overlooking a trading route. That means those elves have had time to do a little taxing of the merchants' caravans in return for safe passage. Maybe gold coins, maybe diamonds and rubies. Whatever it is, it's gotta be worth something. And if them elves ain't there when we get there I say what's the harm in snooping around a bit and seeing what we can scrounge?"

Konowa really couldn't argue with that logic. The life of a soldier in the Calahrian Army was damn hard. Out here it was closer to a nightmare. If his elves had padded their meager pay with a few bribes here and there he wouldn't judge them any the worse for it. They'd been dealt a crappy hand through no fault of their own. Getting a little something back seemed only natural. It made perfect sense to Konowa, yet deep down it filled him with unease. Deep, deep down, he hoped it wasn't true.

The wagon found another rut jolting Konowa forward and back. If the conversation behind continued he could no longer hear it. He gave up trying to listen and shook himself upright while shedding drifts of snow from the folds in his robe. Brushing off more of it he noticed the flakes felt drier and colder than before. He rubbed a few flakes between his finger and thumb and immediately regretted it.

"Son of a witch," he muttered, twisting his head to free his mouth from his makeshift scarf. He brought his stinging fingers to his lips and blew on the skin. When he pulled his hand back bright red drops of blood beaded on the pads of his finger and thumb from several small cuts.

"It's more ice than snow," he said, turning to Rallie.

She pushed the hood of her robe back far enough to see him out of the corner of her eye. A black cigar dangled from her lips, the end of the cigar burning bright orange in the night. "It's worse than you think. This snow springs from the heart of Her forest. It's tainted with metal ore. She failed in Her first attempt to plant Her forest here, so now she's preparing the ground for another try."

Konowa lifted his head and stuck out his tongue. The bitter tang of metal made him grimace.

"She'll kill everything," he said, sitting back down. He'd always believed the Shadow Monarch was mad, but in a controlled, specific way. The enormity of what She was attempting left him weak. "Rallie, She really is insane. She's planning to destroy the entire world."

Rallie's cigar burned brighter as she took several puffs before answering. Her words flowed out with a stream of smoke. "I suspect that in Her mind this makes perfect sense. A world populated with nothing but *sarka har*, their roots ripping into the foundations of all the lands until everything is black forest. It's certainly not what most of us would consider an improvement, but She is working at a distinct disadvantage," she said, pointing to her head.

Konowa turned to stare straight ahead, hunching his shoulders against the cold. "And all because of the Wolf Oaks and the stupid need of my people to find a *ryk faurre*. Nature was doing just fine before we came along. All of this could have been avoided if we'd left well enough alone."

"That's a rather harsh assessment, don't you think?" Rallie asked.

"Harsh? Look around us. Rallie, it's snowing *metal*. Forests of *sarka har* are sprouting up everywhere, some of the buggers have even learned to walk, and we're bound by an oath trapping us in shadow for eternity. No, I don't think I'm being harsh enough. And when we get to Her mountain this all comes to an end."

"So you really do intend to kill Her then?" The tone in Rallie's voice was measured, but Konowa knew an accusation when he heard one.

"Rallie, Her crystal ball is cracked. You said so yourself. She's already killed thousands, and for what? So some possibly sentient tree even more twisted than Her will have a lovely little place in the sun to spread its leaves? She's a poison that needs to be eradicated before She can do any more damage."

Rallie turned to look at him. Her eyes shouldn't have shone that brightly from beneath her cloak. "I don't dispute for a moment the horrors She has unleashed, but when the time comes, don't forget that unlike Her you have choices. She cared for something so deeply that She lost Herself in it. Surely you can understand that."

Konowa sat back a little from Rallie. "It's not the same. All I've ever tried to do is what's right. And look at what I've lost because of Her." He realized his hand had come up to rub the tip of his ruined ear and he quickly brought it back down. "After what we've all lost? No, Rallie, there is only one choice before me."

"You mean like at Luuguth Jor when you could have broken the oath?"

Konowa choked back what he was going to say next. He hated that Rallie was able to make something so simple and clear significantly more complicated just by asking questions.

"Life is messy, Major. We fool ourselves at our great peril if we think otherwise."

"If She doesn't die, how does any of this end?" Konowa finally asked, surprised that he was even considering the possibility.

"I assure you I haven't the foggiest," Rallie said, turning to face forward again. "But it'll be most interesting to find out."

Konowa waited to hear if she had more to add, but judging by the cloud of cigar smoke pouring out from her cloak it was clear she was done talking. The wind picked up, knifing its way through gaps in his robe. Cursing softly, he hunched in on himself to find some warmth. His eyelids closed of their own volition and he began to drift into sleep. He found some small comfort in the fact that with the winter storm still blowing and the horror of the walking *sarka har* now behind them, the regiment was slightly safer from attack. With the current state of the world, Konowa viewed that as a major accomplishment.

TEN

The creature that had once been the man Faltinald Elkhart Gwyn, Viceroy of the Protectorate of Greater Elfkyna, and until a few hours ago the Shadow Monarch's Emissary, struggled to hold on to its sense of being. It moved across the windswept desert, oblivious to the falling snow and the chilling cold.

Its thoughts, once sharp and precise, now spun about a wobbling axis of rage and agony. Were it to rest for even a moment it feared it would simply cease to exist, its energy scattered to the far reaches of the world. Even now, precious fragments of memory and personality crumbled and were lost.

"Diplomacy is not the victory of negotiation, but the failure of war," it muttered to itself. Shards of the life it once lived cascaded through its mind. It saw great halls lit with a thousand candle chandeliers, the light refracting off minutely faceted crystal goblets so thin they sang with just the exhalation of breath. It recalled a map skillfully made by jewelers using the finest gems and metals. It reached out a hand, grasping at something that wasn't there.

The hand closed in a tight fist and it dug deep into the agony and found white, piercing pain and clung to it while the rest of its mind spiraled faster and faster into madness.

I am free! The shackles that had bound it were broken. With that knowledge its anger grew, coalescing into something clear and simple that it could grasp. *The Shadow Monarch betrayed me!* The elf witch struck a deal with the oath-bound soldier of the Iron Elves. But the creature had sacrificed much to be Her Emissary, not that human. It was . . . unfair.

The creature felt a new emotion take hold, one more powerful than its rage or its suffering—revenge. "Talk loudly so that your opponent doesn't hear the assassin creeping up from behind," it said, seeing waiters in crisp white jackets moving silently behind a line of high-back chairs. A single flash of a knife and a guest's soup would grow cold. It laughed, hoping it would soon settle the score with the soldier that had usurped it. Rakkes howled as it laughed and the creature became aware of the growing pack of rakkes surrounding it as it moved across the sand. Hundreds now followed it. The simple beasts looked to it for guidance. More and more rakkes joined as they moved in a northerly direction.

"Diplomacy buys time until the army is in place," it said, looking around at the ancient creatures brought back to life in order to wreak havoc.

The creature smiled, revealing a row of black teeth hoary with frost. The rakkes had picked up a scent and were hunting.

This was an army. Nothing as skilled or precise as the soldiers it had once directed through its efforts at the negotiating table, but these things knew how to kill, and the time for diplomacy was over.

Distant memories of diplomatic missions broke through the whirling chaos of its mind. Armies were often used as leverage, forcing the enemy to concede without blood ever being spilled. It was a quaint notion, and one the creature no longer understood. Its only reason for living, in fact the only thing keeping it alive, was the need to wreak terrible vengeance on those that had wronged it.

The pack picked up its pace and began growling in low, guttural tones to each other. Prey had been spotted. The creature pushed itself forward until it took its rightful position at the head of the pack, its pace unnaturally quick as it scurried across the frozen desert. Its eyes, now frozen orbs of black ice, pivoted within its head with a grating noise of granite on glass. Pain flared in its skull as pure light, and it stumbled before regaining its footing. Forcing its head up, it peered into the darkness. Three hundred yards away a group of three wagons pulled by teams of camels rolled slowly along a caravan path. The creature waited, hoping. A moment later, a column of marching soldiers appeared out of the swirling gloom following the wagons.

The Iron Elves! It had found them. Saliva trickled down what was left of its face as icicle fangs framed its mouth. There would be no ceremony, no elaborate signing of documents, no fake smiles and exaggerated handshakes. This would be a massacre.

It would have its revenge, and the rakkes would feed. Finding control in its pain, the creature wrapped itself tight around its desire to kill. Rakkes slunk away from it as it began to hum with an eerie vibration.

The creature considered ordering the rakkes to spare its usurper, but there would be no need. Its power was great, too strong for any rakkes to defeat. That task would fall to the former Emissary, and it welcomed it.

"I have brought you food."

The rakkes gave full throat to their howls. They stomped the ground and beat their chests. Hackles rose and eyes slitted as their world squeezed down into a single red-hazed need.

"Tear them apart!"

The rakkes raced across the snow-covered sand. All along the column shouts and cries rang out. Camels started and tried to flee as their drivers vainly attempted to keep them under control. The soldiers stopped where they were and began to frantically ram charges into their muskets as the rakkes closed to within two hundred yards. The first shots split the night in a ragged, undisciplined burst. Hot yellow tongues of flames illuminated the hasty line of defense as the column made its stand. Here and there a rakke tumbled and fell, a head shattered, a heart holed, but for every rakke brought down dozens more came after it.

A more controlled volley slashed through the forward ranks of the rakkes at a hundred yards, scything down over a dozen. The surviving rakkes only howled louder and leaped over their dead. Fresher meat was only a short distance away.

The creature looked everywhere for the oath-bound soldier that had stolen its place. It tried to marshal its senses enough to search for it, but the smell of blood was in the air and the rising crescendo of the rakke

pack overpowered everything until it, too, was consumed with the need to rend flesh.

Cries and shouts rose above the charging rakkes as
the men of the column saw their fate moments away. In
a feat of arms made possible by sheer desperation they
managed one more volley as the rakkes crossed the last
ten yards. Rakkes tumbled at their feet in a spray of
blood and flesh and bone fragments, their fur smoldering from the burning gunpowder.

And then the rakkes were upon them.

Screams rose and then cut off abruptly as claw and
fang made short work of the flesh before them. A few
soldiers used their muskets as clubs in one last attempt
to cling to life, but their effort only added seconds. Any
man who turned and ran was borne down by claws in
his back and felt the hot, fetid breath of a rakke in its
ear as the beast's fangs bit down on its neck.

"Where are you?" the creature shouted, wading
through the carnage as the rakkes swarmed over the
wagons like scavenger beetles stripping the flesh from
the carcass of a dead animal. Camels went down under
the weight of several rakkes with a last, defiant braying.
Drivers were pulled from their benches and torn into
bite-sized pieces.

". . . mercy . . ."

The creature turned, searching for the source of the
plea. It spotted a bloody figure a few feet away half-
buried under the carnage. Part of a gnawed rib cage
obscured its view. It strode over and blasted the carrion
to pieces. It looked down. The dead were a mix of elves
and men. It began lifting and tossing the bodies aside as
if they were no more than pieces of wet, dripping cloth.
In its haste to get to the survivor it tore arms from

sockets and spilled innards in sickening heaps until finally it found a dwarf. It reached down and grabbed the dwarf by its beard and pulled it from the pile.

"Where is he?"

Frost began to sparkle along the dwarf's beard as it struggled to breathe. One eye was closed, and it was missing an arm. The wet socket where its shoulder used to be froze over in a black, crackling mess and the dwarf cried out in pain. The creature looked past it to one of the overturned wagons. Artifacts lay spilled in the snow, the gold and gems going unnoticed by the rampaging rakkes. Something about this triggered a memory in it. Library. Kaman Rhal.

"Who are you?"

The dwarf motioned with its one good arm toward its throat and the creature released its grasp, letting it fall to the desert floor. Rakkes moved in to finish it off, but the creature hissed and kept them at bay.

"My . . . my name is Griz Jahrfel, I am a merchant . . ."

The creature searched what little memory remained and realized its mistake. *"You aren't the Iron Elves!"*

The dwarf shook his head. "No. Some of the elves used to be, but not anymore. They work . . . they work for me now," he said, his voice breaking into sobs.

The creature conjured a spear of black ice and stabbed it into the fleshy thigh of the dwarf, who began screaming.

"Where are they? Where?"

"I don't know! If they left the valley they probably headed west along the main caravan route. Stop, please!"

The creature remembered the jeweled map. It had been a thing of much beauty. Precious metals and sparkling gems gleamed before its eyes, tracing borders and marking the limits of the empire it had once helped expand. That the map was worth a fortune meant nothing to it now, but the location of the caravan route did. It saw it clearly and understood. It vanished the spear and walked away.

"Wait! Kill me, please kill me! Don't let them—" The dwarf's words turned into screams as the rakkes moved in.

With blood dripping from their fur and chunks of flesh still hanging from their mouths the pack moved off with the creature urging them on, a strange phrase stuck like a metal pick in what was left of its mind.

Suhundam's Hill.

Konowa opened his eyes and scanned what little he could see of the desert around them. The acorn against his chest thrummed with a cool intensity. It wasn't a warning as much as an acknowledgment of power somewhere out there in the dark. He wondered briefly if it could be Visyna, but suspected it was something he'd just as soon never meet.

The wagon continued its rocking motion as Rallie steered the camels, and Konowa let his eyes close again, telling himself he'd rest them for just a few minutes.

"Double bloody hell!"

He was standing among the Wolf Oaks of his homeland.

I'm dreaming. Again.

He fought the urge to shout or kick or even try to rouse himself from sleep. Based on his previous visits with the Shadow Monarch there didn't seem much chance that he was going to enjoy this, but perhaps he could learn something useful.

All right then, he said to himself, *let's have a look around.*

The forest blurred and suddenly the birthing meadow spread out before him. The sun sat low in the sky casting long shadows from the towering Wolf Oaks surrounding the meadow. Saplings rose arrow straight above the dark, green grass, their leaves unfurling before his eyes as they oriented themselves toward the sunlight. He took a deep breath and was surprised when he didn't feel the crisp cold of a late frost. He took a couple of steps then stopped and looked down. His boots glistened with dew. There was no frost anywhere.

This didn't make sense. The Shadow Monarch bonded with Her Silver Wolf Oak during a late frost. He glanced around the meadow trying to find Her.

A figure sat huddled by a sapling near the edge of the meadow on the far side.

Konowa shrugged and started forward again. He went to shift his musket to his shoulder but his hands were empty. It was just a dream, but all the same, he wanted a weapon in his hands. He reached for his saber, but his scabbard was empty. He stopped and looked down. A twin-headed dwarf battle-ax lay in the grass at his feet.

"Well that's odd," he said, shaking his head as soon as the words came out of his mouth. This was a dream. Odd was merely the starting point.

He reached down and picked the ax up, grunting at the weight. It felt good to hold it, but a guilty feeling kept him from enjoying himself. Axes were viewed as evil incarnate by the elves of the Long Watch. Anything that harmed trees was seen that way. The elves of the

Long Watch weren't known for their sense of humor. Konowa knew his father's choice to transform into a squirrel was partly due to the old elf's desire to tweak their noses and partly because his mother would have disowned him or worse if he'd chosen the form of a beaver instead.

"What are you planning to do with that?"

Konowa turned. Regimental Sergeant Major Yimt Arkhorn stood among the saplings a few feet away. Unlike Konowa he was fully armed with his shatterbow cradled in his hands and the wicked-looking drukar knife hanging from his belt.

"You're dead," Konowa said.

"And a good morning to you, too," Yimt replied. He didn't smile, but looked around the meadow. If he noticed the figure in the distance he paid it no attention.

Konowa gathered his wits. "What happened to you?"

"Think, Major, think. How would I know that? I'm not really me, I'm you, or rather the part of you remembering me. All I know is what you know . . . more or less."

Riddles, lovely. The conversation looked dangerously similar to ones he had with his father, at least until the old elf turned into a squirrel. Konowa decided to try a different approach.

"Any idea why a dwarf ax would be lying around here?"

Yimt shrugged. "Got all my weapons here. Guess that's for you."

Konowa rested the end of the ax handle on the ground and tilted the weapon away from his body to get a better look at the twin half-moon-shaped blades. "So why do dwarves use axes? I never understood that.

You're born miners for the most part. Wouldn't shovels make more sense?"

"Ever try to bash a man's head in with a shovel? It can be done, but it ain't pretty, and it usually takes more than one swing. But that's not why. It's like you said, we're miners."

Konowa waited for an explanation, but none was forthcoming. Apparently, Yimt thought it was obvious. Konowa didn't.

"That doesn't make sense. There's no way you swing these things down in a mine shaft," Konowa said, flicking a finger against one of the blades. A sharp ting rang out that echoed far longer than it should have.

Yimt nodded. "True enough. But mines need shoring up, and that's done with big, thick timbers, and that means dwarves spend a lot of time chopping down trees to use in their mines."

"I didn't know that," Konowa said, but now that he thought about it, it made sense. "Is that why elves and dwarves don't get along?"

Yimt lifted up the brim of his shako to get a better look at Konowa. "What, you mean any better than elves and humans, or humans and other humans, or perhaps you mean you and just about everyone else?"

"Point taken, point taken." This wasn't quite the jovial dwarf that Konowa remembered. Or maybe it was the best he could remember. Dreams were tricky. He knew he'd missed something, but he couldn't put his finger on it.

Yimt tugged on his beard and looked around. "Look, we're being watched, so I have to make this fast."

Konowa looked around the meadow. Dusk had fallen, though he could have sworn it had been early morning only a minute ago. The figure still sat at the far side of the meadow. Something about it looked naggingly familiar to Konowa.

"What?" Konowa asked.

Yimt motioned with his shatterbow toward the distant figure. "Use the ax."

Konowa looked down at the ax, then back up. "That won't solve anything. This is a dream. I *know* it's a dream. Nothing I do here is going to matter when I wake up."

"Then the sooner you get on with it, the sooner you can wake up," Yimt said. "Use the ax."

Mist started pouring between the trees, blanketing the meadow in a white down. A pain began to grow in Konowa's chest. He tried shrugging his shoulders and taking a deep breath, but it didn't help.

Konowa looked at the ax again, then out toward the figure still sitting by the sapling. "Look, I hoped I'd figure something out by this—" He stopped talking. He stood alone, and night had fallen. Konowa gripped the ax in both hands and started walking. The mist swirled around his knees. The pain in his chest wouldn't go away. He rolled his shoulders and got a better grip on the ax. *Yimt is right and Rallie is wrong,* he thought, *there is no other choice. She has to die.*

He reached the Shadow Monarch long before he was ready. Though She was still shrouded in mist he could see Her clear enough that he wouldn't miss.

He raised the ax, ready to swing.

She turned to look up at him. Konowa was now looking at himself.

The ax hung still in the air as he stared at his double. He knew this was a dream, and that it had to mean something else, but what?

"Do it," the Konowa by the tree said. "Swing the ax."

Konowa shook his head. "You aren't real. I know that. So what the hell does this mean?"

His double was gone, and now Kritton sat by the tree. Konowa's hands gripped the ax harder.

"You won't have the guts when the time comes, I know it. You know it," Kritton sneered. "All of this, everything you've been through, and you can't finish things, even when it's just a dream." Kritton started to laugh, his mouth growing large and filling with sharp, black teeth covered in frost.

Konowa swung the blade.

Konowa leaned forward, opening his eyes and ready to strike. "Hell and a handbasket," he said, trying to shake the sleep from his head. His dreams just kept getting weirder. He looked down and saw his hands gripped tightly around his musket. He pried them loose and flexed his fingers.

"You wouldn't believe the dream I just had . . ." he said, then trailed off, realizing the wagon wasn't moving. He blinked and sat up straighter and looked over at Rallie. She was looking straight up. The acorn pressed against his chest was ice cold and he understood what the pain in the dream had been. He looked up as well.

"What—" was all he managed to say before Rallie turned and shoved him hard. Konowa reached out to Rallie to steady himself and managed to grab a scroll of paper from her robe before he was falling off the wagon, face-first into the snow. The shock of the snow against his flesh brought him fully awake. He scrambled to his feet cursing, only to be knocked flat again when Rallie landed on top of him. Before he could try to get up, an earsplitting noise of rending, splintering wood shattered the night followed by the rush of wind and screams. He drove himself up using his elbows and flopped over onto his back. The backboard of the bench on Rallie's wagon was in pieces. Two seconds later and that would have been him.

Soldiers ran and stumbled to get away from it. Two of the camels had broken free from their harness and were galloping off into the night. The other two were little more than bloody heaps on the road, staining the snow a bright red. A single wheel from Rallie's wagon broke loose and rolled down the road like a drunken sailor.

The acorn flared a biting cold, and he heard the thrum of air on wings accompanied by the creaking of wood he'd only ever associated with a ship's masts. He followed the sound and his legs began to tremble of their own accord at what he saw.

A flying tree in the shape of a dragon. His mind refused to accept it even as something deeper and more instinctual in him understood the horror approaching and sparked every fiber in his body to move.

"What is it with these damn trees?!" he shouted. He jumped to his feet as his fear gave energy to his anger. His understanding of the world kept shifting under his feet. The transformed *sarka har* flew in low over the column, dipping its front branch laced with thick, sharp spikes. Three soldiers dove out of the way, but a fourth wasn't as lucky and was impaled through the shoulder.

The *sarka har* flew up until Konowa could barely see it. He followed its movement by the screams of the soldier. When the pitch of the screams changed Konowa knew the tree had let go. A moment later the soldier fell in a blur to impact onto the road with a sickening thud. Konowa didn't bother to wait to see his shade appear, but said a silent good-bye to another Private Grostril, whoever this one might be.

"Rallie, are you okay?" he asked, remembering the scribe and turning to check on her. She was already sitting up and had her quill and the scroll of paper in her lap. Konowa felt relief flood through him to be replaced by a cold emptiness a moment later when she began cursing and tossed the scroll away.

"It's too wet. The ink just smears and won't hold its shape," she said, climbing to her feet. She still clenched a cigar in her mouth, the tip of it burning like a smithy's forge. "My fault entirely for not giving you fair warning, but time was working against us."

"Isn't it always," Konowa said, drawing his saber. "Stay low and try not to move."

"Go, I'll be fine," she said.

Konowa turned and ran onto the road, shouting to the soldiers around him. "Stay low! Load your weapons and fix bayonets, but hold your fire until I give the command."

A piece of wing from a shako fluttered down to land by his boots. He looked up and saw the two *sarka har* circling overhead.

"What in the blue heavens are those?" Viceroy Alstonfar said, trotting up to Konowa with something close to glee in his voice.

"Dead in another minute," Konowa barked, spying RSM Aguom ten yards away rounding up more troops. "Have you seen Private Renwar? We need those damn shades and we need them now!"

Aguom shrugged his shoulders. "No, but I'll find him!"

Konowa slashed his saber in the air. "Send someone. You stay here and get the troops organized. We're going to fire a volley straight up at the things and knock them out of the sky."

"Yes, sir," Aguom shouted back.

Konowa turned and saw the Viceroy was still standing beside him. "You should find a place to hide, Viceroy, the road is not safe."

"I'm not sure the surrounding desert offers any better cover. Better to stay among the column and be one of many than off by myself I think."

The logic of it made Konowa pause. "Where's the Prince?"

Pimmer's face turned a ghostly white. "Mercy, in all the hubbub, I forgot all about him! The future king and I left him alone!"

"We'll find him," Konowa said, not caring a whit if they did or not at the moment. "Right now we have more pressing duties." Turning, he marched over to a group of Iron Elves and crouched down on the road beside them. "Just like before, only we'll be shooting up. On the next pass we'll shoot at the first one that comes."

"But, Major, what are those things?" a soldier asked.

"Dead in another minute," Viceroy Alstonfar said, coming up to crouch beside Konowa. "Listen to the major and follow his lead and you'll all be fine."

Konowa twisted on the soles of his boots to get a look at the Viceroy. The diplomat met his gaze and gave him a big smile followed by a wink. Konowa decided, barely, that he didn't want to make a habit of killing viceroys.

"Nicely put," he finally said, spinning back to face his men.

"Good to keep the men's spirits up," Pimmer said, reaching out and patting Konowa on the back before quickly removing his hand as frost fire crackled to life and stung his bare flesh.

"They're coming!"

Snow swirled and buffeted into trailing vortexes behind the wings of the *sarka har* as they dove. The column lay spread out and vulnerable.

Each tree lowered its jawlike branch. Wicked-looking thorns gleamed like saliva on wet teeth. More thorns sprouted at the end of branches now shaped like claws.

Several soldiers started to get up to run.

"Hold your ground!" Konowa shouted. "You're not chickens being chased by a hawk. You're Calahria's finest. On my command you will fire and you will knock those bloody trees out of the sky. Is that clear?"

The responding "yes, sir" wasn't as enthusiastic as Konowa would have liked, but it would do. The men were back under control.

"RSM, did you hear that?" Konowa said, looking over toward the group of soldiers ten yards away.

Aguom waved. The whites of his eyes were visible, but his voice remained rock solid. "We're ready, Major, just say the word."

Konowa stood up and walked down the road so that he was just in front of the massing soldiers. He stopped where Rallie's wayward wagon wheel now stood forlornly upright, completely undamaged. He turned briefly to look as many in the eyes as he could before spinning abruptly and facing the *sarka har*.

He felt naked in the cold. Every survival instinct told him to run, but he ignored them. Other instincts came to the fore, whispering in his ear to jump into the air and tear the trees apart with his hands and teeth. He settled on something between the two and raised his saber high into the air.

"Ready . . ."

Soldiers ground their knees a little deeper into the snow to steady themselves. In all their training they'd never practiced shooting up into the sky. Several wound up with bloody knees as they pressed hard enough to reach the gravel of the roadway itself. An enterprising few rested the barrel of their musket on the shoulder of the soldier in front of them while three chose to lay flat on their backs and use the very ground itself as a means of steadying their aim.

Unaware or uncaring of the reception that awaited them, the *sarka har* dove. Each tucked in their branch-and-leaf wings with a grating shriek and steepened their dive. A high-pitched whistling began to build, cutting through the wind and the shouting.

Konowa tapped into his anger and forced the frost fire to light his blade. He had no illusions that it would make one bit of difference against these monsters, but he had another motive. "On my command, shoot above the tip of my saber, men, and not a moment before. We'll get one chance at this, so make it count." He could have left it at that, probably should have, but in a night that seemed destined to be his last, he needed to say more. "Remember, shoot just above the saber, not below. I've already had one ear tip trimmed, I don't need a matching set!"

Konowa's own laughter filled his ears, making it

difficult to tell whether anyone else had joined in. Above, the *sarka har* angled their approach and now lined up one behind the other.

They were diving directly at him.

"Aim . . ."

Prayers, curses, and possibly even a song rose from the ranks. No matter where a soldier kneeled or lay it looked like the wooden dragons were diving straight at them. More than a few hands trembled, and at least two soldiers had left their ramrods sticking in the barrels of their muskets, but be they terrified or simply scared, they held their ground and took aim.

Still a hundred yards away and forty yards high, the lead *sarka har* thrust out its wings with a crack like a cannon shot, slowing its descent. The *sarka har* behind it followed suit. A moment later each had lowered its thorn-lined branch in preparation of a raking run along the column.

Konowa filled his lungs with air and opened his eyes wide. Whatever was about to happen, he wasn't going to miss it. He sighted along the edge of his saber blade and squeezed the pommel until he was sure he would crush it.

The lead monster filled Konowa's sky above his saber as the *sarka har* hurtled downward to ten yards away.

"Fire!"

ELEVEN

The massed musket fire of the regiment lit up the night. Thunder and smoke rolled over Konowa as the volley snapped forth like iron rain. Musket balls whizzed above his head, one even grazing his outstretched saber blade setting the lead ball ablaze with black flame. The lead *sarka har* took the full brunt of the volley. Its wings shredded as the musket balls tore it apart while its trunk shattered into splinters as the shots carved through it. It exploded in a searing flash, scattering chunks of flaming debris outward as it continued its dive toward the ground.

And Konowa.

Konowa never considered joining the artillery. To be an officer in that branch of the service meant having a superior understanding of mathematics and physics, especially the calculation of such bizarre, finicky notions as velocity and trajectory. He didn't have the head for that kind of thing. Just how much he didn't was now hurtling toward him as an expanding fireball.

"Son of a—" was as far he got, not out of any sense of sudden decorum, but on account of the wind being knocked from his lungs. The flaming pieces of the *sarka har* crashed into the road three feet in front of Konowa and bounced. A six-foot section slammed into the wagon wheel in front of him which, while saving his life, still hit him at a high rate of speed. The world as he knew it vanished in a tornado of bright and dark, fire and ice.

And then he was floating. Blood pounded in his ears and every joint, muscle, and bone in his body felt pulverized. The wind tore at his uniform and he became conscious that he was trying and failing to get air into his lungs. He convulsed and a gulp of frigid air plunged down his throat, snapping open his eyes.

Sounds and sensations flooded back. He could see the flaming wreckage of the first *sarka har* on the road thirty feet below. He couldn't see the second.

Konowa became aware of a rhythmic creaking and turned his head just enough to catch the up and down beat of a large wooden wing. As his head cleared, the scope of just how much he hadn't thought through where to stand hit him. He was hanging by the waist, probably from his leather belt by the feel of his stomach, facing downward, which meant the second *sarka har* was directly above.

The shouts of the soldiers below began to make it through to his brain.

"Jump, Major, jump!"

"The snow will break your fall!"

"Jump!"

The *sarka har* lurched and Konowa experienced a feeling of momentary weightlessness. He twisted his body so that he could get a better look at the *sarka har*. For the second time that night he wished he hadn't.

The bloody thing was on fire.

The urgent shouts for him to jump rang clear in his ears. He fumbled madly for his belt buckle and began thrashing at the branches that he was tangled up in. The *sarka har* didn't appear to know he was there as it was having an increasingly difficult time staying airborne. With his back now to the earth below, Konowa couldn't see how high they were off the ground, but the rushing wind in his ears and rising emptiness in his stomach told him it was getting closer.

He swung his fists against the branches and with a loud snap he was free and falling. He spun as he dropped and saw a snowdrift rushing up to him as he completed two and a half revolutions. He missed the snowbank by a good six feet, careened off a camel—dead or alive he couldn't tell, they all smelled the same—and skipped off the ground four times in a succession of geysers of snow before sliding to a gentle stop flat on his back.

Time didn't stand still so much as avert its eyes. Konowa was aware he wasn't breathing, but he couldn't tell if it was because he was dead, or that he'd momentarily forgot how. He suspected he was still alive.

"Bloody hell!"

Pain registered in overlapping waves that threatened to take his breath away again. He tried to lift his head and immediately regretted it.

". . . bloody hell . . ."

A rumbling explosion marked the demise of the second *sarka har* somewhere off to his left. He smiled, hoping it hurt as much as he did. A sweaty face appeared above him and it took a moment for its features to swim into view before they promptly went the other way into a throbbing blur.

"Major! That was magnificent! I can safely say in all my years serving in the diplomatic corps I have never seen anything that could come close in sheer spectacle," the Viceroy said, his evident cheer just one more pain for Konowa to bear.

Konowa managed to curl a finger of his right hand and motioned for the Viceroy to come closer. He needed to be quick. His vision was graying around the edges and his body was slipping into a euphoric numbness he recognized as impending unconsciousness.

The Viceroy leaned in and turned his ear to Konowa's lips. Konowa spoke, though his words were little more than a whisper. The light was fading fast, but he had to tell someone one more time in case these were his last words.

Soldiers rushed up to stand around. RSM Aguom arrived a moment later and knelt down on the other side of him. "What did he say, Viceroy?"

Viceroy Alstonfar looked up with pursed lips before responding. Before he could say anything, Konowa rallied enough to say it himself.

"Whatever you do . . . if there are any ashes left of me . . . don't put them in a damn wooden box."

TWELVE

Visyna pulled her hair back and tied it in ponytail, carefully brushing back every wet strand matted to her forehead. Her hands only shook a little. She hadn't had a drink of water in hours, and hadn't slept in well over a day, but it was more than that. She didn't need her weaving to know that blood was going to spill. With each step they took in the company of Kritton and the disgraced elves, a reckoning loomed.

"They're going to kill us," she whispered to Chayii, turning her head slightly to watch the elf's reaction.

Chayii kept walking, her left hand gently stroking the fur on Jir's head as he padded beside her. "They have strayed far from their upbringing. Kritton is a foul influence on them, and I fear that his taint is every bit as toxic as the Shadow Monarch's."

The procession suddenly ground to a halt. Visyna stood on the balls of her feet, her hands by her sides. She didn't know what to expect, but feared the worst.

"We'll rest for ten minutes, no more!" Kritton shouted from further up the tunnel.

The prisoners collapsed to the sandy floor. Visyna was tempted to join them, but she couldn't rest. Their very lives were at stake.

"What are you doing, my child?" Chayii asked, easing herself into a sitting position against one wall. Jir sank down onto his belly and rested his head in her lap and closed his eyes.

"I don't know . . ." she said, letting the thought trail off as she moved up the tunnel.

She was surprised she didn't bump into an elf right away, but they had stayed as far away from the prisoners as possible. After all, it wasn't as if they could run anywhere down here. Still, perhaps there was something to that. Had Kritton warned them to stay back? But why? She was still pondering that when a bayonet loomed out of the shadows and pointed straight at her stomach. She froze, following the steel back to the musket and the elf holding it.

"Get back with the others."

Visyna stood her ground. "I'm just stretching my legs," she lied, cringing as soon as she said it. They had been marching forever, who could possibly need to stretch their legs?

The bayonet retreated as the elf pulled his musket in closer to his body, but kept the weapon pointed at her. He stepped forward until he was three feet away. "He said to watch out for you, that you couldn't be trusted," the elf said.

Visyna offered the elf a sad smile. Kritton would distrust her, and with good reason. Still, in the dim light, this elf looked more like a beggar who needed help than a killer disciple of a traitor. The soldier's cheeks were gaunt and his eyes blinked slowly, as if he was just waking up. His uniform was a patchwork of inexpert repairs. Several buttons had been replaced by bits of wood, and most shockingly, his bayonet had rust on it. She had been around the Iron Elves long enough to know a soldier's first duty was to keep his weapon in perfect working order.

"He told me you were the best soldiers in the Empire," Visyna said, giving her voice a soft, maternal lilt. "He told me that when we found you, everything would be right again."

The elf blinked and took a hand off his musket. "Corporal Kritton said that?"

"Major Swift Dragon said that."

At the mention of Konowa's name, the elf stood up straight and he brought his free hand back down to grip his musket. "Do not mention his name," the elf hissed between clenched teeth. His eyes were now wide open. "He destroyed us."

Visyna stepped back a pace, shocked at the vehemence in the elf. "He feels terrible about what happened, but surely you know he did it with the best of intentions. The Viceroy was in league with—"

The bayonet shot forward and came to rest directly under her chin.

"If you mention his name again, I will gut you," the elf said. Spittle frothed at the corners of his mouth and his hands shook. Visyna could only stare into his unblinking eyes. She was face-to-face with an elf every bit as lost as the *diova gruss*, elves turned mad by their bond with a Silver Wolf Oak like Tyul . . . and the Shadow Monarch.

After what seemed like an eternity, the elf lowered his bayonet and turned and walked further up the tunnel, leaving Visyna alone and shaken. She wanted to feel sympathy for the elf, but her overwhelming reaction was one of concern for Konowa. *His elves hate him. He'll be devastated.* As she collected herself, she realized she wasn't grasping the bigger picture. They wanted to kill him.

She turned and trudged back toward the group and found an empty section of wall to sit down against. A shadow loomed over Visyna and she brought up her hands, prepared to try to weave, but instead of a bayonet there was a goat-hide water skin being held out to her. She blinked and brushed the hair from her face.

"Water?"

She reached out and took the water skin, smiling her thanks at the soldier holding it. Private Hrem Vulhber rubbed his wet hands on his caerna then sat down opposite her, careful to keep the cloth wrap tucked. He rested his back against the wall and eased his legs out in front of him at an angle away from her so that his boots almost touched the far wall. Like all the Iron Elves his kneecaps were now a deep bronze from their exposure to the sun. Visyna glanced at the back of her hand and saw the color wasn't that different from her own.

"Another few weeks and I'll pass for an Elfkynan," Hrem said as if reading her thoughts.

Visyna's cheeks grew hot and she hid her embarrassment by lifting the water skin up to her mouth and pouring a long drink. The water had a sharp tang to it from whatever wine had been in the water skin before, but for all of that it was the best drink she'd had in some time. She wiped her mouth with the back of her sleeve, then leaned forward and gave the skin back to Hrem, careful not to touch his hand. He took it just as carefully and put a small cork stopper in the funnel.

"I saw you try to talk to one of them, not smart," he said. He didn't sound angry, more concerned.

"They were Konowa's brothers. I just can't believe they could turn so bad."

Hrem looked up and down the tunnel before responding. "War is like that. I've seen bad men become angels, and good ones devils. These elves were good. We all heard the stories about the Iron Elves. Their reputation in battle was legendary. Made them sound inhuman, er, inelfen I guess," Hrem said.

"Then how could they be so . . . so lost now?" Visyna asked, trying and failing to understand the rage she'd seen in the elf's eyes.

"Every man, and elf, has his limit. No telling where or when you'll reach it, but you shoot and get shot at long enough, and parts of you just stop working. You see things you can't unsee." Hrem's voice grew quiet as his words slowed. "You feel too much, or maybe, you stop feeling altogether. You do things you never thought you'd ever do, or even could do. Every soldier is different, but in the end, you might win the battles, but you'll never lose the memories of them. It's the kind of thing that can eat you up inside until good and bad are just words with no meaning."

"Are you saying there's no hope for them?" Visyna asked.

Hrem shrugged his huge shoulders, the leather cross-belts over his jacket scraping against the rock as he did so. "Maybe, but I doubt it. If they were going to change, the time was back in the library when Kritton was pointing his musket at Sergeant Arkhorn. When they didn't stop Kritton, they sealed their fate."

The rock behind Visyna's back vibrated as Scolly let out a shuddering snore a few feet away. Yimt's squad were arrayed around her like rag dolls dropped from a great height and left in whatever position they fell. Teeter, the former sailor, had fallen asleep with his chin resting on his chest and his unlit pipe dangling from his mouth. Beside him, the religious farmer, Inkermon, slumped forward with his head between his knees, his hands palm up on the tunnel floor. Curled up in a ball directly across from them, Zwitty moaned and twitched as if caught in the throes of a nightmare. Visyna debated, then decided against coughing loudly to wake him up. He was less annoying when asleep.

A few yards up the tunnel she could just make out the shapes of Chayii and Jir in the dim light. The bengar's head still rested on the elf's lap like a big dog. Visyna tried to reconcile that image with what she knew of the animal's predatory nature and found it difficult. Jir, like everyone else, was a very contradictory creature.

She tried to see past Chayii and Jir, but there wasn't enough light. The elves were not in sight, but she knew they were close by.

She decided to change the subject. "It feels like they're marching us all the way to the Hyntaland," Visyna said, leaning her head back against the wall and wiggling her toes in her sandals. The bottoms of her feet felt like she'd been walking on coals and her shinbones ached.

"Or as far as the coast, at which point we might

need to hold our breath," Hrem said, his voice deadpan but his eyes twinkling.

Visyna smiled up at the ceiling. "I suppose the ocean *might* pose a bit of challenge," she said, although she knew she had to come up with a plan to free them long before then. That elf soldier's eyes hadn't shown a hint of mercy.

"We're still a fair ways away. I don't think we've covered more than twenty-one miles so far."

Visyna brought her head forward and focused on Hrem. He wasn't smiling. "You know this?"

Hrem reached up a hand and tapped a finger against his temple. "No magic required, just the ability to keep count in my head."

"Any idea where we're going? Are they heading us toward the coast?"

Hrem removed his shako and began scratching his head. His black hair was wet and plastered against his skull. The more he scratched the more the hair stood up on end. When he was satisfied with his efforts he put his shako back on his head with a soft thunk. "Near as I can tell, we started heading north, but then there were some twists and turns. I doubt we're going south because that takes us deep into the desert and further away from their homeland. Angling toward the coast makes more sense. I heard the major say they were stationed at Suhundam's Hill, and I know that's due west of the library. If I had to wager on it, other than my life, which is already in the pot," he said, a small grin lighting up his face, "it feels like we're heading west. Makes sense, too. They meet up with that dwarf Griz at their old fort, resupply, and make for the coast."

"Why not head back to Nazalla? There are all kinds of ships there."

Hrem waved away her idea. "True, but these elves are deserters now, just like that bastard Kritton, so Nazalla is the last place they'd want to go. Too many Calahrian forces there. Assuming the city didn't rise up in rebellion . . ."

Images of their recent escape from Nazalla flashed unbidden in Visyna's mind. Private Renwar's calling of the shades of the dead had led to many deaths.

"You're right, but no one but us knows they're deserters, and it was Kritton that killed Sergeant Arkhorn. They could still redeem themselves," Visyna said, knowing as soon as she said it that it was foolish. The elves had cast their lot with Kritton. There was no turning back for them.

"I wish it was different," Hrem said, "but they just went too far over the edge. I actually feel sorry for the poor bastards. They're really just as cursed as we are. They may not be bound by this oath, but they've had to live with being born with a black ear tip and their banishment a lot longer."

Anger welled up in Visyna. *He blames Konowa.* "Major Swift Dragon acted in the best interests of all people when he killed that horrible Viceroy. Do you know the horrors that Viceroy committed against my people? It's true Gwyn turned out to be even worse, but Kon—Major Swift Dragon wasn't to know that. And he certainly couldn't have known his reward for trying to rid the world of such evil would be the loss of his command and the banishment of his regiment out here."

Hrem held up his hands in peace. "I ain't blaming

the major, Miss Tekoy. He was right to kill the first Viceroy even if it did lead to all of this. I know he feels bad about it and wants to do right by these elves, but Kritton found them before he did. Now they think whatever treasure they scavenged out of the library will be enough to buy back their honor. The really sad thing about it is, they could have had their honor back for the price of a single musket ball put in the back of Kritton's head. But they had their chance and didn't take it. Like I said, I feel sorry for them, but because of them, Yimt is dead. If they find themselves on the end of a rope one day, I won't shed a tear."

Visyna bowed her head toward Hrem. "My apologies, Hrem, I should have known better."

"We have faith in the major. He may be as stubborn as a two-headed mule and thrice as ornery, but deep down we know he'll do right by us." The conviction in Hrem's voice surprised her.

"But the oath, the frost fire . . ."

Hrem looked up to the ceiling as he marshaled his thoughts. "I'll admit, I sure didn't expect that when I took the Queen's coin, but I wasn't a babe in the woods either. I saw past the fancy uniforms and marching bands when I joined. Soldiers die. I knew it right from the start. We all did," he said, lowering his head to look around at the sleeping soldiers. "But the thing about soldiering is, we all *know* that it'll always be the other guy that does the dying. That's the trick. People are always talking about hope, but sometimes the best thing you can have is the ability to fool yourself. None of us saw what the oath would do, but if it wasn't that it would have been something else. So you trick yourself into believing we'll find a way to escape these elves, rejoin the regiment, get to the Shadow Monarch's mountain, put an end to Her and break the oath."

It took a moment for the meaning of Hrem's words to sink in. When they did Visyna was aghast. *He really believes they're all doomed.*

"There really is hope, Hrem. Don't give up."

The big soldier said nothing, but looked down at his hands. Flickers of black frost danced in his palms, then went out. "Like I said, Miss Tekoy, sometimes the best thing you can do is fool yourself. If it works, then maybe it was hope all along and you just didn't realize it. Like when I look in a mirror and say 'Hey, I'm a good-lookin' fellow who won't scare children in the street because they think I'm a giant likely to eat them' or something like that."

"I think you're very gallant, and very handsome," Visyna said.

Hrem lifted his head and raised an eyebrow. "Best we keep that between us. I won't tell the wife and you don't tell the major."

Visyna repressed a grin. "And a scoundrel, too."

"That you can tell folk."

"Gladly," Visyna said. "We'll be out of these tunnels eventually."

Hrem looked around them then leaned forward, lowering his voice. "At which point we're going to have to do something about these elves. Is Miss Red Owl going to have a problem with that? They are her people after all."

Visyna glanced over again toward Chayii and Jir. "I think our only problem with her will be staying out of her way when the time comes."

"Good. Now we just need to figure out how we're going to overpower eighty some elves," Hrem said.

Visyna looked down at her hands and delicately weaved the air in front of her. Thin skeins of magic began to glow between her fingers. She looked back up at Hrem and saw his eyes gleaming with reflected light. "I have an idea . . ."

THIRTEEN

Konowa didn't wake up as much as the bruising that covered his entire body dragged him back to a state of consciousness. Pain. Endless pain.

"Ow," he said.

"Back among the living are we?" Rallie asked, her usually gruff voice a full octave more . . . joyful.

Konowa pried open his eyes a crack. It was still dark, still snowing, although not as heavily, and he appeared to be lying flat on his back under a makeshift tarpaulin in the back of Rallie's wagon. "Ask me again in a year," he said. He noted the wagon was definitely the worse for wear, but then who wasn't? Splintered planks of wood making up the wagon bed were bound together with twine. He tried to move and realized he was completely immobilized, swaddled like a newborn babe inside what must have been a dozen Hasshugeb robes and something that smelled like hot manure.

"It was the Viceroy's idea," Rallie said, reaching down and removing the top layer of his cocoon.

"Is that . . ." Konowa started to ask before he was overcome by gagging.

Rallie held up the offending garment. "Camel hide, recently skinned. Apparently it's an old tribal remedy for those who have been injured. They wrap them up tighter than a tick in wet wool in one of these things and before you know it the afflicted are on their feet and running."

"No doubt to get away from the stench," Konowa said, his eyes watering as he gasped for breath. Despite cries of pain from every joint and muscle, he managed to free his arms and push himself up to a sitting position by leaning against what was left of the front board of the wagon bed. It looked the way Konowa felt, frayed and battered.

"And lo, he rises," Rallie said, bundling up the camel hide, then using it as a cushion as she sat down beside him. She popped a cigar into her mouth and drew in a breath. The end of the cigar lit of its own accord.

Konowa stared for a moment then shook his head and wished he hadn't. "Ow."

"Ow, indeed," Rallie said, reaching a hand into her black cloak and pulling out a small silver flask. "You are lucky to be alive, let alone in one piece and without any broken bones. Here, drink this. It'll ease the pain."

He held out his hand, noting that it was shaking. She removed the stopper and handed him the flask. He brought the flask to his lips and tipped it up. The liquid went down his throat like a river of lava. Heat radiated throughout his body, soothing every ache and pain. A smile played on his lips and he closed his eyes, sinking down into the robes.

"What is this stuff?" he asked, taking another sip.

The flask was pulled from his hand and he opened his eyes to see Rallie tucking it back into her cloak.

"For the sake of argument let's call it a very powerful medicinal potion and one not to be ingested in large amounts."

"Magic?" Konowa asked.

Rallie chuckled. "Absolutely not. Mostly Sala Brandy, a few sprigs of this and that, and the oil from a particular mushroom with . . . special qualities."

"I'd like to order a barrel," Konowa said, marveling at how well he suddenly felt. Not healed exactly, but better, as if all the sharp points of pain had been smoothed down and coated in something soft and fluffy.

"A little is good, a lot is deadly," Rallie said, clucking her tongue. "Moderation, Major, everything in moderation."

Konowa sighed. "I'm aware of the concept, just never really been able to put it into practice." He noticed a large bundle wrapped in more Hasshugeb robes down by his feet. "What's in there?"

Rallie didn't look. "That, is pieces from the two dragon *sarka har.*"

Konowa sat up a little straighter and slid toward the opposite side of the wagon. "I've been lying here with those abominations? What if they come back to life?"

"They're perfectly safe. Oh, what was the word he used . . ." Rallie said to herself, taking the cigar from her mouth and studying the end. "Ah. Inert. Not liable to reanimate or explode unless acted upon by a spark generated by a metallic object."

Konowa had no need to ask who. "Did the Viceroy say why he wanted them? Not souvenirs, I hope."

Rallie placed her cigar back in her mouth before responding. "He just said they might come in handy later. I didn't press him on it, but believe me, my curiosity is definitely piqued."

"In my case it's a sense of dread," Konowa said, suddenly feeling very ill at ease. Even dead and in pieces, the *sarka har* were finding ways to torment him.

"To change the subject," Rallie said, her voice adopting a casual smoothness that Konowa immediately found suspicious, "I had meant to ask you before we were so rudely interrupted by those flying twigs, but when you were napping on the wagon you were mumbling to yourself. Dreaming perhaps? The scribe in me is forever curious . . . for my readers back home of course."

Konowa pushed himself back up to a sitting position, wincing as he did so. He took a moment to catch his breath. "I completely forgot about it. Damn, I can barely remember it now . . ." He struggled to recall it, knowing it had been important. Rallie stayed silent though the cigar in her mouth glowed bright orange with a series of quick puffs.

"I remember . . . an ax, and Yimt was there. We were in the birthing meadow. He kept telling me to use the ax, but when I got to the Shadow Monarch and Her Wolf Oak, it wasn't Her." Konowa turned, and ignoring the pain, faced Rallie. "It was me. Yimt was telling me to kill me . . . I think."

Rallie moved the cigar to the other side of her mouth before speaking. "Interesting . . . but that doesn't sound quite right. Are you sure that's what he meant?"

Konowa shook his head, slowly and carefully. "I'm not even sure I'm remembering it right. We talked about mining for a bit, too, though that was because of the ax.

Turns out the reason dwarves use axes in the first place is for cutting down trees for their mines. I didn't know that."

Rallie smiled. "I did, and it appears you did, too."

"But that's just it," Konowa said, "I really didn't know that. Yimt told me something I'd never heard before. How is that possible? Does that mean he was really in my dream? If that was really him, then what was he trying to say?"

Rallie sat up a little straighter and looked out past the tarpaulin to the sky before answering. "A dream is a tricky thing, like trying to catch the wind. You know it's there, you feel it, but the best you can really do is build a sail and let it help you get where you're going."

Konowa thought about that. "I really am not cut out for this. Riddles and puzzles give me a headache." He fished around inside his jacket and found a pocket with a couple of arr beans. He pulled them out and blowing some lint off them held out his hand to Rallie. It wasn't shaking now, he was happy to see.

She reached over and plucked one of the beans from his hand and threw it into her mouth while still keeping her cigar in place. The tip of the cigar began to glow bright blue. Konowa popped the remaining bean in his mouth and his lips puckered at the acidic jolt stinging his tongue. His eyes watered and his head cleared.

"They've got some kick," Konowa said, rolling the bean around in his mouth and enjoying the shock to his system. He still felt some pain in his right shoulder, but it was more like a distant memory, or at least destined to become one.

"You should try them with liquor sometime," Rallie said. "You'll think you can fly."

"Ah, ha . . . ha," Konowa said, memories of his recent flight passing before his eyes to lodge somewhere deep in his spinal column like vibrating harp strings. "I prefer to stay close to the ground. Better odds of surviving when I inevitably fall."

"You do have a knack for that," she said.

Thoughts of falling stirred up other concerns. Everything around him was calm, and he didn't trust it, not after the night he'd had.

Feeling more alert, Konowa brought his left hand to the middle of his chest. The black acorn was still there. Regardless of why the Shadow Monarch had made it possible for him to have this power, it was his to use in aid of the regiment.

Okay, he said to himself, *you're an elf. Despite all evidence to the contrary you're a creature of nature and at one with the natural order.* He closed his eyes and pushed his senses outward, searching for a sign that Her forces were near. He was not going to be surprised by those damn *sarka har* again.

Cold from the black acorn pushed into his chest like a bar of frozen steel, but with that pain came an awareness of the surrounding desert. The metallic snow vanished as his mind explored around rocks and over dunes. The path they were following suddenly appeared before him as if he were looking at it in broad daylight. He could see every twist and turn and every curving sand dune. He pushed harder, and now he felt the world around him. The dull cold of the rocks, the bone-weary exhaustion of the soldiers, the coursing power emanating from Private Renwar at the head of the column, and an ancient power sitting right beside—

Something hit him in the ribs and he opened his

eyes in surprise. He looked over at Rallie who was look-ing back at him with all the innocence she could muster with an eerie blue-flamed cigar clamped between her teeth.

"My apologies, Major, I thought you were going to sleep on me. Now that you're awake it's best you stay awake."

Konowa rubbed the sore spot and managed a gri-mace for a smile. "That's quite all right. You know, I was searching the immediate area and noticing some-thing very interesting. If your elbow hadn't grazed me when it did I think I was about to notice quite a bit more."

Rallie pulled the cigar from her mouth and let out a long, slow stream of smoke. Konowa watched it twist and turn within the confines of the space under the tarp as if it were a living thing. After what seemed an impos-sibly long time, the smoke found its way out and into the night sky. Konowa turned back to Rallie and found her staring directly at him. It wasn't an unfriendly look, exactly.

"So," Konowa said, desperate to change the subject, "I can't help but notice we're not moving. Any reason why my orders are not being followed? Time is slipping away from us. We need to get to Suhundam's Hill." He didn't bother to add because my elves are there, and I have to find them before we leave this desert waste and head for Her mountain. Rallie continued to stare at him for a moment longer then smiled and put the cigar back in her mouth. "We're already here, Major."

"We are?" he said, throwing off the robes and get-ting to his knees before reaching up to push the tarp out of the way and standing up. The cold night air tousled his hair. He brushed a few strands from his eyes and peered into the darkness.

A crumbling pile of rock covered in ragged sheets of snow appeared a half mile away. It looked less a hill and more like the remnants of a rockslide from a long-vanished mountain. There wasn't a smooth line in the entire feature. Every inch of it jutted and fractured like a block of ice repeatedly thrown to the ground.

"Major, really glad to see you up and about!"

"What?" Konowa asked, trying to focus. He looked down to see a young soldier staring up at him, the lad's dirt-smudged face smiling. "Ah, Private Feylan. It'll take more than a damn flying tree to beat me." *Though not by much.*

"Hey, the major is all right!" Feylan shouted. RSM Aguom quickly ran up and shushed the private.

"Keep your voice down. Do you want to bring another orchard of those bloody things after us?"

Feylan nodded, but continued to smile. He stood up straight and saluted. Konowa returned it and turned to face Aguom. "What's our situation?" he asked, walking toward the end of the wagon and staring down at the ground. The jump looked to be about three feet. He debated sitting down and then hopping off, but soldiers were beginning to cluster around. He was their officer, their leader in battle.

Saying a silent prayer then wondering why he bothered, Konowa leaped. He hit the ground and felt every bone joint crack. He stifled a cry, and drew in a deep breath, using it to straighten up his spine. Still, it could have been worse, and his vision was clear. Whatever was in Rallie's medicine really did the trick. He slapped his hand against his side and didn't feel his saber. Before he could turn he heard a clunk on the wood behind him and scabbard and saber slid to a stop at the edge of the wagon. Konowa smiled and grabbed it, strapping it around his waist by its leather belt. *That feels better.* "I don't suppose anyone found my musket?"

"'Fraid not, Major," Aguom said, "but we do have a few spares . . ."

Konowa paused as that sank in. "I suppose we do. If it's still with us, I'd be honored to use Grostril's."

There was a murmur of approval from the troops. Konowa figured they'd approve, but he also wanted to honor the soldier. No one should die because of a damn tree.

"We're in as good a shape as can be expected," RSM Aguom said, waving a hand around to take in the soldiers standing near them. "This weather isn't helping any though, and we're pretty much out of everything except powder and musket balls, and they won't last much longer at the rate we're going. Major," he said, stepping forward and lowering his voice, "if this regiment is going to remain a fighting force we need supplies. If there's so much as a piece of moldy bread in that fort we really need to get it."

"We will, we will." Konowa turned his attention back to Suhundam's Hill. It looked to be three hundred fifty feet at its highest though at this distance he couldn't be certain where the hill ended and the night sky began. He searched for the small fort he knew was up there, looking for a lantern or cookfire glow, but nothing but the metallic sheen of the fallen snow reflected back.

"Stupid bugger," Konowa said, cursing the late Captain Trilvin Suhundam. Recorded as a singular act of uncommon valor, Suhundam had led the spirited defense of a company of soldiers from the then King's Grenadier Guards against more than five hundred Hasshugeb warriors some sixty-five years ago on that mess of rocks. Survivor accounts credited the officer with rallying the troops no less than twelve times when the natives appeared about to overrun them. On the thirteenth, however, Suhundam slipped and fell to his death, at which point the remaining troops conducted what was euphemistically known as a tactical reorientation vis-à-vis their direction of movement—they did the smart thing and took to their heels and ran.

Konowa hoped their experience here would be significantly calmer, but somehow he doubted it.

FOURTEEN

Konowa took a moment to adjust his uniform, aware that as second-in-command he had to look the part in addition to living it. He'd never gone in for the whole spit-and-polish routine that so many officers aspired to. He was more of a spit-and-get-on-with-it kind of officer. Still, his uniform really was looking more like a vagabond's rags these days.

"To hell with it," he muttered, wrapping the Has-shugeb robe around himself and slinging Grostril's musket over his shoulder. The cold was getting worse, even if the snow had tapered off for the moment.

"If you'll hold that pose for a moment I'd like to make a quick sketch," Rallie said from the wagon bed.

Konowa turned slightly and raised his chin, looking off into the distance in what he hoped was a martial pose. Rallie balanced her sketch pad on her knee and poised her quill above it.

"A little less pompous, please. My readers like you; I'd hate for that to change."

Konowa let his shoulders slump. "Fine, it was hurting my neck to stand like that anyway."

"This will only take a moment. Try not to squirm," she said, her quill now flying across the page.

Konowa felt goose bumps on his flesh and put it down to the wind. He surprised himself by realizing he felt good. Physically he was still more bruise than not, but emotionally he really did believe somehow, someway, they were going to make it. There was comfort in seeing Rallie with her quill. Even if she wouldn't talk about it, he knew there was far more to it and to her. It was like having an extra cannon along. He would have still preferred to have canister shot for the three cannons they had pulled all the way from Nazalla, but Rallie's quill and the questionable aid of the dead commanded by Private Renwar would have to do.

"Done," Rallie said, tucking her quill away into the folds of her cloak.

"May I see it?"

"No."

Konowa was momentarily perplexed. "Why not?"

"I meant to say I'm done, for now. I will have more work to do on it later."

That sounded suspiciously mystical to Konowa, but as he was learning by trial and error, sometimes the best course of action was none at all.

"Then I look forward to seeing it . . . eventually," he said. He started to walk forward beside the remaining camels, but caught a whiff of himself and thought better of it. *Stupid animals might think I'm one of them.* He headed in the other direction. The soldiers were now milling around waiting for orders. Remembered images of Regimental Sergeant Major Lorian, and his successor,

Sergeant Arkhorn, shouting and cajoling the troops into order caused a small pain somewhere deep he knew no amount of medicinal elixir would ever cure. He slapped the hilt of his saber with the palm of his hand and smiled as his flesh stung. This was no time to get misty about the past.

The soldiers turned and looked to him for guidance. He set out into the desert a few yards away from the road and motioned for the troops to follow.

Acting Regimental Sergeant Major, Color Sergeant Salia Aguom, and Viceroy Alstonfar stood in the lee of a rocky crag and out of the wind. The two of them were pouring over a map by the light of a small brass lantern. Konowa looked around for the Prince but saw no sign of him.

Pimmer looked up and smiled. "Ah, Major, just the man I wanted to see. The tribal cure seems to have done the trick."

"Yes, remind me to thank you for that later," Konowa said, still smelling of camel and finding it did not get better with age.

The Viceroy took that as a compliment and not an implied threat and motioned for Konowa to come closer. Konowa looked at Aguom, who shrugged as if to say he was just as puzzled. Konowa looked down at the map and saw why.

"That's not a map. It's just numbers and lines of gibberish," Konowa said, reaching out and gently lifting up a corner of the paper to see if the map was on the other side. No, just more scribbling in a language he couldn't read.

"Not gibberish, Major, it's Birsooni," Pimmer said, gently correcting him. "They were a tribe that lived here over a thousand years ago. Nomads wandering the desert wastes. It was known that they created a unique code for oasis, wadis, water cisterns, and other important features, but little more than fragments of their maps have ever been found. And I found a stack of them in the library!" Pimmer said, his voice rising with obvious joy. "Judging by the discoloration, the feel of the fibers, and the color of the ink—goat's blood if I'm not mistaken—this one is the most recent by a good two hundred years. Not nearly as valuable as the others, I'm afraid, but in this inclement weather I thought it better to risk this specimen and preserve the others. Still, isn't it marvelous! Here in my hands is proof that the Birsooni navigated by numeric code."

Marvelous wasn't the first word that came to Konowa's mind. "I certainly haven't seen anything like it, Viceroy. Does it give you any details about Suhundam's Hill? Any secret paths or tunnels we might use?"

Pimmer smiled as he nodded his head. "I'm almost certain it does, but I can't make sense of one single bit of the thing." He winked at Konowa and lowered his voice as he continued. "Actually, calling the Birsooni nomadic is being rather charitable. Seems their maps weren't quite as useful as they'd intended. The history of the other tribes of the Hasshugeb are filled with accounts of the Birsooni wandering hither and yon. The nastier accounts suggest they simply couldn't find their way back home, which is the only reason they became nomadic in the first place. One day they set out on a raiding party against another tribe's caravan and were never seen again. For all we know their descendants are still out there today somewhere, still trying to find their way back to their homeland. Quite poetic, really."

A metallic-tasting snowflake landed in Konowa's open mouth, but he couldn't quite bring himself to close it. *How in blazes did the Calabrian Empire survive this long? Everyone in power must have been dropped on their heads at birth.*

"So no help for our immediate situation then?" Konowa finally asked, turning slightly to spit out the bitter-tasting snow.

"Definitely not," Pimmer said, his eyes shining. "I was just showing the sergeant here. It really is a remarkable find . . ." He trailed off as he finally seemed to notice Konowa's expression. "Oh, but not to worry, this map should provide us with everything we'll need to know," he said, pulling a small, folded piece of paper from inside his swaddling robes. "It's Birsooni, too, but the cartographer was more traditional in his approach, to a point."

Konowa reached out a hand and took the piece of paper without saying a word. He opened it and saw a finely detailed sketch of the fort in plan view. A wide, straight road sloped all the way down from the fort's one gate on its northern face to the desert floor. It was by far the quickest and easiest way up to the fort, but going that way uninvited would be certain death. Anyone in the fort would have a clear shot the entire way up. What Konowa was looking for was an escape route, something small and hidden. The Grenadier Guards had found one all those years ago, so he knew it had to be there somewhere. He found it lightly traced on the southern exposure. It had far fewer twists and turns and headed straight for the rear of the fort, where it disappeared under the wall. A secret doorway in and out. Perfect.

Less perfect, however, was that parts of the path appeared to have either been erased or never drawn in. There was more gibberish written in the margins, but at least this was something he could work with.

"This should do nicely, thank you," Konowa said, fighting the sudden desire to hit something, preferably rotund and smiling.

"Think nothing of it," Pimmer said, his smile suggesting he certainly didn't. "I hope you weren't thinking you'd have to walk up to the front gate and knock?"

Not anymore I'm not, Konowa thought, rubbing the back of his sleeve against his mouth. "No, not at all. Well, now that we have this it's time we were moving. Will the Prince be joining us?"

Pimmer took one last longing look at the Birsooni map then rolled it up, careful to shield it from the wind and snow. "The Prince is indisposed at the moment, but conveys in his absence that you are to take whatever measures necessary to secure the fort."

A diplomat through and through, Konowa thought, grudgingly admiring the man's ability to lie with absolute sincerity. *So the Prince was still sulking?* Konowa found he just didn't care. He knew what had to be done, and Prince or no Prince, it would be done.

"Very good," Konowa said, spitting out the last of the bitter-tasting snow and nodding to Pimmer. "I'll confer with the RSM here and we'll get moving within the quarter hour. Perhaps you should check on the Prince and make sure he doesn't do something fool—adventurish and wander off on his own."

"Not to worry, I left a soldier in charge of his camel this time," Pimmer said. "I need to be here with you when we reach the fort."

Konowa had seen this before. Officers that spent their lives behind desks and conference tables get a rare taste of battle—aren't torn in two by a cannonball—and suddenly they feel alive. The fear and the excitement of being shot at and missed acts like a drug. Suddenly, they *understand* warfare in a way no one else does, and they are overcome with a fevered need to be in the thick of it. The inevitable outcome is always bloody, definitely for the soldiers who pay the price, and sometimes, happily, for the fool who caused their suffering. Konowa wasn't about to let that tragedy play itself out here. And it wasn't just for the sake of the troops. He genuinely liked Pimmer and realized he was the first Viceroy he'd met he didn't want to kill. Mostly.

"That won't be possible, Viceroy," Konowa said, thinking fast. "I'll need you at the rear with the Prince. If the fort is no longer held by the elves there could now be a Hasshugeb tribe in there. I don't speak the language, you do. I can't risk having you out front getting shot before you get a chance to talk."

"I do make a large target, I'm afraid," Pimmer said, looking between Konowa and the RSM. Neither one laughed. "But rest assured, Major, it isn't vainglory that necessitates my being up front with you. It's a bit more pedestrian this time. Not only am I the only one who can speak the language, I'm the only one who can read it, too. The writing on this map contains details of the path up to the fort not drawn here. The cartographer chose to keep some aspects of the route secret and so instead of drawing them chose to put them down in writing, ensuring only a native would be able to decipher it. Rather clever, actually. Much smarter than the other Birsooni's attempt I dare say."

Konowa interrupted before Pimmer could pull the other map back out. "Can't you just tell me what it says now?"

Pimmer was already shaking his head. "You'd think that, but there was a real mind at work here. Certain details of the path are missing on purpose. The writing that accompanies the map fills in the blanks, but they aren't simple instructions.

"You see, these lines are riddles. And not just your run-of-the-mill children's game either, but riddles referencing ancient tribal legends. Absolute genius. I mean, look at this part here," he said, showing the map to Konowa and Aguom, who dutifully looked. "What, for example, would you do when you come to a fork in the path and you read 'The lamb with wolves' teeth suckles from the camel on a moonless night'?"

Have another drink was the first thought that entered Konowa's head, but he kept it to himself. "I'll admit, I can't begin to imagine what that means, but does it really matter? I can see the fort from here. We simply have to climb up. With or without the map and its secrets that really shouldn't be that hard."

"Except for the booby traps."

That got Konowa's attention. Aguom stiffened. Soldiers trained to fight an enemy they could see. Hidden traps though were like snakes lying in tall grass. There was something fundamentally unfair about them, although the enemy of course thought differently. "It says that? What kind of traps?"

Pimmer rubbed his chin in thought. "Well, in this particular case the camel can only refer to Suljak Emyan, who was famous for carting about a massive main tent that could be seen for miles in the desert like a great camel's hump. One moonless night, or so legend has it, his guards made the unfortunate mistake of allowing a Guara assassin into his tent thinking the man was one of the Suljak's servants. You can guess what happened next," Pimmer said, making a slashing motion with his hand across his throat.

Konowa offered Pimmer a weak smile. "I'm still not clear how this helps us. What's the trap?"

"No way to tell from here, but I suspect it will be something that looks innocuous enough but will in fact be quite deadly."

Konowa still wasn't convinced, but it was time to move. "Very well, Viceroy, I can see the benefit of having you with me. Please collect whatever you'll need and report—return here so that we can begin."

Pimmer smiled and reached out to pat Konowa on the arm then appeared to think better of it and turned it into a wave that meandered into a salute that only the most charitable, or farsighted, would consider military. "I shall go fetch my pistol and be back in a moment."

Aguom coughed. "You aren't carrying it with you now?"

Pimmer made a patting gesture on his robes. "Afraid not. In fact, it seems I've left my saber back at the camel, too. Takes a bit of getting used to carting all these weapons around. I don't know how you do it."

Konowa made sure not to catch the regimental sergeant major's eye lest one or both of them burst out with something they'd regret. "As a general rule, Viceroy, you might wish to keep your pistol and other weapons on your person and in a position to use at a moment's notice. As you've seen, things are a bit dicey out here. There's no telling where or when we'll be in battle next."

Pimmer straightened up at the idea and fixed Konowa with a hard stare. "Then it's time we get going," he said. "You know, up until your arrival my battles were fought with the quill, strategically planned tea breaks, and wine-soaked dinner parties for the coup de grâce."

"I think it's safe to say those days are over for the foreseeable future," Konowa said. "A saber in hand is your best friend now."

"What a wonderful phrase and terrible thought," Pimmer said, then turned and strode off to fetch his gear.

Konowa watched him go and then motioned to Aguom to follow. They walked a short distance away so they were well out of earshot of the troops.

"Right, I'm splitting us into two groups." He knew it was risky to divide their strength when about to face the enemy, but he didn't see he had much choice. Marching the entire column at Suhundam's Hill meant following the caravan track that wound its way directly below it and well within range of muskets or arrows.

"A good move, sir, if you don't mind my saying so," Aguom said. "If we took the whole column straight on we could find out the enemy is somewhere out there in the desert and we'd be pinned up against the rock. Splitting us up gives us options, and in the snow and the dark the enemy will have a hard time seeing us, hopefully at least until it's too late."

Konowa stepped back a pace and studied the RSM. "I knew sergeants were the backbone of the army and put there to keep officers from making too many mistakes they might not live to regret, but I didn't know they were tacticians, too. I've been remiss in not consulting with you sooner."

"Kind of you to say, Major, but I actually picked it up talking to another officer with us."

Konowa looked past him to the assembled soldiers a short distance away. "What, the naval ensign in charge of the guns? Where did a fish learn how to fight on land?"

Aguom shook his head. "No, sir. He was killed by one of those flying trees. A branch went right through his neck. Quite a mess." Aguom pointed at his own neck indicating where the branch had struck and killed the naval ensign.

Konowa reached up toward his own neck then brought his hand back down. Without intending to he hunched his shoulders and tucked his chin in a little. He realized Aguom was staring at him and reluctantly Konowa forced himself to raise his head and expose the flesh of his neck to the cold night air. He had a new-found sympathy for turtles. "If not the ensign then . . . wait, you don't mean the Viceroy?" Pimmer was clearly bright and capable enough in a maddening, eccentric way, but he didn't know command of soldiers in the field.

"No, sir, not the Viceroy. It's Lieutenant Imba, sir."

Konowa didn't recognize the name. "We have a Lieutenant Imba? Where did we pick him up and where's he been hiding?"

The RSM looked at the ground then back at Konowa. "He was one of the volunteers from the 3rd Spears. He was afraid you wouldn't let him join if you knew he was an officer, so he begged me to keep his secret. He took off his rank and blended in. His men admire him greatly. I know his clan. Fishermen for the most part and warriors when necessary."

Konowa looked back toward the soldiers. "Lieutenant Imba, to me."

A soldier detached himself from the group and started over. The remaining men began looking everywhere except at Konowa. *They all knew,* he realized, kicking himself for not spotting the deception back in Nazalla, but he'd had too much on his mind. As Lieutenant Imba marched he carried himself like an officer, a confident one at that. There was an easy grace to his gait. Almost as tall as Konowa, he never averted his gaze as he approached. He held his head up just a fraction higher than was comfortable in order to jut out his chin and throw his shoulders back. The result was subtle yet powerful. He conveyed authority without appearing aggressive. Konowa knew he stomped around like a bull half the time. It had worked, especially in the early going of his career when he was determined to prove elves weren't all a bunch of flower-sniffing dandies, but maybe it was time for a more thoughtful approach to life's challenges . . . although perhaps not too thoughtful.

Imba came to a smooth stop in front of Konowa and saluted smartly. Unlike most of the men, he had not wrapped himself in a Hasshugeb robe and stood before Konowa in a threadbare uniform and bare feet. His musket rested perfectly against his left shoulder and gleamed as if he had guard duty at the Queen's palace. Konowa stared at his face, mentally tracing each ceremonial scarring band under clear, unblinking eyes. He knew they were made without the aid of any drug or liquor to ease the pain. Ragged scars were a sign of squirming as the blade bit into flesh across the cheekbones and Konowa wondered how many he could stomach before throwing up, passing out, or taking a swing at whoever was doing the cutting. Imba had seven scars under his right eye and six under his left. Every one was ruler straight.

The acorn grew colder, but Konowa didn't need its warning. The man before him was a true warrior.

"So, it's lieutenant, is it?" Konowa asked.

Imba's voice was clear and unapologetic despite his words. "Yes, sir. My apologies for the deception. I shall place myself under arrest until such time as a court-martial is convened and I am tried and convicted for dereliction of duty."

Konowa looked up to the sky as if considering the idea. Another time and another place not that long ago that's exactly what would have happened, and the most likely result would have been execution by firing squad . . . assuming he didn't die first from a thousand lashes. But that time and place no longer existed. Konowa brushed a few snowflakes from his face and returned his gaze to Lieutenant Imba.

"Yes, well, under the unique circumstances, I'm inclined to view this as a significant but correctable oversight on your part. As of now you will resume the rank of lieutenant. We've been a regiment running on wings and prayers from the outset so another officer is a useful addition. I want you, with the RSM's assistance, to take the column up the road toward the fort. That includes the cannons. I know we don't have any shot for them, but no one in the fort will know that. Miss Synjyn will follow in her wagon with His Highness bringing up the rear. You will assign the Color Party to stay with the Prince and keep him safe."

If Imba wondered at the strangeness of the order he

didn't show it. "Yes, sir. Thank you, sir. If you don't mind my asking, where will you be, Major?"

Konowa pointed toward the fort. "I'm taking ten men and the Viceroy with me across the desert and coming at the place from the backside."

"Will ten men suffice?"

"Lieutenant," Konowa said, drawing his saber and holding it up near his face to examine the blade, "if it weren't for the look of the thing I'd run right up there by myself and to hell with the consequences."

Choosing to take that as a signal, RSM Aguom motioned to Lieutenant Imba and they both saluted and marched back toward the troops. Konowa continued to stare at his blade as snowflakes fell on the steel. A quick burst of frost fire burned it clean and he reluctantly sheathed it. He looked back toward Suhundam's Hill. *Please, let there be something up there I can take a swing at.*

FIFTEEN

Blood will spill this night," Konowa said. The assembled soldiers grew quiet. Konowa let that thought hang in the cold air for a while. Only a few flakes were falling now, which seemed to make the night darker, more sinister. Even though it was hell to march through, there had been something oddly comforting about the snow.

Konowa turned and looked toward Suhundam's Hill. It had to be clear to every soldier present that it wouldn't be an easy nut to crack if they had to take it by force. Faced with the prospect of assaulting a fortified position on a rocky hill definitely focused their attention.

Konowa continued. "His Majesty has asked me to convey his best wishes in the coming hours and knows you will do your best. He is currently deep in study, pouring over the many documents and artifacts that were recovered from the library in hopes of finding ways to defeat the Shadow Monarch and break the oath. While this is unlikely," he quickly added, knowing it was the best lie he had to offer, "there is always hope. And cunning."

"Lieutenant Imba," Konowa announced, drawing a few murmurs of feigned surprise from the ranks. Imba stepped forward and turned to look at the gathered troops.

"*Some* of you are no doubt aware that Lieutenant Imba has been with us since Nazalla, serving quietly among the ranks. I'm sure you've guessed the reason for this subterfuge by now." Konowa was certain, in fact, that they hadn't because he was crafting his reasoning as he spoke. "The enemy is wily, and they can no doubt pick out myself, His Majesty, and the Viceroy from some distance. This is good. They will see all of us march toward Suhundam's Hill and believe the entire regiment is coming straight at them. They'll be in for a surprise.

"Two soldiers will dress up like the Viceroy and myself and march with the regiment with Lieutenant Imba in actual command. The Prince will remain to the rear and appear to be . . . incapacitated." Konowa doubted he'd be able to remember all these lies if ever called to explain this later. "While the regiment goes forward I, along with the Viceroy, will lead a group of ten men across the desert and climb the hill up a secret pathway. If necessary, we expect to catch whoever is in the fort completely by surprise."

As plans went it sounded pathetic and Konowa was trying to think of an alternative when he noticed the bustling sound of the regiment had quieted. He turned as Private Renwar appeared out of the dark.

Neat trick. Konowa kept his expression neutral.

"Where would you like me?"

Konowa looked past Renwar to see if he could detect any of the fallen, but it was too dark to see. He felt relieved. "Private Renwar," Konowa said, ignoring the fact the soldier hadn't formally addressed him, "I wasn't sure if you were still with us. Your . . . charges, have been rather absent of late."

The air cooled around them, an impressive feat considering the already freezing temperature. Konowa refused to be intimidated. *This is still my regiment.*

"We are here, but even in death there is a cost to battle. The pain we suffer grows. To kill Her creatures compounds that pain. It's my duty to ease their suffering."

The use of the word "we" struck Konowa. *He's really going over to the darkness.* Aware of the regiment hanging on every word, Konowa had no choice but to keep things light. "A noble attitude, and one we all share, living and dead. That said, we all still have our duty. I need you to continue leading the column toward the fort. If there's going to be a fight, I'd like the . . . others to create a distraction while my group sneaks up on whatever might be up there from behind. Is that understood?"

"There is no need. We can kill every living thing in our way," Renwar said. There was no emotion in his voice. It was a simple statement of fact. Konowa couldn't tell if it was meant as a larger threat or not, but it was chilling regardless.

Konowa sensed the unease building among the troops. He bowed his head for a moment as if in deep thought then raised it, revealing a big smile. "Well of course we can, we're the Iron Elves," he said, deliberately raising his voice and putting on a big smile. He turned and caught the eyes of some of the soldiers, nodding his head in recognition even though in their bundled state he couldn't tell one from another. "I pity any foe who opposes us this night, especially any villainous rum casks or wine barrels we might find up there."

Heads nodded and a few soldiers even cheered. Any chance for rest and drink, no matter how brief or where the respite might come, was always welcome. RSM Aguom looked to Konowa to see if he wanted him to instill some order, but Konowa shook his head. Let the lads enjoy the moment. Their dead comrades followed them everywhere led by the increasingly unsettling Private Renwar. Even Konowa wasn't immune to the growing sense of dread that hung around them like an invisible fog. No, if the troops could find some joy among all this horror then Konowa wanted them to wring every drop out it.

"Any chance there'll be any women up there, too, Major?" one of the soldiers shouted out.

"That depends," Konowa said, pausing for effect.

"On what?" several soldiers asked at the same time.

Konowa made a show of adjusting his shako on his head and straightening out his uniform. "On if you find female rakkes attractive."

Laughter rolled from the ranks, a release of tension by men knowing that in the next hour they might very well be dead, or worse. Konowa casually looked over at Private Renwar. The soldier's face remained impassive, his gray eyes locked in on Konowa's.

You and I have a problem.

Konowa held on to his smile, grinning so hard his jaw ached. *This is my regiment, and don't you forget it.* "At the very least they make good rugs," he continued, letting his gaze slide away from Renwar's unblinking eyes.

"Lads, the truth of it is, I don't know what we're going to find up there, but whatever it is, I absolutely know you'll handle it." Konowa motioned to Aguom to take over and the RSM started barking orders.

Konowa turned and walked a short distance away. He doubted his speech was worthy of Rallie's quill, and that disappointed him. Her readers back home wanted to hear about glory and adventure, and he understood that, but it was the quiet, impromptu little talks like the one he just gave that made the difference. Throughout history it was small banter, a quick laugh and nod of understanding among a few tired, hungry, and scared soldiers like these that turned the tide and won the day. Maybe if more folks back home knew that, they'd be less eager for the empire to push its boundaries further. The truth of it was, talk of queen and country sounded good when you were far from danger and warm and fed and chatting up a barmaid and no one, except maybe her husband, was lurking in the shadows waiting to bash your head in. Out here, however, with rakkes threatening to tear a soldier's throat out with their fangs and claws, dark elves shooting vicious black arrows, and *sarka har* learning new and more lethal ways to kill, it didn't have the same impact. The call of duty that every soldier did carry with him deep in his gut like a precious white diamond was nothing more and nothing less than the desperate hope to live to see another day. Wake up to a new dawn enough times and one of those days a ship would take you back home. Walking off that gangplank and setting up shop in the nearest tavern, a soldier could spin tales of derring-do leavened with a touch of modesty about how he wasn't really a hero, which only made him sound even more of one.

The soldier had been there, and everyone else hadn't, and they knew it. The screams might still echo somewhere deep in the soldier's skull and a loud noise might make him start and reach for the musket he no longer carried, but the audience around him would see a gallant warrior, a man who had stood before the enemy and held his ground. Even the stingiest bartender would slide him another round with just the smallest shake of his head indicating that his money was no good there. Konowa had experienced that more than once when on leave, but as good as it felt, his heart yearned to be back with the regiment, somewhere out in the wilds, wherever that might be.

"It is a bit steep, isn't it?" Viceroy Alstonfar said, startling Konowa.

"Sorry, what is?"

"That," Pimmer said, pointing up at Suhundam's Hill.

Konowa realized he'd been staring at the hill without realizing it. Now he looked at it and began to realize the challenge that lay ahead. Suhundam's Hill looked like a mountain that had been shorn off a much taller mountain and then dropped smack in the middle of the desert. Rock slivers thrust up from the desert floor in sharp lines of gray, black, and white to form a pointed pyramid towering several hundred feet above the ground.

"Steep? It's a bloody mountaintop without the rest of the mountain," Konowa said. "Why couldn't the stupid bugger go and get himself killed heroically on a nice piece of flat sand and not a place where a mountain goat would think twice about climbing?"

"They don't actually have mountain goats in this

part of the world," Pimmer said helpfully. Konowa turned to glare at the Viceroy, who kept any other observations to himself.

Konowa paled at the thought of climbing up there, not the least of which was the knowledge that the higher he went the farther he had to fall back down. Still, there was no other choice, and at least this plan gave them an advantage. Most of the men were probably uneasy with the idea of his handing over the regiment to an until then unknown junior officer from another regiment while he took a small group on what could be a suicide mission.

Konowa would never say it in front of them, but he wanted to reach the fort before the regiment, especially before Private Renwar and his legion of the dead.

If the original Iron Elves were up there, Konowa hoped he could deal with whatever issues might arise and keep tempers cool.

If he was with the regiment and Renwar, there was no telling what could happen.

Rallie had mentioned Renwar's calling of the shades when they had departed Nazalla and the slaughter that had ensued, and that was before he had become their de facto leader. Now, the scared wisp of a boy commanded a power of incredible violence, or at least appeared to. Konowa thought it equally possible the Shadow Monarch had more control than Renwar thought.

When Konowa was completely honest with himself he wondered how much that was the case with him as well.

"The men are ready," Pimmer said, his voice a theatrical whisper that sounded louder than if he'd just spoken normally.

Konowa put on a brave face and turned to see who the RSM had chosen. Deep down Konowa wanted that crusty old dwarf and his ragtag group of misfits, but they were gone, perhaps forever. Konowa inspected the assembled troops.

"An excellent cross-section of men if I do say so myself," Pimmer said. "Every one of them up to the task ahead."

This was too much for Konowa. He turned to stare at the Viceroy. "You know these men?"

Pimmer nodded solemnly. "I made it a point to learn the names of all the soldiers in the regiment. The variation in ethnic backgrounds is remarkable."

Konowa couldn't tell if this was the man's attempt at humor or sarcasm. "You know their names? All of them?"

"Certainly. It's one of the reasons I joined the diplomatic corps. Memory like a jar of honey," he said, tapping a finger against his temple. "Everything sticks."

Even though he was certain the Viceroy meant nothing by it, something about his smile irritated Konowa.

"Fair enough," Konowa said, taking a few steps in the snow and letting the sound of his boots crunching on the metallic flakes soothe his nerves. He marched in a small circle and came back to where he'd stood before, a smile now fixed to his face. "All right, here's the drill. We'll double time it across the open ground until we get around to the far end of the hill. There's a secret path there that will lead us straight up the backside of the rocks and into the fort."

Instead of waiting for questions he simply turned and started trotting. He could have walked, but all the time standing around had allowed the cold to seep into his bones and he was freezing. He quickly realized, however, that moving across snow laden with metal ore was like trying to push through icy cold, liquid pain. Cursing under his breath, he slogged his way forward, swinging his legs from the hip as he pushed through the fresh snow. The sound of heaving breathing sounded in his ears and a moment later Pimmer was trudging beside him.

"Follow me, Major, I'm built for this kind of thing," he said as he moved past. Not to be outdone, Konowa tried to stay in step but was quickly left behind as Pimmer surged ahead. The soldiers quietly stepped out from behind Konowa and followed the much wider path left by the Viceroy. Leaving his wounded pride in a snowdrift, Konowa followed suit as the last soldier passed him by.

"I never knew it snowed in the desert," the soldier said, slowing to keep pace with Konowa. He was short and stocky and looked like a butcher's apprentice with his red cheeks and double chin. He'd wrapped himself in two robes, one red and one beige, which made it look as if his stomach had been slashed open.

Konowa snorted. "It doesn't. This is just for our benefit, Private . . ."

"Meswiz, sir. I was just thinking it's a shame Miss Tekoy isn't around to work some of her weather magic is all."

Konowa said nothing. After a few more steps, Meswiz got the hint and carried on ahead of him. Konowa let him go, then moved over onto the well-trodden path set by Pimmer and found the going much easier. His feet, which had been frozen, now felt like they were on fire. He was certain an evil mix of sand and metal-ized snowflakes had fallen down his boots and were currently grinding the soles of his feet to pulp. He kept his head down as the wind blew more of the gritty mix around them. Konowa wondered what it must feel like to be wearing a caerna in weather like this, but after the initial shock of being issued the cloth wrap back in Elfkyna, the regiment had taken to it as a source of pride. It was one more thing that set them apart from the rest of the army, and that was something to be proud of.

Konowa was still thinking about that when he walked straight into the back of Meswiz. "Sorry," he muttered, reaching up to adjust his shako as he looked up to see where they were.

A black mass loomed before them. He craned his head skyward. The swirling snow only added to the illu-sion that he was looking up at a mountain, and the ef-fect was not welcome.

Konowa blew on his hands to get some warmth back into them. The wind rattled about the foot of the hills, chaffing at the rocks in a grating whine. "Load muskets and fix bayonets," he said, grounding his own musket and loading a ball and charge. For a moment, there was only the well-drilled movements of men loading their weap-ons, and Konowa felt at one with them, and more impor-tant, at peace. The scrape of ramrods down barrels drifted to his ears like music. He smiled as his shoulder twinged with the effort of jamming the ball home. He kept at it until he heard the satisfying thud of it setting against the charge at the bottom of the barrel. Drawing the ramrod out, he nodded to himself as he hefted his musket. This he understood. This was why he lived.

"I think it best that I lead," Pimmer said, his voice cutting through the wind. Konowa locked his bayonet into place with a solid click and felt more than heard ten bayonets lock into place at the same time. This wasn't a parade ground, no sergeants were watching, yet the men had timed their movements to the second with his. Konowa risked a look and saw ten brothers before him.

"Your keenness is impressive, Viceroy, but there might be more than booby traps ahead. For all we know, the place could be crawling with rakkes or something worse," Konowa said, remembering the flying *sarka har*. "If we lose you, we lose the only person who can read that map of yours. I'll lead, and you'll follow me."

"Major, we can't afford to lose you either. I'd like to take the lead," Private Feylan said. His voice was quiet, almost a whisper, but there was determination in it. "The Viceroy can call out any warnings to me as we approach them. Like you said, we don't know what's up there."

"You only get corporal's stripes if you're alive to sew them on," Konowa said, admiring the determination in Feylan's voice. "We're walking into the complete unknown. The first man up these steps is the one that's going to meet that unknown head on."

Feylan ran a finger around the collar of his jacket. "Someone's got to be first."

"So it seems," Konowa said.

Even in the dark, the determination in Feylan's face was apparent. He stood up a little straighter and just a hint of frost fire glittered on his bayonet. "The thing is, we'll take this fort, then make for the coast and board a ship and then it's off to the Hyntaland. When we get there, we put paid to the Shadow Monarch once and for all. With Her out of the way a fellow can think about his future. Mine's out at sea on a ship. So the way I see it, the sooner we climb these steps and find out what's up there, the sooner we are to being done. Sir."

Emotion caught in Konowa's throat and he turned his head. *He sees a future after this. He sees hope.* Konowa turned back and coughed before speaking. "Viceroys wanting to lead, lieutenants hiding in the ranks, and privates wanting command of a ship of the line. Why not? Very well. Private Feylan has the lead," Konowa said, looking at the soldier with something close to fatherly concern, "but I want you to stay close and listen hard to Viceroy Alstonfar. This isn't the wide-open sea. We won't be able to cross the T going up this path. The only way we'll able to fire in support will likely be over your dead body, so keep both eyes peeled and your ears perked."

Feylan came to attention and saluted. "You can count on me, Major."

Konowa nodded as he looked at the other soldiers. "Same goes for all of you. Eyes wide, mouths shut, and ears on swivels. If all goes well we'll find the place empty, but we might not."

"It could be your elves are still there, too," one of the other soldiers said.

It was a thought that Konowa was doing his best to banish from his mind. For reasons he wasn't entirely sure of, he hoped his elves weren't up there. Now that he'd come this far in search of them, he wasn't ready to see them again.

"Probably have a nice fire going, maybe even a hunk of meat roasting on a spit. Wait, do elves eat meat?" a soldier asked. His voice squeaked, and Konowa doubted the lad was a day over eighteen.

Pimmer turned as if preparing a long sermon on the dietary habits of elves, but Konowa growled and the man simply adjusted his saber and kept his mouth shut.

He turned back to the map and his face brightened immediately. "Private Feylan, the first three hundred steps appear to be clear of any dangers, but the three hundred and first might put a cramp in your plans for a bridge of your own."

"Can you tell what it is?" Feylan asked. Konowa admired the way his voice barely shook. Maybe the private *was* cut out for command after all.

Pimmer shook his head, bringing the map in closer until his nose was almost pressed against it. "Could be any number of nasty things, I'm afraid. Won't know for sure until we get up there and have a look around. I would suggest you pay close attention to your count as we ascend."

Konowa could tell by the look on Feylan's face that his confidence was waning.

"Just count quietly to yourself and take it slow," Konowa said to him, giving him a wink. "We'll be doing the same just to be safe. When you get over two hundred stop where you are and we'll check the map again. Just to be sure," he said, looking over at Pimmer who was now turning the map upside down.

"What? Oh, yes, always wise to measure twice and cut once," Pimmer said, then his mouth dropped open. "Goodness, that's not offensive to you, is it, what with the inference about cutting wood?"

"Viceroy, when it comes to trees, I say cut twice and to hell with measuring."

Pimmer started to smile, then stopped and decided to look down at his map again. After a moment he gave it a quarter turn. "Ah, that's better. Yes, now it's making sense."

Konowa lowered his voice as he tilted his head to get Feylan to lean in. "On second thought, stop when you get to a hundred steps."

SIXTEEN

T he creature raged at the scudding clouds driven before an unceasing wind. The sky churned gray and black, echoing the chaotic thoughts in its mind. It leaned into the wind, heedless of the metallic snow scouring the desert floor like an army of teeth. The rakkes, their bloodlust whetted to a shrieking frenzy after ripping through the caravan, charged forward heedless of the deteriorating weather. With every mile covered more rakkes joined the pack until it appeared that a dark crescent was sweeping all the land bare.

Nothing survived the onslaught.

Not wildlife, not Hasshugeb tribes, and certainly not Her dark elves seeking to end the creature's existence.

The creature, however, felt no triumph. Insanity swirled in an ever-expanding vortex in its mind. More and more of its being was fragmenting, scattered on winds that no mortal could feel. In its fury at being cheated out of destroying the Iron Elves at the caravan, the creature was tearing itself apart. Only its need for revenge kept it from losing itself entirely. That one crystalline thought fixed and shone in the center of its madness like a diamond.

Suhundam's Hill.

The Iron Elves.

Major Swift Dragon.

The soldier usurper.

Endlessly it repeated the mantra.

As it did a new, cunning thought began to form. The shades of the dead still aided the Iron Elves. No matter how fierce the rakkes, they were no match for such enemies . . . alive.

Frost fire arced and spit across the creature's body. The snow, stained with black ore, flew to it and began circling around it. A whirling storm of thick sheets of metal ice bands formed, each one rotating faster and faster. The earth cracked and buckled beneath its feet. Rakkes screamed and ran.

A high-pitched shriek rose above the siren wail of the spinning metal ice as the pull of circling bands began to tighten their orbits until they were cutting into what remained of its body.

Ribbons of flesh were gouged out of it like a plow cutting through loam. Each slice was a new exploration of suffering. Bone chipped and disintegrated while blood misted and crystallized, then fractured into ever smaller pieces.

It kept moving even as its body and mind were honed down to a razor-thin existence. It drew more of the storm toward it until it vanished entirely in a maelstrom of gale force winds. For a moment, it was only energy, spinning itself tighter and tighter until the pressure became too much.

The wind died.

Everything went silent.

The spinning stopped.

The explosion released energy and agony. The bands of metal ice fractured, scything the air for hundreds of yards in every direction. Bits of the creature stained the shards.

Rakkes vaporized in a hail of ice and metal. Bodies flew apart, sliced and cleaved so minutely that it was impossible to tell what they had once been.

A remnant of the creature coalesced in the center of the blast. A cold, dark spinning core of black energy. It reached out with its mind, finding pieces of itself all around. It called to them, and shades of dead rakkes by the hundreds answered the call.

The surviving rakkes picked up their pace, their bloodlust unabated. The shades of the dead rakkes flowed between this plane and the next.

They were the creature's revenge.

The creature would have smiled if it still knew how.

It had transformed itself. It had taken its pain and agony and multiplied it hundreds of times over.

Finally, after decades of servitude, it had an army to call its own.

Konowa rubbed his right shin and climbed back to his feet, waving for Private Feylan to continue. The soldier was moving quicker up the rocky path than Konowa expected. The footing was treacherous as every rise was slicked with ice, as Konowa's shinbone could attest. Worse, no two were quite the same, so he couldn't find a comfortable rhythm. Whoever had hacked the steps out of the rock had done so quickly and with little care or concern for craftsmanship. The more Konowa thought about it the more he wondered about the likelihood of there being any booby traps at all. Considering the condition of the steps he doubted the workers would have had the time or the skill to set anything more dangerous than the uneven steps themselves.

"That's a hundred, Major," Private Feylan whispered. He stood just a yard ahead of Konowa, one boot resting on the step above, his musket held at the ready. Snow swirled above their heads providing a pale, reflected light tinged with the blue of the returned Jewel of the Desert. It made everything feel even colder, which was quite a feat.

Konowa nodded, hiding his chagrin. He'd been so busy trying to navigate the winding path without breaking a bone he'd lost count. He turned and looked at the Viceroy, who had the map out and held at what appeared to be a new angle.

"Problem?" Konowa asked.

"Wrinkle is more like it. I can't quite make out a letter here, and I suspect it's rather important. No matter, we're good until the three hundred and first step. Of that I'm almost positive."

Konowa looked back up at Feylan, whose eyes grew considerably wider. Konowa offered him a tired smile. "You're doing fine. Just slow it down a bit. We'll beat the regiment to the fort by a good hour as long as we do it carefully. Now hold there for a second, I want to do a head count."

Private Feylan nodded and turned back to face up the path. Slinging his musket over his shoulder, Konowa eased himself around using both hands on the rocks near him to steady himself. A thin sheet of ice covered the rock, giving his hands little purchase. He pressed harder as a boot heel began to slip out from beneath him.

"Oh, hell," he muttered, ramming the palms of his hands against the ice and willing his body to stay upright even as his other boot began to slip as well. He tried to dig in, but only resulted in slipping faster. For a moment he treaded air, madly trying to find some footing. An idea formed from desperation sprang to mind and frost fire flared out from his hands to cover the rock and the step beneath him. His boots thudded down into the rough ice crystals and didn't move.

Konowa's sigh of relief was cut short as the butt of his musket banged against a boulder.

He cringed, but the noise was dull and didn't carry. He deliberately looked past Pimmer, who was staring at him with mouth agape and caught the eye of the soldier behind him. "Everyone still with us?" Konowa asked as nonchalantly as he could.

A low murmur sounded followed by a few muffled aye's before the wind drowned out the rest. A moment later the soldier nearest Konowa gave him a thumbs-up.

Konowa carefully spun himself back around to face up the stone stairs and gave Feylan a hand signal to continue. The soldier set out at once, but definitely with more caution. Konowa kept a close eye on where Feylan stepped and tried to place his boot in exactly the same spot while counting off the steps under his breath.

Before Konowa was ready they reached the two hundredth step. Again they stopped and Konowa did another head count while the Viceroy continued to spin his map for yet another new angle in a most disconcerting fashion.

Three hundred and one remained the magic number. All the soldiers were accounted for, so they pressed on until Konowa counted out two hundred and eighty. He reached out a hand and grabbed a hold of Feylan's robe and pulled. The private stopped and turned.

"We're getting close," Konowa said, keeping his voice low. He motioned for Feylan to sit down as he leaned back against a boulder and caught his breath. Thus far the path, though steep, had run more or less in a straight line. Up ahead, however, Konowa could make out a sharp turn and then blackness.

The wind had a nasty trick of funneling down the path directly into their faces, carrying with it minute particles of sand and rock along with the metallic-tinged snow, stinging his face and making it even harder to see the way ahead.

Pushing his senses forward would be of little help here. If there really was an ancient booby trap up ahead the original builders would have had to have made it out of rock or metal. It certainly couldn't be anything alive . . . or could it?

Konowa closed his eyes and drew his thoughts inward, grasping the cold power of the oath bond and then strengthening it with his need. He pushed outward, opening his eyes to stare sightlessly as his mind surged far ahead, questing the rocks above them for something waiting to attack.

Something warm and sweaty loomed in front of his face and Konowa snapped back to himself to find Pimmer weaving in front of him like a ship tossed on a storm. "Major, are you . . . are you all right?" he asked, his breathing ragged.

"Fine, thank you, Viceroy. I was just checking to see if there was anything with large claws and teeth around the next rock, but I sensed nothing. How are you?"

"I . . . oh my, this is far more vigorous than I anticipated," he said, sliding down against the rock face opposite Konowa. "Maps . . . don't really impart . . . a true sense of altitude I'm afraid."

"Let's hope they're better at telling us what the first booby trap is," Konowa said, motioning for the rest of the soldiers to take a knee. The command had to be relayed back down the line as the path was too narrow for all of them to squeeze together in a circle.

Knowing that was his cue, Pimmer pulled out the map, turning his body so that it blocked the paper from the wind. Konowa pushed himself away from the rock and leaned over for a better look. Pimmer fished around in his robes and retrieved a small brass storm lantern. He wrapped both hands around it and gave it a shake. When he took his hands away, Konowa was amazed to see it had lit.

Pimmer saw him looking and held it closer so Konowa could see. "A little find in the library. Can't say that I understand how it works, but that's science for you."

"It's not magic?"

"I shouldn't think so," Pimmer said. "Looks like there is a liquid and perhaps some crystals inside it. When you shake it they get smashed together and you get light. Lasts for a good ten minutes or so until you shake it again. There are several cases in nature of creatures having the ability to produce their own light from tiny fireflies to, well, dragons."

"When all this is over you'll have to tell me all about it," Konowa lied, pointing to the map. "What's around the next bend?"

Pimmer smiled and set the lantern down and focused his attention on the map. "If I'm reading this right," he said, tracing a finger along the paper, "the key to step three hundred and one is to avoid it altogether."

"Beg pardon?" Konowa said. To their credit, the soldiers around them said nothing, knowing Konowa would look out for them.

Pimmer shrugged. "I'm doing my best, but deciphering the code is tricky, Major. Still, my advice is sound. Whatever happens with the three hundred and first step is nothing we want a part of, so it's a simple matter of not stepping on it and we should be fine."

"Are you going first then?" a soldier asked.

"Who said that?" Konowa asked, looking around sharply.

"Me, sir, Private Otillo," the soldier said. He didn't have the good sense to look sheepish.

It was clear insubordination. However naïve about the job of soldiering the Viceroy might appear, he was still the ruler of this land and Her Majesty's sworn representative. Konowa knew he'd been letting a lot slide since the ramifications of the oath had become clear, but the men were starting to take advantage. Before he could call out the soldier, however, Pimmer responded.

"There's nothing else for it. The map is tricky and I won't be a lick of good to someone a few feet ahead of me as I try to piece the puzzle together."

Konowa waved away the offer. "Viceroy, we've been over this. No one questions your bravery," he said, looking squarely at Otillo, who had just done so, "but your unique talents will no doubt be needed many times in the coming days as we travel toward the coast. You aren't going first."

Pimmer stood up with some effort and straightened his robes. It took a moment as he had to readjust his pistol and saber. When he finally had everything in place, he stuck out his chin and pointed a finger at Konowa. "Then I must pull rank on you, Major, and insist that I go first."

"This isn't the time or place, Viceroy," Konowa said, reining in his exasperation as best he could. "You might outrank me, but out here I—"

"Excuse me, Major," Private Meswiz said, his voice a high-pitched whisper. "Feylan's gone."

Konowa and Pimmer both turned and looked up the path. It was empty.

"What in blue blazes is he thinking?" Konowa said. "All right, stay sharp and keep quiet. Follow me." Konowa turned and headed up the steps two at a time and to hell with the ice.

He rounded the bend expecting the worst and found Private Feylan standing proudly on a step. When he saw Konowa he mouthed three hundred and one.

"Are you mad? Get off that thing," Konowa hissed.

Feylan backed up to the next highest step. "It's okay, Major, all this ice has frozen everything solid. If there are any mechanisms they're not moving. It's perfectly safe."

"Are you trying to get yourself killed? We have no idea what these traps might be. Anything could set them off. Maybe it's not pressure on the step at all. Maybe it's some kind of magical trigger. Have you forgotten the white fire already?"

Feylan's grin withered on his face. "Oh . . . I hadn't thought about that. Sorry, sir. I'd be okay if someone else wants to take the lead for the next part."

Now it was Konowa's turn to grin. "Oh, no, you've got the keenest sense for danger now, I reckon, so you lead on. Viceroy," Konowa said, turning his head slightly to speak over his shoulder. "How far to the next booby trap?"

"Looks like five hundred and thirty-three steps this time," he said, his voice far from confident.

"You heard him," Konowa said, motioning for Feylan to get moving. "Count like your life depends on it."

Feylan nodded, slowly turned, and began creeping up the steps with significantly more care than before. Konowa let him get a few steps ahead then started after him, careful to step over the three hundred and first step. He knew without looking that the Viceroy and all the soldiers following would do the same. Nothing focuses one's attention like impending death.

They reached and passed three more suspected booby traps without setting anything off.

Pimmer grew more confident with each success, his voice growing louder as he discussed the intricacies of the map detail until Konowa had to shush him. Konowa, on the other hand, grew increasingly nervous the higher they climbed. The soldiers were starting to relax, and Konowa didn't like it.

He suspected that Pimmer had missed something critical in his deciphering of the map, but he had no idea what. The builders of the path couldn't have expected a snow and ice storm to gum up the works, so maybe it really was as simple as that, but Konowa didn't believe it.

He continued following Private Feylan closely, keeping the soldier within arm's reach so that if something did spring at them he'd have at least a fighting chance of pulling the lad back to safety. Of course, that assumed whatever trap was sprung didn't get Konowa, too.

The higher they climbed the more Konowa's guilt grew. Feylan was pushing his luck as he passed through each booby-trapped section, and unlike before, his confidence that the ice had rendered everything safe had eroded. It went unsaid, but Private Feylan would be Corporal Feylan at the top of the stairs. All he had to do was survive.

They reached the next trap. Konowa double-checked the count in his head to make sure it was right and nodded to Feylan. The soldier stepped over the trigger and waited. When nothing happened, Konowa did the same. They each let out a small sigh. Konowa turned and pointed down at the step to the soldier behind him.

"Don't step here," he said.

The soldier, Otillo, muttered and Konowa turned to follow Feylan.

A soft click of a metal latch releasing cut through the wind.

Konowa reached out to grab Feylan even as the sound of stone sliding on stone reached his ears.

He was too late. Konowa's hand touched Feylan's robe as a sharp snap echoed off the rocks around them.

SEVENTEEN

No one move!" Pimmer hissed, his voice carrying far more authority than Konowa had ever heard.

Feylan stood stock-still with Konowa's hand frozen on his shoulder.

"You must have triggered it, Major," Feylan said. "It sounded like it was behind me."

Konowa looked down at his boots, but could see nothing that indicated a trap. "No. I counted the right number of steps. I didn't touch anything."

"You've got the elf ears, sir, but I'm telling you I heard it right behind me."

Konowa started to doubt himself. His hearing was far from perfect. Too many musket volleys and cannon blasts had taken their toll. Maybe Feylan was right. A thought dawned on Konowa and he twisted his body to the left so that he could look back down the steps while keeping his boots rooted to the stone. Pimmer was picking his way carefully through the men on the stairs as he climbed up to Konowa. He stopped a few steps below him and right behind Private Otillo. Konowa counted the steps back to Otillo.

"You stupid, stupid arse. You're standing on the trigger."

Otillo looked down then back up. Unbelievably, the soldier's voice still sounded defiant. "Everything's iced up. It should have been fine." Konowa could see why Otillo had been bounced from his previous regiment. The lad refused to learn.

It was all Konowa could do not to fly back down the steps and throttle him. The fool had risked his life and all of theirs because of his don't-give-a-damn attitude.

"Viceroy, what do we do now?" Konowa asked.

"This is most distressing. I'll need a moment," he said, burying his head in the map as he studied it.

"Quickly," Konowa said. "We're rather exposed out here."

"Yes, yes, I do understand the urgency." He looked up from his map and the expression on his face already told Konowa the answer. "There's nothing on here about what to do if a trap is triggered."

"Then I'll just jump," Otillo said, crouching in preparation.

"No!" Pimmer shouted. "You could be standing on a swing lever—"

Otillo jumped. The sound of iron pins scraping across stone echoed off the rocks a moment before the stone step he was standing on gave way. The stones plummeted into a dark chasm. Otillo's momentum would have carried him to safety, but the second part of the trap now released. An iron bar buried in the rock debris and hinged to the stone step swung up and over as the weight of the stones fell. The bar caught Otillo square on the top of his head with a sickening crack, spraying blood ten feet into the air.

Otillo fell without a sound. A moment later the sound of crashing rock reverberated from the hole.

Ignoring Pimmer's shouts to stay still, Konowa raced to the edge of the hole and looked down. It took a moment for his eyes to adjust. Even with his elven vision it was difficult to see all the way down, and for that he was thankful. He saw enough to know Otillo was dead. Black frost was already limning his body.

"I tried to warn him," Pimmer said. "I . . ."

"It's not your fault, Pimmer," Konowa said through clenched teeth, not caring that he hadn't addressed him by his title in front of the men. "He didn't listen, and it cost him his life."

"It's just that I—"

"We need to keep moving. Now." Konowa knew his anger was driving his actions, and for the moment he was going to let it. One of his men had been killed because of stupidity, and because he didn't take his commanding officer's warning seriously enough. That was not going to happen again.

"Viceroy, if it's safe, climb up and over the rocks and get back on the steps here. Move."

Folding up his map, Pimmer clambered over the rocks piled high on either side of the stone stairs and past the gaping hole where Otillo fell. The remaining soldiers quickly followed suit until everyone was bunched up on the far side. Konowa held up a hand for Feylan to wait.

"Otillo's death is my fault. I told him not to tread on that step and he didn't listen."

A couple of the soldiers started to protest this, but

he cut them off with a curt wave of his hand. "The next time I give an order and it's disobeyed the soldier won't have to worry about a booby trap because I'll take his head clean off. Is that understood?"

Konowa looked each of them in the eyes. Everyone nodded, including Pimmer.

"I'll keep lead," Feylan said. It wasn't a question.

"You can only push your luck so far," Konowa said, prepared to choose another soldier to take over for Feylan.

"I've come this far and I want to see it through. I don't know who set these traps, but they aren't going to beat me. I'll get us to the top. Safely."

Konowa could tell the soldier wouldn't be easily swayed. He could give him a direct order to go to the back of the line and he'd obey, but there was something in his voice that told Konowa that Feylan needed to do this.

"Very well. Private Feylan has lead. Let's go."

They moved out silently, each footstep a well chosen affair. Their pace was definitely slower, but Konowa wasn't going to chasten them. They were all shaken by Otillo's death, especially because it had been so senseless. It was a harsh lesson to learn, but they were all very keen on counting now.

After a hundred steps Konowa thought about calling for a break. Climbing on ice-coated, uneven steps was bad enough, but looking and listening for signs of a booby trap made it exhausting. Every nerve and muscle was screaming with tension. A small rock tumbled down past Konowa and he almost pulled his saber to stab it.

Easy, easy, he told himself.

He turned his attention back to Feylan, watching

where he put each foot. Feylan's right boot raised and started to swing forward to the next step, but then paused in midair and came back down. Konowa tensed and put up his hand to signal to Pimmer behind him to stop. Feylan crouched down and brought his musket to rest on his hip, the bayonet pointing straight ahead. After several seconds, he quarter-turned so that Konowa could see the side of his face. His jaw was clenched as he whispered out the side of his mouth.

"Rakke. Boulder. Five yards ahead on the right."

Konowa drew in a breath and froze in place. *How was that possible?* He hadn't sensed a thing. He focused on the black acorn and felt its cold power. Yes, there was danger. He'd become so accustomed to the pain of the cold that he hadn't even noticed it. He inched up the step until his chest was pressed against Feylan's back and he could rest his chin on his shoulder. He let his gaze travel up the steps and then to the right.

The back of his neck shivered uncontrollably. Feylan was right. Not five yards ahead a rakke crouched on a rock looking down the path they were climbing. How had the beast not seen them?

"Well spotted," Konowa whispered.

Feylan moved his head just a fraction to the left. "I see three more behind it. And I think there are more behind those."

The shivering moved to Konowa's stomach.

He counted over a dozen rakkes perched on boulders. As he looked further up he realized that what he'd taken for more rocks were in fact rakkes. Scores of them. Thoughts of the bravado he'd displayed just a couple of hours before when he'd come up with this plan made him feel foolish. Instead of charging full speed with his saber flashing he wondered if he had just led them all to their deaths. Otillo had already paid the price. Were the others next?

A weight pressed against Konowa's back and the warm breath of Pimmer thawed his good ear. "Did we find something?"

For a reply, Konowa pointed with his chin while trying to shrug Pimmer's mouth away from his ear. If they were all about to die the current tableau wasn't exactly the way Konowa wanted to meet his fate.

"Oh, yes, I see," Pimmer whispered, patting Konowa on the arm. "Not to worry, I think I know how to deal with this." Without another word Pimmer bent down, picked up a small rock, stood up, and threw it at the nearest rakke.

Konowa was so shocked he couldn't move. *Was the man truly off his nut?* The rock missed and rattled around among the boulders. The rakkes appeared not to notice. Before Konowa could act, Pimmer threw a second rock. This time it hit the rakke on the top of its skull and bounced off.

"Stop him, Major," Feylan whispered, his musket shaking. "He's going to get us all killed."

Konowa brought his right arm forward ready to ram an elbow into Pimmer's face when the rakke moved. Holding his blow in check, Konowa stared in amazement as the rakke leaned forward. *Maybe it thought it was the wind,* Konowa hoped, knowing that not even a rakke was that stupid. The rakke continued to lean and Konowa was sure it must have seen them. He was starting to call up the frost fire when the beast did the most curious thing and tipped right over and sprawled face-first into the rocks below its boulder.

"Bloody hell," Feylan said, momentarily forgetting to keep his voice down. "Is he chucking magic rocks?"

Konowa wondered the same thing. The acorn still throbbed with a cold warning. That rakke must have froze to death, but something up ahead was very much alive. He turned to look at Pimmer, who was standing erect and smiling grimly. "Just as I suspected," he said, and pushed past Konowa and Feylan and walked up the steps toward the rakke.

Konowa lunged after him and caught him a few steps up. "What game are you playing at?" he hissed, trying to pull him back.

"It's dead, Major," he said, gently patting Konowa's hand on his arm. "They all are."

Konowa risked a look at the nearest rakke. A wooden stake was strapped to its back by a length of frayed rope wrapped around its chest. There was a large, fist-sized hole at the base of its skull and its fur was matted with dried blood. The rakke was dead. Someone had placed it on the boulder like a trophy, or a scarecrow. He looked up the hill and now that fear wasn't clouding his vision he saw that the other rakkes were dead. Every single rakke had been propped on or staked to a boulder.

Throwing caution to the howling wind, Konowa reached out and grabbed the rakke by the shoulder and tried to heave it over onto its back. He got it partway up, but the wooden stake jammed between two rocks prevented him from turning it all the way over. It didn't matter, he got a clear view of its face. Both eyes had been gouged out, its fangs had been pulled, its throat slit, and its tongue had been pulled down and out through the gaping wound. The wounds looked fresh, like they had been inflicted only a few days ago.

"My elves did this?" Konowa asked. Rakkes were cruel and vicious and, most disturbingly, extinct. They had no reason existing in this age. Still, he knew that even at his most battle-crazed, he could never do what he saw before him. Not this. Not torture. He could kill, of that he had no qualms, but there was a bright, burning line deep inside of him that he had never crossed, and had no intention of ever doing so.

"Why did they do that?" Private Feylan asked, his voice quiet again. "What's the point in torturing them? They don't know nothing." The rest of the soldiers had moved up the path to see what was going on and were now staring silently at the corpse.

Konowa's mind raced. *Why indeed?*

"A warning, I should imagine," Pimmer said. "A rather graphic and horrific warning to be sure, but perhaps an effective one . . ." he said, his voice trailing off as if he didn't really believe it.

Konowa wanted to believe it was a warning, but his instincts weren't cooperating. Whoever did this had acted as cruelly as the rakkes themselves, but something about it was worse. Rakkes were stupid creatures controlled by dark forces. If his elves did this then they were responsible.

"Perhaps we should be moving," Pimmer said at last, his voice thankfully firm. Konowa wasn't sure he could deal with sympathy right now.

Without a word he brushed past Private Feylan and took the lead up the stone stairs. Feylan said nothing. Something was alive up here, and they hadn't found it yet.

Each step higher brought more rakke bodies into view. For every one set out on a boulder there were several more dumped among the rocks. Many appeared to have been tortured. Several had been beheaded. He'd seen enough bodies on battlefields to be hardened to death, but even he wasn't prepared for what waited around the next corner.

"Oh . . ."

A rakke lay tied spread-eagle on the steps, its hands and feet cut off, the stumps black with frozen blood. Two bayonets protruded from its eye sockets, its fangs were splintered, and sections of its hide had been peeled back exposing the muscle beneath.

It was still breathing.

Konowa understood shame and guilt and the rage it built inside an elf. He'd lived with it all his life bearing the Shadow Monarch's mark. After losing the regiment he thought for a time he might lose himself in the Elf-kynan forest. And now he'd condemned the reincarnated Iron Elves to a bond beyond death, and when given a chance to break it, chose not to.

But nothing he'd felt, nothing he'd experienced, could ever justify this.

"Do you see some—" Private Feylan started to ask, poking his head around Konowa's shoulder. He turned away and began to vomit, the sound churning Konowa's stomach. He might have been sick himself if he'd had anything to eat in the last day.

He drew his saber from its scabbard and stepped forward. Anger at Otillo, at his own foolishness, and his brother elves and what they had become poured out in a savage thrust through the beast's heart. It convulsed once and then went still. Black frost glittered on the exposed portion of the blade and soon the rakke's body was engulfed. Konowa stood perfectly still, watching.

After several seconds the body of the rakke was consumed and the tip of Konowa's saber rested against the stone step.

"Major?"

The wind, or maybe it was the sound of the blood in Konowa's veins, roared in his ears. He wanted to scream, cry, punch, and curl up in a ball all at the same time.

"Major Swift Dragon?"

Konowa blinked. Mechanically, he sheathed his blade and forced himself to turn away. Viceroy Alstonfar's face swam into view.

"I did this to them," Konowa said. "It's because of me they were banished here. They did this because of me."

Pimmer stepped back in surprise. "Absolutely not. Every man and elf has a choice between good and evil. Circumstances might stack the deck one way or the other, but you still pick the card."

Konowa looked into Pimmer's eyes, searching for the lie. He saw only compassion and honesty. "You really believe that?"

"With every ounce of my being, and that's a lot of belief."

Konowa smiled in spite of himself. "I could have used you in the forest a while back."

"I'm here now, and my advice is that we get off these rocks and in the fort posthaste."

A gust of wind buffeted Konowa's shako and he realized he was shivering. "Wise words." He turned and started to climb the steps, not sure he was prepared for what he might see next but knowing he had to face whatever it was. The rest of the climb happened in a blur. Dead rakkes littered the ground wherever he looked. Eventually, he simply looked down, watching his boots. He forgot about counting. He forgot about the regiment marching across the desert floor heading toward the fort. Thoughts of what his elves had become were still playing in his mind when a shadow loomed before him. He looked up in surprise to see the wall of the fort towering directly above him.

The bottom twenty feet of the wall were comprised of rough-hewn boulders joined together like massive blocks. As Konowa craned his head back he saw the stones grew smaller and had been worked more, although the overall appearance was still of something put together rapidly.

"We made it," Private Feylan said, coming to stand beside Konowa. The other soldiers soon appeared and huddled together. Their faces were pale masks of grim concentration. Konowa imagined they were trying desperately, as he was, to forget what they'd just seen.

"We're not in yet," Konowa said, looking to Pimmer.

"But we will be soon," the diplomat said, walking up to the wall and tracing the cracks between the blocks with a finger. He began counting the blocks from right to left and referring back to the map in his hand. "I do believe I've found it," he said after a minute, stepping back from the wall and pointing to a block four feet tall and three feet wide. He looked down at the ground, took another step back, looked up and counted the blocks again, nodded, and stamped his right boot twice.

"Was something supposed to happen?" Private Feylan whispered to Konowa.

Konowa said nothing, only raising an eyebrow at

Pimmer, who gave the map another look, spun it ninety degrees before turning it back, and moved over three blocks to the right and pointed at another block of similar dimensions. "Yes, definitely got it this time." The block shifted back an inch with a puff of dust that was quickly whipped away by the wind.

"Gentlemen, our way in," he said, stepping forward and giving the block a kick with his boot. It swung backward and disappeared in the dark as if it were on hinges. He reached into his robe and pulled out the small storm lantern. "Now it's my turn," he said. He shook the lantern and as its light bloomed he stooped down and walked inside.

Konowa watched the light in the square hole dim as Pimmer walked deeper inside. He realized he was cringing, waiting to hear a loud crack as another fiendish device sprung. When no scream of pain issued forth from the secret passage Konowa pinched the bridge of his nose and blew into his hands for warmth.

"He just . . . he just walked right in," Feylan said, pointing to the opening with his musket. "Just kicked it open and went in like it was his town's tavern."

"Seems he finally figured out which way is up on the map," Konowa said, then cursed himself for disparaging Pimmer in front of the troops. "Which of course he knew all along. I do believe the Viceroy likes to jest," he said.

Feylan and the other soldiers looked at him with obvious skepticism, but they kept their opinions to themselves.

"Okay, grab him before he wanders too far," Konowa said, pushing Feylan toward the opening. The private nodded and followed after Pimmer. He reached the wall and without pausing ducked inside.

"All right, the rest of you, in you go. Take it slow, and don't go far. We still don't know who or what might be in there."

The soldiers walked silently toward the opening, each of them lost in thought. One by one they crouched down and entered the passageway until only Konowa remained outside the wall. He hunched his shoulders against the cold. For several minutes, he simply stood there.

Finally, he took one last look down the rocky slope before turning and walking inside. A trail of black frost stained the ground in his wake.

EIGHTEEN

Scolly fell to the tunnel floor, the sound of the musket stock striking his cheek still echoing off the walls.

"Stop it, you'll kill him!" Visyna shouted, jumping up from the wall and running toward the fallen man. The same elf soldier that had threatened Visyna earlier stood over Scolly, his musket raised for another strike.

Hrem was only a second behind her. "Try that again and I will kill you!"

The elf looked between Visyna and Hrem then down at Scolly. "If he wanders off again, he dies," the elf said, spitting at the soldier, then spinning on his heel and walking away.

Hrem reached down and lifted Scolly to his feet while Visyna came close and examined the bruise on his face without touching it. "How do you feel?"

Tears were running down Scolly's cheeks. "I just wanted to know where we are going."

Teeter came up to them and took Scolly by the

elbow, but not before giving Visyna a cold stare. "If you don't use your damn magic soon it's going to be too late. C'mon, Scolly, let's go sit down."

Visyna tried to think of a response, but couldn't. Teeter was right. If she didn't do something then what good was she?

She sat back down against the wall. Hrem joined her a moment later. "Don't worry about Teeter, he's just upset."

"He's right though," Visyna said. "I have to act. You see what these elves are like."

Hrem looked down the tunnel then back at her. "So what did you have in mind?"

"How good is your command of the frost fire?"

"I'm one of the few in the regiment who seems to be able to control it, but I'm no Renwar," he said, his voice a mixture of pity and relief. "What he did when we left Nazalla was way beyond anything I'd know how to do. I don't even know exactly how I do control it. It's sort of like breathing, I just do it."

Visyna hid her disappointment. "But you can call it up when you want, right?"

For an answer Hrem held out a hand. Black frost covered his palm. As she watched the crystals grew and transformed into ugly, black flames before he closed his fist and doused them. "I could kill someone with it if I touched them, but I couldn't throw it if that's what you're thinking."

"Could you make a wall? Some kind of barrier that you could place around Kritton and the elves?"

Hrem thought about that. "Never tried anything like that. Even if I could, though, how would that help? Flame won't stop musket balls."

"Not flame," Visyna said, "but ice. If I could teach you to weave, maybe you could do it. It wouldn't have to be for long, just enough time for Chayii, Jir, and me to do the rest."

Hrem looked at his hands then at her. "Do you want to try now?"

"No, it's too confined down here. We'll have to wait until we get out of this tunnel."

"Does that mean you're able to weave down here?" he asked.

Visyna nodded. "My ability never left. The ancient power in the library was just too caustic to weave." She tried to think of a way to explain it. "Think of nature as one giant fabric. Everything has a life force, an energy like a thread that weaves and bonds with everything else. I find these threads and weave them into something I can use, crafting a spell from the very life around me."

Hrem's eyes widened. "Do you mean you take some of our life when you cast a spell?"

Visyna smiled and held up her hands. "It doesn't work that way. I take only what is free. It's like the heat from a fire for warmth. All life gives off energy as it lives. I find that energy and use it."

"What if you can't find enough energy around you? Couldn't you tap into someone?"

"That would be horrible," she said, her voice rising before she remembered where they were. "It would be as if I plunged a knife into you and drained your blood. I weave the energy that lives all around us, but I do so with care. I seek to strengthen and help, not hurt. I only take what is available and will harm no living thing."

"But could you do it if you had to, if there were no other way?"

Visyna thought she understood what he was getting at. "I wouldn't be able to use your energy even if I wanted to. The oath is far too strong in all of you now."

"These elves aren't bound by the oath," he said.

She understood his implication. She could weave their energy, killing them in the process. "Even if my weaving were strong enough, I couldn't kill in that fashion." The very thought of it made her skin crawl.

Hrem raised a hand and held his thumb and forefinger apart an inch. "Then don't kill them—weaken them. Drain some of their energy, enough that we can get away when the opportunity presents itself."

It was an intriguing idea, but already she saw a flaw. "Even if I could do it, and I'm not saying I could, I wouldn't be able to affect Kritton. He is oath-bound like you. The Shadow Monarch's power makes it too difficult for me to work with it."

Hrem smiled. "I'll take care of Kritton."

She sat back against the tunnel wall. Choices whirled about inside her head, each one dark and filled with unforeseen dangers. A dull pain settled in her breast bone. Is this what it felt like for Konowa? Faced with nothing but terrible choices? A sudden longing for him filled her. Her heart went out to him as she understood in a way she hadn't before the constant nightmare of choosing the lesser of two evils.

"You say it so easily," she said.

"For that piece of filth, killing him will be easy. Doesn't mean I like it, but it's something that has to be done. In the end, it's going to come down to him or us, and I'd rather it be us."

"It's just that it seems so barbaric, all this killing.

There should be another way." She knew she sounded naïve, but didn't care.

Hrem's voice grew stern and he leaned toward her as he spoke. "Begging your pardon, but have you tried talking to a rakke? The only thing they understand is brute force. And as for Kritton and the rest of these elves, we tried talking to them back in the library and you saw what happened. No, the time for talking is long past. Kritton has to die, and if the other elves get in the way, they will, too. Maybe you don't like it, but it won't be the first time you've killed."

"Actually, it will."

Hrem sat back in surprise. "You've been in the thick of the fighting since we set out . . ."

Visyna shook her head. "I've done what I could to aid the regiment with my weaving, but I've never directly taken a life." In her months with the Iron Elves, her weaving had certainly made it easier for the regiment to kill its enemies, but they had been monsters, creatures spawned by wickedness. What Hrem suggested was something new. It was a line she had never crossed.

Could she drain just a little energy? And at what cost?

"Are you sure?" he asked.

"I would remember."

A brown carapaced beetle no bigger than a fly crawled across the sand on the tunnel floor near her foot. She stared at it. Without meaning to she sought out its life presence in the web of energy around her. She glanced up at Hrem and saw that he had seen it, too. He looked at her and shrugged his shoulders a fraction.

It's only an insect, she told herself, forcing her attention back on the beetle, but in her heart she didn't believe it. It was a living creature, part of the natural order.

"They're living, breathing men with families. They deserve a chance," Hrem said.

And there it was. She knew what he was saying was true, and that she was being overly sensitive, but she also understood this is how it begins. Once she began weaving the living energy of another life she would lose a part of herself forever. It dawned on her then that if she were ever to see Konowa again, this was a sacrifice she would have to make.

"Keep watch," she whispered, leaning forward to concentrate on the beetle. She brought her hands in front of her and concentrated on the energy coursing around her. The men of the squad were easy to pick out, their energy laced with the darkness of the oath. She quickly found the slender thread of the beetle's energy and with soft, smooth strokes began to tease it apart, looking only to weave a single strand of it in the hopes of slowing it down.

The beetle continued to crawl across the floor, unaffected by her efforts. Her face flushed and she flexed her fingers and started again. She found its thread and gave a gentle pull.

Crack. The beetle's energy unspooled like a dropped ball of yarn. She looked past her fingers to see the insect dead on the floor, its tiny body broken in two.

"Impressive," Hrem said, reaching out and picking up the bug with his huge hand. He studied it for a few seconds then incinerated it with frost fire.

Visyna couldn't breathe. "I was . . . I was only trying to slow it down," Visyna said, dropping her hands in her lap. "Its energy was too thin." It was a bug, and she knew Hrem would think she was foolish, but she didn't care. She had just killed a living creature. Tears welled up in her eyes.

Hrem nodded. "Then slowing down a bunch of elves should be easy."

Visyna looked at him in shock. "It's murder."

He returned her stare. "Then so be it."

The sound of footsteps echoed off the tunnel walls.

"On your feet," Private Kritton ordered, coming to stand in front of Visyna's small group. A makeshift bandage of torn blue cloth covered his left shoulder. A dark, wet stain in the center of the cloth attested to the wound from Chayii's thrown dagger back at the library. Even now, Visyna felt an urge to want to help the elf. She chided herself for the thought. *Let him suffer, he deserves it.* He'd shot Yimt in cold blood. He'd poisoned the elves with his mad need for redemption. It was clear he would never stop until something, or someone, stopped him.

No one moved. Kritton's eyes narrowed as he looked them over, then without warning he lashed out with his boot, kicking Scolly hard in the ribs. The soldier yelped in pain and curled up in a ball clutching his rib cage. "I said on your feet, now."

Hrem was up in an instant, moving far faster than a man of his bulk should move. Frost fire burned in his hands. Several elves appeared with muskets cocked and ready to fire. Each muzzle was aimed at a different member of Yimt's old squad. There was no way they'd miss.

"Easy, Hrem, he's not worth it," Visyna said, gently laying a hand on his arm. Frost fire arced from his sleeve to her skin. The shock of the magic stung her hand, but she kept it there for several seconds, wincing at the pain.

Teeter helped up a whimpering Scolly, while Zwitty and Inkermon rose to their feet on their own. They grouped close together, each one's fists clenched. Their bravery was all the more impressive because even as they prepared to fight they swayed on their feet. Chayii remained crouched by Jir, her hands buried deep in the fur on the back of his neck. A deep, rumbling growl echoed throughout the tunnel.

"You have something to say, big man?" Kritton asked, wincing as he clutched his left arm to his side.

"Don't touch him again. Don't touch any of us again, ever."

Kritton sneered. "Or what? Your precious major isn't here to save you now. All I see are a bunch of misguided fools doing the bidding of a bastard in league with Her."

"Funny," Hrem said, his voice low and steady, "I was going to say the same about you lot."

"It'll be the last thing you say," Kritton said, his right hand falling to rest on the hilt of Yimt's drukar.

Seeing it worn by Kritton angered Visyna, but she knew she couldn't afford to indulge that emotion, not here, and not now. A few growls from the rest of Yimt's squad suggested they were not as likely to hold their feelings in check. If Visyna didn't do something soon things would spin out of control.

"It would help if you told us where we are going," she said, surprised that her voice sounded calm.

Kritton and Hrem continued to glare at each other.

Scolly coughed and doubled over gasping. Teeter kept him from falling and helped him stand up again.

When he did they all saw blood trickling from his mouth.

"You pathetic bastard," Teeter said, letting go of Scolly and taking a step forward. He pointed a finger at the elf. "You don't know where you're going, do you? All you know is you fouled it all up and now you're taking these elves with you."

Kritton broke his stare with Hrem and turned on Teeter. The elf's jaw was clenched. "Shut your mouth."

Teeter took another step. "You're a coward and a liar, Kritton. All you're doing is running. That's all you've *ever* done. There's a noose waiting for you now so you're running and you're taking these elves with you to the gibbet. Yes, that's right," Teeter said, turning to look at the elves. "Desertion, murder, and looting are all hanging offenses, or do you think they'll pardon your crimes for some long-lost baubles and beads?"

No, no, no, Visyna thought, *please don't provoke him.*

"*Our honor will be restored!*" Kritton shouted, his voice trembling. "Everything we've done has been necessary. We've destroyed Her forces wherever we found them. The rakkes . . . the rakkes paid for the humiliation we've endured."

The elf soldiers looked uncomfortable at Kritton's mention of the rakkes, though Visyna couldn't understand why. The tension in the tunnel was growing. Hrem turned his head slightly and looked at her. She felt trapped. She had to try to weave some magic now.

Teeter refused to back down, continuing to shout insult after insult at the increasingly agitated elf. Visyna took in a slow breath and held it. With her hands down by her side, she sought out the life energy around her. She found the elves easily.

Avoiding Kritton's aura, she began to weave, careful to keep her movements as small as possible. Sweat broke out on her forehead and her neck grew warm as she focused. The wrongness of what she was doing filled her with dread.

She had just begun to tease apart the strands when the oath magic flared and caused her to lose focus. Teeter's clenched fists were wreathed in black frost. He was still yelling at Kritton and didn't appear to notice.

"Teeter, let it go!" Hrem said, recognizing this new danger. Zwitty gasped.

The elves shuffled back a couple of steps before Kritton barked at them to stay where they were. His eyes narrowed. "Do you see? This is the curse Swift Dragon brought down on the regiment, and if he has his way, it will be your fate, too."

Teeter was no longer yelling, but his anger remained. "Get out of here and take your kind with you," he said, his voice low and menacing.

"You don't frighten me," Kritton said, "or do you forget that I'm just as cursed as you?"

The frost fire blossomed into ice-black flame and began crawling up Teeter's arms. His jacket shimmered and the buttons gleamed as the fire took hold. The ground beneath his feet sparkled as if he stood on broken glass.

"Put it out, Teeter—you know what happened to Zwitty," Hrem said.

"I had it under control just fine," Zwitty said.

"I'm not doing anything. Not until they leave," Teeter said. His face was cast in a flickering light of sharp shadows as the black frost fire reached his shoulders and covered his chest. He wavered where he stood.

Visyna stifled a cry as she sought out his energy in the web around her. The oath magic was spiraling out of control.

"Hrem, do something," she said.

He held out his hands and shrugged. "I can't do what Renwar did. None of us can."

She looked over at Chayii, but she shook her head.

Teeter took a step toward Kritton. "Run . . . now." He was completely wreathed in black flame. The temperature of the air plummeted and the tunnel filled with white mist from their breath. The fire grew in intensity, feeding off Teeter as it did. Kritton backed up several steps.

"This would have been your fate!" he shouted, turning to look at the elves. "This is what I am trying to save you from. This is why everything we did was necessary!"

"Put out the fire now!" Hrem shouted.

Teeter turned to look at him, then at the others. Even through the flame Visyna could see he was trying to smile. "I plan to."

He spun, and opening his arms wide, lunged at Kritton.

Smoke and flame filled the tunnel as several muskets fired at once. Visyna screamed and covered her ears too late as the blast assaulted her senses. Hot, acrid smoke and burning embers slapped her face. She reeled backward and would have fallen if not for slamming into the tunnel wall.

There was yelling, screaming. Inkermon crashed to the floor with two elves on top of him. Scolly dove on top of them, his fists a blur as he pummeled the back of an elf's head. More elves charged past her knocking

her off her feet in the process. She slid down the wall,
scraping her back and landing sharply on her tailbone
bringing tears to her eyes.

"You bastards! You bastards!" Hrem shouted, tearing into the elves and scattering bodies everywhere. His
fists swung like massive sledgehammers, dropping elves
into crumpled heaps. Black frost sparkled on several of
their uniforms, but did not burst into flame. Visyna
struggled to her feet determined to help, but a body fell
on her legs pinning her in place. Frost fire crackled and
sparkled on her legs and she screamed, pushing the
body off. It was Zwitty. Blood trickled from a long gash
above his right eye.

This time she did get to her feet, but the fight was
over. Elves had them penned in from both sides, their
muskets ready to shoot them all down. She rubbed her
eyes, blinking and shaking her head as her vision slowly
readjusted.

Teeter's body lay sprawled on the tunnel floor, the
frost fire consuming it rapidly. In a matter of seconds it
was gone. The air started to warm, and her breath no
longer misted in front of her face. More tears filled her
eyes as Teeter's shade materialized briefly and then
faded, leaving only a cold, empty space.

"We go, now!" Kritton shouted, his eyes wide with fear
and anger. He kicked at elves to get them moving, motioning them to haul the human soldiers to their feet.
Visyna willed herself to move. Scolly and Inkermon
helped Zwitty up as she fell into step with Hrem.

"There was nothing you could do," Hrem said. His
knuckles were bloody and the left sleeve of his uniform
was ripped from shoulder to cuff.

She knew it was true that there was nothing she

could have done, but hearing him say it made her feel guilty all the same. She began to trace a tiny pattern in the air with her hands, seeking out the threads of the elves around them. Hrem looked over and tilted his head in question.

"No more of us die," she whispered.

He nodded, and they kept walking.

NINETEEN

A cold shock rippled through Private Alwyn Renwar as he led the regiment toward Suhundam's Hill. His vision fogged and the ground beneath him spun. He drove his wooden leg down hard for support, breaking through the ore-stained snow crust.

More Iron Elves had been killed. The ranks of the dead shuddered, the feeling moving through Alwyn like an ice flow. No one alive should ever experience this. It was cold, and loss, and hopelessness, and it eroded away a little more of his humanity.

He started to seek out who they were, then stopped. He no longer wanted to know. Soon enough, the shades of the dead soldiers would appear, their cries adding to the chorus of agony and fear that marked the existence of all the fallen. What made it worse was remembering a time in the very recent past when these same men had lived and laughed and smiled. To know them now as nothing but shadows of unending torment and despair was a burden he couldn't bear much longer.

Death, he knew, would be no release. For him, insanity offered the only way forward.

"And how are you doing this less-than-ideal evening?"

Alwyn turned, surprised to see Rallie standing behind him. He saw the column of soldiers a few yards behind her, waiting.

"More of them have died," Alwyn said, turning away again.

"You mean of us, don't you?" Rallie asked, walking to stand beside him. Despite the wind, her cloak barely rippled. "You are still among the living, yes?"

"Am I?"

For an answer, Rallie reached out with her quill and jabbed the point into the flesh of his hand. He yelped, snatching his hand away and shaking it. A warm, soothing sensation enveloped his hand before frost fire sparked and burned the feeling away, leaving him cold and shivering.

"Either you have excellent reflexes for a dead man, or you're still very much alive," she said.

Alwyn studied her through his gray eyes, seeking out her energy. An ancient power radiated from—"Oww!" he said, feeling the sting of her quill jab him again, this time in the earlobe. As before, a feeling of warmth began to spread throughout his body before the oath magic overwhelmed it. Alwyn shook himself as anger surged inside him.

"The wind took it," she said, staring him directly in the eyes as if daring him to contradict her. Power coursed through Alwyn. He was the destroyer of Kaman Rhal's dragon of bones. It was he who blasted the Shadow Monarch's emissary to pieces. Who was Rallie to—"Oww!"

"It's like it has a mind of its own," Rallie said, removing the sharpened end of her quill from his shoulder. It had pierced the cloth of his uniform and his cotton undershirt underneath. This time instead of warmth there was heat as the point entered his skin dead center in the middle of his acorn tattoo. He felt frost fire tracing the outline of the tattoo and its motto "*Æri Mekah* (Into the Fire and Right the Hell Back Out)" but unlike the previous two times it did not consume the power he felt from her quill.

Rallie held the quill loosely between her fingers, twirling it slowly. Alwyn raised his hands in surrender.

"Who are you?" he asked.

She didn't answer right away, but started walking. Alwyn watched her for a few steps then followed after her. He caught up with her and fell into step. His tattoo continued to burn, but now it was a tolerable heat. In a very strange way he found it comforting, as if one small part of him was still him.

"The major will be waiting for us, so I think it best we keep moving," she said.

"You're not going back to your wagon?"

"One of the lads used to drive a beer wagon. I'm not sure camels are quite the same as dray horses, but I think he'll get the gist of it quick enough. Besides, with one damaged wagon wheel it's not a very smooth ride. So I decided I'd take the chance to stretch my legs. And I'd like the company."

Alwyn tried and failed to read Rallie. He looked for fear, or mockery, but all he sensed was genuine interest on her part.

"Sometimes what you see is what you get," she said.

He walked in silence, only partially listening as Rallie

somehow got onto the subject of distilleries. The regiment trailed them at a distance. A new feeling enveloped him. He was never alone, not anymore, but right now he felt a degree of peace and solitude as he walked beside Rallie. There was something soothing about her voice.

"Are you casting a spell on me?" he asked, suspicion rushing his words and making his tone sharp.

"I have been called mesmerizing in my day," she said, "positively captivating even. But no, no spell beyond the simple act of keeping a friend company. There's a power in that greater than anything I've ever encountered."

Alwyn turned his head to see if she was laughing.

"Well, in a deeply emotional way," she explained, resting a hand over her heart.

Before Alwyn could stop himself the words rushed out. "Everything is pain. I'm losing my friends, Rallie. I'm losing my grasp on this world. Soon there won't be anything left to keep me here."

"Nonsense. You're just feeling sorry for yourself."

Alwyn had expected sympathy, perhaps shock on her part at his plight, but not this. "That's what you think this is? I'm becoming the living dead, cursed for eternity with tormented shades as my companions, and you think I'm feeling sorry for myself?"

Rallie pulled the cigar out of her mouth and jabbed it at him. He recoiled.

"As I keep having to explain to you, you're not dead, not by a long shot." She put the cigar back in her mouth and clamped down on it as a gust of wind raced across the desert kicking up sand and snow. "Your survival instinct still works. It's your brain that's giving you problems. You're overthinking things. Wallowing, as it were, in a sea of woe. I can't help the dead, but the confused and despondent I can still help . . . if they're prepared to help themselves. I was telling the major something similar. Start with hope and build."

Alwyn thought about that. *Was there still hope?*

"I don't know if I know how to do that, Rallie. What hope is there for them? For me? We're all bound by Her magic."

"Magic done can be undone. That's why we're going to meet Her on Her mountain. Which is why we're currently trekking across this desert. You're getting yourself twisted in knots about grand, horrible things when what you need to be doing is putting your attention on the here and now."

"But the shades—"

"Will remain that way unless you and the rest of the living do something about it," she said, cutting him off. Her voice softened as she continued. "I know they're suffering, as are you. For now, it can't be helped. You're their emissary now, and they look to you for answers, so give them something to do."

"What do you mean?"

Rallie swung a hand around taking in the emptiness. "Put the buggers to work. They're dead, but that's no excuse for lying around moaning and lamenting that state of affairs. They need focus, and you can give it to them. You know what's at stake. You know what has to be done to free the regiment from Her oath. So buck up, chin up, and get moving."

"It's not that simple, Rallie," Alwyn said.

"That's the human mind for you, always trying to show how complicated things can be. Don't think about it, just feel it. Better to do something and fail than nothing and wonder."

For the first time in a long time, it was as if a dark, smothering veil had been lifted from his face. Thinking about his situation only made it worse. So maybe Rallie had a point. Stop thinking and start acting. Alwyn drew in a breath and planted his legs firmly in the snow. Rallie stopped and turned to look at him, a smile apparent behind the glowing end of her cigar.

His heart filled with emotion, not all of it sad. There was a way forward. How it would all work out he didn't know, but right now that didn't matter. Right now he was alive, and that was enough.

"I miss Yimt," he said at last, unsure what else to say.

"I miss the rascal, too," she said, "but I hate to think what he'd be saying to you if he were here instead of me right now. I'm not sure ears as tender as yours could survive being exposed to that kind of verbal abuse."

Alwyn actually smiled.

She started walking again. He matched her step for step, marveling at how his view of the world could change so fast.

"You never answered my question," he said. "You know, who *are* you?"

"I didn't answer only because I don't mean to," she said, cheerily puffing away on her cigar. "A woman is entitled to her secrets, especially if she can't remember some of them."

Alwyn didn't believe that.

"Eventually you have to tell us." He paused before continuing. "Don't you?"

"Do you know what kills cats?" Rallie asked.

"Curiosity?" Alwyn answered.

"Not really. It's usually the horse and buggy that runs them over *because* they thought they heard a lot of mice scurrying on the road."

"I'm not sure, but I think that means I should change the subject," Alwyn said.

She stopped again. A feeling of dread came over Alwyn. Shades of the dead materialized all around him. He shuddered, but steeled himself. He might be their spokesman, but he *wasn't* dead. Not yet.

"It's just been changed for you. There's the fort," Rallie said.

Alwyn looked. The hill jutted out of the desert like a broken bone, the jagged top the battlements of the fort. Letting his gaze fall he took in the base of the hill, searching the snow-covered debris for signs of life.

"Are those rakkes?" he asked, spotting bodies spread out in front of the hill.

"They were," Rallie said.

He tore his gaze away from the hill and focused instead on the shades of the fallen. Their hands started to reach for him and the cold, unending pressure of their agony began to gnaw at him from the inside. His mood darkened, and the warm feeling he'd had from the playful banter with Rallie began to retreat, but then he felt the tattoo on his arm begin to burn hotter, as if a fire were being stoked. It was little more than a single match in a blizzard, but it was enough for him to remember that he could still make choices.

He stood to his full height, the charred and blackened branches of his wooden leg creaking with the effort. *"Go. Seek out our enemies. Now!"*

The shades didn't move.

"Try again," Rallie said.

Alwyn looked at the shades. He felt the anger well up inside him. They were soldiers, damn it, and they had a duty to perform. "The regiment needs you. You are still part of it. Remember that," Alwyn said.

The shades continued to stand their ground. RSM Lorian rode forth on Zwindarra until he was only a few feet away. "Our pain in this existence grows, yet we appear no closer to our goal."

Rallie started to step forward, but Alwyn held up his hand to stop her. This time, he let his anger boil forth.

"RSM! You know better. You all know better. We're soldiers. We fight until the battle is won, and this battle is far from over." He stepped forth and placed his hands on his hips. "You weren't cowards in life. Being dead changes nothing. Remember who you are," Alwyn said, pointing to individual soldiers. "You, and you, and you . . . you're Iron Elves. Live up to that name!"

The air around them crackled as the temperature fell. Alwyn's breath misted and his lungs burned with the cold. The shades of the Iron Elves grew straighter in front of his eyes. He blinked. They were standing at attention. A moment later, they vanished. Alwyn waited several seconds before letting out his breath.

"Now that's something Yimt would have been damn proud of," Rallie said, whistling softly.

"I thought I went too far," Alwyn said.

"So did I, my boy, so did I. Remind me never to play poker with you."

The sound of crunching snow preceded acting-RSM Aguom as he marched up to stand a few feet away. Alwyn remembered that he was still a member of Her Majesty's Imperial Armed Forces and turned and stood to attention.

"Stand easy," Aguom said, looking around nervously.

He pointed toward the hill. "Was there a battle here?" he asked, taking in the carnage before them.

"Something like that," Rallie said.

Aguom looked like he wanted more of an explanation, but let it go at that. "Lieutenant Imba wants to know what the situation is. He's preparing the regiment to advance in line. Should they fix bayonets?"

"Yes," Alwyn said.

"Do you sense something?" he asked.

Alwyn closed his eyes and rested his chin against his chest. The wind played with the edge of his caerna, but the sting of the icy snow against his one good leg barely registered. Something darker and colder had his attention.

"What is it?" Rallie asked. Alwyn heard a rustle of paper and knew she had a scroll in her hand, her quill at the ready.

"The shades have found our enemy," he said, opening his eyes as he raised his head. "Hundreds upon hundreds of rakkes in one mass."

"What, where?" Aguom asked. "We slaughtered hundreds at the canyon. The rest scattered to the four winds. How can they be gathered up into a force again so quickly?"

"They are driven by Her Emissary. Its power was not destroyed."

"But you killed it. We saw you tear it to bits," Aguom said. "How could anything survive that?"

"Madness," Alwyn said, seeing the path that he might one day walk himself.

RSM Aguom recovered quickly. "No time to waste then, we'll double time it to the fort and set up our defenses. Once we're in there we'll be able to hold them off."

"I'm afraid we won't be going to the fort," Alwyn said.

A howl carried on the wind from somewhere off to the west. It was answered by several more to the east.

"We are already surrounded."

TWENTY

Konowa found Pimmer twenty yards inside the tunnel leading from the outer wall of the fort. Despite being out of the wind and snow the man appeared to be shivering. He was standing just inside a chamber. The glow from his small storm lantern cast enough light that Konowa could make out the figures of the soldiers all grouped against the wall nearby. After the horror he'd just witnessed he was feeling helpless and angry and seeing his men not spread out and ready to face danger gave him the perfect chance to vent.

He strode into the room, the first curse ready to be whispered with force at such a complete breakdown of discipline. Then he saw what had stopped the men in their tracks.

"This was the garrison's torture chamber," Pimmer said, his voice flat.

Konowa took it all in in an instant. The chains, the metal spikes, blood-and-gore-stained walls, and the smell of death. It threatened to overwhelm him. His senses were still reeling from the tableau on the slope outside the fort. He looked at his men and saw they were on the verge of cracking. He didn't blame them, but this was no time for sympathy and understanding. They could be moments away from battle with who knew what. He had to snap them out of it, and fast.

"Of course it's their torture chamber," Konowa snapped, reaching down and picking up a metal device that looked like it might have been used for boring holes in bone. "What did you expect, a barracks with warm sheets and a hearth? Maybe a nice little tavern with drinks and a chatty barmaid?"

Some of the soldiers shuffled their feet. Others looked at him then looked away. Pimmer blinked and looked surprised. "Major, I just meant that—"

"We don't have time for this," Konowa said, cutting him. He could deal with hurt feelings later. Right now he had to get his men focused on the task at hand. "And what in blazes are you lot doing there gawking? You should know by now that monsters come in all shapes and sizes." He whirled on Feylan. "Feylan! If you want those corporal stripes, you'd better start acting like one. We still have no idea who or what is in here with us. If you can't get the men together and prepared to fight when I'm not here to watch then maybe you're not the leader I thought you were."

Feylan's face grew red as the insult stung, but it had the desired effect.

"You heard the major," Feylan called out, batting at the shoulder of the soldier nearest to him. "Smirck, Meswiz, Rasser, get across the room and cover that doorway. Dimwhol, watch the way we came in. We don't want something sneaking up on us from behind. The rest of you grab a brand and light it then keep your eyes and ears peeled."

Konowa nodded as the soldiers hurried to obey. In moments, the chamber was filled with warm, yellow light. "Viceroy, there's nothing here for us. Let's get upstairs and find out if anyone's home."

Pimmer looked down at his map then back at Konowa. "Yes, quite right." He took a breath and stood up a little straighter. "Right. Through that door, gentlemen, and up those stairs will take us to an entrance onto the main courtyard of the fort."

"Good, good. Now listen, all of you," Konowa said. He expected all eyes on him, but instead several were nervously staring at the torture device he still held in his hand. He bent down and placed it on the floor, wiping his hands on his trousers as he stood back up. "Look, we've made it this far. We lost a good man, but the rest of you pulled through, and that's pretty bloody amazing. None of us expected what we found out there, or in here, but you've handled yourselves well. I'm damn proud of you."

Konowa kept his face neutral, but allowed himself a sense of satisfaction as his words worked their magic. The soldiers before him grew bigger before his eyes. Chests expanded, chins jutted, shoulders rolled, and spines lengthened. Their demeanor changed into something more like the battle-hardened warriors they knew themselves to be.

"All of you," Konowa added, looking straight at Pimmer when he said it. Konowa worried buttons would start flying about the room if the diplomat's chest swelled anymore, so he turned back to his men. "But we're not into the woods yet." He paused as he realized he'd used one of his father's old expressions. For humans and dwarves, they felt safe once they were out of the forest. Elves, naturally, felt the opposite. What surprised Konowa was that he should feel that. He looked around the room they were standing in and decided perhaps it wasn't that surprising after all. Almost any forest would be preferable to this.

"I'll take the lead," Private Feylan said, moving toward the doorway.

"Private Smirck can handle this," Konowa said, drawing his saber. Feylan looked disappointed, but Konowa knew he'd get over it. The young soldier had proven his mettle more than enough. If he kept volunteering he'd eventually do himself into an early grave. "Slow and easy, Smirck. We still don't know who, if anyone, is in here with us."

"Yes, sir," Smirck said. He turned and faced the doorway head on. He rolled his head from shoulder to shoulder, ran a finger along the edge of the bayonet attached to his musket, then eased himself forward as if a rope were tied to his waist pulling him backward.

Konowa let two more soldiers follow then fell in behind them, confident the rest would fall in behind him. No one would linger in that room. He started climbing and realized at once that the stairway had been carved out of the rock with the same lack of attention to detail as the one outside the fort. No two steps rose at the same height, making their progress a jarring one. Bayonet's scrapped against the rock walls spraying sparks of black frost. Someone behind him tripped, which set off a chain of muttered curses.

"Terribly sorry," Pimmer whispered. "Bit hard to see in here. These brands seem better at casting shadow than they do light."

Konowa inwardly groaned. He counted to five and let the curse on his lips fade. Best to just keep moving and get to the top of the steps as quickly as possible. He pushed his senses outward and tried to determine if anything was waiting for them once they reached the top. He couldn't detect anything. He was mostly relieved, but disappointed, too.

The soldier in front of Konowa stopped moving. He looked over his shoulder at Konowa and pointed forward. Konowa moved up and around him, losing a good chunk of his Hasshugeb robe on the end of the man's bayonet in the process. It was an even tighter squeeze to get past the next soldier and Konowa felt a momentary panic of being trapped under all this rock, and then he was past him and the feeling retreated. He reached Smirck, who was crouched down with his ear pressed against the keyhole in a wooden door at the top of the stairs.

Despite feeling no warning of danger, Konowa waited until Smirck rose and gave the thumbs-up. It never hurt for a second opinion. He patted the soldier on the back and Smirck reached out and pushed against the door. It didn't budge. He turned to his left and put his shoulder to it.

"Push," Konowa whispered.

"I am pushing . . . sir," Smirck grunted, his voice straining.

"Let me at it," Konowa said, grabbing Smirck by the belt and pulling him back from the door. Squeezing around him, Konowa looked the door over, wondering if there was another latch or bolt somewhere keeping it in place. A horrible thought came to him. The door was bolted and locked on the other side. Konowa's stomach sank. How could he have been so stupid? Of course

doors would be locked, especially those leading to torture chambers.

Furious at himself, he leaned against the door and
pushed with all his might. It didn't even budge. He
stepped back and looked down at the keyhole again. It
was a simple iron plate, perhaps three inches by five
inches, bolted into the wood of the door, with a narrow
slot for a key. Assuming there weren't additional bolts
holding the door secure on the other side, a competent
locksmith should be able to open it in under a minute.
Konowa didn't know any locksmiths, but he knew
someone even better.

"You ever do any robbery in your younger days,
Smirck?" Konowa asked.

Smirck had the decency not to look offended. "I
thought of that, too, sir, but I just used to roll drunks
in the alley behind the pub. Couldn't pick a lock if I
had a key, but I think Dimwhol used to be a second-
story man." He turned to the soldier behind him. "Ask
Dimmy if he can pick a lock."

The message was relayed down the stairs. A minute
later hushed whispers rose back up toward Konowa.
Smirck listened and then turned to relay the information. Konowa could tell by the look on his face it wasn't
good news. "Sorry, sir, says that was his father, but, um,
we do have a master lock pick with us."

Konowa brightened. "Well get him up here, now.
It's a tight fit but he can squeeze by."

"I don't think so . . ."

Konowa sagged against the door. *Of course the Viceroy
can pick locks. He's a diplomat. He's probably versed in all manner
of subterfuge and skulduggery.* And he was now at the end of
their column on the stairs.

"Are you okay, Major?" Smirck asked.

Konowa tried counting to five again. It didn't help. He stood up and away from the door. "Tell everyone to get ready." With that he turned and faced the doorway. Black flames danced along the edge of his saber and frost crinkled beneath his boots. He drew back his hand, fixed his gaze on the lock, and thrust his saber forward.

The door swung open before his blade hit the lock. Konowa tumbled forward to sprawl facedown on the stone pavers. The sound of his saber clattering on the stone echoed around him. His shako rolled along the ground, the last portions of the wings falling off in a cloud of feathers. The shako came to an abrupt halt against the toe of a boot. Konowa scrambled to his feet.

He wasn't alone.

TWENTY-ONE

Konowa could make out two elves standing ten feet away, one crouching behind the other. They were backlit by the falling snow so that their faces were in shadow, but the pointy ears were a dead giveaway.

The one in front held a bow and arrow pointed directly at Konowa's heart. The bow was at full draw and the elf's hands were rock steady. He was dressed in what appeared to be palm leaves, twigs, weeds, and other natural litter to be found in the desert. Konowa knew Her dark elves chose to garb themselves in leaves and other material harvested from the *sarka har*, but he couldn't recall seeing any dressed like this.

Konowa reluctantly took his eyes off the arrow still pointed at him and assessed the other elf. Unlike his partner, this one wore robes of the Hasshugeb tribes and was currently smoothing nonexistent whiskers on his face.

"Father?" Konowa said, not trusting his eyes.

Standing before him and finally transformed back

to elf form from that of a squirrel, Jurwan Leaf
Talker continued to work at whiskers no longer there.
"What . . . how did you get here? You're elf again?
What happened?" He heard boots on the stairs behind him stepping out into the courtyard and held up
his hand toward the other elf. "Easy, lad, easy. Tyul,
right?" he said. "Nothing to worry about, we're
friends. You remember us, right? We were on the big
boat together. I'm his son, Konowa. Father, tell him to
put down the bow."

The bow remained at full draw, the arrow unwaver-
ingly fixed on Konowa's chest. The muzzles of muskets
slid into his field of vision on either side of him as his
soldiers took aim.

"Father, time to climb down from the tree and be an
elf again. Tell him to lower his damn bow. Now!" Jurwan blinked and then bolted for a nearby ladder leading
up to a wooden walkway that went all the way around
the inside of the fort a few feet below the parapet. He
was up it in a flash and gone from sight.

Konowa stood openmouthed. It wasn't the reunion
he'd imagined.

"The two of them are a few bricks short of a wall at
the moment," Yimt said, stepping out from behind the
door to stand between Konowa and Tyul. "Mute as
monks. Haven't got a word out of either of them." He
pointed at Tyul and wagged his finger. "What did I tell
you about shooting arrows at friends? *No.* Bad elf. *Very
bad.*"

Tyul eased the bowstring forward and slowly lowered the bow. Konowa realized his mouth was still hanging open and he shut it slowly. He resisted the urge to
wrap the dwarf in a bear hug. Yimt was a mess. He no

longer wore his shako, his beard looked more like an eagle's nest of twigs, and his uniform seemed more holes than cloth. The nastiest-looking hole was one centered right in the middle of his chest. It looked very much like a wound from a musket ball. "You little devil. Where in the hell have you been? We all thought you were dead."

A chorus of shouts started to build as the soldiers recognized the dwarf, but Konowa quickly silenced them with a sharp wave of his hand. He looked past Yimt and took in the interior of the fort.

It appeared smaller and less imposing on the inside. Truth be told, it was less a fort than four stone walls roughly mortared together to form a box thirty feet by thirty feet. The walls themselves rose no more than twelve feet, but situated as they were on top of the rocky hilltop, they were still imposing to anyone trying to launch an attack from the outside.

Dilapidated wooden shanties lined the interior walls serving as barracks and storerooms. A large fire pit scarred the courtyard in the far corner. Stores lay tumbled in heaps wherever Konowa looked. Smashed-open crates with packing straw strewn everywhere, broken earthenware jugs, split burlap sacks, and wooden barrels with their staves kicked in. The elves stationed here had clearly grabbed what they could, tried to destroy the rest, and then taken flight. Judging by the amount of supplies still scattered about, it was equally clear that the Hasshugeb warriors had not yet looted the place or Konowa suspected there wouldn't have been so much as a nail left.

He looked back at Yimt. "Did you find anyone here at all?"

"Quiet as a tomb," Yimt said, "which I gather you've seen for yourself." He used a thumb to point back the way they came.

Konowa nodded. The shock of seeing first his father and now Yimt alive was wearing off and his mind began to function again. "Visyna? Where is she? The rest of your squad? My mother? Jir?"

"All still alive last time I saw them," Yimt said.

Konowa was glad the soldiers were behind him. His eyes teared up. *Visyna was alive.* The image of their first meeting in the forests of Elfkyna came back to him. She'd tried to skewer him with a blade, but the memory was a fond one. She was fire, but it was the kind that tempered his spirit and made him strong.

He took a moment to cough so that he could wipe the tears away without anyone noticing.

Yimt waited until Konowa signaled he was okay, then made a point of coming to attention and saluting. It wasn't easy for him, his face grimacing as his right arm came up. "Regimental Sergeant Major Yimt Arkhorn requesting permission to rejoin the ranks, sir!"

Konowa returned the salute then held out his hand. Yimt looked momentarily surprised, but smiled and shook his hand. The dwarf's grip was hard and steady. Relief flooded through Konowa. He had the regiment's steel spine back.

"We need to talk in private, Major," Yimt said, keeping his voice low so that only Konowa could hear him.

Konowa turned and faced the troops. "Corporal Feylan."

Feylan snapped to attention while struggling to wipe the smile off his face. The other soldiers perked up on hearing Feylan's new rank. "Get men to the front gate and see if you can spot the regiment. I want the rest rounding up whatever supplies are here and stacking them by the gate." Konowa lowered his voice as he continued. "And see if you can't coax my father down."

"Grab some gravel in your fist and shake it," Yimt said to Feylan. "Sounds like nuts. It works, but make sure you've got something to feed him otherwise he has a tendency to bite."

"Er, yes, RSM," Feylan said. "I'll get one of the lads on it." He saluted then spun on a heel and started barking orders. The troops scattered to their tasks.

"Bright lad, that Feylan," Yimt said. "He's got the knack of delegating already."

"Wants to join the navy if you can believe it," Konowa said.

"Hot buttered nuns, is he daft? He'd be wasted on a ship," Yimt said, his cheeks flushing red. "I leave this regiment for a few days and the lads start losing the plot. Good thing I'm back." Yimt scuffed one of his boots in the snow then looked up into Konowa's eyes. "How is he?"

Konowa had been hoping he wouldn't ask about Private Renwar, but he couldn't keep the truth from him. He knew time was precious, but he took it anyway to bring the dwarf up-to-date on everything that happened. Yimt's eyes grew wide at the description of the bone dragon and of the marching and flying *sarka har*, but when Konowa mentioned Private Renwar's transformation, he hung his head.

"I'm sorry, Yimt," Konowa said, feeling a bond beyond officer and sergeant. "Rallie thinks there's hope for him yet, and I hope she's right, but he just keeps drifting further away from this world and into the next."

Yimt lifted his head. His face gave nothing away, but Konowa knew the hurt he must be feeling.

"He wasn't made for this life. Oh, he's tough enough in his own way, in ways I never could be, but a boy like that deserves more, you know?"

Konowa reached out and placed a hand on Yimt's shoulder. "We all do. And maybe, with a little skill, a lot of luck, and you giving the troops a good kick and bellow now and again, we might all just get it."

Yimt flashed a smile, his pewter-colored teeth gleaming. "I like the sound of that, Major. And truth be told, trying to march two squirrelly elves across the desert just doesn't compare to a proper regiment. Of course, seeing as there ain't one in sight I guess the Iron Elves will have to do."

Konowa managed to keep the smile on his face as he spied Pimmer walking toward them. "Very nice to meet you, RSM," the diplomat said, extending his hand. "I've heard many tales about you in the short time I've been with the regiment, and if even half of them are true, well, I'd love to hear a few more."

Yimt reached out and shook his hand, ignoring the black frost that sparked when their flesh touched. "An honor to meet you, Viceroy. Not every day you meet a diplomat on a scouting party," Yimt said, looking at Konowa out of the corner of his eye. "And well armed, to boot."

Pimmer beamed and winced at the same time as he gently took back his hand and patted the pistol tucked into the leather belt keeping his robes in place. "Well, it's not exactly safe out here. One never knows when danger is going to rear its head. I find it best to be prepared for all eventualities." He looked over at Konowa and hurriedly added, "And the major has been giving me a crash course in military tactics. It's all been quite fascinating."

Before the conversation could detour any more Konowa interjected. "What happened to you and the others? And how in the world did you find my father and Tyul?"

Yimt limped over to an empty wooden crate. "Sorry, sir, not quite up to snuff at the moment, but I'll be fightin' fit with a little breather." The dwarf sat down hard on the crate, which groaned in protest but did not break. "Your father and Tyul saved my skin. The beasties, rakkes that is, had me cornered and I'm not afraid to say I was in a spot of bother. Your father and Tyul diced those monsters up like so much onion. Course, neither one of them is quite sound in the noggin. I thought the young one was going to do me, but instead he shot the rock right out of my hand. He's completely daft, but the lad can shoot."

Konowa looked over at Tyul. He was sitting in the middle of the courtyard and appeared to be meditating, or maybe sleeping. "So my father hasn't said anything?"

"Not that I can make sense of. Every so often he'll start chittering away about something. I thought maybe it was elvish, but I think it's squirrelish. Still, the fact that he's not actually a squirrel anymore has to be a good sign. And he's wearing clothes now."

Konowa decided that yes, it was an improvement. He had his father back, at least part of the way. The old elf was tough. If he managed to make it this far, he'd eventually make it the rest of the way home to himself.

"So then . . . what happened to you?"

Yimt pointed to the hole in his uniform over his chest. "Courtesy of that yellow-bellied coward of a snake, Kritton," he said, spitting out the words.

Konowa was still staring at the frost-burned scar tissue visible through the hole when what Yimt said registered.

"Kritton? He's here?!" Konowa asked in disbelief. "How?"

"Can't say I know how he gets around these days, but I can tell you about the why." Yimt took the next several minutes to explain the scene in the library. "Buggers were looting the place like rats in a cheese shop. They had wagons-full of more knickknacks, bric-a-brac, and artifacts than you could shake a stick at. But even that would be excusable," Yimt said, showing his rather expansive view on a soldier's right to grab a few items in the course of a good battle, "if Kritton hadn't got it into their heads they needed revenge. He's turned them. Any one of 'em could've put a musket ball up that elf's backside and been a hero, but not a one made a move. And the weaselly elf bastard shot me."

Konowa closed his eyes for a moment then opened them, looking past Yimt. "We saw the mutilated bodies. I recognized a lot of the muscle cuts. We learned how to skin deer that way back in the Hynta. Kritton is poison all right, but they didn't have to drink his swill. They made their choice. I can't worry about that now. The regiment is just outside the fort."

"But how on earth did you survive a musket shot at close range like that?" Pimmer asked. "Were you wearing armor beneath your uniform?"

Yimt smiled, showing off his pewter-colored teeth.

"In a manner of speaking. A dwarf rib cage is like iron, hell, it actually *is* part iron. It's all the crute we chew. If he'd shot me in the gut it would have been a very different story, but lucky for me the bastard aimed right at my heart."

"Incredible. You're indeed full of surprises, my friend. Do you have any idea where they were headed?" Konowa asked.

Yimt scratched at his beard. "I think they're trying to head back home."

"There's no way the tunnels go all the way to the coast. They'd have to surface somewhere . . ."

Konowa looked around him. "Viceroy, any indication on your map of any other secret entrances into this place?"

Pimmer turned over another empty crate and with some difficulty kneeled down and spread the map out on it. He held out the storm lantern, which Konowa grabbed and positioned over the map.

"I've spent some time looking over this, but I'm afraid I just don't see anything indicating a tunnel leading into the fort."

"What's this bit of scribble over here?" Yimt asked, pointing a finger at a small rock formation outside of the fort a few hundred yards off its southern side.

Pimmer leaned over for a closer look. "That's just the privy. In Birsooni it translates as hole of dark earth, which I took to refer to midnight soil, which we all know means sh—"

Konowa coughed. "They wouldn't build a latrine outside the fort like that. Couldn't that also mean tunnel opening? Everything would look dark down there without light?"

"But why all the way out there? Why not bring it right into the fort?"

"Geologic reasons perhaps," Yimt said. "Might have been too difficult trying to tunnel through this stuff. Everything looks like it was done fast and with less than a master stone mason's attention to detail."

"Whatever the reason, that could be a tunnel," Konowa said. "If it is, then we need to explore it."

Pimmer rubbed his chin as if debating his next words very carefully. "Not to throw a damper on things, but won't that take time, time we don't have?"

Now *you worry about time.* "We'll make time," Konowa said, making sure his tone gave no room for argument. "RSM, when the regiment arrives, I want that rock pile searched. If it's a tunnel entrance, I want to know what's down there. Viceroy, look at that map again. If there are any other oddities on there that could mean a tunnel or hole or anything like that, I want to know." His words were coming out faster than he intended, but he didn't care. Visyna and Kritton were both alive, and they were somewhere nearby. He knew it. And he was going to find both of them.

"This does shed new light on things," Pimmer said, standing up and wandering off with his map held close to his face. Konowa watched him walk over to where Tyul was sitting and plop down in front of him. He spread the map out between them, sheltering it from the snow with part of his robe, and began talking. The elf ignored him though Pimmer didn't seem to notice.

Konowa turned back to Yimt, who was staring up at him with a questioning look.

"What?"

"It's just that the last time I saw you look that happy, you were killing something," Yimt said.

Was Konowa going mad? He'd just walked through a field of horrors and this is how he reacted? But it wasn't that. He struggled to understand the feeling swelling inside him. It was . . . balance. All his life he'd been angry, thinking that one day he'd find peace and be able to come to terms with the world and his place in it. But he'd had it all wrong. He'd been miserable with his anger, but it gave him purpose. To lose it would be to rob him of something important. He needed his anger, but he needed more, too. He needed to be part of something. For a long time the regiment had served that role. It was his family. The time in the forest during his banishment had been hell. He realized that despite his outward bravado he wasn't so different from everyone else. He wanted to be part of something more than himself. Maybe he could find it with Visyna. All he knew for certain was that the time was coming when he would have to make choices. Permanent, inviolable choices.

Konowa looked at Yimt and decided he could risk revealing a little of what he was experiencing. "What do you call it when you suddenly realize something that makes your whole life make sense? Everything just comes into view like a fog has lifted?"

Yimt snapped his fingers. "You, Major, just had what they call in technical terms an *e-piff-anny*. It's named after some lass from way back. It means you came to an abrupt understanding of something. It's like when you wake up after a night at the pub and for a minute you don't know why your bed is wet and lumpy and your beard smells like the wrong end of a goat, not that there's a right end, and you suddenly remember the wife chasing you out of the quarry with a battle-ax yelling at you not to come back until you sober up."

"Ahh, that sounds . . . possible," Konowa said, surprised that he actually got the gist of what the dwarf was saying if not the full meaning. "Um, I'll probably regret this, but a goat?"

"Turns out I stumbled into the local cheesemonger's shop a few doors down and took a table of cheese curds as a big bed. Wound up buying seventy-five pounds of a right tangy cheddar. Lucky for me the wife had put up some prune preserves, because after two weeks of eating cheese I was—" Whatever Yimt was going to say was thankfully interrupted by a shout from the front gate.

"Major, you'd better get over here!"

Even before Konowa made it to the front gate he knew it was trouble. He sprinted the last few yards and came to a stop by the soldiers standing guard. They were all pointing down to the desert floor.

"Rakkes, sir, hundreds and hundreds of the buggers! They're swarming in from all over."

The chill that ran down Konowa's spine had nothing to do with the black acorn. The regiment had yet to reach the bottom of the hill, but the rakkes already had.

"They just came out of nowhere, Major. One minute it was quiet and the next they were everywhere."

Konowa gripped the edge of the wooden gate. The snow-covered desert plain below the hill was dotted with hundreds of rakkes. They bounded through the snow from every direction, all homing in on the regiment now stranded several hundred yards from the bottom of the road leading up to the gate. Deep in the heart of the swirling dark mass of rakkes, a vortex of black light spun on a wobbling axis. Images of a twisted, mangled figure walked in the center of it. The rakkes kept well clear of the spinning darkness. Konowa cursed under his breath.

"What is that thing?" Corporal Feylan asked, using his musket to point.

"One viceroy too many," Konowa said. Corporal Feylan brought his musket tight into his shoulder ready to fire.

Konowa reached out a hand and knocked the muzzle down. "That's a thousand yards if it's a foot. You couldn't hit that thing if you tried that shot for a month straight. And I doubt it would even notice a musket ball going through it."

Feylan looked like he wanted to try anyway, but he grounded his musket. "We can't just stand here, sir. We have to do something. The regiment is marching right into a noose. They'll be ripped to shreds."

"Easy, Feylan, you're not thinking. One, there's damn little the handful of us could do from up here, so I'd rather not draw attention to ourselves at the moment."

Feylan lifted his musket again, his nostrils flaring. "But that's the point, Major. If we draw their attention the regiment will have a chance."

Konowa grabbed Feylan by the collar and pulled him forward just past the front gate. "What do you see right down there littered all over the rocks?"

"It's more dead rakkes."

"But they're not just dead, are they? They've been *tortured*. Their bodies were mutilated and set out on display. Now who do you suppose all these new rakkes are going to think did that?"

"Whoever's up here in the fort . . ." Feylan said, his voice trailing off.

"Exactly," Konowa said, letting go of the soldier's collar and patting him on the shoulder. "We're relatively safe in here as long as we don't do anything stupid. Even if the rakkes do climb up the hill they'll have a devil of a time trying to get in. This fort isn't much, but it's on top of a chunk of steep rock, and that counts for a lot." He put his hand on Feylan's shoulder and gave it a firm squeeze. "Sometimes, lad, the smartest thing you can do is nothing at all."

"But . . . you mean we just sit here and watch?"

Konowa pointed toward the desert floor. Black frost etched jagged lines in front of the oncoming rakkes. Icy flames rose from the ground then guttered out. In their place stood the shades of the regiment's dead. The deathly remains of Regimental Sergeant Major Lorian sat astride the great, black warhorse Zwindarra. Konowa shivered in spite of himself. "We let the Darkly Departed do what they do best."

Lorian charged, leaning forward over Zwindarra's thick neck. The horse glided more than galloped across the snow and smashed into three rakkes. Blurred images of slashing hooves and Lorian's ghostly saber flashed among the rakkes and blood splattered the snow in great swathes.

The other shades followed suit, cutting through the rakkes with a fierce abandon Konowa couldn't remember seeing before. Something, or someone, had definitely fired them up.

"Major, a word?"

Konowa turned. Pimmer stood behind him with his pistol in one hand and a brown-leather-wrapped

telescope in the other. The Birsooni map was folded
and tucked in the front of his belt and his small brass
storm lantern now hung from a loop of heavy twine
around his right shoulder. In his layers of Hasshugeb
robes the diplomat looked like a desert warrior ready
for anything.

"You were right," Pimmer said.

"About?" Konowa asked. He really didn't have time
for this, but hearing "you were right" granted the man a
little leeway. It wasn't often Konowa heard those three
magic words.

"The map. It turns out that notation does mean
tunnel. I think you'd better look." He handed Konowa
the telescope and pointed to the ladder leading up to
the southern walkway.

"That's good to know, but exploring it will have to
wait at the moment," Konowa said, turning back to
watch the unfolding battle on the desert floor below. At
first he thought a fog had rolled in, but realized it was
the freezing mist of spilled blood. His stomach heaved.
The black vortex continued to move forward, but as of
yet had made no obvious signs of joining the fray. That
worried Konowa. A hand on Konowa's arm spun him
around to face a stern-looking Viceroy. "I'm afraid I
didn't make myself clear. I know it's a tunnel because
people are emerging from it as we speak."

Konowa grabbed the telescope from Pimmer's hand
and tore across the courtyard. "Keep a close watch on
that twisted Emissary, but don't do anything. I'll be
back!" he shouted over his shoulder. He skidded to a
stop at the foot of the ladder and leaped, barely touching the rungs as he vaulted up the ladder and landed on
the wood plank walkway attached to the wall. It shook

alarmingly, but he barely noticed as he ran across it to where Private Meswiz stood clinging to the top of the wall. He pointed down toward the desert.

"They started popping up like rabbits by that pile of rocks. At first I thought I was seeing things, but they're there all right."

Konowa peered into the night. "Are you sure? Maybe it was just rakkes roaming around. I can barely see anything."

"I know I saw people with muskets, sir, at least, I'm pretty sure that's what they were."

Konowa pulled the telescope open to its full length and sighted it where the soldier was pointing. Everything was black.

"What's wrong with this thing?"

"The lens cover . . ." Private Meswiz said.

"Damn it," Konowa muttered, ripping the cover off and re-sighting the telescope. He struggled to find the spot again. "I don't see . . . wait, there are figures there." *Something about that one looks familiar . . .* He moved the larger tube to bring the image into focus.

He lowered the telescope.

Kritton.

TWENTY-TWO

Do you see? This is what that fool Konowa has brought down upon us all!" Kritton said, throwing his hands around to encompass the snow-covered desert. He glared at Visyna. There was a certainty of purpose in his eyes that would brook no dispute. In someone else it might have been viewed as fierce determination, but Visyna knew this was something different, something lethal.

He's losing control, she realized. It was only a matter of time before he tried to kill them all.

Kritton continued to rage, all the while flailing his arms around. His uniform hung in tatters from his lean frame. His hair was unkempt and his caerna was little more than a rag.

She lowered her head and turned away, partly to avoid antagonizing him further, but also to protect her face from the wind-whipped snow buffeting her. After the warm confines of the tunnel, she was finding it difficult to catch her breath in the cold. None of them were dressed for this weather, and all of them were tired, hungry, thirsty, and nursing wounds. They wouldn't last more than an hour or two in these conditions.

She waited, bringing her hands in tight to her chest to warm her fingers in case she had to begin weaving. Kritton cursed and walked away, shouting orders to the elves to keep their muskets pointed at the prisoners. Visyna searched their faces, looking for a sign of compassion, of regret, or even shame, but all she saw were masks of indifference. The look in their eyes was as cold as the steel of their bayonets. Visyna had no doubt in her mind they would kill all of them without hesitation.

Hrem appeared beside her a moment later. "I think I was right. There's a fort just ahead of us on those rocks. That has to be Suhundam's Hill."

Visyna squinted into the wind. What at first she took to be more darkness resolved itself into the outline of a jagged collection of rocks topped off with a squat, square box. "We need to act before we get inside there. Kritton is coming apart."

"Elves could die," Hrem said, his gaze still fixed on the fort.

"They made their choice. It's time we made ours," she said, echoing his words from earlier. She tested the air around her. Now that she knew what to look for her fingers easily found the elves' threads in the storm. She gasped when her touch found one more surrounded by a cold, black power. Could it be? "I think Konowa is here," she whispered, looking up at the fort.

"That means the regiment is here, too," Hrem said, glancing around them before looking back to the top of the wall. "I thought I saw movement up there, but I figured it was just the wind. If the regiment is already inside the fort then Kritton is going to walk himself right into a trap. All we have to do is stay calm and let it happen."

Visyna couldn't believe their luck. *Would it really be this easy?* Kritton barked more orders and the elves and their prisoners began to move. In this weather it would be easy for one of the soldiers to slip away into the night unseen, but where would they run? With no shelter from the storm they would freeze to death out here. She looked at the huddled group of soldiers and realized none of them would be running anywhere. Zwitty, Scolly, and Inkermon were keeping each other upright in a swaying, stumbling fashion. Chayii walked with one hand firmly gripping Jir's mane. The elf stopped and started to swoon, then caught herself and stood up straight.

"Hrem, I must help Chayii. If she collapses, her hold on Jir will, too, and he'll attack. Keep the others together."

Hrem nodded and slid over to steady the trio while Visyna matched her pace with Chayii and casually slipped her arm around her waist. The elf was shaking.

"You must keep your hands free to weave, my child," Chayii said, turning to look at her. Chayii's face was gray and her lips were turning blue.

"You're turning to ice," Visyna said, gripping the elf more tightly and hoping to get some warmth into her.

"Jir is becoming increasingly difficult to hold, and the weather is not helping. I don't think I can make it to the fort."

No. Visyna looked around to make sure no elves

were close. "I think I felt Konowa up there. I'm certain I sensed him. We just have to make it inside and we'll be fine. Everything will be fine."

"My son is there?"

Visyna squeezed her waist. "You just have to hold on a bit longer."

At these words Chayii stood up a little straighter. Jir looked up at them and purred, his ears pointing straight up and his muzzle to the wind, sniffing the air. Could he sense Konowa, too? she wondered. A moment later the bengar's purr turned into a snarl.

Visyna took her hand from Chayii's waist and sought out the threads again. There were more, hundreds more.

"Rakkes!"

"Where?" Chayii asked, coming to a halt. The elves around them heard her shout and stopped, too. Kritton was there in a flash, eyes boring in on her.

"I warned you, witch," he said, raising the butt of his musket in preparation to strike her.

Before it could fall, the shrieking cry of a rakke sounded off in the distance. It was answered at once by dozens more. The sound grew to a fury far outstripping the storm. Kritton lowered his musket.

"Back to the tunnel. We need to go back there, now!"

"It's too late for that," Hrem said, walking up to place himself between the elf and Visyna. "Didn't you hear those things? They're behind us, too. Our only chance now is to make it to the fort. The rakkes will never get us in there."

Mention of the fort snapped Kritton's head around to look at the rocky hill. Visyna noticed the elves were watching the storm now and paying no attention to the rest of them.

One of the elves said something to Kritton in elvish and pointed toward the fort, but Kritton shook his head. "The plan was to meet at the foot of the path leading up to the main gate. The dwarf Griz Jahrfel will be there."

"Kritton, if Griz Jahrfel is anywhere around here, he and the rest of his band of thieves are probably rakke meat by now," Hrem said. "Listen to them. We have to get to the fort."

Kritton raised his musket as if to fire. "You forget who's in charge here! We will not go back in that fort!" Kritton shouted.

By now all the elves had formed a small square facing outward. This was exactly the chance Visyna had been looking for, but now that there were rakkes nearby she wasn't certain if she should take it. She believed in her heart that Konowa was in that fort, and wanted nothing more than for him to charge out with the regiment to save them, but she already knew that was impossible. A regiment can't move that fast, and it would be suicide to bring them out of the security of the fort.

She made up her mind.

While Hrem and Kritton continued to argue she moved over to stand in front of Zwitty, Scolly, and Inkermon. She turned to them as if offering them aid.

"Tell me if Kritton comes this way," she said.

"What are you up to?" Zwitty asked, his weasely face a scowl of suspicion.

"Saving your lives," she said.

Ignoring the threads of life around her, Visyna focused instead on the weather. She closed her eyes and focused her attention skyward, picking out a single snowflake fluttering in the air several hundred feet up. Using it as her focal point, she began to draw more flakes to it, hoping to create a microstorm that would blind Kritton and the elves long enough to cover their escape.

Instead of massing together into a billowing pile, however, the flakes melted and froze together, forming a spinning chunk of ice. She grimaced, feeling the sting of the Shadow Monarch's taint in the storm. Her dexterity was hampered by the pain. The more she wove the larger the ice grew. It was already man-sized and growing faster as it fell. The horror of what she had set in motion dawned on her. This wasn't going to be a blinding storm, it was a single chunk of solid metallic ice.

She saw Kritton's life force clearly in the storm. It was bound in the Shadow Monarch's oath and pulsing with a black energy. It troubled her that it was so similar to that of Konowa's, but unlike Konowa, she knew Kritton wasn't going to change. There was more than just the oath staining Kritton's energy. His rage and his need for revenge were consuming him, making him as toxic as the rakkes around them.

Visyna turned and opened her eyes. Kritton was still yelling at Hrem, but he paused in mid-sentence and looked at her. He saw her hands and his eyes grew wide.

He knows.

Kritton began to bring his musket up to his shoulder again. He was going to fire. Time stood still. Visyna knew what she had to do, but unlike the beetle in the tunnel, this would be no accident. She lowered her hands, removing the last of her hold on the falling ice. It occurred to her then she had the power in her to divert the ice so that it wouldn't fall directly on Kritton, but she didn't. A part of her was screaming that this was wrong, and that there would truly be no turning back, but her survival and that of the group meant more.

She made a choice.

There was a rush of air, a blur, and then a spray of red mist as the ice slammed into Kritton's skull. The ice didn't shatter then, but carried on to pulverize Kritton's body into a four-foot-deep crater in the frozen desert floor.

Visyna cried out. The violence of Kritton's death shocked her. Blood, snow, and ice exploded in every direction. A chunk of ice struck Visyna in the stomach, knocking her backward into the three soldiers, sending all four of them tumbling to the snow.

Visyna gasped for breath, her arms and legs twitching as she tried to regain control of her senses. A hand appeared out of the dark. She reached for it, yelping as the frost fire singed her bare flesh. Hrem hauled her upright then quickly let go. Scolly, Zwitty, and Inkermon staggered to their feet. Jir padded into view with Chayii still gripping his mane.

"That was one hell of an ace you had tucked up your sleeve," Hrem said. There was a fierce grin of satisfaction on his face that Visyna couldn't share. He held up his other hand. Yimt's drukar was clenched in his fist. *Did he want to give it to her as a war prize?* She'd just murdered another living being. She knew she had done it for all the right reasons, but it still didn't change the fact of what she had done. She shook her head and turned away.

A musket fired. Everyone ducked, but the shot had been aimed away from them. Rakkes yowled. A rock sailed overhead. The elves were all turned to face out-ward. More muskets fired.

"The rakkes are closing in," Hrem shouted. "We have to try for the fort. Can you do more of that weather stuff?"

Visyna was still reeling. It wasn't remorse, but more shock that she had deliberately taken another life. She tried to probe her feelings further, wanting to feel something beyond disbelief, but her mind was too full of images of blood-splattered ice and the horrible sound of crunching bone. She knew it would stay with her the rest of her life.

"Not like that, but I should be able to keep us partially hidden in the storm." She suddenly felt the need to explain herself. "I can't kill them all, Hrem. I did what I had to do to stop Kritton, but I can't take the lives of all these elves. Even if I had the power I don't think I could do it."

"You won't have to," Hrem said, looking away.

Visyna followed his gaze. The elves were disappear-ing into the snow, firing their muskets as they went.

"Are they running away?" she asked.

"Don't know and don't care," Hrem said. "After what you did to Kritton, they probably figure they're safer with the rakkes. If anything, they should prove a nice distraction for us. We're a lot smaller group. We have a better chance of remaining undetected."

A volley of musket fire made further conversation impossible. Visyna ducked again. Rakkes screamed in pain from somewhere close.

"You're risking our lives," Zwitty said, pointing a finger at Hrem. "You really think one of these elves won't put a musket ball in our back as a parting gift? They were ready to end every last one of us down in that tunnel. We set out toward the fort on our own and they might just fire a volley at us."

"Would you rather stay here and wait for the rakkes?" Hrem asked.

"I don't think that's a good idea," Scolly said, looking at Zwitty. "Those rakkes are terrible."

Zwitty looked at Scolly, opened his mouth, and then closed it in a frown. He lowered his hand. "No one wants to meet up with those damn rakkes, I'm just saying it's our lives if you're wrong, Hrem."

"It's our lives regardless," Visyna added, marshaling her energy. "We have to get to the fort, it's the only chance we have. I should be able to weave a small storm within the storm that will keep us hidden."

"Can you control it?" Zwitty asked. The concern in his voice was obvious. They had all seen Kritton's death. Cannon balls weren't that destructive.

Visyna knew her cheeks were burning. She hadn't meant to create a massive chunk of ice, but in the end it saved them. She saved them. "I won't be focusing my energy above us, only around us. You'll all be fine, just don't touch me, and don't stray outside the area I protect."

"And if we did?" Zwitty asked.

Visyna said nothing, simply looking over at the crater where Kritton had been standing.

The musket fire lessened. Visyna could still see a few of the elves through the snow, but it was as if her group no longer existed. Now that Kritton was dead, maybe his toxic concepts of honor and revenge would no longer sway the elves. She wanted to believe that was true, but she had already made up her mind she wasn't going to stay here to find out.

She noticed Chayii still holding on to Jir and walked over to them. "Konowa must know we're here. We just have to make it to the walls and we'll be safe."

"You have a lot of faith in my son," Chayii said. It was a statement. Visyna detected no sarcasm.

"I do, but I also have a lot of faith in myself, and in you and Jir and the rest of the squad, even Zwitty."

Chayii's eyebrows went up and Visyna tilted her head. "Well, faith that he doesn't want to get left out here all alone."

The elf smiled. "In that case, my faith in him equals yours."

Visyna paused, listening to more musket fire. Before she could stop herself she blurted out the question she knew she had to ask. "Do you want me to save them? The elves?"

Chayii stood up straighter. Her eyes peered deep into Visyna's and for several seconds she said nothing.

"No," Chayii said. Her voice was free of any emotion. "They are beyond our help."

"But Konowa . . ." Visyna started to say, then paused. She wanted to say that Konowa's whole life had been about finding his elves. And now that they were so close, they were about to slip away.

Chayii smiled at her. "I think you already know the answer. These are not Konowa's elves. They were once, but not anymore. If by some miracle they were to survive, Konowa would have no choice but to court-martial every one of them. You know what the penalty for their crimes is? He would have to sign their death warrants."

Visyna knew it was true. "Is there nothing else we can do?"

"We can save ourselves, my child," Chayii said. "That will be difficult enough."

There was a cold logic to what Chayii said that Visyna couldn't dispute. Hrem strode up to them with the other three soldiers close behind. The musket fire began to pick up in intensity again, and this time it didn't slacken off. Rakkes roared and called to each other all around them.

"We really need to go," he said.

Visyna looked one last time at Chayii, who turned away to face the fort. It loomed before them like a dark block. It seemed impossibly far away. She knew she was cold, tired, hungry, and scared and did her best to ignore it. The snow swirled around in patches, providing sporadic views of the desert. She caught glimpse of packs of rakkes and bodies sprawled in the snow.

"Stay close." She began to weave the air, pulling at the threads around her. Musket fire crackled all around her, making it difficult to concentrate. The responding screams and roars from the rakkes only made it worse. She shook her fingers and rolled her head from side to side. She went deeper into herself, ignoring the chaos and searching for something solid to hold on to.

Konowa. She smiled and growled at the same time. He was less base and more a potent element in an alchemist's cauldron, but he was energy and life. The key, and one she wasn't sure she'd ever fully comprehend, was to get the mixture of who he was just right. She had no illusions that she could ever change him . . . at least not completely, but however far he'd drifted from his origins he remained a creature of the natural order. That was enough.

Visyna pictured him in her mind, seeing the elf that

he was. She accepted the darkness and the violence that was in him, knowing the choices he'd made had been as difficult as they had been necessary. It didn't mean she agreed, and it certainly didn't mean she wasn't going to help him become a better elf, but for now she found it in herself to accept him the way he was. She'd killed an elf this night because he couldn't change. The regret weighed heavy on her heart. She would move heaven and earth to help the elf she loved find the strength that Kritton could not.

The ground around her erupted in a geyser of snow and sand. A single column of tightly swirling snow a foot thick climbed twenty feet into the sky. She gasped and slowed down her weaving, allowing the column to settle at a height of six feet.

"The Creator be praised," Inkermon said, wonder and fear evident in his voice.

Visyna wanted to say his so-called creator had nothing to do with it, but that wasn't helpful.

"Could you ask him for a little help?" Visyna said, turning her concentration back to the column of snow.

"What, pray to him? Now?" Inkermon asked.

"I could use it. We all could." She risked a quick look over her shoulder. The soldier appeared stunned.

"No one's ever asked before," Inkermon said. He stood up. His knees wobbled, but he stayed upright. "I'm always ridiculed. I have only ever tried to spread the word and offer them a path to redemption."

"Mercy, Inkermon, don't get all weepy on us," Hrem said. "I can't speak for the rest of them, but I admire a man with firm convictions. Just maybe keep in mind other men might have different ones."

"There is only one true . . ." Inkermon started to

say, then let the rest of his words get taken by the wind. "A prayer right now would be appropriate. Yes, I will call on his aid that we may yet live to do his bidding."

Visyna smiled. She had no idea who or what might exist beyond this world, but if they wanted to throw a little help their way she wasn't going to turn it down. She shivered and lifted her hands out in front of her. With a flick of her right wrist she began to tease apart the column, unfurling it like one of Rallie's scrolls. As she did she coaxed it into a curving wall, bringing it around to fully enclose them in a five-foot-diameter space.

"Not a lot of room in here," Zwitty muttered.

"Can you ever give your mouth a break?" Hrem asked.

"Look, I'm not saying I want to be on the other side of this thing," Zwitty said, his defensive whine in full pitch. "I'm just saying it's tight quarters is all. She's the one that said we can't touch her while she's doing her spells. That's not going to be easy trying to get to the fort now, is it?"

"It will be challenging," Chayii said, her grip loosening on Jir's mane as she crowded in to stand in front of Visyna. The bengar sniffed at the swirling snow a foot away from his muzzle, but had the sense not to touch it. The soldiers shuffled close to stand beside and behind her in a crescent.

"This is the best I can manage," Visyna said. It truly was. The dawning realization that she now had to maintain this wall while walking several hundred yards over increasingly difficult terrain and surrounded by rakkes made her question if she could really do it.

"Not much though, is it," Zwitty said, clearly

unable to contain himself. "Now that boulder of ice you used to crush Kritton, now that was some good magic. This, though, it's just a bit of snow swirling around, isn't it?"

Before she could shout a warning, Zwitty yelped.

"That could have scoured the skin right off my bones!" he shouted. "It's scalding!"

Visyna felt his hand briefly touch the wall without having to see it. "Do not touch it. The longer the wall is maintained, the hotter it will become. I should warn you, it will likely become very warm in here."

"I'm still freezing my—Well, it's freezing right now so a bit warmer would be just fine," Hrem said.

Let's hope that's all it becomes, Visyna thought, easing back on the pace of her weaving. It was going to be a delicate balance. The rakkes would sense the use of magic, so all the swirling snow in the world would only mask them for so long. She'd need to keep them hidden with enough of a barrier to dissuade any curious rakkes from trying to see what was inside.

"Hrem, you're all soldiers. We need to walk at a steady pace."

"That I can help you with. All right, ladies and gentlemen. Nice and easy. I'll give the cadence and you just follow along. Ready? By the right . . . and by that I mean your right foot . . . forward . . . march."

As Hrem called out a soft "left, right, left, right" Visyna used the tempo to help her weaving. She soon had a comfortable rhythm going. Chayii kept her hand on Jir, but for now he seemed perfectly content to pad along with them. He still favored his wounded shoulder, but it didn't seem to be slowing him down.

"Left, right, left, right, I see the fort straight ahead,

left, right, left, right," Hrem said, saying the words at the same tempo as the cadence.

"Any sign of rakkes?" she asked. "I have to concentrate on this. It's difficult to see beyond it."

Hrem didn't answer right away. "Well," he said, dropping the cadence, "we're about to find out just how hot that snow is. Can you brace yourself?"

Visyna risked a quick push of her senses beyond the wall and immediately regretted it. "There's hundreds of them!"

"I can't see all that, but I can see enough. We don't even have any damn weapons," he said.

Sweat began dripping off the end of Visyna's nose. She blinked and more drops stung her eyes. She couldn't afford to wipe her hands across them so she rubbed her face into the cloth of her sleeve while still maintaining her weaving. It was already hot inside the circle and they had barely traveled twenty yards.

"Just stay close . . . and keep moving," Visyna said, really talking to herself. She already knew she couldn't keep this up all the way to the fort.

A rakke howled from just outside the swirling wall of snow.

A moment later, Visyna felt the creature impact the wall. Its screams were cut short as the small group continued moving forward and over the rakke's smoking body. Jir growled and barred his fangs at the sight of the rakke, but other than giving the corpse a good sniff, he left it alone. Visyna stepped over it while doing her best not to look, but the smell of singed hair and flesh made her gag.

"Well, that's all right then," Zwitty said, his voice startlingly loud inside the small area. "Any rakke stupid enough to try to get through this is in for a nasty surprise. Good. But could you turn down the heat a bit?"

"I can't," she said, wiping her eyes again. She licked her lips and tasted salt. Her skin felt like she was lying in the sun at high noon. "I'm sorry. It's only going to get hotter."

There was a commotion on the other side of the wall and several rakkes began screaming in pain. Fortunately, none of them fell down in their path, but now the snow and sand beneath their feet was turning to mud. Walking was becoming increasingly difficult. *If anyone slipped they would fall through the wall.* If that didn't kill them, the slavering beasts on the other side would. They were all walking a tightrope with just one wrong step meaning a horrible death. "I'm going to have to stop," she said. Her legs were shaking and she was having a hard time walking. Between the fear and her exhaustion it was becoming a challenge just to stand upright.

"Are you mad? We've barely——" was all Zwitty managed before the sound of a thump suggested Hrem had knocked him off his train of thought.

"The fort is still quite a piece away," Hrem said.

"I know," she said, lifting her sandals out of the mud one at a time only to sink back down again. "I just can't keep this up. I'm sorry, I thought I could but I can't." It was as if the muscles in her legs had been replaced with solid lead.

"You've done everything you could, child, no one is blaming you," Chayii said, her voice calm and without a hint of accusation.

I am, she thought to herself. Her hands were cramping and her hold on the spinning wall was faltering. If she didn't dissipate it soon, she might lose control of it completely and risk all their lives.

Her right foot caught as she pulled it from the mud and she stumbled. She fumbled her hold on the storm. She struggled to get it back, but it would take more strength than she had left to pull it in tight and keep it strong. The best she could do now was focus it outward, pushing the swirling snow and heat further away while still keeping it swirling around them. Visyna knew before long she would lose even that ability, and when that happened, they would be completely exposed.

And when it happens, I will have killed us all.

TWENTY-THREE

"Viceroy, I want another exit, now!" Konowa shouted. His right knee was throbbing after jumping the last six feet off the ladder, but pain could wait. He limped across the courtyard of the fort, his mind a whirl of conflicting emotions.

Visyna is alive! And his elves . . . he sped up his gait and to hell with the stabbing sensation in his knee as he tried to process everything. After all this time, they were just a few hundred yards away. Everything and everyone he'd wanted and searched for were now on the outside of the fort.

But it wasn't what he expected.

The soldiers he thought of as his sons and brothers weren't the elves out there, but the raggedy-arsed collection of human misfits he'd led into battle from Elfkyna to the Wikumma Islands to here.

The smell of leather, polished copper, and sawdust snapped him back to the here and now. He'd come to a stop under a tattered canvas awning tacked to the inside of the fort's west wall and held up by two broken cart shafts at the other end. It created about the saddest, leaky, and sagging roof he'd ever seen, but it did serve to keep most of the snow off Pimmer, who had taken refuge underneath it. The spot had clearly been a workshop at one point. Everything from boot soles to leather and canvas straps, bits of brass and pewter, and clay jars littered the ground. Pimmer sat on an overturned bucket while his ever present map was spread out on a door resting on bricks, which created a more than adequate table. His small brass lantern gave off a surprising amount of light.

RSM Arkhorn sat off to the side on a tangled mound of coiled rope, chain, and burlap sacks. He was turning the handle of a small grinding stone set upright in a wooden yoke while holding a piece of copper sheet to it. A rat-sized pyramid of copper dust already filled an earthenware basin set at the base of the grinding wheel.

"I think Kritton's dead," Konowa said. "Visyna killed him. Or at least, I think she did. Dropped a huge chunk of ice on him." The image still shocked him. Between the snow, the dark, and the distance he couldn't be sure, but even if his eyes couldn't confirm it, something in his heart did . . . or at least, very much wanted to. That huge chunk of ice had come plummeting from the sky and hit someone. He had no idea she could do that.

Yimt stopped grinding. "Blast. I was looking forward to putting a permanent crimp in his spine myself. You're sure he's dead?"

"If he's not, he's at the bottom of a crater with his head in his boots."

Yimt let out a low whistle. "I owe that lass a pint. Is she okay?"

"As far as I can tell," Konowa said, starting to pace then stopping when the pain in his knee flared up. "I saw a storm. She weaves weather so it had to be something she made. It hid everything from sight, but that's about all it's probably good for. There are a lot of rakkes between her and the fort. We have to find a way to help her."

Pimmer looked up from the map. The expression on his face wasn't encouraging. "We've gone over this a hundred times from a dozen different angles and there's no other way in or out except the main gate and the entrance we used."

Konowa wasn't satisfied. "They must have built more bolt holes. There has to be another way."

Pimmer shook his head. "I'm sorry, Major, but I don't see it. And even if there were . . ." he said, shrugging his shoulders.

"Meaning what?" Konowa asked, the pain in his knee forgotten.

"Meaning," Yimt said, "what would we do with it? There's hundreds of yards between us and them, and then there's a vertical climb to get up here. And that's not counting the rakkes. There's precious little we can do for them by charging outside these walls without a plan."

Konowa couldn't believe what he was hearing. "This isn't like the regiment. They have the Darkly Departed. They're trained soldiers. Rallie's with them. They'll be fine. Visyna's out there alone." As soon as he said it he paused and rubbed a hand against his forehead. "Visyna and your squad and my mother and hopefully Jir are out there alone. They're the ones that need our help."

"As I was saying, Major, we'd be little more than fresh meat for the rakkes if we venture out without a plan. However," Yimt said, looking over at the Viceroy, "we've been working on something that should put a lit fuse up their keisters. We were concocting it with the lads in mind, but now that Visyna and her group have arrived I'd say they could use it more."

The two of them smiled. Konowa found his hand reaching for his saber of its own accord. Yimt Arkhorn and Pimmer Alstonfar had come up with a plan to inconvenience hundreds of rampaging rakkes.

And they'd done it together.

"Tell me," he ordered.

When they finished, both looked at him for his response. For several seconds, Konowa was absolutely speechless. Finally, he nodded and took his hand off the pommel. "Let's do it. Now, explain to me again why I'm the one who's going to be set on fire?"

Kritton.

The elf's shade appeared before Alwyn. It was a dark spectral being in searing pain, yet it wasn't like the other shades of the deceased Iron Elves. Kritton's shade exuded an awareness and a presence the others did not, not even RSM Lorian.

"Take your place among the fallen and defend the regiment," Alwyn said. He phrased it like an order, but would Kritton obey? Alwyn's relationship with the shades was a precarious one. He walked on the edge, just one slip away from joining them wholly. But as long as he still lived he wasn't one of them. He did command the dead, but only because they chose to follow. He had bargained with the Shadow Monarch and won them a freedom of a kind, but they remained dead, and in servitude. Alwyn saw the futility of it. "Rakkes have encircled us and Her Emissary approaches."

Alwyn turned from the shade, expecting it to obey, and focused his attention on Her Emissary. It took him a moment to realize he was wrong. *Her Emissary no longer serves the Shadow Monarch.* The realization would have filled him with hope a few days ago, but now he knew the cost behind it. The Shadow Monarch's former servant was utterly mad and destroying itself in the process. It was literally and figuratively flying apart, and growing more dangerous in the process. How do you destroy something like that?

"I have always defended the regiment," Kritton said, his voice an icy tendril worming its way into Alwyn's mind.

Alwyn blinked and turned back to Kritton's shade. "Then do so again," he said. "As the oath bound you as you lived to the regiment, and through it, the Shadow Monarch, it binds you now to me. You must feel this."

"You can't understand what I feel," the shade of Kritton said, moving forward so that it stood only a foot away. *"You are not elf. You are not one of the tainted ones soiled by Her vile touch. You were not betrayed as I was."*

"This is not the time or the place to discuss betrayal, Kritton," Alwyn said, finding it easier now in the face of Kritton's anger to exert his own power. "You are bound by the oath as we all are. You have no choice."

"You lie! I hear it in your voice. I do have a choice. I may not have the power, but I have the choice. You yourself tried to break Her oath. Yes . . . I feel this."

Alwyn focused on Kritton. Power arced between them in ugly barbs of harsh light. Kritton's shade began to scream. It flailed and tried to break free, but it was no match for Alwyn.

"Stand and fight with the others. You know this is our duty. We are all soldiers of the Iron Elves. Forget the oath that cursed us and remember the one you made with the regiment. All of us must fight."

"I do not accept that!"

Alwyn raised his hand to strike Kritton down, then paused. He felt Rallie's power being exerted to keep the rakkes at bay. The shades of the dead should have been more than sufficient to handle them, but they had fallen back and were no longer attacking. The living soldiers of the regiment were yelling and pleading for the shades to resume the battle, but the shades now refused to move. They were waiting for something.

They were . . . afraid.

"They do not want this fate any more than I do, any more than you do," Kritton said. *"And you know this."*

Alwyn thrust a hand and drove it into the heart of Kritton's shade. He felt it scream as he closed his fingers tight. "You are right, Kritton, but I remind you again that we took the oath, and now we will see it through." He released his grip and withdrew his hand. Kritton's shade wavered and blurred before resuming its remembered shape of the elf.

Several shades drifted closer to the war of wills between Alwyn and Kritton. Would any of the other shades come to Kritton's aid? Was their pain so unbearable that they would rather flee than fight?

Alwyn looked the dead in their eyes, steeling himself for the empty horror he saw there. "Our only chance is if we stick together as one. We are all Iron Elves, living and dead. There is no other way."

The shades appeared to accept this, and a moment later a cheer went up from the regiment as the dead moved forward and began to attack again. Alwyn noted, however, that none ventured near the approach of the thing that had once been Her Emissary. The creature's spiraling madness spread fear before it like a tornado.

". . . *the advantage is yours . . . for now,*" Kritton said, moving off to join the other shades.

Alwyn watched it go, but knew he had bigger problems to deal with. Gwyn, though the thing drawing near no longer resembled the man in form or being, managed to hold some core of itself at the center of its own storm even as the rest of it was torn away.

Is this to be my destiny, too? Alwyn wondered. Will I become little more than a maddened collection of violence and death? He half-expected Rallie to appear at his side and tell him he was being foolish, but she was busy, and in the end, he still had a duty to perform. And that, he realized, was what would keep him sane. He was a soldier. He was an Iron Elf. As long as that was true, he could never become the monstrosity Gwyn had.

He adjusted his caerna and brought his hand up to adjust his spectacles, then remembered he no longer wore them. He brought his hand down and knocked on his wooden leg for luck, then limped forward to meet the threat.

"And how is this better than my plan?" Konowa whispered, scrambling over an ice-slicked rock and sliding down the other side to land awkwardly and fall to one knee before catching himself. "We're still outside the walls risking life and limb." He stood, brushed the snow off his trousers, and strode after Yimt. *How the blazes does anyone with legs so short move so bloody fast?* The dwarf had a knack for navigating among the tumbled rocks of Suhundam's Hill like a mountain goat.

"Almost done, sir," the dwarf said, easily bounding up and over another boulder. Yimt spooled out more twine from a bobbin slung from his belt. A continuous line now led all the way back to the secret entrance they had come through just a short twenty minutes before.

Konowa ignored the view from below as Yimt's caerna blew in the wind, and instead marveled that he could move so nimbly after having been shot in the chest. Dwarves had a reputation for toughness, but just how tough Konowa had never fully appreciated. It was truly impressive.

"That's how I feel," Konowa said, letting gravity pull him the next few yards before digging his boot heels into the snow to slow himself down as another pile of rocks loomed before him.

"Think low and wide, Major," Yimt whispered back over his shoulder. "The idea is to spread yourself out over a bigger area, and keep your body close to the ground. Makes a fellow more stable, especially a lanky one like you."

"I'll be low and wide and splattered all over these rocks if you don't slow down," Konowa grumbled. He finally gave in to his heaving lungs and stopped at the next boulder. Unlike the slow, tense climb up to the fort of a few hours ago, this descent was barely controlled chaos. Konowa's body was now bruise on top of bruise. If he ever lay down he seriously wondered if he could haul himself back up again.

Yimt turned and trotted back up to where Konowa had halted. "Your orders, if you recall, sir, were to, and I quote, 'Get down the damn hill as fast as you can bloody well move.'"

"Yes, you're right," Konowa managed, bending over double. His face was flushed and he'd already undone the top four buttons on his jacket despite the cold. He straightened back up and started to move off, but Yimt placed a strong hand on his arm and held him in place.

"If you don't mind my saying, Major," Yimt said, steering Konowa toward a small rock where he could sit down, "you haven't really conquered the whole patience is a virtue thing."

"They're surrounded by rakkes out there," Konowa said, struggling to get up from the rock and reluctantly giving into this body and allowing himself to rest for a moment. "Patience won't do them any good if they're dead."

Yimt lowered his chin to his chest for a moment as if in deep thought. When he lifted it again he gave Konowa a look he'd never seen before. Konowa wasn't looking at a sergeant in his regiment—it was the disgusted and disapproving face of a father.

"Then go, charge out there like a mad, brave fool and see what it gets you. You're as worn out as a butterfly in a windstorm right now. You're no good to anyone like this, least of all your missus."

Missus . . . ? Konowa stood up though it was no easy feat. His thighs screamed and he almost tipped over. "You're not out in the desert with two elves too far out on a branch. I'll check the regs, but I'm fairly certain

I'm still your commanding officer." It was surreal to hear those words coming from his lips. It sounded precisely like something the Prince said, but maybe he was allowing his feeling for the troops to breed too much familiarity. He *was* their commanding officer, but the comradeship and friendship he felt with them, especially Yimt, blurred the lines.

"And while you're at it, you can check my paybook. Do you know why I've been busted back down to private more times than a unicorn has virgins lining up to ride it?" Yimt asked, his voice taking on a hard edge. "I mean, besides the drinking and brawling and general disregard for military rules and discipline?"

Konowa said nothing, deciding a smart remark wasn't needed at this juncture.

"Because I've saved more bloody officers from themselves than deserved it. Most of 'em didn't even have the decency to give thanks. No, their egos were a little too bruised for that, so when I stopped a lieutenant from leading his company across the path of another regiment about to fire a volley I was brought up on charges of insubordination. And when I fired at a shrubbery that was hiding a band of archers and sprung an ambush before we walked into it, a captain busted me for not maintaining fire discipline."

"I'm not like that," Konowa said, his feelings hurt that Yimt would lump him in with these other incompetent officers.

"No, Major," Yimt said, "you're *worse*. You really *do* care about the men, and yet you still charge hither, yon, and beyond, saber flashing, hair flowing, and setting an altogether bad example."

"Bad example?" Konowa wasn't standing for that.

"The hell, you say! I lead from the front. I've never backed down from a fight."

"Aye, and that's an admirable quality in a soldier, but an officer also has to use his brain once in a while. What do you think all those young impressionable lads get in their heads when they see their officer deep in the thick of every fight? I'll tell you what," Yimt said, cutting off Konowa's response. "They think they have to live up to your example, and so they start charging around like mad hatters, too. But here's the thing—they ain't you. Let's face it, *you* ain't you either. You're banged up more than a round-heel on payday. But you've got the knack, same as me. The two of us get into trouble all on our own, but we figure a way to get back out again. We've both been shot at and hit, missed, and learned a few tricks. A lot of these lads, they don't have what we have. They can get themselves into trouble, but getting *out* ain't going to be as easy for them."

This was something Konowa had never really thought about before. "But I can't just sit back and watch. I'm not the Prince."

Yimt shook his beard and snow fluttered to the ground. "A few weeks ago I would have said that was a good thing, but you know, that royal pain in the arse *does* use his gray matter. Oh sure, he's got lofty plans, but I'll be buggered if he hasn't put a hell of a lot thought into each one. *He* thinks about what comes next. Probably learned it from his mum. You could learn from him. Think more than one step ahead. Remember, when you charge there are a lot of soldiers that are going to follow in your footsteps. Know where you're leading them, and for that matter, know what you're going to do when you get there."

The nearby howl of rakkes reminded Konowa of the urgency of their task, but he held the urge to simply charge forward in check. "You know, for a loud-mouthed, highly opinionated, rule-breaking malcontent, you offer some damn good advice."

Yimt's metal-stained teeth flashed in the night. "And you're not the dandiest, wouldn't-know-his-arse-from-a-hole-in-the-ground officer I've ever met . . . though you do vie for that distinction at times."

"Let's just pretend that was a compliment and get on with it."

Yimt motioned with his thumb. "Just waiting for you to catch your breath, Major. Got three more of the sorry things right here."

Konowa looked and saw three rakke bodies now half-covered in snow. "They piled the things everywhere." He stood up and walked over to the bodies, using his boot to kick off the snow from each one. Grunting with the effort, he then propped each frozen corpse into as close to a standing position as he could manage as Yimt piled some rocks around them to keep them in place. His hands stung as he handled the snow-crusted rakkes, but there was nothing for it. An uneasy feeling washed over him as he realized he was doing something very similar with the bodies of the rakkes that his elves had done.

"This ain't the same thing," Yimt said as if reading his thoughts. "We're just trying to save some lives." He took the twine and wrapped it around the nearest arm of each rakke. When he was done, they were all tied together. Without pausing, he lifted the flap on the haversack he had slung over one shoulder, reached a hand inside and came out with a dollop of axle grease used for wagon wheels.

"There's a part of me that says this is desecration," Konowa said, not feeling sympathy for the rakkes, but something dangerously close to it.

"Part of you is right," Yimt replied, quickly smearing grease on the rakkes' chests and heads, if they still had a head. "But the way I see it, for all the evil they did in their short, brutish lives, they get to make amends by helping us now. Makes what we're doing here almost noble." He took some of the fur on top of a rakke's head and used the grease to pull it up into a spike then stood back to admire his work.

"You think this is something you'd tell the grandchildren one day?" Konowa asked, opening the haversack he was carrying and scooping out a small handful of copper shavings. He sprinkled some on each body, making sure to trickle a small pile on the grease-coated twine as well. The copper shavings stuck to the grease despite the wind.

"There are things I won't tell myself," Yimt said. "As for the rest of it, I imagine I'll wind up being a plucky warrior saving poor benighted officers left, right, and center. Yup, they'll think their gramps was a real hero."

Konowa clapped the dwarf on the shoulder. "He is."

"You'll make an old dwarf cry with that kind of mush," Yimt said, absently pulling up the hem of his caerna to rub the grease off his hand. The howling of rakkes turned both their heads.

"How much more twine do we have?" Konowa asked.

Yimt lifted up the bobbin and pulled the last foot of twine from it. "Out of twine and out of time."

Konowa rolled his eyes and looked out across the desert. "I can see all kinds of shadows moving out there. I see the storm Visyna is controlling, too. Maybe two hundred yards away." The thought of her being so close filled him with anxiety. Was she okay? He wanted to run out there right now to her, but he knew if they were going to have any chance of making it back to the fort they had to follow through with this plan.

"I wish I had my shatterbow with me," Yimt said, sliding a large chopping ax out of the leather straps that held it to his back.

"We'll be moving too fast to reload. If your plan works, your ax and my saber should be more than enough. If they aren't, it won't really matter."

Yimt hefted the ax in his hands and gave it a few twirls. He deftly spun it around his body as if it were an extension of his arms. Images from Konowa's dream in the Shadow Monarch's forest came back to him and he was tempted to ask Yimt about it, but the sound of the rakkes was growing louder. Time was definitely up.

"So," Konowa said, "I'll find Visyna and the squad and lead them back here. When you see my signal, light the twine."

Yimt looked him over. "Now that the rakkes from here to the door are done, a liberal dusting of you should do it."

Konowa untied the bundled Hasshugeb robe that hung from the belt at his waist and draped it over his shoulders.

Yimt reached forward and opened the flap on Konowa's haversack and stuck a hand inside. He took the copper shavings and dust and began patting them all over Konowa's robe, ordering him to turn with a swirling motion of his main finger where upon he patted down his back as well.

"And this won't hurt?" Konowa asked.

Yimt gave him an extra hard pat and turned him around to face him. "More than anything else you've been through in the last few days? Naw," Yimt said, "can't imagine it will feel more than a bunny nibbling on your fingers."

Konowa decided to inquire about the kind of rabbits Yimt had encountered another time. "Right. Somehow, it seems like I should be sending you out running across the desert," Konowa said, looking down and noticing how the copper shimmered in the reflected metallic light of the falling snow.

Yimt held out his right hand palm up. A small, black flame burned in the center of it. "Gotta hand it to the Viceroy. He knows as much about metals and alchemy as a dwarf. That pencil pusher has one devious mind." The admiration in his voice sounded sincere.

"I think it's part of the job requirement," Konowa said, reaching out with his own hand and the black flame that burned there. The two shook, black sparks whirling up into the night.

"You know all those things I said about thinking ahead and not always charging headlong into battle?" Yimt said, looking up at Konowa with an unblinking stare.

"I wasn't listening," Konowa said, giving the dwarf's hand a squeeze then letting go. He turned and worked his way down through the last jumble of fallen rocks and hit the desert floor at a run. He unsheathed his saber and it immediately glistened with black frost.

"I didn't think you were," Yimt shouted after him. "Now go do what you do so well, Major. Stir up that hornet's nest!"

TWENTY-FOUR

A wind blew among the *sarka har* on the mountaintop, rattling their branches. Leaves heavy with ore and dark power twisted and ripped away, twirling through the air like miniature scythes. A few of the blood trees snapped and splintered, their trunks too rigid to cope with the strain. The Shadow Monarch ignored the whirling debris around Her and pulled Her robe closer. It was cold up here, even for Her. She sat on the leeward side of Her *ryk faur*, sheltered by its massive, gnarled trunk from the worst of the wind. Great, knobby branches hung low around Her, offering further protection.

She closed Her eyes and leaned Her head against the Silver Wolf Oak's trunk. She felt the strong, urgent vibration of the ichor pulsing through the tree and took comfort from it. Her *ryk faur* would live. The early frost would not kill it. She saw the birthing meadow sparkling with white frost and felt the anguish as the tiny sapling screamed in terror and pain as the frost burned it. She turned to plead with the elves of the Long Watch to save it, but there was no one there.

The Shadow Monarch sat up, crying out as She reached to soothe the sapling. Her hands came to rest on the ulcerating trunk of the tree. It was sick. It was a thought She knew, yet refused to accept. The contradiction made Her angry, and She looked around for a place to vent Her rage.

A constant trickle of ichor bled down the side of the Silver Wolf Oak to collect in a pool near the Shadow Monarch's feet. She stared at the shimmering surface, feeling the power flow from the tree. She tried to find Her children as She had before, but the surface of the ichor would not settle. The mountain shuddered and rock cracked as the roots of the *sarka har* drove deeper in search of sustenance.

Growing angrier, She focused all Her thought on the pool, willing it to cooperate. An image began to appear, but it wasn't of elves but of a city of humans. Celwyn. She'd never been, but She knew it from the minds of Her Emissaries. A loud snap overhead made Her look up as a heavy branch from the Silver Wolf Oak splintered and fell to the ground, shattering. Ichor splashed Her, and She smelled the taint of death.

Using Her anger, She called on the power in the depths, urging the roots to dig deeper still. The mountain shook and several *sarka har* fell into chasms that opened wide beneath their trunks. Undaunted, She reached out to the shimmering vision of Celwyn.

Large, lush trees lined cobbled streets. Huge parks with vast meadows buzzed with life. Everywhere She looked, the land mocked Her with its verdant energy. She saw the image of Her *ryk faur* reflected in the pool of ichor and the contrast drew a slow hiss from between Her teeth.

She felt its branches come down to gently rest on Her shoulders. Two snaked their way down Her arms to wrap lightly around Her wrists. She plunged both hands into the ichor up to Her elbows. The cold shocked her, but cleared Her mind. She felt the natural order and began to tug on the web of roots deep underground, directing them to a new destination. She withdrew Her hands and watched. The branches slid back up Her arms and away.

She sat like that, unaware of the passage of time or the growing cold. Frost sparkled on Her cloak and in Her hair, turning it gray and brittle. The view of Celwyn shimmered and then changed. She blinked. Darkness erupted from the earth throughout the city as Her *sarka har* sought to conquer this new land. She smiled, and leaned back against her *ryk faur* as the screams and cries of a people echoed in Her mind.

The Shadow Monarch closed Her eyes. Soon, there would be nowhere else for Her children to run. Soon, they would have to come home. They would have to come back to Her.

Visyna stumbled again, and this time she knew she wouldn't be able to keep control of the storm around her. The stinging threads began slipping through her fingers at an increasing rate. Her fingertips burned and she stifled a scream, doing her best to use her weaving to shape what little of the storm she still controlled.

"I'm losing it," she said, knowing her warning was

obvious as the wall of swirling snow that had protected the group disappeared into the larger storm around them.

Cold air rushed into the bubble, chilling her to the bone. The pain in her fingers turned into pins and needles. She pressed her hands under her armpits and dared to look around. Rakkes were emerging from the snow wherever she looked.

"Everyone stay close. Don't get split from the group and don't try to make a run for it!" Hrem shouted, coming to stand beside her on her left. "We're stronger as a group and they know it!"

Three dozen rakkes began beating their chests and thrashing in the snow as they built themselves into a frenzy. The fur on Jir's back stood straight up and his lips peeled back to reveal his fangs. The growl that emanated from deep within his chest sent shudders up Visyna's spine. Against a few rakkes she would have given the bengar a better than average chance of defeating them, but there were far too many. He couldn't kill them all, though he would die trying.

Visyna freed her hands and tried to call up some threads from the surrounding storm, hoping against hope that she could yet weave something more out of the chaos, but her efforts were in vain. She sank to her knees, her energy spent.

She felt a hand on her shoulder and looked up to see Chayii. The elf smiled at her. "I would have been proud to call you my daughter-in-law," she said, gently reaching down and grabbing Visyna by the elbow, helping her up.

"He would have had to ask first," she said, wiping away a tear.

"He would have," Chayii replied.

The rakkes howled and moved in closer, though none yet dared to charge the last ten yards.

"Release the animal!" Zwitty hissed. He stood so that Hrem covered him on one side and Scolly on the other. "He wants to get at them anyway. This is the perfect time."

"There are too many rakkes," Visyna said, looking to Chayii for support.

She shook her head slowly. "I can't hold him any longer, child—his rage grows too strong. He will hunt, and what will be will be." She leaned down and whispered something into the bengar's ear, patting his mane as she spoke to him. Jir's growl turned into a deep, rumbling purr. For a moment, Visyna hoped he might stay with them, but then Chayii stood up and released her grip.

Jir shook his head and brought his left paw up to his eyes and rubbed it across them. He then extended his legs, stretching and arching his back as if waking from a sleep, which perhaps he was after Chayii released her hold on him. His muzzle sniffed the air and the purring grew louder.

"Has he gone stupid?" Zwitty asked. "There are rakkes everywhere. He's acting like he doesn't even see them."

"He sees, he smells. He knows they're there," Chayii said, leaning against Visyna. The old elf was even more tired than she was. If the wind got any stronger it would blow them both over.

A rakke charged forward a couple of steps in a show of aggression, throwing its head back and gibbering into the sky. Jir twisted his head around and began to lick the fur around his wounded shoulder.

"I can't believe I'm with Zwitty on this, but why isn't Jir tearing into them?" Hrem asked.

"Elves have a great affinity with nature and all its creatures," Chayii said, talking slowly, "although I suppose my son is not the best example. It is how we came to bond with the Wolf Oaks. It is also, unfortunately, why we face the evil of the Shadow Monarch now. Konowa did, however, bond with this creature. As their spirits are very much alike, his influence on it did not materially change its basic personality of a predator."

Visyna understood at once. "But you did!"

Chayii stood up enough to look at her and smile. "He is still very much a predator, and a wild one at that, but during the time I held him in thrall I was able to impart a certain degree of . . . patience. Something, sadly, I had less success doing with my own son."

"How in the hell does that help us now?" Zwitty asked.

"You will see soon enough," Chayii said.

The rakke that charged ahead of the others grew bold when no response came from the group. It gnashed its teeth together and bounded ahead another yard. The other rakkes howled their encouragement and began to shuffle forward. Visyna knew a mass charge was imminent. The longer the rakkes remained uncertain the better their chances were of coming up with some kind of plan to save themselves. She raised her hands and began to weave.

"I thought you couldn't?" Hrem asked, raising his own hands and balling them into fists.

"I can't," Visyna said, "at least, not enough to push them away, but they don't know that." She made a show of waving her hands about her before crouching down in the snow and scooping up two handfuls of the tainted snow. It burned her hands, but it also warmed them enough for her to be able to tease a gossamer thread of power from the air and create a thin, shimmering wall between them and the rakkes.

Many of the rakkes scurried back a couple of yards. The lead rakke crouched lower and grew silent, but it didn't retreat.

Good, Visyna thought, amazed that her plan was actually working, but knowing it wouldn't for long.

"We need to stall them a little longer," she said. "Inkermon, start praying. Out loud. Hrem, if you can keep control of the frost fire, call it up now. Make a big show of it. Grunt and yell. You see how they are. Try to do something similar."

The big soldier looked down at his hands then back at her. "I can't act."

Visyna choked back a curse. "Forget acting. Just get angry. Stomp around. Yell."

"Imagine someone got between you and a bowl of stew," Zwitty said, his wheedling tone cutting through the building tension.

Hrem roared. Visyna gasped. The soldier spun on his heel and swung his fist at Zwitty's head. Zwitty leaped backward, took a couple of awkward steps, and fell to the snow. The rakkes nearby howled with renewed fury. Zwitty scrambled back to the group on his hands and knees.

"You could have got me killed!" Zwitty said, jumping to his feet and waving an arm at the surrounding rakkes.

"And?" Hrem asked. "Guess I can act a little after all." There was no humor in his voice.

"This isn't helping," Visyna said.

"What should we do?" Scolly asked.

"Make snowballs."

"Snowballs?" Zwitty asked as Scolly bent over and began scooping up snow in great handfuls. "You really think that's going to stop a rakke?"

The temptation to punch the private in the nose now had her clenching her fists until she remembered she was supposed to be putting on a show of weaving. "They might if you toss a few to Hrem and the frost fire lights them and then he throws them at the rakkes."

"Clever," Chayii said, patting Visyna on the arm.

Jir padded a few feet toward the closest rakke, but still he gave no indication that he was aware of it. The rakke roared and raised its arms high above its head in a threat display. Jir turned as if noticing the creature for the first time. And then he did the most remarkable thing.

"He's cowering," Visyna said, not sure she believed her eyes. The fearless bengar was actually belly down in the snow and slowly slinking backward. The rakke recognized the posture and charged.

"No," Chayii said, "he's *acting*."

Jir's demeanor changed in an instant. His ears flattened against his skull and his fur rippled as muscles bunched and tensed. The rakke was two strides away when Jir leaped, a blur of black and red fur against the snow. There was a scream that cut off short, the sound of ripping leather, and a spray of blood. Jir landed on his front two paws and let his rear ones softly come down a second later.

The body of the rakke lay sprawled in the snow, its head resting in Jir's jaws.

The other rakkes retreated several steps and their constant screeching and bellowing calls ceased. Jir had bought them some more time, but how much? More rakkes were appearing who hadn't seen Jir's horrific demonstration. Their roars would soon enough encourage the others to move forward again.

"Now what?" Zwitty asked.

"We start moving again toward the fort. Hrem, toss the snowballs about seven yards ahead of us and then a few to the sides. Jir can keep a watch and go after any that come in too close."

Scolly handed Hrem a snowball. Hrem strode forward from the group and held his hand out at arm's length. The rakkes fixated on him immediately. Hrem roared, and the snowball burst into black flame. He moved his arm around so that as many rakkes as possible could get a look and then he threw. The ball made a graceful arc trailing black frost in the air. It hit the snow with a sharp crack and Visyna realized it had instantly frozen the powdery snow into solid ice. Black flames and sparks flared for a few seconds before burning out. The rakkes near the flames screamed and pulled back several more yards.

"Move!" Visyna shouted, forcing her fingers to weave what little threads she could manage.

They started forward. Inkermon prayed, Scolly and Zwitty made snowballs and passed them to Hrem, who lit them with frost fire and threw them as quickly as he could. Visyna did her best to prop up Chayii while weaving as Jir circled the group, snarling here and there at any rakke that came too close.

"It's working!" Hrem shouted, tossing a snowball and hitting a rakke directly in the chest. The creature screamed as black flames washed over it and it ran off into the night. "We're going to make it."

A rock sailed out of the dark striking Hrem a glancing blow on the side of the head. He didn't fall, but bent over in pain clutching the wound. The rakkes lunged forward. Jir attacked, his claws sweeping in lightning fast arcs designed more to wound and frighten than to kill.

The charge faltered, but did not stop. There had to be fifty or more rakkes around them now, and even creatures as primal as these knew that with numbers like that they could overwhelm their prey.

"They've figured out how to get to us," Zwitty said, not bothering to hide the rising fear in his voice.

"They're predators," Chayii said by way of an answer.

Scolly and Zwitty started throwing snowballs though neither one lit them on fire. Inkermon's prayer grew louder, but if it was having an effect Visyna couldn't see it. She only caught a few words, but noticed that the soldier was invoking a lot of salvation, righteous fury, and a quick death. She hoped that last part was directed at the rakkes and not them.

A growing roar filled the air from the direction of the fort. The rakkes turned to look even as they continued to charge.

The sound reached a crescendo and a dark form burst through the circle of rakkes, its body covered in bright green spots of fire.

The reaction of the rakkes was immediate and stunning. They yipped and gibbered with fear and ran, everything else forgotten. They flayed and scrambled over each other to get away from the figure now stumbling around in their midst. Green flame flickered all over the creature, obscuring its true shape as it swung its arms as if trying to beat out the fire.

That's when Visyna noticed it was also waving a saber and cursing a blue streak.

"Konowa!" Visyna shouted, running toward him. She pulled up several feet short from him. He was wearing the tattered and smoldering remains of a cloth robe that was smoking furiously as it burned up with hundreds of tiny green flames.

"Has a spell been cast on you?" she asked, surprised that she could sense no foreign magic at work.

"Ow, ow, bloody, ow!" Konowa shouted, ripping what was left of the robe off his shoulders and diving into the snow, where he began to roll over and over. "A bunny nibbling my fingers my arse! Ow!" he shouted some more, some of the choicer words being lost as his face went beneath the snow.

He finally sat up, covered in snow, his saber still waving dangerously around him. "I am going to kick that dwarf right in the—Jir!" he managed to say before a blur raced past Visyna and thundered into Konowa, sending them both, elf and bengar, tumbling in a snowy heap.

Their reunion was short as Konowa staggered to his feet, an excited Jir threatening to bowl him over bounding all around him, the wound in his shoulder completely forgotten. Frost fire arced between them but Jir didn't appear to notice.

"Major!" Hrem said, stepping forward and clamping a huge hand on Konowa's shoulder. "It's great to see you, sir. Where's the rest of the regiment?"

Konowa was still brushing himself off and didn't appear to hear the question.

"Are you all right, my son?" Chayii asked, holding out a hand toward him then reluctantly pulling it back as black frost sparkled on his uniform.

"Mother. Oh, just a little hot under the collar is all . . . Look, no time to explain. We have to move, now." He started to turn back toward the fort then stopped and looked at his mother again. "Father is back to his elf self, well, almost."

This time Chayii did step forward and embrace her son. Frost fire glittered where her arms wrapped around him, but she held on.

"I missed you, too, but um, this isn't really the best time," Konowa said. His troops stood staring at him with open mouths.

Chayii let go and stepped back, but not before reaching up and brushing a strand of hair from his forehead. Visyna felt a pang of longing, wishing it was her in Chayii's place right now.

Visyna began to lower her head and start walking. She so desperately wanted him to run to her and sweep her up in an embrace and to hell with the frost fire. The thought made her angry. *I'm no delicate flower,* she told herself. She lifted her head up, threw back her shoulders, and walked right up to him and stopped.

"You, Konowa Swift Dragon, are my elf." After everything she'd been through, all the pain, all the fear, and all the uncertainty, she was certain about this. She'd found him. She reached up, put her hand around the back of his neck, and pulled him down toward her. Frost fire needled into her hands, but it could have been dragon teeth and she wouldn't have let go. Their lips met. The kiss was unlike any she had ever experienced. It was cold cold lightning, sweet and clear like fresh spring water. His right arm curved around her waist pulling her in close. The frost fire sparked across her back, but she barely noticed. She was lost in a feeling so wondrous that pain would have to wait. She could have stayed there in his arms forever, but long before she was ready to let go, he pulled away. She could still taste him on her lips.

"Ummm, I fwink my wips are nuwmb," he said, his cheeks flushing red.

"Mwine twwo," she said, not caring one bit.

Whistles and approving clucks suggested the nearby Iron Elves approved.

"There's still the matter of the rakkes," Hrem said, dabbing at the side of his head where a thin trickle of blood was seeping from the wound. "How many soldiers are out here with you, Major?"

"Fwowwow me," Konowa said, then stopped and rubbed the back of his hand against his lips before trying again. "Follow me, and I'll show you." This time Konowa did turn and began striding toward the fort. Jir bounded to his side and butted his head against his knee, almost knocking him over. Konowa reached down with his hand and scratched the bengar's head, leaving a patch of glittering frost on the animal's fur.

Visyna smiled. She took hold of Chayii's arm and they followed with the soldiers bringing up the rear. They were surrounded by ravenous monsters intent on their destruction, caught up in the complex web of a demented elf witch, and in the middle of a snow-covered desert, yet her overwhelming feeling was of absolute bliss. She had her elf, and he felt the same way about her as she did about him. Nothing in this world or any other could surpass how good that made her feel.

"I remember when Yimt first told me about you," Chayii said as they walked along. "I must admit I did not approve."

Visyna could only smile. Her cheeks actually hurt because she couldn't stop grinning. "And now?" she asked, knowing the answer.

"And now I'm wondering when I will have grandchildren."

Visyna's grin vanished. "We, uh, we only just—"

Chayii squeezed her arm and smiled at her. "I tease," she said, "for now."

Visyna noticed that Konowa had slowed to try and overhear their conversation. She took the opportunity to change the subject.

"What was that green fire and why were the rakkes so frightened of it?" she asked.

Konowa slowed enough to walk beside her. "Copper dust and shavings. It burns green. Seems rakkes associate that with some kind of nasty bug that they instinctively fear. Wish I'd known this a few months ago."

"Rakkes were extinct a few months ago," Visyna said.

As if to put a point on her thought a rakke bellowed into the night. Several returned the cry. They were gathering for another attack.

"They're stupid, but persistent," Konowa said. "We need to move faster."

Visyna reached out and touched his arm, knowing it would sting. "Everyone is tired and hurt. We're lucky to be standing at all."

Konowa slowed. He turned and looked at her. His face was drawn and he looked every bit as exhausted as she felt. "I know, and I'm sorry, but we really have to get out of here."

"And you came out here by yourself, for us?"

Konowa smiled. "Not exactly. I did bring one other soldier along to help."

The ground began to slope upward and she saw the dark outlines of large boulders ahead of her. A shadow detached from the side of one and began to move toward them.

"Konowa," she said, moving to place her body in front of Chayii's.

"You don't have to worry—he's not dangerous unless he starts talking."

Like the ghost he should have been, Yimt materialized out of the snow and came to a halt, his metal teeth shining like polished diamonds. "I ain't dead, in case you were wondering."

For a minute, the dwarf disappeared as Hrem and Scolly mobbed him. Inkermon and Zwitty eased forward cautiously, their right hands extended for a quick shake, but Hrem reached out and pulled both of them into the scrum and whatever ill-blood existed between the soldiers and their sergeant appeared, at least for the moment, to be forgotten.

"All right, let him breathe," Konowa ordered, breaking up the reunion. The pile parted and Yimt straightened his caerna and caught Visyna's eye.

"Miss Red Owl," he said, turning to Chayii, doffing his shako and bowing his head toward the elf. "Miss Tekoy," he said as he repeated the gesture. "I understand you did this world a great service."

"It was him or us," Visyna said. She saw Konowa's eyes go wide, then he nodded in approval. She nodded back, wishing Konowa was congratulating her for anything else. Taking a life should never be a happy occasion.

"Damn straight," Yimt said. "It's what I've been trying to get through this lot's thick melons from the day I set eyes on them." He paused as he looked over the soldiers and his smile vanished. "Teeter?"

"He went down fighting," Hrem said, his voice catching.

Yimt nodded. "Aye, that he would. Well," he said, clapping his hands together, "we'll drink to him later. Right now we need to get climbing."

"You might want this," Hrem said, holding out the dwarf's drukar.

Yimt's mouth opened and closed, but no words issued forth. He reached out a hand and took the blade, staring at it the way Visyna had at Konowa. "I never thought I'd see this again," he finally managed.

"Sorry we couldn't get your shatterbow, too," Hrem said.

Yimt waved away the apology. "Lil' Nipper served me well, but when Kritton shot me, I lost my grip on it and it cracked when it hit the floor. It was tough, but I had to leave it behind. I did, however, find a rather nasty little surprise in the library that more than made up for it," he said, his eyes twinkling.

Two rakkes emerged out of the darkness and charged straight at the group, ending the conversation.

Jir's claws flashed and one of the creatures fell to the snow, its legs tangled in its own spilled intestines. The second met its fate at the end of Yimt's drukar as the dwarf buried the blade deep into the creature's chest.

The smell of hot blood filled the air, and the rakke howls grew in ferocity.

"Still works," Yimt said, trying to pull the blade out.

"Now we really need to go," Konowa said, directing them toward the rocks. "It's steep and it's slippery, so watch your step but move as fast as you can."

"A little help," Yimt said, struggling to pull the drukar out of the rakke's chest.

Hrem walked over and placing a boot on the rakke's rib cage heaved and freed the blade.

"Always nice to have a big, strong man around," Yimt said, patting Hrem on the forearm. "Now get your arse up that hill and mind you don't trip on the twine. Oh, and watch out for the dead rakkes. They're with us now."

Visyna looked at the dwarf. "There are rakkes up there, too?"

Yimt looked like he was about to explain, but Jir's growl changed his mind. "Let's hope we have all the time in the world later to chat. For now, up you go," he said, shooing her toward the rocks.

"Wait, aren't you coming with us?"

The soldiers turned when she asked the question, and she could read the concern on their faces. Having just discovered their sergeant was alive, they weren't about to lose him again.

"Steady now, boys and girls, your old sergeant isn't leaving. I'm just going to lag behind a tad to keep these critters from getting too frisky and galloping up after us."

"I'll stay with you then," Hrem said, stepping down from a rock and coming back toward Yimt.

"Your heart's as big as your head, and it's to your credit, but there ain't room among these rocks for a big job like you. You just get along and help the others. I'll be fine, and I won't be far behind." He stood up a little straighter. "So now's the time to follow the twine."

"Yimt of the warm breeze, it is very good to be in your company again," Chayii said.

"You flatter me, madam," Yimt said, "now get your pretty little self up those rocks and take the rest of this rabble with you."

"Everyone, start climbing," Konowa said. "Now. And believe it or not, that's actually an order."

Visyna's face flushed, and the familiar urge to snap back at Konowa danced behind her teeth, or maybe it was just the aftereffects of the kiss. This time, however, she wasn't looking for a fight, but for a way to draw him closer. She longed to feel his body pressed up against hers again. It was beyond infuriating that now that they were together in both presence and emotion, they were still apart because of the oath. She wondered if that fact made her desire for him that much stronger, but she didn't think so. She wanted him, and she knew he wanted her, too.

"Now off you go," Yimt said, twirling the drukar in his hands and either not knowing or not caring that it was spraying blood everywhere as he did it. "I will be right behind you."

Visyna reluctantly turned her back and began climbing. She held out her hand and guided Chayii over a cracked boulder. There was a path of sorts to follow that Konowa and Yimt had made on their way down along with a grubby-looking piece of twine laying on top of the snow. She paused as she looked at the twine closer. It appeared to be flecked with copper as well.

"Do you know why green fire or insects would frighten rakkes so much?" she asked Chayii.

"Are you asking if I was alive when rakkes still roamed the earth?"

Visyna mentally cursed herself. "I wasn't trying to imply . . . I just meant . . ." She sighed and looked at the elf. "Well, yes, I guess that is what I am asking."

Chayii brushed some snow from her hair and considered the question. "I was not there. There are many things in this world older than I, child."

Visyna accepted the soft rebuke with a smile. "But I doubt few as wise, or as kind."

"I have my moments," Chayii said.

From a few feet below them, Yimt bellowed. "C'mon you mangy bastards! You want fresh meat, I'm right here! Maybe a little gamey, but nothing you brutes can't choke down."

Visyna turned to look. Yimt was standing on a boulder, his drukar casually resting over his shoulder, his other hand firmly on his hip, and his caerna waving merrily in the wind.

"Oh my," Visyna said,

"Indeed," Chayii said. "Quite impressive."

Visyna didn't think her cheeks could get any hotter. "We should probably keep climbing," she said, desperate to change the subject.

"Yes, I suppose we should," Chayii replied, lingering a moment longer to watch the dwarf. She turned back to climb and saw Visyna looking at her. "I very much love my fool of a husband, but as we say in the Long Watch, 'You may admire another tree's nuts as long as you don't harvest them.'"

I was wrong, Visyna realized. *My cheeks can get hotter.*

TWENTY-FIVE

Up on the hill, Konowa waited by the first dead rakkes, wanting to make sure no one overreacted when they saw them. Even frozen stiff and partially covered in snow, the creatures were still fearsome to look at.

"Just keep following the twine," Konowa said, ignoring the questioning looks as the soldiers passed by the first bodies.

"Did you kill all these, Major?" Scolly asked, stopping and carefully prodding the leg of one rakke with the toe of his boot.

"They were already dead when we got here, must have frozen to death standing around asking too many questions," Konowa said.

Hrem clearly got the message and grabbed Scolly's arm, pulling him away. "C'mon, we need to keep moving."

"But I want to know what happened to the monsters," Scolly said.

"Just be glad they're dead and can't hurt you anymore," Hrem said, nudging the soldier on.

"Weren't they dead before and then they came back again?"

Konowa turned and looked at the corpses. Scolly was a full horn short of a unicorn, but he hit on something that worried Konowa. The rakkes had been dead. Extinct, gone and never to be seen again, until they came back. What would stop the Shadow Monarch from reviving them again and again? The answer was always the same. To hell with his dreams—if he had an ax in his hands when the time came, he'd cut Her down like any tree in the forest.

Yimt's war cry, sounding much like first volley in a barroom brawl, echoed off the rocks. The rakkes' reply drowned out anything after that.

"Okay, Sergeant, you little rascal, let's see if you think it feels like nibbling bunnies," Konowa said.

"What was that?" Visyna asked as she helped Chayii past the rakkes.

Konowa started. "Ah, nothing. You'd better hurry, it's about to get very exciting around here."

"Yes, because up until now our day has been fairly uneventful," she said while his mother clucked her tongue at him.

"Right, sorry," he muttered. He watched them go by, making a solemn vow that whether he continued in the service of the empire or not, he would, as a general rule, ensure that neither his parents nor his love interest accompanied him out in the field. It just wasn't good for his elfhood.

". . . between the eyes you smelly furball!" Yimt shouted, arriving at Konowa's position huffing for breath.

"I've been called worse," Konowa said, drawing his

saber as he brought forth the frost fire. His saber lit at once, giving off a shimmering black, translucent light.

"Probably with cause, too," Yimt said matter-of-factly, "but in this case I was directing my keen observations at the hairy brutes not that far behind me."

Konowa spied them. "They appear to be suitably enraged, well done," he said, taking a quick look behind him for the best footing.

"I do have a gift for the oral-torical," Yimt said, resting splay-legged on a boulder while he sharpened the blade edge of his drukar on the rock between his legs. "You know, sometimes I think my talents aren't fully utilized in the infantry."

"Do tell," Konowa said.

"Well, I've been wondering of late if a change in career might be called for. I'm not as young as I used to be. Now don't get me wrong, Major, I do enjoy the fresh air and the travel and even the chance to meet the natives, although it loses something when you usually end up having to shoot them."

As eager as the rakkes were to rip them to shreds, judging by the mewling and howling, the recent deaths of many of their brethren had instilled a degree of wariness as they stalked their prey. Still, they continued to climb up the rocks, oblivious even to the macabre sight of their mutilated brethren. They were out for blood. Their claws clicked on the rocks as they came on, growing louder as they jockeyed for position to be the first to sink their fangs into the fresh meat barring their path.

"I've been thinking along those lines myself," Konowa said, a sense of relief filling him as he spoke the words aloud. Maybe it was time to hang up his saber and try his hand at something new, that is, if they did manage to survive this *and* destroy the Shadow Monarch. "What would you do if you left the army? Between the two of us, we've served longer than most of these boys we lead combined. It's hard to imagine doing anything else."

Yimt held up his drukar blade and admired the edge. "Well, that's just it, isn't it? After a lifetime of honing our skills in battle, what to do after you parade for the last time and walk out the barracks gates a free dwarf or elf?"

"I've a feeling you've got an answer."

"Barrister," Yimt said.

"Hold that thought," Konowa said, as three rakkes were overcome by bloodlust and began scrambling over the boulder just a couple yards below them.

Yimt stood up on his rock and hefted his weapon. "Step forth, oh ye wretched and rabid rabble, and prepare to be judged."

Whether the rakkes understood anything Yimt said was impossible to tell, but his voice was enough to send them into a frenzy. They charged.

Konowa reached forward and touched his saber on the hem of Yimt's caerna. The coating of copper dust immediately burst into hundreds of tiny green flames. The night turned a sickly green as the flames roared to life.

Yimt leaped from his rock, looking for all the world like a green comet crashing to earth. He landed between two rakkes and dispatched them with quick, powerful blows of his drukar. Konowa fought the urge to join him, knowing his job was to wait.

Rakkes roared and screamed with fright as they

tried flee. Yimt was a glowing green nightmare among the rocks, bounding from boulder to boulder, cutting down the creatures with brutal precision. Unlike on the desert floor, however, the rakkes were hemmed in by the rough terrain and couldn't escape fast enough. Konowa lost count after the seventh rakke went down.

"You're flaming out!" Konowa shouted, noticing the green glow was rapidly dying. "Get back now."

The rakkes appeared to be noticing it, too. Already, several of them were curving around to climb the hill on either side of them.

"They're flanking us, Sergeant!" Konowa shouted again, getting ready with his saber.

"Coming!" Yimt yelled, turning and running back up to Konowa's position as the last of the green flames went out. He leaned forward with his hands on his knees and gulped in air. "Definitely getting a bit long in the beard for this."

Several rocks crashed into the boulders around them. "I think they're starting to figure this out," Konowa said, ducking as another rock sailed overhead.

"Maybe, but we're slowing them down, and that's what matters," he said, standing up straight and drawing in a deep breath through his nose. "Okay, I'm ready."

Konowa couldn't help but stare. "Your caerna . . ."

Yimt looked down. "Appears to have burnt right off. Think they'll dock my pay for damaging military property?"

Konowa touched his flaming saber to the rakke corpses and the copper shavings caught fire, illuminating the night once again. "I'll make certain they don't," he said, leaping to the next rock and making his way up.

"In fact, I'll make sure you get a special stipend specifically for uniforms so you never have to go without ever again."

"Very kind of you, Major," Yimt said as he stepped past him and ran ahead. His short, powerful legs and muscular buttocks pumping vigorously as he climbed. "I don't mind telling you, now I really do notice the chill."

"I imagine you would," Konowa said, doing his best to keep pace, but not too fast. Behind him, the sound of rakkes scrambling over the rocks told him the green fire wouldn't slow them down much longer.

They reached the next rakke corpse and Konowa simply lit it and kept going. The idea of making a stand at each one was no longer viable. Rakkes were ascending the hill all around them. He was sure a few had even got ahead of them, but their fear of what they thought the green fire really was held them back just enough.

"So a barrister?" Konowa said, finding the idea of the dwarf putting on the robes and powdered wigs of the legal profession fascinating and frightening. He stepped on a rock and slipped, twisting his knee. The pain simply added another layer to the blankets of agony covering his body. He bit off a curse and kept going. "Why spend your days in a courtroom with judges and rules? You don't strike me as the type to prosecute some poor lad who stole a loaf of bread."

"Prosecute? Major, I have my pride." Yimt said, huffing as he bounded over a jumble of rocks. "I'd be representing the wrongfully accused."

A couple of rocks bounced off boulders nearby. Konowa turned to look over his shoulder, but the rakkes were still far enough back to make their aim wild. "Okay, barrister, convince me."

"Another time, Major. Shadows up ahead on the path," Yimt whispered, pointing forward. Konowa saw them.

"Is it our group?"

"I don't think so, because they are coming down."

Konowa took a hurried look around and didn't like what he saw. They were hemmed in by boulders on all sides. There was nowhere to run, and they were out of copper-covered rakkes. Growling and scraping noises echoed from all sides. They were completely surrounded. He looked up and could see the fort's wall a little over thirty yards away. So close.

"Our best bet is to scream bloody murder and charge," Yimt said, shifting his drukar from hand to hand.

"I thought that was a bad trait."

"There's a time and a place for everything, and in this particular time and place, a good old-fashioned berserker charge is just the ticket."

Konowa flexed his fingers around the pommel of his saber and rolled his shoulders. They still had the frost fire to call on, and they were close enough to the fort that maybe help would arrive in time. It would have to do.

"Ready?" Konowa asked, moving up to stand beside Yimt.

"Time for these rakkes to hear my closing argument," Yimt said.

Konowa groaned, but smiled. "You might want the Viceroy to write up your briefs. On three. One . . . two . . ."

A volley of musket fire lit the night, its sharp

cracks cutting through the snow-deadened air. Rakkes screamed. Konowa stuck his head over the rock in front of him. Corporal Feylan stood fifteen yards away with Yimt's squad.

"Hurry, Major, there's a lot more coming up behind you."

The pair climbed over the rocks and the fallen rakkes before running as fast as they could up to the squad. Yimt's soldiers were already reloading their muskets in preparation for another volley. Konowa looked behind him and saw they were in no immediate danger.

"That's enough. Let's get back inside," he said. "The regiment is still out there on the plain."

A touch on his arm made him look down.

"Probably good for them to blow off a little steam," Yimt said in a low voice. "With everything they've been through, I imagine it feels good to give a little back."

Konowa thought about that. They hadn't just seen hell, they'd been battling their way through it from the very beginning. So many good men had fallen. There were wives who would never see their husbands again, small children would grow up without ever knowing their father, and mothers who would grieve for their son for the rest of their lives.

He studied the faces of the soldiers. They were gaunt, their skin chalky white with cold, and their eyes red-rimmed. These were men who had to look over their shoulders to see where they had passed their breaking point, and still they were ready to stand and fight.

Konowa knew time wasn't in their favor, but to hell with that. "Good shooting, men. A few more volleys should keep them out of our hair for a while. On your own time, tear those bastards a new one."

There were smiles and grunts of approval as the soldiers continued reloading their muskets. The sound of ramrods rattling down barrels as his soldiers tamped down lead ball and black powder was music to his ears. This was the release they'd been longing for. Finally, and at least for the time being, they had the upper hand.

More rakkes appeared and clambered up the rocks to be met with a withering rain of lead shot. The soldiers began cheering and calling out to each other as they picked apart the charging rakkes.

The sharp vibration in his chest as the muskets spit out their lead balls put a grin on Konowa's face. The rotten-egg smell of the smoke filled his nostrils. He tasted the bitter powder on his tongue and the constant ringing in his ears kicked up an octave.

The rakkes fell by the dozen, but there seemed to be two more ready to take the place of every one that died. The cheering fell away, and soon the joy of exacting an ounce of revenge became a grim task as wave after wave of screaming, roaring predators climbed over the rocks to get them.

"Major," Yimt said, "they aren't going to stop."

Konowa shook his head in disbelief. The beasts just kept coming. He'd once thought the walls of the fort would be easily defended, but with an enemy like this nothing was safe.

"RSM, get these men inside, now."

Yimt began barking orders and the soldiers started backing up, taking turns covering each other as they retreated to the safety of the fort. Konowa was the last to step inside, realizing that the fort wouldn't be a safe haven at all. If they didn't get out of it soon, it would be their tomb.

TWENTY-SIX

I want everyone ready to move in ten minutes!" Konowa shouted as he emerged from the steps leading up to the fort's main square. Passing through the torture chamber again had made his mood very grim. "Grab whatever you can carry and get by the front gate."

Musket fire sounded along the top of the fort's walls as soldiers shot down at the massing rakkes. Konowa knew it wouldn't delay the beasts for long, but hopefully just long enough.

"Major, you had better see this," Pimmer said from the gate.

Konowa trotted over. "How's the battle going?"

For an answer, the Viceroy pointed down to the plain below. A single soldier was marching into the open and straight for the whirling madness that had once been Faltinald Gwyn. Frost fire blazed all around the soldier, creating a barrier that no rakke dared approach.

"That's got to be Renwar," Konowa said.

Yimt appeared at Konowa's elbow. "I'd recognize that gimpy walk a mile away. What in the hell does he think he's doing?"

"He's challenging Gywn again," Konowa said, admiring the soldier's courage. "I told you, Renwar already ripped him apart once before."

"But did that monster look like that the last time?" Yimt asked.

Konowa didn't answer. The creature moving toward Renwar looked like nothing so much as a whirling, black storm. Konowa could feel the malevolence of it from here.

"Surely the shades of the dead will aid young Renwar," Pimmer said. No sooner were the words out of his mouth than several shadows flickered into being near the creature on the desert floor.

But something about them was wrong.

"Those aren't the Darkly Departed," Yimt said, starting forward. "Bloody hell. They're shades of dead rakkes!"

Hundreds of them appeared, emerging from the storm-whipped vortex and flying outward like shrapnel. They were met at once by the shades of the Iron Elves in massive explosions of black frost and earsplitting cracks. The desert floor gleamed as it iced over. Shadows merged and fragmented in close-quarter combat. The air vibrated with screams and howls as huge chunks of darkness ripped open and then closed as the fighting between the dead escalated from this plane to the next.

The living rakkes took the opportunity to descend on the Iron Elves, charging across the ice with wild abandon. Volley after volley of well-aimed musket fire scythed through their ranks. Limbs and heads flew through the air as the beasts were chopped apart by the lead shot. Blood droplets froze in the air and fell like red glass beads to roll around on the icy ground. Rakkes died by the dozens, but the beasts refused to retreat and launched fresh assaults over the bodies of their fallen.

"You cagey bastard," Konowa said, his fury rising as he focused on the swirling entity that had once been Viceroy Faltinald Gwyn.

"We have to do something," Yimt said, turning to look at Konowa. Konowa halted before he'd taken two steps toward the roadway leading down to the desert. His first reaction was to run all the way down there and wade into the beasts with nothing but his saber and his anger. He turned, and with an effort, sheathed his saber, allowing the frost fire to die out. Musket fire from the Iron Elves manning the fort's walls was crackling like wet pine in a fire. Already, he could hear the shrieks and growls of the rakkes on the far side of the fort.

"The fort is untenable, and the regiment is in trouble. We're between a rock and an even harder rock. We need to be able to create some kind of diversion," he said, frustrated that he couldn't think of anything big enough that would pose a threat to the mass of rakkes attacking the regiment.

"Your father's a wizard and Miss Tekoy's a witch," Yimt said, though Konowa could tell by the tone of his voice he didn't have much hope in that regard.

Konowa kicked the stone wall of the fort with his boot.

"Unless he's stopped speaking squirrel I don't think he'll be much help, and Visyna is exhausted. Damn it! There has to be something else." *I was wrong to leave the regiment*, Konowa realized, horrified that he might very

well watch its destruction and not be able to do a
bloody thing about it.

"There's nothing for it then," Yimt said, standing to
his full height and straightening his uniform. He
clutched his drukar in his right hand and pointed toward the battle below. "We'll just have to charge down
there and take 'em on head on."

Konowa looked at the dwarf. "That's suicide and
you know it."

"Aye, but it's the best kind. Maybe we'll buy them
enough time to get away."

Konowa was already shaking his head even though
he still had no better idea. "We'll call that plan B. I still
want something we can do that gives us at least a five
percent chance of survival."

A small cough alerted Konowa to the presence of
Pimmer. "Five percent you say?" he said, offering the
two of them a smile he probably only brought out just
before revealing the existence of the Calahrian Army
outside the opposing diplomat's capital city. "I think I
have just the thing."

Alwyn felt the presence of the dead rakkes before he
saw them. The shades of the dead creatures tore
through the wall between this world and the next, staining the air around them with a toxic mix of mindless
fear and ravenous hunger. The cries of the living soldiers sounded distant and muted compared to the reaction of the shades of the Iron Elves' dead.

They charged headlong into the dead creatures,
meeting frenzy with the controlled violence of seasoned

soldiers. The dead of the Iron Elves slashed and burned their way through the dead creatures, tearing their shadowy forms into fragments that shattered and bled darkness into the night. Frost fire sparked off them and burned holes in the ice on the ground, creating deep, black holes. Wails of absolute agony ebbed and flowed as the battle raged.

Frost fire consumed rakke shades, eating their essence until nothing but disembodied screams of pain remained to echo in the night. The temperature continued to fall as death swept across the mortal plane. It beckoned to things dead and gone eons before rakkes ever walked the earth. Huge, multilegged creatures with spike-crusted claws scrambled into being, lunging and stabbing at the shades of the Iron Elves and forcing them to slowly retreat.

The vortex around the creature continued to grow, its scouring winds tearing and scattering anything and everything they touched. It fed on the darkness, drawing ever more power as time disgorged dead after dead onto the field of battle. Each new creature was more twisted and broken than the last, its memory of what it was so fragmented that it could only piece together parts of what it had once been. What remained as strong as ever, however, was the rapacious need to feed, and these monsters of tentacle and spike, fang and barb, flew at the shades of the Iron Elves with abandon. The shades fell back, and Alwyn let them, knowing that not even they could withstand this force. There was only one way for this madness to stop.

Alwyn took in a breath and breathed out frost fire.

"I challenge you, Gwyn!" Alwyn shouted, and strode forth to meet the darkness head on.

TWENTY-SEVEN

K onowa, this is madness," Visyna said, standing at the front gate of the fort. Except the front gate wasn't there anymore. The two large wooden doors had been ripped from their hinges and repurposed by Viceroy Alstonfar. "The Viceroy is a very creative man, but this is just lunacy."

Konowa couldn't disagree, but he didn't see what choice they had. He stepped aside as soldiers ran back and forth from inside the fort. They were scrambling to load as many supplies as would fit on the hastily constructed wooden contraption now resting on the top of the snow-covered roadway leading down to the desert floor. Armloads of anything and everything were being tossed onto the Viceroy's invention, though Konowa thought a more apt description would be "disaster waiting to happen." In this regard, he and Visyna agreed, but he couldn't let her know that.

"Careful, Major, coming through," a soldier said, tottering under the weight of a large wooden cask.

Anything of possible value, especially foodstuffs, were being hurriedly bundled and loaded as RSM Arkhorn barked orders that would sound more at home in a grocer's shop: "Try to find a bag of flour with a few less rat droppings in it! Don't go mixing the tins of boot polish with the tins of jam. Some of us will be wanting toast later, and if I open the wrong tin in the dark guess who'll be eating every bite!"

The crackle of a musket volley drifted up from the desert floor below, adding urgency to the loading. It was a clear reminder that living men were down there among all the shades. Smoke from volley after volley mixed with flashes of light and bursts of frost fire were making it difficult to see what was going on. The urge to charge down there rose up in Konowa again and he fought it by pacing. He looked down at the plain again. The Iron Elves with the Darkly Departed and Private Renwar would have to hold off Gwyn and his monsters for a little longer.

Konowa tore himself away from the view and faced Visyna. "It's our only option," he said, looking at the toboggan and wishing it wasn't. While Konowa had been outside the fort bringing Visyna and her group inside, Pimmer had been hard at work crafting what was little more than thirty feet of sled with a bow made of wood planking, and everything nailed and banded together with cobbler's supplies. It did not fill Konowa with confidence, but there really was no more time. More musket fire and a rising gibbering howl of maddened rakkes emphasized his point.

"I know it is," Visyna said, leaning forward and giving him a quick kiss on the lips. The frost fire stung, but he thought he could get used to that.

"All aboard who's going aboard," Pimmer shouted.

Konowa turned. His mother was placing his father and Tyul onto the toboggan and getting them settled in. His father was still not talking. Konowa knew it was risky, but he hoped that thrusting the elf into the heart of a battle would snap him out of it. They were going to need him.

Pimmer ran past to direct a soldier where to put some sacks then hurried over to Konowa. "We're just about ready, Major. I think you can call the soldiers down from the wall."

Konowa heard their musket fire and shook his head. "Not until the very last moment."

"We are rapidly approaching that moment," he said. "Once *The Flying Elf* starts sliding, there'll be no stopping her."

Konowa brought his right hand up to his ear and rubbed a knuckle in it. "*The Flying Elf?*"

"HMT *The Flying Elf,* actually." When Konowa didn't respond, Pimmer elaborated. "Her Majesty's Toboggan, of course."

"Of course. And the name?"

Pimmer's smile lessened a little. "A bit cheeky, I know, but after I relayed your experiences with the flying *sarka har,* Miss Tekoy insisted."

"And can you steer this . . . elf?"

Pimmer's face clouded. "All I had time for was the basic design. We'll just push it down the slope until it starts to move then hop on and hold tight. Our great luck in this is that the road leading down to the desert floor runs straight with a three-foot wall on either side, creating a nice, deep furrow. Now that it's filled with snow we should stay well centered all the way down. I am a little concerned about the angle of transition between the road and the desert when we reach the bottom. There appears to be a large snowbank down there, but I think we'll manage with a fairly gradual transition."

Konowa looked down to the bottom. "More ice than snow I'd say."

"Best not to think about it too much," Pimmer offered.

Konowa agreed. "Right. We're going now." He looked around and spotted Yimt waving his drukar in the air as he spurred the men on. "RSM! Get the men formed up and make sure we have everyone. We're not coming back. I want this sl—this toboggan moving in one minute."

"Corporal Feylan!" Yimt shouted, pointing at the young soldier with his drukar. "I want everyone right here in thirty seconds. Get the men down from the walls, now. Any dawdlers will have the honor of welcoming the rakkes to this place. In light of what happened around here, I imagine death will be almost instantaneous."

"Yes, RSM, right away," Feylan said, running off to round up the soldiers still inside the fort.

"So whose butt did he kiss to make corporal?" Zwitty asked, walking up with a single loaf of moldy bread in his hand.

"Corporals and higher sit at the front of this device. Want a promotion?" Yimt asked.

"Just asking," Zwitty said, scurrying away to place his loaf of bread on the pile then jumping on well away from the front.

"Shame he didn't dawdle," Yimt said, watching the soldier the whole time.

A musket fired from inside the fort. Privates Vulh-ber, Erinmoss, and Inkermon came running. "It's the rakkes, sir! They're climbing over the walls!"

Bloodcurdling roars echoed inside the fort as the beasts vaulted over the top and descended into the yard. A couple of muskets fired, dropping one rakke where it twitched and growled in agony, and taking off the left arm of another at the elbow.

"Do we have everyone?" Konowa shouted.

"All accounted for, Major," Feylan said.

"Good. RSM, get this toboggan moving!"

"All right, laddies . . . and ladies," Yimt said, grab-bing hold of a wooden crate roped onto the toboggan. "Start pushing!"

A collective groan went up as backs bent to the task. Konowa tried to do the mental calculation of how heavy this toboggan with all its supplies and passengers was and came up with bloody damn heavy.

"It's not moving!" someone shouted.

More rakkes poured over the wall and started bounding across the fort's small yard. A single musket fired in response. If a rakke went down Konowa couldn't see it in the mass of furry beasts closing in on them.

"Then keep bloody pushing!" Yimt shouted back.

A blur off to the left caught Konowa's attention and he was shocked to see Pimmer running for all he was worth toward the toboggan. "What are you doing, man? This was your idea! Get on!"

Pimmer jumped on and the toboggan broke free and began to slide across the snow. Konowa pushed until he thought his eyes would pop out of his head. The toboggan inched forward, slowly picking up speed. Blood pounded in his ears. *I'm getting too old for this,* he decided, easing off for a moment to catch his breath. The toboggan leaped ahead a few feet and his heart raced as it started to slip away from him.

"Jump on! Jump on!"

Konowa pumped his legs and dove, landing head-first in a bag of flour that burst open on impact.

He came up gasping for air. "Do we have everyone?" he shouted, turning to look behind him. Rakkes screamed and picked up pieces of wood and threw them at the toboggan. Too late he wondered what would stop the rakkes from simply sliding down the hill after them?

Jir bounded up beside him and dug his claws into the stack of supplies. He stuck his head up into the wind with his mouth open and his tongue hanging out. His stubby little tail wagged furiously.

"Cover your ears!" Pimmer shouted, using his thumb to point back at the fort.

Konowa looked, then flinched as the fort vanished in a black orange flash. The explosion rocked the toboggan and set it hurtling even faster down the slope. Rakkes and rubble rocketed into the air. Konowa had seen gunpowder explode before, but never this much. It sounded like a thousand thunderclouds detonating at the same time. The walls of the fort buckled and flew outward, scattering cartwheeling chunks of masonry down the hill and toward the toboggan. Body parts and bricks began falling all around them.

People screamed. Something heavy hit Konowa in the back between the shoulder blades, knocking him forward again into the flour. He pushed himself back up and looked down at his side to see the grinning, severed head of a rakke staring back at him. He picked it up by the smoldering hair on its head and flung it over the side.

He became aware of a new sensation, that of falling. He turned and faced forward as the toboggan whooshed down the snow like the bow of a ship plunging into the trough of a monster wave.

The rock walls whizzed past much closer than Konowa thought was safe. He squinted into the wind and saw that due to the prevailing wind the snow had drifted more to the western side of the road, creating a ramp that was angling them toward the east side, and the rocks that lined it.

"Everyone lean left!" he shouted, throwing his body sideways. The whole toboggan lurched and began to tilt as it climbed up the snowdrift on the west side.

"Too much! Back to the right!"

The toboggan lurched again and a loud crack sounded from somewhere beneath him.

"She's breaking up, Major!" Pimmer shouted from somewhere behind him. "She can't handle the strain!"

"We're almost there!" Konowa shouted, trying to reach for his saber then forgetting the idea when he realized he'd have to release one of his hands from its death grip on the supplies. The toboggan hit a bump—it might have been part of a rakke—and became airborne. The bottom of his stomach fell away and he suddenly felt as light as a feather. It wasn't a good feeling.

The desert floor appeared through the snow. It was close, and on an angle that looked more vertical than horizontal. A cluster of rakkes stood at the bottom of the snow-covered stairs looking up.

"Rakkes dead ahead off the bow!" Corporal Feylan

shouted, embracing his naval ambitions in his excitement. "Brace for impact!"

In the final second before toboggan, Iron Elves, and rakkes met in what would be recorded as the first and last battle of the HMT *The Flying Elf*, Major Konowa Swift Dragon, brevet naval captain, said a silent prayer to blind, dumb luck.

"Viceroy!" he yelled, the wind and snow stinging his face. "You know how to make a distraction!"

TWENTY-EIGHT

Konowa's understanding of physics was, as he was the first to admit, more of a complete misunderstanding. The looming change from the steep descent down the snow-covered road to the flat snow-covered desert rushing toward him was blocked by a huge mound of accumulated ice and snow. It looked less like a soft pile of fluffy snow and more of a hard, ice-encrusted ramp. He chose to keep his eyes open as he'd already lived his life once and a lot of it he would just as soon forget. He wanted to see the next few seconds, especially if they were to be his last.

What saved Konowa and the riders of HMT *The Flying Elf* was luck in the form of the combined body mass of thirty-five rakkes. The toboggan launched itself into the air and immediately took a nose-down position as it sailed through the air toward the desert floor. At that angle it would have shattered on landing, but the rakkes took the initial impact of the toboggan, absorbing the force of over two thousand pounds traveling faster than an eight-team horse carriage.

A rakke's skull, though heavy and thick to protect what little brain it had, wasn't designed to withstand the blunt impact of that much force. Konowa had never seen a body disintegrate two feet in front of him before. The spray of rakke material stung his face with a wet mask that dried instantly in the wind.

If the creatures screamed, Konowa couldn't hear them. He did, however, feel the force of the wood pulverizing them as it shuddered toward touchdown. More rakkes appeared and while these, too, were smashed by the toboggan, the body parts now flying through the air were considerably larger and posed a real danger.

"Duck!" someone shouted entirely unnecessarily. Even Jir had had the sense to crouch down as limbs and heads began flying overhead.

HMT *The Flying Elf* touched down some thirty feet away from the foot of the road and rebounded at once, throwing up a hundred-foot-tall geyser of ice, snow, wood, and more rakke parts. This time Konowa did hear screams, but he had no time to check who they were. He was too busy holding on. His hips then his legs flew up into the air, and for a moment, he was doing a handstand before the toboggan slammed down again and Konowa did, too.

Three more bounces and one more handstand occurred before Konowa was able to remain firmly on the pile of supplies. Rakke howls rose and fell away as the toboggan roared across the snow, bowling over the creatures with little regard and minimal drag on its high rate of speed.

"That was marvelous!" Pimmer shouted, his voice filled with glee.

"Miraculous is more like it," Konowa yelled, rising

up slightly to look beyond the next group of rakkes running to get out of the way. Three didn't, but one did. Konowa stuck out his boot and caught the rakke at the base of its skull with his heel as they flew past and immediately regretted it. The crack he heard had been the rakke's spine and not his ankle, but he was still seeing stars for the next several seconds.

"Everyone keep your hands and legs inside!" Visyna shouted. "We're traveling much too fast."

Konowa was still grimacing with pain so he didn't bother to look over his shoulder. He had a feeling she was looking right at him.

"Shades!"

The shades of dead rakkes flitted in and out of sight up ahead. Maybe they're still trying to get the hang of it, Konowa wondered, hoping that provided enough of an advantage to allow the toboggan to slide through. He risked taking his right hand off the supplies and grabbed his saber, drawing and calling on the frost fire as he did so.

The part of him that was forever six years old grinned while the rest of him tried to convince himself this really had been the best and only plan of action. The blade of the saber sparked to life with frost fire and began trailing an eerie icy black tail of flame and frost like a comet falling from the heavens. Unlike the living rakkes, however, these shades moved to intercept the toboggan. Konowa suddenly realized there was no way he'd be able to swing his blade in a wide enough arc to cut a swath big enough for them to pass through safely.

"I hope this works!" he shouted, swinging his saber down to lodge it into the table top acting as the bow. Black flame engulfed the wood and the entire front of the toboggan, sending huge, flickering tongues of frost fire back along the toboggan. Jir yelped and stuck his head beneath his front paws while screams and shouts rose from those immediately behind him.

"What are you doing?" Visyna and Pimmer shouted at the same time.

Konowa didn't bother to reply. The answer was about to happen . . . now!

The first shades of dead rakkes hit by the flaming toboggan exploded in a shower of sparks. Their shadowy forms fractured and disintegrated like smashed crystal as the black flames consumed the tumbling pieces until nothing remained. The toboggan barreled on, making living and dead rakkes one and the same.

"A most novel idea, Major," Pimmer said, crawling up beside him. "We appear to be through the rakke wall. Any thoughts on how to put out the flames?"

His grin vanished. "Oh . . ."

The flames, fed as much by the wind as the supply of rakke shades, were quickly clawing their way back along the supplies.

"I am sorry about this," Konowa said, meaning it. He hadn't set out to destroy the man's pride and joy. "We'll just have to jump off and let it burn out."

"That sounds wise, especially considering I saved a few kegs of black powder and loaded them on the toboggan."

Konowa looked down below him. He could just make out the curve of a keg at the bottom of the pile. "How could you be that stupid?"

Pimmer looked crestfallen. "I'm afraid I placed them on the bottom to provide some ballast and keep our center of gravity low, like on a ship."

"Everyone jump off!" Konowa shouted, turning and looking back down the length of the toboggan.

The looks he received were a mix of horror and incredulity. Even Jir perked his head up as if to see if he was serious.

"It was a mad plan to start with, you don't need to embellish it!" Visyna shouted back. "We're still going too fast!"

Konowa couldn't help but notice how attractive she looked with her hair blowing wildly in the wind. He'd have to remember to tell her that. Later. "There's black powder on here. When the frost fire hits it it's going to explode!"

"You arse!" Visyna shouted. She glared at him for a second then began weaving the air. Konowa felt the power of her control over the elements around them. It suddenly started snowing much harder. Big, fluffy flakes pasted him like a cold, wet wool blanket.

"I don't think that's going to put out the fire," he said, taking a quick look at the front of the toboggan and the growing bonfire there.

"This isn't over!" Visyna shouted, grabbing a hold of Chayii. His mother just looked at him with disappointment in her eyes, a look he'd seen far too often. And then the two women in his life stood up and dove off the side of the toboggan and into the snow.

"The Viceroy did it, not me!" he shouted after them, knowing that was the six-year-old part of him again. "I'm just trying to help!"

"And to think you were complaining about a little bit of copper fire a few hours ago," Yimt said, his face and beard a mask of snow.

"This was the only—Look, I'm still in charge here!"

Konowa shouted, anger rising that he was being scolded by apparently everyone. "And I order all of you off the damn sled!"

"Damn toboggan," Pimmer offered helpfully.

Konowa grabbed the diplomat under both arms and held him up. "Thank you for pointing that out. Try to roll when you hit the snow." He heaved, his anger sending the diplomat flying in a graceful arc, which ended in an explosion of snow.

He turned to look back at the rest of the passengers. "Anyone else need assistance?"

Yimt began kicking supplies and soldiers off the toboggan with equal force. "Never a dull moment in the service!" He jumped, grabbing a flailing Zwitty in one hand and a metal tin in the other. The rest followed in a melee of limbs, prayers, and curses, the latter aimed, he was certain, directly at him.

By now the flames were licking all around Konowa. He knew he was impervious to their effect, but he had no such protection from gunpowder. "Time to go, Jir," he said, motioning for the bengar to move. Jir growled, and the hair on the back of his mane stood straight up. "This is no time to get squirrelly," Konowa said, and shook his finger at him. "Jump or I'll boot you off."

Jir growled again and bared his fangs. Konowa realized the poor creature was terrified.

"Look, I don't like it either, but we have to get off this thing. Everyone else is gone, it's just you and me, and I'm not leaving you behind." He held out his hands and motioned for Jir to come to him.

Konowa doubted the bengar understood the words, but the tone in his voice must have registered. Jir stopped growling and slinked over to rest his head

against Konowa's thigh. Frost immediately arced between Konowa and Jir and the bengar stood up in surprise. Konowa lunged, grabbed Jir by the mane, and
pushed him over the side as the bengar flailed the air
with his paws.

"You can thank me later!" he shouted, after the
howling bengar landed on the snow, snout first. He
skidded along like that for a few yards before emerging
from a growing snow pile and began running after the
toboggan as it pulled away. "Thought they always
landed paws down."

Konowa turned to face forward again and was surrounded by black flame. It was surprisingly peaceful, as
if he'd just dived into a cool lake on a hot summer day.
The feeling only lasted a moment.

"Right, this is going to explode," he said to himself,
and prepared to jump. He was halfway to throwing
himself off the side when the battle somewhere out in
the snow between Private Renwar and Her Emissary
caught his attention. The acorn made a grating sound
as it constricted with an icy burst of energy. Konowa
bent over double with tears streaming down his face.
He struggled to right himself as the toboggan continued to tear through the battlefield. He wasn't steering,
but the pull of the conflict between Renwar and Gwyn
was drawing him and the toboggan toward them. The
power in the night was astounding. It was as if all the
breathable air had been replaced with raw energy, and
he wasn't breathing it so much as absorbing it.

The toboggan began to pick up speed as it homed in
on the dueling pair and Konowa knew his time was now.
The temptation to ride it out and draw even closer to the
swirling battle of power almost kept him on the toboggan.

Almost.

With a scream he didn't pretend was anything but, he flung himself off the side. He'd lost count of the number of times he'd experienced the sensation of flying and falling, but he knew if he never felt it again he'd be entirely okay with that. The snow-covered desert floor came up and punched him in the face and everything went white, cold, and suffocating for a while.

After what could have been an eternity or a few seconds he lifted his head and sucked in some air, choking down a mouthful of the bitter-tasting snow in the process. He gingerly climbed to his hands and knees as the earth pivoted and spun beneath him. He shook his head, which didn't help one bit. Everything was vibrating, and not in that warm, slightly drunk-feeling way. This was harsh and unsettling. He stood up, surprised to see his saber still clutched in his hand.

"Where's my . . . damn shako?" he muttered, poking around in the snow with the point of the blade in the vain hope of finding it. He turned around in a small circle intent on finding the hat while a voice deep inside was screaming at him to pull himself together. "Not without my shako," he said to no one, then dry-heaved.

Sweat dripped off his nose and his whole body began to shake. "Think I should sit . . . sit down," he said, starting to walk instead. That's when the sights, sounds, and smells of battle assaulted him all at once. He staggered and had to use his saber as a cane to stay upright. Rakkes howled and screamed. Musket volleys rippled and snapped through the air as the acrid smoke of gunpowder mixed with the falling snow turning everything a dusty, pale gray.

He heard shouts, saw shadows, felt the cold wind

on his face. It occurred to him then that he was still sweating a lot as more liquid poured down his face and dripped off the end of his nose. He reached up with his left hand to wipe the sweat away and thought it felt awfully sticky. He looked at his fingers. They were covered in blood.

"Oh . . ."

Got to keep moving, he thought, even as his knees buckled and he sat down in the snow. The weight of the world pressed down on his shoulders. He watched the snowflakes spin and float in the air. That was him. Weak and blown about by the wind. He shook his head again. *No,* that wasn't him. He had purpose. He had strength. Still, right now that was just so many words.

". . . just close my eyes for a minute," he said, aware that the ground was shaking. Something loomed over him and he looked up.

A rakke stood two yards away. His shako was clutched in its claws. It opened its mouth and peeled back its lips to reveal the full length of its fangs.

Konowa tried to lift his saber, but his right arm stayed limp at his side. The rakke stepped forward, looking around as if trying to detect a trap.

"Run," Konowa mumbled, not sure if he was talking to himself or the rakke. It didn't matter. He couldn't move and the rakke took another step toward him.

Something hard and impossibly cold pressed against his breast until he thought it would burst through and shatter his chest. Still, it wasn't enough. He watched the rakke approach, the shako still dangling from a claw. He ignored the creature's milky eyes and its drooling fangs. All his attention was on the shako.

"That's not yours," he said, his voice little more

than a hoarse whisper. Images of a locket and four words inscribed inside—*Come back to me*—kept him from slipping into unconsciousness.

The rakke seemed to understand what he meant. It looked down at its claws and brought the shako up to its face. It sniffed at the hat and then tore a chunk out of it and threw it to the snow, spitting out the piece a moment later.

Konowa got one leg underneath him and tried to stand. "You really shouldn't have done that," he said, struggling to stand upright. He wobbled and collapsed back down, the strength from anger not enough this time.

The rakke growled and took another step forward. Its arms could now reach Konowa. One swing and his throat would be torn open or his intestines spilled in the snow. That's all it would take for him to be so much red meat going down the gullet of a rakke.

"I haven't had a bath in weeks," Konowa said, doubting the rakke's taste buds would care. He took in a breath and cursed under it. *Not exactly the most poetic of last words.* He was still thinking of something better when the rakke screamed and vanished in a burst of frost fire.

A shade stood where the rakke once had. Konowa blinked.

"Kritton? You saved me?"

The shade of Kritton stepped forward and swung its blade. *"No, I didn't."*

TWENTY-NINE

I *am the master!*

Never in the creature's past life had it ever believed that statement in its entirety. It had served senior diplomats, and then the queen of Calahr, and finally the Shadow Monarch, and though it had exerted much power and control over the destinies of others in those roles, it had always had a master to answer to. What few memories remained of that time only served to fuel the uncontrollable rage that now consumed it. How could it have been so weak, so powerless, so . . . human?

It continued to tear itself apart, ridding itself of everything superfluous and soft. The human frailties that had defined Gwyn eroded in the fierce storm of its madness. All that remained was pure, unadulterated power. Its world was now one of unbearable pain, yet within that suffering it found an existence so euphoric that it sought even more ways to hurt itself. It scoured and tore every last shred of humanity from its being, whittling itself down to nothing but a collapsing mass of absolute agony.

The vortex of its madness swirled faster and faster, rending the fabric between the planes of the living and the dead. More and more creatures long vanished from the world poured through the tear, taking up ethereal form and attacking the shades of the Iron Elves with raw, wild glee, unfettered again after millennia.

I do this! I control this!

Its core grew smaller even as its power expanded. Its rage and power flew around it in a blur, spinning so fast they created a vacuum. There was no longer any air to breathe within its boundaries, but it had long moved beyond the need for it.

I am the master!

The voice that answered back shook it to its core.

"You are mistaken," Alwyn said, "and I am here to put things right."

"Are you all right?" Visyna asked, helping Chayii to her feet while brushing snow from the elf's hair.

"I appear to be," she said, her voice shaking as she smoothed out her Hasshugeb robe and straightened up. "Your weaving has saved us again. The snow is much deeper here."

"I hope the others landed as softly as we did," Visyna said, not entirely sure her weaving had really had that much of an effect. The burst of fear- and anger-induced energy brought on by Konowa's latest recklessness had fueled her power to weave the snow in the wake of the toboggan. She doubted she could do it again, although knowing Konowa she didn't rule it out. He could charm one second and infuriate the next.

"I hope so, too, my dear," Chayii said, reaching up and brushing some snow out of Visyna's hair. "You work well with the natural order. I suspect the elf-line runs in your family."

"Actually, I don't think one's bloodline really matters when it comes to caring about the world around us. You either do or you don't. It just feels right to me."

Chayii paused in brushing Visyna's hair and looked deeply into her eyes. "So wise for one so young. Do not tell my son, but I hope my grandchildren take after you."

Any other time Visyna would have blushed, but being in the middle of a battlefield didn't afford her that luxury. "We must move," she said, grabbing the elf by the arm and heading off after the toboggan. It was easy enough to follow its tracks in the snow along with bits of crates, sacks, uniforms, and, eventually, soldiers.

"Friend or foe?" Corporal Feylan shouted. He held the back half of a broken musket in his hands and appeared dazed.

"Shoot first, then ask," Yimt said, appearing out of the gloom and placing a hand on the soldier's arm. "But in this case it's all right. Ladies," he said, taking a quick bow. He held his drukar in his hand. The blade was slick and dripping.

"Are you okay?" Visyna asked, walking closer. Yes, there was definitely blood on the end of his weapon.

Yimt followed her gaze and then looked back up. "Just my luck I landed on a rakke and the poor thing broke my fall. I am glad I found you. We're scattered about like dandelions in a windstorm. Ah, there's a few more now."

"Is everyone all right?" Hrem asked, running up to

them. He had Scolly and Zwitty and three other soldiers in tow. Visyna wasn't surprised. The big soldier was a natural leader with the added advantage of being easy to spot.

"Better and better," Yimt said, punching Hrem affectionately in the biceps. "We're still missing a few, but we can't stay here. We'll keep following the trail and see if we can't round up the stragglers on the way. If you haven't already done so, grab some kind of weapon. I don't care if it's a piece of ice or a knitting needle, but we're deep in the middle of nowhere safe. Miss Red Owl, Miss Tekoy, please stay behind Private Vulhber. He makes a lovely wall. The rest of you, heads on swivels and if you think you see a rakke or worse, shout it out. Now, by the left if you still remember how it's done . . . march."

As they walked Visyna found herself tussling between two emotions. On the one hand she felt relieved that Sergeant Arkhorn so quickly and easily took command of the situation, but she was surprised to feel a degree of resentment, too, at the loss of the authority she had earned just a short few hours before. In the end, she was content to let things be as her thoughts turned to Konowa.

"I hope he's all right, because when we find him, I might just punch him in the nose," she said.

"He was like this even as a child," Chayii said, keeping her voice low. "The incident in the birthing meadow when he was not chosen by a Wolf Oak only added to what was already there. I realize now he will never truly be at peace until this has come full circle. He will face the Shadow Monarch, and one of them will die."

Visyna was taken aback by Chayii's matter-of-fact

assessment of the fate of her son, but she didn't disagree with it. "Perhaps there will be another way."

"Perhaps," Chayii said, but she didn't sound like she believed it, and Visyna wasn't sure she did herself.

"Heads up! Movement on the left flank."

Visyna turned. Two shadows emerged from the dark and resolved themselves into the Viceroy and Jurwan.

"Look who I found, or rather, who found me!" the Viceroy said, his voice booming as if trying to get the attention of a barkeep on a busy night. He walked with one arm around the elf's waist. Jurwan clutched his left arm tight to his chest and appeared to be in pain. Blood glistened between the fingers of his right hand.

Two more shadows emerged ten yards from the pair and angled toward them at a growing rate of speed.

"Rakkes!" Visyna shouted, her fingers flailing uselessly in the cold air. She couldn't pull so much as a single thread to weave. She stomped the snow in frustration as the rakkes closed in. The Viceroy nonchalantly drew his saber and began to whistle loudly and with little sense of rhythm. Jurwan removed his right hand from his wounded left arm and waved it into the air, scattering drops of blood everywhere.

The rakkes roared and ran even faster toward them. Five more rakkes appeared from the other side, boxing the hapless pair in.

Yimt was already charging toward the rakkes with Hrem right behind him, but they wouldn't reach them in time.

"Yimt. Hrem. Stop!"

The command cut through the night like a sliver from a single hair threaded through the smallest needle. If Visyna hadn't been standing right beside her she doubted she would have heard it, but Yimt turned, startled. Hrem stopped, too, after plowing into Yimt and sending them both to their knees in the snow.

"Chayii, why?" Visyna asked, as the rakkes covered the last few yards to the Viceroy and Jurwan.

"My husband is up to his old tricks again," she said, her tone a mixture of pride and annoyance.

A fifth shadow slid through the night. It moved so fast and so silently that Visyna couldn't keep it in focus. A soft, subtle voice carried on the night air, and while she couldn't understand its language, its meaning was clear; this was the power of a Silver Wolf Oak unleashed.

Tyul cut through the rakkes like lightning falling from the sky. He appeared, he destroyed, he disappeared. The creatures had no chance to defend themselves and no time to scream.

As the last rakke collapsed, Tyul came to a standstill, standing quietly in the snow as if he'd been there all along. No other living thing except perhaps Jir could look so calm and yet exude so much potential for violence. It was in the smooth, calculating grace of his stance. She would have found that attractive but for looking in his eyes. The elf was gone. What remained was little more than pure, natural force, a predator of the natural order driven and sustained by the power of a Silver Wolf Oak.

The smell of hot blood filled the air and Visyna brought her hand to her nose.

"What is—" she started to say, but Chayii held up her hand to silence her.

She took a slow, careful step toward Tyul, but the elf simply turned and disappeared into the night. Visyna looked down at the snow where he had stood and could see no sign that he had ever been there.

"A single company of lads like that and the Empire could rule the world," the Viceroy said, walking up to them as he sheathed his saber. He stopped when he looked at Chayii and his smile froze on his face. "But of course, his affliction is a most tragic one and not something to be used for gain." He sounded genuinely concerned if a little wistful.

"I see my husband does not share your concern equally," she said, turning her gaze on Jurwan. "No doubt he cut himself deliberately so that the rakkes would smell his blood and come running, unaware they were being drawn into the hunting ground of one of the *diova gruss.*"

Visyna had heard that term before and remembered it meant lost one. It definitely fit Tyul. It wasn't that the elf was insane, at least, she didn't think so, just that he was so in tune with the natural order that he had become part of it as much as the wind and the rain. He would strike down rakkes and any other ill-conceived creatures that marred the world and upset the natural order.

"Chayii," Visyna asked, "what will happen to Tyul when there are no more rakkes to hunt?"

The elf hung her head before answering. "Eventually, they lose themselves so completely that they can't bear to feed on anything, knowing their very existence mars the world. They starve to death in one final act of guardianship of the natural order, giving back their bodies to the earth."

"That's crazy," Zwitty muttered, drawing everyone's attention his way. He looked guilty, but met their gaze and glared. "Well, isn't it? What good is anybody dead to anyone?"

"I've often wanted to find out," Yimt said, eyeing Zwitty as if sizing him up for a coffin. "But as with so many joys in life, that will have to wait. We need to keep moving. Anyone seen Inkermon? He jumped about the same time you lot did?"

Hrem shook his head. "It was all a white blur. He's got to be around here somewhere though."

No one mentioned the obvious, but Visyna could tell they were all thinking it. With rakkes roaming everywhere his odds of survival were slim. He was no Tyul.

"Well, if that creator of his put any sense in his brain he'll follow the tracks and catch up. Let's go."

Visyna fell into step, watching Chayii gently take her husband's arm and rest her head on his shoulder. Jurwan still wasn't talking, but it was clear from his tactic with Tyul he was regaining his elfness.

A forlorn shako, a broken musket, and other bits of uniform and equipment surrounded several black marks in the snow where Iron Elves had perished. Yimt took the time to quickly sift through each one, muttering under his breath as he did so. In each case he picked up something and put the object in a haversack he'd found and slung over his shoulder.

"What's he doing?" Visyna asked Hrem.

"Collecting something from each soldier, hopefully something personal their family back home might know and appreciate receiving, especially when there won't be any body."

"Damn," Yimt said, standing up from the last spot. He was holding a small white book in his hand with a torn cover.

"Inkermon's holy book," Hrem said, his voice low and rough.

Visyna waited for him to say more, but he didn't. She thought about it, and realized that for soldiers like Hrem and Yimt and Konowa, the squad, the regiment, was another way of saying family.

"Everyone stay sharp, we're coming up on the main battle," Yimt said, pointing with his steel bar toward the front.

Visyna had been feeling the pull of the energy in the air for some time and her head began to swim.

"I see a rakke!" Scolly shouted, harkening Yimt's advice.

"Pointing would help," Yimt growled, trying to follow Scolly's eye line.

"It's standing over there by the major."

Everyone looked. Up ahead in a rockier area that hadn't received the heavier snowfall, Konowa sat limply in the snow, looking up at the creature. He wasn't defending himself.

"Help him!" Visyna cried, not knowing who or what could.

"My son, my son," Chayii said, her voice trembling.

The rakke stepped forward, ready to kill him when it disappeared in a violent flash of frost fire. The shade of an Iron Elf stood over its body.

"The Darkly Departed are handy to have around, I'll give them that," Yimt said, starting to chuckle. His laughter died as the form of the shade sharpened.

Visyna screamed.

Kritton raised his ethereal blade and swung.

THIRTY

The swirling mass that had once been Her Emissary tore itself into ever tinier pieces, scattering its rage and influence among the shades of the dead rakkes. Alwyn had expected to fight the creature as he had before at the canyon, but he realized now that was impossible. It had devolved into a burning black core of hatred no bigger than Alwyn's fist, but around it swirled an ever-growing maelstrom of shadowy death, each element a fearful particle of what Faltinald Gwyn had become.

Worse, the tear opened into the realm of the dead was expanding, and the creature's manic anger was drawing more and larger monsters through into this world. Alwyn leaned forward, pushing the wall of frost fire that surrounded him into the path of the shrieking vortex. The pain in his stump flared and he winced. Tears welled in his eyes. His wooden leg creaked with the stress, its many interwoven limbs splintering as he moved through the magical storm.

The storm reacted with fury to his presence, its

howling winds buffeting Alwyn as he closed the distance to its center. Screams from the living and dead
mingled in a chaotic thunder. Alwyn tried to draw in a
breath, but as soon as he opened his mouth he felt ice
form on his tongue. The cold dug into him like metal
forks, twisting and stabbing into his flesh as each step
brought him closer to the creature.

"I am the master now!" the creature screamed, focusing its attention on Alwyn.

"Then why do you fear me?" Alwyn replied, standing up to his full height and fixing the pulsing black
core with his gray eyes. He had its full attention, which
meant the others would have a chance. The thought
struck him as oddly comforting. He did still care about
others, and he knew they still cared about him.

He stepped forward, leading with his wooden leg.
The wood chipped and cracked as it was flayed by the
storm. Black frost crystallized along the length of the
wood, extinguishing the last trace of the more whole-
some power once placed there by Miss Red Owl and
Miss Tekoy. So be it. With the wood now sheathed in
protective black ice, he leaned forward and kept
walking.

He'd expected pain, and he got it. It was a new kind
of agony, like thousands of knives nicking his flesh one
sliver at a time, but it wasn't the pain that hurt him. He
wasn't just being eroded away by the force of the spinning storm. Bits of who he was, what he believed, what
he desired, were being frayed and blown away by the
grinding, howling wind.

He caught fleeting visions of thoughts that were
once part of the thing at the center of the storm. Pain,
horror, misery, and death dominated, but there were

other, kinder thoughts. He saw a beautiful jeweled map and an intricately carved table that looked like a dragon. Alwyn began to sift through the storm as he strode toward its center, collecting what pieces he could, however small, containing joy and hope. He let his own fears and angers get torn away as he did his best to replace them with the bits of goodness he found. The task was an uneven one, but he only needed to sustain himself a little longer. The seething core was now just yards away.

Here, near the center, the storm spun slower, but the madness grew denser, making it difficult for Alwyn to focus. Insane laughter filled his lungs. *Is this me? Am I becoming it?*

He stopped a yard away from the black core. It hung in the air in front of his eyes, an infinite blackness so crazed it repeatedly shattered and re-formed under the pressure of its own insanity. He tried to remember why he'd come and couldn't. The blackness deepened and his understanding of this world and the next blurred. He shuddered, his body and his being slowly disintegrating in the storm. The fabric of his uniform melted away, leaving him naked and exposed.

Something small and white flew past, just at the edge of his vision. It came around again and stuck into his arm. He felt a hot fire begin to burn, its heat spreading out from the point of impact. As it spread, it redefined his shape, his form, and he understood who and what he was again. He looked down and saw Rallie's quill sticking out of his arm, dead center in the acorn tattoo: *Æri Mekah* . . . Into the Fire.

He smiled and looked up at the blackness before him.

"Your pain is at an end," he said, reaching out with both hands and grabbing the blackness between them.

The fury of the storm spiked, the wind screamed, and the very air fractured as the madness that was Faltinald Gwyn began to collapse. Alwyn squeezed, crushing time and space into an ever-dwindling point of nothingness. Everything Alwyn ever knew and loved was ripped away as all his energy focused on destroying the creature and closing the tear. Claws and fangs lashed and cut him, gouging flesh and bone and memory. Obsidian-like blades of frost fire cauterized and healed the wounds, replacing flesh and blood with icy flame.

Tears rolled down his face forming icicles on his cheeks. He closed his eyes and squeezed harder, taking the pain from the creature, amplifying it with his own, and building a wall in the tear between this world and the next. Everything dead became caught up in the whirlwind as Alwyn focused all his might. The monsters broke apart and flew back into the darkness, followed by the shades of the rakkes. Still, the maelstrom did not weaken.

He slipped, as the branches of his wooden leg broke. He dropped down to his one knee and his grip on the creature faltered. The wall began to crack as the dead on the other side saw an opportunity to be free again.

"Help me," he cried, though he couldn't be sure his voice had made any sound at all.

Shades of the Iron Elves appeared at his side. He opened his eyes as they moved to the wall to buttress it, but even they were not enough. The creature sensed this, and the storm began to spin even faster. Alwyn cried out and would have let go, but a voice came to him from a distance.

"Kick him in the arse and be done with it, Ally. I know damn sure I never taught you to give up!"

Yimt!

Alwyn turned, blinking tears out of his eyes.

The dwarf stood on the edge of the storm. He was looking straight at Alwyn. The tears in his eyes were unmistakable.

"I knew from the moment I laid eyes on you that I'd have my work cut out turning you into a soldier," Yimt said, "but I always knew I would. You ain't about to prove me wrong now, are you?"

Alwyn laughed and cried at the same time. "Yimt! You're alive!"

"Well, what the hell else would I be? You didn't think I'd let some mangy rakkes get the better of me now, did you?"

Alwyn found the strength he needed. He squeezed one more time, and this time the creature was unable to resist. The monsters and shades of the rakkes were cast deep in the abyss of the distant past. He absorbed the creature's pain, robbing it of its power.

"I . . . there's so much I want to say," Alwyn shouted. His entire being was agony, but he still managed to smile. Yimt was alive.

"Save your breath, Ally," Yimt shouted back, his voice breaking up between sobs. "I'll say it for both of us. You're the skinny, overly sensitive, whiny, yet tough as bloody iron son I never had. I'm damn proud of you."

As the life force in his hands flickered with its last moments, Alwyn smiled. He crushed the last particle that had been Gwyn and the tear between the worlds was closed. The storm around him began to die, and as the air cleared he was able to get one, perfect look at Yimt. The dwarf stood military straight, giving Alwyn a salute.

Alwyn saluted back as the toboggan engulfed in black flame slid to a halt beside him. The frost fire reached the kegs of black powder and exploded, banishing the darkness in a burning white sun brighter than a thousand stars.

Snow flashed and vaporized. Everything went pure white then black as the night shattered. A sizzling wave of cold and hot air washed over Visyna, stealing the breath from her throat. Bright splotches of color swirled before her eyes as icy shards of frost fire crackled and slivered amidst searing-hot tongues of red-orange flame. A moment later, the booming sound of an explosion tore through the air, crushing everything flat in its path.

It felt as if the ground had risen up and slammed into her instead of the other way around. Alternating currents of bitter cold and caustic heat roared overhead, twisting and turning in the sky. Visyna tried to lift her head, but it was pinned to the ground as much by her exhaustion as the rolling blast wave of the explosion.

Unable to breathe and too weak to move, her vision began to gray and she experienced a growing numbness throughout her body. *No, not like this!* Fighting every urge to close her eyes and drift into unconsciousness, she pulled her arms back until she could prop herself up on her elbows. Straining like she was in labor, she hauled her body up to a sitting position.

She brought one arm up to shield her face as she peered ahead, trying to find Konowa. There was so much flickering light and shadow that it took her a minute to find the spot she'd last seen him. She realized suddenly she hoped to see his body lying on the ground. It sounded perverse even as she thought it, but the logic was sound. If he was dead, there would be nothing left, but if he was only wounded, he would still be there.

She scoured the ground ahead looking for any sign at all of the body of the elf she loved. She found him a moment later, but despite the horrors she had already witnessed, she wasn't prepared for what she saw.

THIRTY-ONE

I'm dead. Surprisingly, it didn't feel strange to think it. He tried out the concept again. *I'm dead, I'm really dead.*

Something distant and loud echoed in the space around him, but he couldn't put any meaning to it. Everything was dark, not black exactly, more like the absence of . . . anything.

He tried to move, but the process by which that happened escaped him. For all that he didn't feel trapped. It was as if he knew he could travel wherever he wanted, but he had no desire to go anywhere or do anything, so the fact that he couldn't move was moot.

The noise sounded closer. It was more distinct now, like a huge drum being beaten . . . or a cannon firing. He thought it strange he could hear that in the afterlife, but then again, why not? The Blood Oath meant he wasn't really gone, not all the way.

The thought was comforting. He realized he wasn't ready to leave this world, not yet. His nose itched and he wanted to scratch it, but his arms still wouldn't move. *Wait a second. If my nose is itchy . . . oh bloody he—*

"*—EELLLLLLLL!*" Konowa yelled, his eyes flying open. Spots flickered in front of his eyes making it impossible to see anything clearly. He kept yelling, knowing that the moment he stopped he was going to experience something he had no desire to feel. He yelled until his whole body was rigid and shaking and his throat on fire. Finally, he closed his eyes and took in a breath, and with it the pain.

". . . mother," he whispered, tears welling in his eyes and rolling down the side of his face. If he'd had a pistol in his hand and the energy to lift it he would have put it to his head and ended it all. Never in his life had he felt pain like this. This wasn't possible. It was as if he was being frozen from the inside out. He could feel tiny, razor-sharp pieces of frost growing like crystal inside his body. The agony was so pure he could have cut diamonds with it.

"I'm here my son, I'm here," Chayii said, her voice coming to him like a rope to a drowning elf.

"What's happening?" he asked, unable to open his eyes again as the pain robbed him of the ability to do little more than breathe.

"The blade is still in you, my son. That is why you are suffering. Hold on a little longer."

Konowa tried to make sense of what she was saying. *What blade?* He couldn't remember how he got here, everything was fuzzy and out of order. His memory lay scattered about his mind like a spilled deck of playing cards. Images flashed in his mind, of sliding, of black fire, of rakkes, of—

"Kritton!" He opened his eyes again and forced

them to look to his left. A dark, shimmering, ethereal blade protruded from his shoulder. The shoulder itself was sheathed in black ice like an armor suit. That's what saved me, he realized, also understanding that it was the power of the frost fire that now kept the blade firmly lodged in his flesh. The blade faded in and out of sight, and as it did the pain ebbed and flowed like the tides. "Pull it out! Bloody hell, pull the damn thing out!"

Now that he knew the source of the pain he found strength in his limbs. He thrashed and cursed and spit and dug his heels into the dirt as the pain wracked him. He tried to reach the blade to pull it out himself, but when his hand grasped the shadowy pommel it closed around nothing. It was as if the blade really was just shadow. There was nothing to hold on to.

"You see our dilemma," Pimmer said, coming into view. "We've tried all manner of ways to remove the blade, but thus far none have worked."

"We haven't tried my idea yet," Yimt said, barging forward. The Viceroy started to object then thought better of it and disappeared. Yimt knelt beside Konowa and laid a hand on his right arm. Even through the pain, Konowa could tell the dwarf had been crying.

"You remember Ally took that black arrow in his leg. He lost the leg, but he survived. Miss Red Owl, er, your mother, helped with that."

Konowa felt colder still. "You want to cut off my arm?"

"This thing is killing you. If we don't do something soon you're going to be a solid block of ice."

Konowa knew it was true. He could feel the frost fire inside him. It had never done that before.

His back arched as a new surge of pain raced

through his body. "Okay," he panted, "let's call that . . . plan B. Mother, can't you do some magic and get it out?"

She leaned forward so that her face was above his. "My child, this is beyond my power, and even if your father were himself, I do not think he could do it either."

"Visyna?"

There was a pause before Chayii answered. "She is . . . too weak right now. But have faith, we will find a way."

"Renwar," Konowa said, his mind reeling through the list of people he knew with magical powers. It was surprisingly large. "He's part of their world. Can't he pull it out?"

The silence that greeted his question triggered something in Konowa's memory.

"The explosion . . ."

"There's a massive crater where Ally was fighting that thing," Yimt said. His voice deepened with the effort to recall the events. "You should have seen him, Major. Bravest lad I ever knew. He did himself proud."

Even in his pain, Konowa could hear the hurt in Yimt's voice. "I'm sorry. If I hadn't lit the sled on fire—"

Yimt squeezed his arm. "You did what you had to do, Major, just like Ally. He'd already made his choice long before that sled exploded. Besides, if he is dead . . ."

Konowa understood. If Alwyn was dead, they would see him again.

"Could one of the other shades get this thing out of my shoulder?"

Yimt coughed before answering. "They're gone. When we all picked ourselves up after the explosion the

DD and even the rakke dead just vanished. Can't find a trace of them anywhere."

A cannon boomed nearby. "The battle is still going on?" Konowa asked.

"Still hundreds of regular old rakkes running around. We're holding them off, but that's about it."

Something wasn't adding up. "How are the cannons firing? We ran out of shot for them."

"That was the Viceroy's second idea. He took chunks of those dragon *sarka har* you went flying with and stuffed them down the cannon barrels. Not exactly standard procedure, but credit where it's due, those things tear up rakkes like a hungry dog with a bone."

It was an image Konowa could have done without. "The regiment. We need to get out of here."

"We're working on it," Yimt said. He looked away for a second and then back at Konowa. His smile was alarming. "Miss Synjyn is coming. She'll get you right as rain."

Everything went black. When Konowa opened his eyes again, Rallie was kneeling on his left side. She held a sheaf of papers in one hand and a quill in the other. The end of a lit cigar glowed cherry red clenched between her teeth. He coughed and blew cigar smoke out of his lungs. "So what's the verdict?"

Rallie looked up from her papers. "I'm drawing you a new reality, one that doesn't include a sword of shadow stuck in your shoulder."

"You can do that?" Konowa asked.

"I really don't know, but it's a cinch we're all about to find out. Now, you might feel a little sting when I do this."

Yimt placed his knee on Konowa's right shoulder and

his hands on his head, pinning him securely to the ground. Hrem appeared and grabbed hold of both his ankles.

"Sting?"

"Would you rather I tell you it's going to hurt beyond belief?" Rallie asked.

"Not now," Konowa said, wishing he hadn't asked.

"Count of three?" Rallie asked.

"Sure, just give me a-argh!" he screamed, as she began to draw on the paper and the blade in his shoulder vibrated with tension.

"Hold him steady. If he moves too much I could accidentally draw part of him out of existence."

Konowa choked back his next scream and grunted. Every time he thought the pain couldn't get worse it drove another spike into him. Black frost flickered around the hands of Yimt and Hrem where they held him, but neither let go.

"I do believe it's working," Rallie said over the scratching of her quill.

Konowa wanted to shout his dissent, but he was afraid to move at all. Batting an eyelash hurt too much. "Let me know . . . when you're sure," he gasped.

"That's it, Major, you're doing fine. Miss Synjyn will have you stitched up like new in no time," Hrem said from down by his feet.

Konowa looked down his body and saw Hrem had his eyes closed.

"Anything wrong?"

"He just doesn't like to see the insides of people is all," Yimt said. "Me on the other hand, I find it downright fascinating. Get to see what makes a fellow tick. Not every day you can say you got to see the inner workings of an officer."

Konowa risked a look over at his shoulder and felt the blood drain from his face. The shadow blade remained intact, but a large chunk of his shoulder was missing. He could see the pure white bone of his shoulder joint. Black tendrils of frost fire intermingled with shadow snaked all around it and deep into his flesh.

"Rallie?"

"It really is crucial you stay as still as possible," she said, her quill moving even faster as she drew across the page. "In order to remove the blade, I first have to remove all the parts of you infected by the blade, *which*," she hurriedly added, "I plan to put back when the blade is gone."

"Oh, is that what you're doing?" he said between gasps. "Carry on."

"See, no problem," Yimt said. Konowa felt the pressure on his head shift as Yimt leaned over for a better look at the wound. "Reminds me of a beef joint, but very little marbling. Not very tender I'm afraid, but probably good for stew if you let it simmer for a day."

"You wouldn't like me," Konowa said, a tiny smile reaching his lips. "We elves are gamey."

"I've heard that," Yimt said, as if this was an entirely normal and acceptable topic of conversation. "Now take a big slab of human meat like Private Vulhber there. You've got to figure there's a good ten pounds of top sirloin running along that spine of his. Lot of prime cuts in a lad that size."

"Have you ever tried orc?" Konowa asked, flinching as another wave of pain spread out from the wound.

"Now that's gamey," Yimt said. "Just about broke a tooth on some orc jerky one time. Nasty stuff. You could soak it for a week and it'd still be as tough as boot leather. But here's something most people don't know. Orcs have the most tender—" Whatever Yimt was going to say was cut off by Hrem's shouting.

"Would you two please stop! I'm going to be sick."

Konowa looked down at him and sure enough, the big soldier looked wan and about ready to pass out.

"Easy, Hrem, we're just chitchatting here. Keeping the major preoccupied is all. Pick a different subject if you like. Come to think of it, all this talk about food has built up an appetite. I've been thinking about trying out a new recipe—"

"Or silence," Hrem said, his breaths coming in short bursts. "Silence might work."

"Not to worry, gentlemen, the deed is done," Rallie said.

Konowa looked over as she flourished her quill and tucked it away up a sleeve. He had the oddest thought that her arm must be covered in ink stains, but then he was looking at his shoulder.

The blade was gone and his shoulder was whole again, but with a nasty-looking black scar running across it. The cascading waves of pain were gone, too. Every muscle in his body relaxed and he felt his back touch the ground again. It was as if a thousand ropes under tension had been cut and he sank into a puddle of relief.

The frost fire had already disappeared. He tentatively moved the fingers of his left hand.

"They work. Hurts like hell, but they work."

Rallie leaned back and took the cigar from her mouth, blowing out a thick stream of smoke. "I'm tempted to remind you of the aphorism about quills being mightier than the sword, but you can read all about it when I write my next dispatch."

"Help me up," Konowa said, struggling to lift his shoulders from the ground. They wouldn't budge. "Sergeant, you can stop holding me down, Rallie's finished."

Yimt appeared at his side, his hands held out for Konowa to see. "Not me, Major."

Rallie leaned over and looked closely in his eyes. He had to turn his head to avoid being burnt by the end of her cigar. She leaned back and sighed. "I had hoped to avoid this, but it could have been worse."

"What?" Konowa asked.

"I did my best to redraw everything back as it was, connecting all the little fibers and bits to where they were before. Still, that kind of work is hard on a body. I've never actually done anything like this before, well, I don't think I have . . ."

Konowa shared a look with Yimt and decided to ignore the last part. "Rallie, I can't be flat on my back while the regiment fights. They need me." *And I need them.*

"A few hours, a few days, it's hard to say. But you will recover, of that I'm sure," she said, slapping the sheaf of papers in her hand.

Konowa shuddered. It felt as if someone had just shook him.

"Sorry about that," Rallie said, gently rolling the papers up. "There's a residual connection after something like this. Should dissipate shortly. In the meantime, I suggest we all get moving. The supply of exploding *sarka har* is limited."

Yimt and Hrem lifted him up and carried him to Rallie's battered wagon, which he gathered must have been parked nearby the whole time. Amazing he hadn't smelled the camels before now, but then his mind had been on other things. They eased him into the back and laid him down on a blanket before throwing another one on top of him. His saber, the tattered remains of his uniform jacket, and a shako that may or may not have been his followed.

"If anyone tries to tuck me in I swear I'll order you shot at dawn."

"Shh," Yimt said, "you're not the only patient here."

Konowa looked over. Visyna lay beside him, wrapped up in another blanket. Her eyes were closed. He desperately wanted to reach over and brush her hair and kiss her forehead. "How is she?"

"Exhausted," Chayii said, coming to sit between the two of them. "As are we all, but she has taken much of the burden upon herself. Were it not for her none of our group would be here now. She is a strong one, Konowa, and a good one."

The last part was said with such implied meaning that even Konowa couldn't miss it. "Do I at least get to propose, or has that been taken care of, too?"

"I have no doubt that you will pursue your courtship with her as you see fit," his mother said, shaking her head as if she already knew it would be some form of disaster, "but hear me now and hear me well. If you let this one get away I might just have *you* shot at dawn."

Somewhere not far enough away, Konowa heard Yimt trying not very hard to hold in a laugh. The temptation to bellow at him only lasted a second as happier thoughts filled his mind. It was crazy, especially when in the further distance he could hear musket fire and howling rakkes, but he believed he could see a future when all this was done. A future with Visyna. How any of them got there in one piece was a mystery still to be solved, but his determination to do so was greater than ever.

Rallie clicked her tongue and the wagon groaned and started moving. Konowa did his best to accept his current state and enjoy the ride, but all the while his mind raced with possibilities of what might be. He vowed to stay awake and allowed himself to close his eyes for only a second as the wagon rocked and swayed across the ground.

He woke up two days later on the deck of a ship, and in a world thrown into total chaos.

THIRTY-TWO

"Two days?" Konowa asked. His head throbbed, along with the rest of his body, and he'd only been awake for ten minutes. This was worse than drinking Sala brandy with the Duke of Rakestraw. At least he had fun when he did that before paying the price. He reached up and removed the wet cloth from his forehead. It dawned on him that his body was responding again, even if it did so through a curtain of dull, aching pain. He sat up in bed, noticing that he'd been placed in what must have been a senior officer's quarters on one of Her Majesty's ships of the line. He was tempted to wonder if this was one of his dreams, but the smell of the ship told him it was all too real. "I've been out that long?"

"You had quite a snooze, but considering your recent adventures it's amazing you're conscious at all," Yimt said, plopping down on a small wooden stool by the bed and grinning at him. He handed him a tin cup filled with water. "Besides, you didn't really miss much. We held off the rakkes and marched to the coast."

Konowa took the cup with his left hand and downed it in two gulps. He was impressed he held on to it without spilling. He looked over at the black scar on his left shoulder and flexed the muscle. It hurt, but it worked. Maybe he really had needed all that sleep. "You make it sound like a walk in the park, but somehow I doubt it was that," Konowa said, looking closer at the dwarf. A fresh, pink scar creased the dwarf's right cheek. "I don't remember that being there last time we talked. And, Viceroy," Konowa said, shifting slightly to address the diplomat standing quietly by the closed door, "you appear to have acquired a couple of additional war wounds yourself." His uniform was a mess of rips and tears. The man was a far cry from the bloated spit-and-polish bureaucrat Konowa had met back in Nazalla. Pimrald "Pimmer" Alstonfar had been in the field, and it looked like it agreed with him.

Pimmer blushed. "Just doing my part. I really didn't do anything heroic."

"In that case, how about you two get me up to speed on what's going on?" Konowa said, looking out the one porthole in the room and seeing only darkness. The room itself was lit by a hanging lantern that created far more shadows than Konowa felt comfortable with. He turned back to see Pimmer's crestfallen face and realized his mistake. "But of course that can wait a few minutes. Regimental Sergeant Major, I suspect the Viceroy is being a bit too modest. Perhaps you could tell me how he comes to look like a gypsy warrior instead of one of Calahr's civil servants?"

Pimmer beamed as Yimt recounted the last two days. It was as much as Konowa had expected.

"Rakkes hounded us the whole way. Persistent, I'll

give them that. Just won't give up those things, but the Viceroy has picked up a few of your bad traits, Major. He led three bayonet charges into them. Scattered them to hell and gone. They definitely weren't in the mood for his style of negotiating."

Konowa tried to imagine the diplomat trundling across the snow and laying waste to a horde of marauding rakkes and the really startling thing was, he could see it clearly.

It was Pimmer's turn to return the compliment. "My efforts pale in comparison to that of the RSM here. His leadership and savvy saw us through one tight squeeze after another. And he is quite simply a maestro with a drukar. Such precision . . . I dare say, he could trim the fuzz off a bumble bee in midflight."

"Indeed," Konowa said, deciding to change the subject before the two praised each other to godlike status. "I see I'm on a ship. I take it we made it to Tel Martruk?"

Pimmer jumped in. "And not just us, but a good portion of the Calahrian fleet. They managed to rescue most of the force that landed at Nazalla and came down the coast looking for us. Seems Her Majesty's Scribe had something to do with that. Do you recognize this ship? It's the *Black Spike*. Seemed appropriate to put the Iron Elves on it again. I understand you two share quite a history."

Memories of the island assaults flooded Konowa's mind and he quickly pushed them aside. "That we do. RSM, what's the roster? How many?"

At this the room grew eerily quiet. "Counting the 3rd Spears, the gun crews, civilians like your parents, Miss Tekoy and Miss Synjyn, we muster sixty-seven."

The number burned into Konowa like a brand. Just

a few short months ago they'd started with close to three hundred. "And the shades?"

Yimt's jovial demeanor faltered. "Nary a peep since that explosion. Ally's gone. Just . . . gone, and it looks like he took Her Emissary and all the dead with him. Even when someone new goes down, their body turns to ash, but we don't see the shade."

Konowa wasn't sure he was ready to face it, but if he didn't ask now it would only be worse later. "Who did we lose on the march to the coast?"

Yimt scratched at his beard. "Lieutenant Imba and most of the 3rd Spears. Only five of them made it. And we lost half the gun crews."

It was a heavy blow. Imba had been a true leader, an officer destined for so much more. The bravery of the 3rd Spears was already legendary, and their duty with the Iron Elves would only cement that reputation, and rightly so. Konowa could tell there was more, though. "Who else?"

Yimt sighed. "Several soldiers are missing, including Private Inkermon. And Tyul has yet to turn up. Your mother is sick with worry about him. She sent Jir out looking for him, but we haven't seen anything since. Not sure we'd get that elf on the ship anyway. He's gone so far round the bend he can see the back of his own head."

Konowa sat up fully in bed, ignoring the pain. Jir would turn up, he knew it. He had to. That bengar had kept him sane during his banishment. As crushing as it was to come so close to his elves and not see them, to lose Jir would hurt so much worse. His loyalty and companionship meant more to him than he liked to admit. Through Jir he did connect with nature, even if it was in its most predatory state. The bengar actually made him more elf than he otherwise would have been. *No, Jir will return.*

"Why haven't you sent out search parties for the missing soldiers?" Konowa asked.

A cannon broadside boomed in the distance before Yimt could reply. Two more followed in quick succession. "That's why. The town is deserted. About the only thing left alive in it now are rakkes. The ships have been shelling the waterfront to keep the buggers at bay. I hate leaving anyone behind, but orders is orders. We're setting sail within the hour. That's why we had to come and wake you, recovered or not."

It was a blow to realize just how quickly the Empire was collapsing, but it gave Konowa renewed strength. "About bloody time. We should land on the Hyntaland in a few days with good winds. You know, I've wanted to throttle His Highness more times than not, but he's finally seeing things right."

Pimmer held up his hands. "Major, I think it important to remind you that you're still recovering from a multitude of grievous wounds. You need to avoid exerting yourself as you recover. Any aggravation could have serious repercussions to your health."

"Not to worry, Viceroy, this is good news. I feel great."

Pimmer's smile froze on his face. He looked to Yimt for help.

"Am I missing something?" Konowa asked.

"You could say that," Yimt said, slowly getting up from the stool. He stood braced as if he'd just walked into a pub expecting a fight. "Here's the thing, it's about our destination . . ."

Konowa waited for him to finish. When he didn't he looked back at Pimmer. The man held up his hands and shrugged as if to say "I tried." "We're not sailing to the Hyntaland, are we?" Konowa asked.

The man held on to his frozen smile. "Not as such, no. The Prince has determined the wisest course of action is to head for Calahr and assemble a much larger force before tackling the Shadow Monarch."

Konowa's following curses were drowned out by a broadside fired by the *Black Spike*. The entire ship shook and groaned as its heavy cannons let loose against the rakkes in Tel Martruk. The acrid smell of black-powder smoke filled the room.

Konowa threw off the covers and swung his legs over the side of the bed. The pouch with the black acorn in it swung from the leather thong still tied around his neck. A brief stab of cold reminded him it was there, not that he needed any reminding. The cost of the oath was a permanent weight on his shoulders.

He set his feet down on floor and almost smiled at the feel of the cool wood beneath his feet. It was the closest he was likely to come to bonding with a tree. He stood, fighting off the light-headedness that threatened to topple him. He looked down at himself and except for the leather pouch was completely naked. "Where's my uniform?"

"Now, Major, please, you have to understand," Pimmer said, moving to stand at the foot of the bed. "The regiment is all but depleted. Even the shades are gone. The Empire is in utter turmoil. Everyone, including the Prince, understands the need to finish this business with the Shadow Monarch once and for all, but it needs planning, and resources. If we just sail straight there with this ragtag collection of ships and soldiers the outcome could well be disastrous."

Konowa stared at the Viceroy. "I'll walk out of here like this if I have to."

Yimt came into view with Konowa's uniform. It looked clean and repaired. He wondered when anyone had had time to put needle to thread, but he was grateful. He really would have stormed out of the room naked, but he suspected his argument for going straight to Her mountain would have more weight if he were wearing more than a snarl. "I had a feeling you'd be a bit motivated to go have a chat with His Highness so I got your things ready for you."

Konowa looked away from Pimmer and down at the smiling dwarf. "Is that also why I can't see my saber among my things?"

"Got it out with one of the lads for sharpening. Should have it back to you, oh, right about *after* you've had your talk with him."

Konowa held Yimt's stare for several seconds then grabbed the uniform out of his hands and began to get dressed. "I know what I'm doing," he said, struggling into his trousers.

"Do you now?" Yimt said, helping him on with his boots. "Because from my perspective, and admittedly it isn't quite as lofty, it appears that you're about to go charging wildly."

"Then why are you helping me?" Konowa asked, stomping down harder than he needed to adjust his boots. If anyone was wondering if Major Swift Dragon was up, they'd know it now.

"A good old-fashioned charge is sometimes exactly what's called for. I just think you'd be wise to consider what you intend to do when you get to the other end of your charge. See, starting a charge is easy. You're better than most at it. Someone lights a fire under you and off you go. It's how it ends that can get sticky."

Konowa fought with the sleeve of his jacket. "I really thought he'd changed, at least enough that he wouldn't do something as stupid as this. Was he always this pig-headed, even in school?" Konowa asked, turning back to Pimmer.

"Well, it would be highly indelicate of me to comment on—"

"Pimmer!" Konowa shouted, ramming his arm into a sleeve then pulling it back out when he realized he was putting his jacket on back to front. "The fate of the world is at stake. We don't have time to gather more forces. If we don't do this now there'll be nothing but dark forest from here to the horizon and beyond."

Pimmer moved closer, lowering his voice. "I know this, Konowa, but we've received word that the royal court is under siege and Her Majesty ails. The Empire is besieged within and without and the Queen wants her son and heir home where he can better attend affairs of state."

Konowa snorted, then looked down at his uniform to make sure he didn't get anything on it. "Let's be honest, at least among each other. If the Queen has summoned her son home, it's to keep him safe."

The diplomat stood up straight and his voice took on a more commanding tone. "It wasn't just His Royal Highness. She summoned all of us home. The Iron Elves, too."

Some of the steam firing Konowa left him and he sat down on the bed. "What is she thinking? We need to face danger, not turn and run from it."

"I think," Pimmer ventured, looking toward the door as if to ensure it remained closed, "she wants to save as many as she can, including you."

"But this will only ensure more die. No," he said, standing up again and taking his shako from Yimt's outstretched hand. "She is wrong, and the Prince is wrong. We are the key. We need to strike now."

Pimmer took a moment before responding. "And you can't be dissuaded?"

"Not as long as I've got breath in my lungs."

Pimmer smiled and gave a quick salute to Yimt. Konowa looked between the two of them. "What in blazes are you two up to now?"

"As Her Majesty's representative it was my sworn duty to make the case for returning to Calahr with all due haste per royal decree. Having made my case I can report, in due time, that it was unsuccessful. Now, we simply need to convince the Prince."

"You couldn't have just told me this at the start?" Konowa asked.

"That was my idea," Yimt said, brushing away a few dust motes from Konowa's uniform. "I told the Viceroy that after your two-day nap you'd be a bit slow off the mark unless we gave you the proper incentive. I'd say we succeeded."

Konowa placed his shako on his head and walked to the door. He stopped with his back to Pimmer and Yimt. "Next time, you could try telling me the truth right off. I might just surprise you." He opened the door and stepped out. As he walked away the conversation behind reached his ears.

"He seems a bit upset with us," Pimmer said.

"Naw, he's just temperamental. Besides, time is

fleeting. Did you see how fast he got out of bed? Can't boot an officer in the butt like you can a soldier. You have to find other ways to motivate 'em."

Konowa kept walking, his fists clenching as he did. Yimt was right, he felt *very* motivated. He stormed on deck looking for the Prince. He was surprised to see it wasn't snowing. It was cold, though, and the wind hummed in the rigging and snapped the sails, urging the *Black Spike* to heave anchor.

Rallie, Visyna, and his mother materialized in front of him as if they'd been waiting there the whole time, which, he imagined, they probably had.

"The last time we were on this boat the three of you did your best to keep me from harming the Prince, and I appreciate it. This time, however, is different."

The answer he received threw him off guard.

"We know, Konowa, and we are with you," Visyna said, moving forward as if to embrace him, but stopping a yard short. "He must be made to see reason. The Shadow Monarch must be stopped now before Her power can grow any stronger."

Konowa looked to his mother and then Rallie. Both nodded in agreement.

"Where is he?"

"Right behind you," the Prince said, walking around Konowa to stand on his left. He looked at the three ladies and touched his hand to the brim of his shako. "Shall I guess, or is there any point? You've all heard we're to sail to Calahr at once and not to the Hyntaland."

Konowa drew in a breath in preparation to convince the Prince through sheer force of argument, but never got the chance.

"Does anyone else hear that?" Rallie asked, looking skyward.

Konowa stomped his boot on the deck. *What was Rallie doing?* He opened his mouth to speak, but was stymied when the Prince turned his back to follow Rallie's gaze.

"Is that wings?" the Prince asked.

"Not just any wings," Rallie said, her gruff voice rising an octave in obvious delight. "I'd know that drunken collection of feathers anywhere."

True to his name, Wobbly the messenger pelican wobbled into view out over the harbor. His flying prowess, or complete lack of, was obvious. He bobbed and weaved like the drunken bird he was, using up far more sky than any other bird. Konowa figured he flew probably twice as far as he had to on account of all the weaving.

"Wobbly!" Rallie cried. Everyone turned to follow the pelican's flight.

"It's wounded," Pimmer said, stepping out on deck.

"No, just drunk as usual," Rallie said, walking to the edge of the ship's railing. Wobbly made a few less than smooth course corrections and began to home in on the ship.

Konowa glared at the Prince one more time then turned to follow the final approach of the pelican. At seventy-five yards out he leveled his wings and started to glide. He slipped a little to the right, dipped his left wing, and steadied himself on the wind.

"He's coming in awfully fast, isn't he?"

At twenty yards he flared his wings and stuck out his webbed feet. Konowa tried to follow his path to see what he was aiming for, but the only thing obvious was the large sail canvas.

Thump!

Wobbly hit the main sail and began a panicked flapping of wings as he tried and failed to gain any purchase. Giving up, or growing exhausted, he slid down the sail until he hit the main spar, bounced off it, did a complete somersault in the air losing several feathers in the process, and landed flat on his back on the deck, his wings outstretched and his webbed feet paddling the air.

"You ever think of using an owl instead?" Konowa asked.

"Can't trust them," Rallie said, walking forward to pick up the pelican and cradle it in her arms. "Too smart for their own good. Now Wobbly here is a bird you can trust. A drunk, but a trustworthy one."

Wobbly's bill opened wide letting forth a belch Konowa could smell from five yards away. A regurgitated vial popped out of his gullet, which Rallie deftly grabbed. She then set the pelican back down on the deck. "Could someone please fetch him a bowl of grog, thank you."

Konowa was growing increasingly frustrated that his showdown with the Prince was being delayed. He started to open his mouth again, but stopped when he saw the look on Rallie's face as she opened the vial and read the small scroll that had been rolled up inside.

"Rallie, what does it say?" Visyna asked.

Rallie turned to look at the Prince. She pulled back the hood of her cloak. Tears glistened in her eyes. "It is with deepest regrets that I must inform you that Her Majesty, the Queen of Calahr, is dead."

THIRTY-THREE

Konowa willed himself to remain calm. The death of the Queen was tragic. He'd met the old girl once and been impressed with the sharp intelligence peering out from a fat, soft face. Would the Prince blubber and go hide in his cabin? Perhaps he'd put on a brave front, or worse, express happiness that he was finally King. After his inconsolable pout brought on by the destruction of the Lost Library of Kaman Rahl, would this be the final straw to break his royal back, or maybe, just maybe, turn him into a man.

Sympathy tempered Konowa's anger while he waited. The Prince had lost his father years before, and now his mother. As strange as his parents were, Konowa found comfort in knowing both were still alive. He didn't want to think about the hole they would leave when they were gone.

A muffled sob made Konowa turn. Pimmer stood with his mouth open, his eyes wide with shock. Visyna went over to him and helped him to sit down on a nearby crate. The man was absolutely undone. Konowa's respect for him lessened a little, and he felt bad about that, but what kind of diplomat went to pieces like that?

"Pimmer, I am so sorry," the Prince said softly, with far more caring than Konowa could muster. And why was he apologizing to him?

A cluster of soldiers and sailors had formed around them. When they saw Konowa looking at them they started to leave, but he motioned for them to stay.

"Does it say how she died?" the Prince asked, his voice calm, and giving nothing away.

Rallie paused before answering. "She was murdered. An agent of the Shadow Monarch." She wiped the tears from her eyes and put a cigar in her mouth, which instantly lit. She took two draws on the stogie before continuing, her next words mixed with a thick cloud of smoke. "The message goes on to request His Highness's immediate return to Celwyn for the Queen's funeral and for his coronation as the king of the Calahrian Empire."

At this she paused, and Konowa assumed it was emotion. When she resumed, he realized it was more likely shock.

"However, due to the current unrest sweeping the Empire and the encroachment by creatures of the Shadow Monarch into Calahr itself it is advised that His Highness does not attempt to return at this time. His safety, and that of the royal court and the very citizenry itself, can no longer be guaranteed."

Konowa couldn't believe his ears. By the gasp of surprise by those around, neither could anyone else.

Rallie continued. "Dark creatures now run rampant

in the countryside. Citizens from small villages and farms have fled and are now harboring in the larger cities. The risk of plague has now been added to our woes."

The Prince waved her to silence. "It is as we feared, and why so many of you have counseled for sailing directly to the Hyntaland and the Shadow Monarch's mountain. In light of this news, I concur. We must—"

"No!" Pimmer shouted, jumping to his feet and crossing the deck to stand in front of the Prince. "You must return. You must take up the crown."

If events turned any faster Konowa was going to have to sit down. "Viceroy," he said, walking forward, "you know why we *must* go to Her mountain. I understand you're upset, but—"

"No, you don't," Pimmer said, never breaking his gaze at the Prince. "If there is no King, the Empire won't simply crumble, it will explode in an orgy of rebellion and war. Do you have any idea how many different races and tribes are kept from each other's throats by the presence of Imperial forces? Do you know why just a few thousand siggers in their green coats can pacify a nation of hundreds of thousands? It's because of the symbol. The power of the throne. As long as it's strong, it exerts enormous influence. But leave it vacant and chaos will reign."

"Pimmer," the Prince said, reaching out and grabbing him by the arm. "I know you're hurting. I am, too, but if this is about—"

Pimmer yanked his arm away. "This is not about that! This hasn't been about that in a very long time. I never wanted the throne. We agreed on this."

Konowa had been to the theater where the twists

and turns hadn't been this convoluted. Was Pimmer admitting to being the real heir? It struck him how much the Queen and Pimmer looked alike. There was that same twinkle of smarts carefully hidden by a heavy exterior . . .

Son of a witch.

"Viceroy, perhaps we can continue this conversation in private," Rallie said.

Of course Rallie would know, Konowa realized. She had been Her Majesty's Scribe for decades.

"There is no private anymore," Pimmer said, looking around him. "The fate of our very existence balances on this fulcrum in time."

"Told you," Yimt said from somewhere in the crowd. "The full crumb."

Pimmer rounded on Prince Tykkin. "This is about your destiny, your duty. If you do not take the throne, it won't simply be the Empire that falls, but all living things in it. Is that the legacy you want?"

"And if we do not destroy the Shadow Monarch what then?" Konowa asked, unable to contain himself. "You told me yourself it was the right thing to do," he said, knowing he was betraying the man's trust and not caring.

"It was, but now it isn't."

The Prince raised his hand for silence. Konowa bit back his next retort and waited.

"Events continue to move faster than we anticipate. We have suffered the most unfortunate luck to lose the wrong monarch. Therefore, I have no choice but to set sail for Celwyn and to assume the crown." He turned and stared at Konowa, forcing him to remain silent. It was as if the man had suddenly grown. He seemed bigger, stronger.

"We've had our differences, you and I. I doubt there's any other officer in this army or any other who exhibits such constant and repeated insubordination. Your attitude toward authority is deplorable."

If there was a compliment in the offing the Prince was taking a long road to get there. Konowa opened his mouth to speak, but he felt three pairs of eyes on him and shut it again. He chose to believe he did it through his own willpower, and not the combined force of the three women a few feet away.

"Furthermore, you are reckless and have a short temper. It's quite astonishing you've only been court-martialed once."

Konowa felt the first flicker of frost fire dance in his clenched fists, but with a restraint that was causing the blood to pound in his ears he remained silent.

"I could go on, but time is short, and I think I've made my point," the Prince said. He pulled down on the hem of his coat and jutted out his chin. "It is therefore my great privilege and honor to hereby hand over command of the Iron Elves to you. Congratulations, Colonel Swift Dragon."

Murmurs of pleasure broke out all over the deck. A nearby cannonade fired by another ship seemed perfectly timed to echo in martial salute. A few even shouted "Long live the King," threatening to turn a solemn moment into something else. The Prince held up his hands and things quieted down.

The Prince turned to take in the growing crowd. "Ladies and gentlemen, we are witness to a truly rare occasion. Colonel Swift Dragon has been rendered all but speechless."

Konowa found his voice. "I thank you for this

honor, Your Highness, but it has little meaning if we are still going to Celwyn and not the Hyntaland."

"Glad to see your rise in rank hasn't changed you," the Prince said, a slight mocking tone in his voice. "Of course, you are right. *If* you were accompanying me to Celwyn."

Now Konowa dared hope. "I'm not?"

The Prince smiled. "My duty is clear, as Viceroy Alstonfar pointed out. I must return to the capital and assume the throne. The Empire must be defended. If Calahr falls, all falls. Your duty, and that of the Iron Elves, is equally clear. The Shadow Monarch must be destroyed. I place this vessel under your command. Make all haste to your homeland and use whatever means necessary to dethrone the Shadow Monarch."

Konowa stood to full attention and saluted. "Yes, sir!"

The Prince looked at him, a bemused expression on his face. And then he did the most startling thing. He held out his hand.

Konowa looked down at it. "Sir? The oath, the frost fire."

"King's prerogative."

Konowa smiled and grabbed the man's hand. Frost fire crackled between their palms. The Prince winced, but squeezed tighter. He leaned forward and whispered in Konowa's ear, "If we should never meet again, I still think you're a scoundrel and a disgrace . . . and I'm honored to have served with you. Thank you."

"We will meet again," Konowa said, squeezing just a bit harder. "And you're arrogant and vain and it will be my great privilege to one day greet you as His Majesty, the King."

They stepped back and released their grip. This time the surrounding soldiers and sailors did cheer.

"Very well, it is time we parted ways. I leave you to your task, may fortune favor you."

"And you, sir," Konowa said, saluting again.

The Prince returned his salute. He turned and addressed Viceroy Alstonfar.

"Unfortunately, it would appear the Hasshugeb Expanse is no longer part of the Calahrian Empire, which means your viceroyship is at an end."

"That is a correct interpretation of the political situation," Pimmer said. He stood calmly, one hand resting on the pommel of his saber, the other on the butt of a pistol stuck into his belt. Konowa smiled. In the short time he'd known him, Pimmer had gone from bureaucrat to warrior. Give the man a few months in the field with the right instruction and he'd be an excellent leader.

"As king, I will be choosing my advisors. I would like my first chosen counsel to be you."

Pimmer nodded his head. "That is a wonderful offer, and some day I look forward to accepting it, but with the king's permission, I would like to enlist in the Calahrian Army."

The ship grew silent. The Prince leaned forward a little. "Pimmer, everyone knows of your bravery. You impressed a lot of people, myself included. You have nothing to prove. Come back with me, help me in Celwyn."

"I will, Your Majesty, in time. Right now, however, the most pressing need lies to the north, and with your permission, I will accompany the Iron Elves."

"Not as viceroy you can't," Konowa said, interjecting himself into the conversation. "I'm sorry, but we only have room for soldiers." He looked at the Prince and winked.

"Quite," the Prince said. "Very well. Viceroy

Pimrald Alstonfar, I hereby strip you of your title and standing in the Calahrian Diplomatic Corps and induct you into the Calahrian Army with the rank of Major, second-in-command of the Iron Elves regiment."

A week ago there would have been a riot. Now, there were cheers. Major Pimrald Alstonfar smiled and saluted, knocking his shako clean off his head.

"He's all yours, Colonel," the Prince said. He then turned and motioned to Rallie. "As you were Her Majesty's Scribe your services now belong to me," the Prince said.

Konowa expected some sort of comment from Rallie, but she simply bowed her head in acceptance.

"Which is why," the Prince continued, "I am ordering you to accompany Colonel Swift Dragon and the Iron Elves to the Hyntaland. I'll be as eager as the rest of your readers to hear how events unfold, and their forthcoming victory in the battle against darkness."

This time the cheers were raucous. It never ceased to amaze Konowa how fatalistic and cheery a soldier could be at the same time. Still, he felt it, too. They'd all suffered and lost so much because of Her. Revenge, even if it appeared suicidal, appealed to them.

He risked a glance over at Visyna, hoping desperately not to see her frowning. Her smile put a grin on his face. Not giving a damn about decorum, he walked over to her and kissed her as sparks flew.

He pulled back after a moment, his lips and tongue tingling. Soldiers started crowding around and she and Rallie and his mother disappeared from view.

Konowa stood still for a moment, taking it all in. *I have the Iron Elves back.* The fact that they numbered just a handful and none were from the original regiment mattered not at all. As the soldiers clustered around him to offer their congratulations, Konowa smiled and shook as many hands as were offered. Young Corporal Feylan, the nautical lad; hulking, salt-of-the-earth Private Hrem Vulhber; rock-steady Color Sergeant Salia Aguom; the childlike but determined Private Scolfelton; and the irrepressible Regimental Sergeant Major Yimt Arkhorn. He looked into their eyes and was proud of what he saw. They were dirty, tired, hungry, and scared, but they were Iron Elves. These were his men, his brothers. A pain unassociated with the black acorn lingered in his heart as he thought of the others he'd lost. His smile faltered for a moment as he searched and failed to find the faces of so, so many.

He took a deep breath and let it out slowly. Their numbers had been steadily whittled away. Months of hard living and even harder fighting had taken its toll on those that still remained. The scars, whether physical or somewhere deep inside, would probably never heal, not entirely. Their Empire was falling apart at the seams, and victory looked less and less likely the closer they got to Her mountain. But for all that, they had each other.

Konowa grinned, and started to laugh. His soldiers laughed with him. From somewhere in the small crowd, a soldier's voice rose up above the din, and his words were taken up by every Iron Elf present:

We do not fear the flame, though it burns us,
We do not fear the fire, though it consumes us,
And we do not fear its light,
Though it reveals the darkness of our souls,
For therein lies our power.
Æri Mekah!

THIRTY-FOUR

Visyna stood on the harbor side of the ship with her forearms resting on the railing. The wind in her hair felt good, as did being on the ship and knowing they were leaving this place. She waved as the Prince, escorted by a company of troops, walked across the pier to board the HMS *Ormandy* to take him back to Calahr. He never broke stride, but he did doff his shako in response.

"Our future king," Konowa said, walking up to stand beside her at the railing. She felt the sudden urge to slide closer and have him wrap his arms around her, but the frost fire made it too difficult.

"A future king," she said, turning to him. "I wish him well, but the time of his Empire is over. My country is free."

Konowa held up his hands. "You're right, I'm sorry. Old habits."

"Speaking of old habits, can't you get rid of that acorn? You did before in Elfkyna," she said, watching his face carefully.

He smiled, removed his shako and placed it between his thighs, and reached into his jacket and pulled the leather thong up over his head. He then placed it inside his shako and set it on the deck of the ship. "Give me your hand," he said, holding out his.

She did, and immediately withdrew it when black frost arced between their fingertips. "I don't understand, you removed the acorn."

His smile remained, but she saw the sadness in it now. He unbuttoned the top four buttons of his jacket and pulled back the lapels while pulling down on his undershirt. A black, acorn-sized stain marked the skin above his heart. "It's in me. The only way I break this oath and Her hold is to destroy Her." He placed the acorn back around his neck.

"Then we need to be going," she said, standing up straight and stepping away from the railing. "She's come between us long enough. One monarch's reign has ended, now it's time the other's does, too."

"Have I told you how attractive you are when you're feisty?" Konowa asked, moving to stand as close to her as he could without touching her.

"No, and I expect that to change," she said, breathing deeply to take in as much of his scent as possible. She wet her lips. "Bellowing orders like a mad bull might work in the army, but as my elf you'll need to learn more subtle techniques to get what you want."

Konowa looked at her with a hunger she longed to feed. She knew it matched her own.

He leaned forward and brought his lips to the very edge of her ear. His breath on her skin made her entire body shiver. "Are you saying you want to tame me?"

"Not . . . not when we're alone," she said, her voice husky with desire.

He started to whisper something else when there was a loud thump and the ship rocked. She stepped back and looked around. "What was that?"

Konowa had his hand on his chest and his eyes closed. "Nothing good."

The water in the harbor began to churn, but the wind hadn't picked up. "You're the only weather weaver I know. Can you tell what this is?" he asked. Men were running around the deck of the ship shouting. Iron Elves appeared along the railings with their muskets at the ready. From belowdecks the ship's gun crews were yelling and hurriedly reloading their cannons.

"If I could weave I might have an idea, but I've exhausted myself. I'm sorry," she said.

He moved forward and smiled at her. "You've nothing to apologize for. I heard what you did. Everything from when you, my mother, and Rallie took off in her wagon from the party in Nazalla until we met at the fort. You didn't just survive, you saved a lot of lives."

She returned his smile. "I guess I've picked up a few things from watching you."

The ship rocked again from another unseen blow. "All right, that's got to stop," Konowa said, his hand drawing his saber halfway out of its scabbard. "Can anyone see anything?"

The answer came in two parts. Ice began to form on the water although the temperature above it hadn't dropped. Moments later, long, black branches shot up from the water on the seaward side of the ship and clawed up the side of HMS *Black Spike*, tilting the ship to starboard.

Pandemonium broke out on deck. Soldiers fired their muskets wildly at any branch they could see. Musket balls whizzed and ricocheted but did little damage. "Hold your fire, hold your fire, you daft buggers!" Yimt yelled. A few more muskets fired before order was restored. The ship rocked as more branches snaked up the side and latched on.

"They're underneath us," Visyna said, looking down at her feet. She could accept horrors that came at her in the open, but something about an unseen enemy beneath her was chilling. She stepped away from the railing.

Konowa turned to look at her. "And you wonder why I hate trees?"

Rallie and Chayii appeared on deck with Jurwan between them. The elf wizard was still not talking, but his eyes followed events with an obvious interest and it seemed he was close to returning to normal. Visyna hoped so.

"If you've got any more tricks up your sleeves, now's the time," Konowa said to the women. He walked over to his father and peered into his eyes. "We could really use your help, Father."

The ship lurched and mooring lines snapped.

"They're trying to pull us away from the dock," Visyna said, stumbling back toward the railing. She caught herself and looked down into the water. It was black and frothing, like boiling oil. She pushed herself upright and caught movement on the dock.

"It's Jir and Tyul!"

She turned to point, but only Chayii heard her. The elf ran over to stand beside her.

A thunderous broadside fired from the *Ormandy*

across the way shook the night. Both of them jumped. Wooden buildings near the dock exploded in a shower of splinters. Jir and Tyul went to ground, but were immediately back up and running for the ship. Rakkes cut them off and a melee began. The elf was a blur of slashing precision while the bengar tore through the creatures with savage efficiency.

But it wouldn't be enough. There were too many rakkes. More and more joined the horde surrounding the two. The rakkes finally had a chance to bring down two of their tormentors and they weren't going to let them get away.

"Don't shoot!" Chayii yelled, waving in a vain attempt to get the attention of the Prince's ship.

"It's their only hope," Visyna said, doubting even that could save them. She could only see Jir and Tyul sporadically now as still more rakkes streamed through the smoldering ruins of the buildings and toward the dock.

The ship rocked again and the brittle, caustic tang of frost fire filled the air. She turned and saw Konowa with his saber drawn, slashing at branches while Rallie drew furiously on a sheaf of papers. Jurwan stood between them, watching, but not helping.

When she turned back, Chayii was gone. Visyna looked over the railing and saw the elf walking effortlessly down one of the mooring lines to land on the dock and start running toward Tyul and Jir. Rakkes filled the space between and musket fire from the *Ormandy* lashed the dockside.

"Chayii, come back!"

The elf never turned, but kept running. Half a dozen rakkes closed in on her in a converging arc. The ship rose several feet in the air then fell back, sending up an icy spray that coated everything. Visyna lost her footing and started to fall as the ship tilted further to port. The deck shook as cannons tore loose from their stations and slid free. Screams and shouts and the groaning and splintering of wood mixed with the howl of rakkes and sharp crack of muskets.

Making up her mind while still falling, Visyna let her body go limp and slid through a gap in the railing. She grabbed a mooring line and slid down it, burning her hands red in the process. Once on the dock she ran after Chayii, still not knowing what she was going to do. She felt as a hollow as a reed. Her body was running on reserves she'd never tapped before.

Shouts rang out behind her as men noticed the two women running on the dock. *So this is what it's like for Konowa*, she thought, pumping her arms as her legs carried her across the open space. No plan, just absolute exhilaration.

She reached Chayii as the rakkes closed in to five yards. Reaching down, she picked up a broken piece of barrel stave to use as a weapon. The downside of Konowa's approach to things became rapidly clear.

"What are you doing out here?" she shouted at Chayii, moving closer until they were back to back as the rakke's circled them.

"I could not leave Tyul or Jir out here alone. They are innocents. They follow where we lead. It is our duty to protect them," she said.

Visyna suddenly understood Konowa's frustration with the elves of the Long Watch. They really did think in the most altruistic terms, even to the point of risking certain death. And she had run out to join her!

"Chayii, Jir and Tyul are two born killers! We need *their* help," she said, swinging her broken stave in front of her, knowing it would do little to slow down a charging rakke. She thought about yelling back to the ship, but more branches had shot up from the water to grapple it while other ships were firing their cannons, making it impossible to hear in the rising storm of noise.

"I did not come out here without a plan, child," Chayii said. Her voice was surprisingly calm.

"Well then do it!"

Chayii turned and placed a hand on Visyna's shoulder. "Tell my son . . . that I would have enjoyed spoiling your grandchildren very much."

Before Visyna could reply Chayii turned and raised her hands to the sky. She began chanting in elvish and immediately the world around Visyna changed. Deep, powerful voices from somewhere far away filled the air. She recalled hearing and feeling something like this before, when Tyul had used his oath weapon, but this was different. Something else added its power to the heavy thrum, something close.

"What are you doing?" she asked, aware that the fabric of the natural order around her was beginning to tear.

The old elf continued to chant, ignoring her. Rakkes howled and bared their fangs, but none dared come closer. It began growing lighter. At first, Visyna couldn't place the source, but then realized the main mast of the *Black Spike* was glowing. She blinked and looked again. For just the briefest of moments she could have sworn a massive tree had stood where the mast was.

"Chayii?"

"I do what I must, child," she said, her voice filled with something Visyna thought sounded like joy. "We are the stewards of this world. If, through our sacrifice, we can save it, then it is a small price to pay."

Visyna's objection was blown away in a burst of pure, golden light. She turned and marveled at what she saw. The mast of the *Black Spike*, once the very trunk of Jurwan's *ryk faur* from which the ship was named, dissolved into a million gleaming specs of energy. They swirled as if caught in a wind only they could feel before coalescing into the shape of a shimmering, translucent Wolf Oak standing proudly on the deck of the ship.

The leaves of Black Spike began to fall, twirling and spinning faster and faster. A glowing white acorn was attached to each leaf.

"Your time here is over," Chayii said to the rakkes. "Be one again with the *mukta ull*." A gibbering wail rose up from the rakkes. Visyna turned in time to see Chayii's hands spread open. The next moment a wind blew over her from behind, knocking her to the ground. The leaves and their acorns flashed above her in brilliant streaks of light. Each leaf and acorn struck a rakke with the force of a cannon ball, cutting off the howls of fear.

The rakkes died where they stood. One moment they were there in all their primal fury, the next, there was a burst of light, and then for the briefest of moments, the ghostly afterimage of a Wolf Oak sapling.

Before she could get up, the wind reversed direction and blew out to sea. She heard Jir yelp in fear and looked up to see the bengar and Tyul tumbling helplessly in the grip of the wind, borne aloft on still more of the shimmering leaves. It carried them all the way to the *Black Spike* and dumped them onto the deck, Tyul landing lightly on his feet and Jir on all four paws.

The ship heaved and rose high on a roiling wave of water. The *sarka har* clawing at the *Black Spike*'s hull tore and shattered. The wind howled and the heavy ropes mooring the ship to the dock snapped like thread. The *Black Spike* began drifting out into the harbor, picking up speed as it moved. The massive image of Jurwan's Wolf Oak was bent by the wind, acting as a main sail.

"Konowa!" She reached out her hands, determined to weave the weather and battle the forces taking him away from her again, but already she knew her strength wasn't up to the task. She watched silently as the ship disappeared into the night and was gone.

It was several moments before Visyna realized everything had gone quiet. Not a single rakke howled. No shouting, no screaming, no muskets firing. She sat up. Darkness had returned. She rubbed her eyes and turned to Chayii.

"Oh, Chayii." The elf lay facedown on the dock. Visyna grabbed her shoulder and gently turned her over. She felt it as soon as she touched her body.

Chayii was dead.

She sensed a presence near her and looked up. A misty image of a forest played before her eyes. It was gone so fast she wasn't sure if it was real or her imagination. She chose to believe its truth; Chayii walking among the trees, singing softly as she tended to the forest.

She blinked and turned away, staring out to sea. She gently let Chayii's body down and got up, and walked to the dock's edge. Splintered wood, torn ropes, and great chunks of sailcloth littered the dockside and floated on the ice on the water, as the only indication that the *Black Spike* had been moored there. A large, churned path through the ice marked its passage out to sea.

The sound of running feet made her turn. Several soldiers from the *Ormandy* approached, their muskets held at the ready as they looked about for rakkes. A sergeant came up to her and touched his hand to his shako. He was bleeding from a cut above his left eye, but he didn't seem to notice.

"More rakkes on the way, ma'am. His Highness says for you to board the *Ormandy*."

Visyna nodded numbly and allowed herself to be lead toward the ship. She saw two soldiers move to pick up Chayii's body, then pause and look at her.

"Please" was all she could manage. The soldiers bent down and with surprising gentleness picked up the elf and began to carry her to the ship.

Visyna followed them and boarded the *Ormandy* without another look back. She crossed the deck and stood at the starboard railing looking out to sea. The cold, salty air changed something inside her and she stood taller as she gripped the railing, feeling the rough grain of the wood on her palms.

"I will find you, Konowa Swift Dragon, I will find you."

THIRTY-FIVE

D amn it, Father, snap out of it!" Konowa
shouted, turning and stomping away
a few paces before spinning on a heel
and marching back toward Jurwan. The
deck of the *Black Spike* was a windswept mess, which
made Konowa's pacing all the more challenging. There
was no main mast anymore. In its place was a tangle of
sail, spars, and rigging and the impossible image of his
father's shimmering *ryk faur*.

The ship should have been crawling along, but instead it was driven by a wind that seemed solely focused
on the tree that was and wasn't there. It was pushing
them north at a speed no hurricane could ever match.
The ship creaked and groaned with the strain. Konowa
heard the captain ordering his sailors to bring down all
but the smallest of sails, but it made no difference he
could see. The *Black Spike* was being driven by something
none of them understood.

Except Jurwan.

Konowa approached his father again. "Please, Father,

we need you. Mother . . . mother is dead." Saying it out loud hurt more than simply knowing it in his heart, but he had to get through to his father.

"Colonel," Major Alstonfar said quietly, coming up to stand beside him. "Could we talk over here, please?"

Konowa glared at his father, who simply looked straight ahead as if nothing out of the ordinary was happening. "I liked you better as a squirrel," Konowa muttered, then turned away and followed Pimmer until they were out of the wind behind a pile of collapsed sail.

"I understand your frustration and concern over our situation, but telling your father your mother is dead is a bit extreme, don't you think?"

Konowa looked at the man and realized he didn't know. "She's dead. She gave her life to tap into whatever energy or life force was left in my father's *ryk faur*. I've never seen it done before, but I've heard them talk about it. It's the ultimate sacrifice for an elf of the Long Watch." Bitterness swelled within his chest, but he fought against it. Her sacrifice hadn't been for trees or plants or the bloody natural order. She'd saved flesh and blood. He was desperately proud and devastated at the same time.

"My mother . . . gave her life for us. Many of the Long Watch have given their lives to save the trees they bonded with. It's why we're in this mess now. The Shadow Monarch poured all her misguided compassion into the Silver Wolf Oak and look where it got us."

Pimmer looked stunned. "She's really dead? I am so sorry. I thought . . . I thought you were trying to shock your father into talking."

"I am, but not even the death of his wife seems to

be enough," Konowa said, forcing himself not to dwell on what he'd just lost. His mother was gone, and Visyna and Jir were back there and he had no idea if they were alive or dead.

"Her act was truly courageous. She saved us from certain death," he said. "I am sure the *Ormandy* and all her crew are fine."

"The Prince," Konowa said, suddenly remembering. "If he didn't survive that would mean you—"

"No," Pimmer said, cutting Konowa off. "The Prince survived, I am certain. He will take the throne."

Konowa wanted to object, but there seemed little point. Whether Tykkin was dead or alive was no longer in their hands. They were headed to the Hyntaland. The state of the Empire would have to take a backseat to the coming showdown with the Shadow Monarch.

"Major, gather up all sergeants and corporals and meet me in my cabin in five minutes. Oh, and find Private Vulhber, tell him he's a corporal now. We have a battle to plan and judging the speed of our travel, we don't have much time to get it sorted out."

"Very good, sir," he said. "Ah, and Her, ahem, His Majesty's Scribe?"

Konowa looked up at the night sky as gray clouds whipped past before looking back at Pimmer. "She's already RSVP'd," Konowa said, pointing behind the man to Rallie, who was already walking toward Konowa's cabin.

"Indeed," Pimmer said, turning. He saluted and quickly walked off to assemble the senior staff, such as it was.

Konowa stepped back out into the wind and let the salty air sting his face. It hurt, and he liked that. It made him angry, and anger gave him power. He felt the fire burning inside him and let the flames build. When he reached Her mountain, a forest was going to burn.

Konowa looked back at his father. Did he know his wife was dead? He started to walk toward him again and paused as the wind shifted. It took him a moment to realize it hadn't been the wind, but the direction of the *Black Spike* itself. The ship was tacking to port, and heading west.

Konowa walked toward the bridge to speak to Captain Milceal Ervod, but the sailor was already walking toward him.

"We've changed direction," Konowa said.

Ervod motioned for Konowa to duck into a passageway. Once inside, Ervod pulled a map from inside his tunic and held it up against the wall. "Near as I can reckon, we're here, just north of the Timolia Islands," he said, pointing to a patch of blue ocean.

Konowa leaned closer. "Are you certain? We only left Tel Martruk a few hours ago."

Ervod pulled at the end of his nose in a nervous gesture. "By rights, we should still see the lights of the harbor, but we aren't traveling by any wind I know."

Konowa wondered if there was a subtle accusation there, but he really didn't care. His mother's sacrifice was propelling them to the Hyntaland, or at least, it had been. "What lies to the west of us?"

Ervod unfolded more of the map. "Assuming I'm right and we are north of the Timolians, then a westerly course will take us through the Xephril Straits. Two major rivers empty into the straits, the Kantanna and the Ottawota, which merge into the Greater Kantanna further inland."

Konowa knew the river. Its headwater was the Shadow Monarch's mountain in the Hyntaland. "Is the river deep enough to take us all the way to the mountain?"

Ervod shrugged. "The Imperial Navy has only charted the tributary openings in Rewland along the coast. It's my understanding that the agreement reached with your . . . the agreement reached with the elves denied the navy access further north."

"That doesn't surprise me," Konowa said. "When the elves of the Long Watch see a sailing ship like this they see mass murder."

Ervod went pale. "Colonel!"

"They do make exceptions, and in the case of our current mission I don't think they'll mind. In fact, I don't care if they do. If this wind takes us up the river and saves us having to march the whole way, I'm all for it."

"You mean, we might end up in the middle of a battle on a river?"

Konowa shrugged. "It would seem anything is possible these days."

Major Alstonfar appeared in the hatchway. "Ah, here you are, Colonel. Captain. The men and Miss Synjyn have assembled."

Konowa went to pat Ervod on the back then thought better of it. The man was jumpy enough. "If our course changes again, let me know. Otherwise, assume we're going upriver and plan accordingly." He plucked the map from the captain's hands and followed Pimmer back out and across the deck.

He started to head into the passageway to his cabin when he heard something. It was so distant, so quiet, that he wasn't sure it was there at all. He was about to brush it off when he heard it again.

"Colonel?" Pimmer said.

"Do you hear that?"

"What? All I can hear is the wind and the ship," he said.

Konowa shook his head. "No, something else." He strained to hear it again and this time picked up something. It was coming from the direction of his father. "Go on ahead. I'll be there in a few minutes." Without waiting for a reply, he walked toward his father, who he realized had been facing in the direction they were now headed before the ship changed course. As he got closer, he heard the sound again. It was . . . droning, or maybe chanting. He walked up to his father and looked closely at his face. His eyes were closed, but his lips were moving. Konowa leaned in. The chanting wasn't coming from his father, but his lips were moving in perfect time with it. Either Jurwan heard it, too, or he was somehow controlling it.

Konowa looked up where the main mast used to be. He'd assumed everything that had happened on the dock until now had been his mother's doing. Tyul, crazy bloody elf that he was, had climbed the shimmering tree and was sitting in one of its top branches, rocking back and forth. How he got there let alone stayed there defied more than Konowa was prepared to consider. Tyul's bond with his Silver Wolf Oak must be playing a part. Konowa shook his head and looked back at his father and found himself staring into his open eyes.

"I know she is dead, and I will grieve in time," Jurwan said.

Konowa jumped backward, almost falling on the deck. "Damn it, Father! You could scare an elf out of his skin like that! How long have you been back?"

Jurwan sighed and rolled his shoulders as if just waking up. "I was never away, I just wasn't here."

Konowa groaned. "I forgot how fun it is to talk with you." He started to reach out to hug the elf, then remembered and stopped. "I missed you."

Jurwan reached forward and wrapped his arms around him, squeezing him tight. Konowa was too surprised to react at first, but when he did he hugged him back. No frost fire sparked between them. When Jurwan let go there were tears in his eyes. "I am sorry about your mother. She was always strong-willed. You two are so much alike."

It was the first time Konowa had ever heard his father say that. Before today he would have laughed to hear the comparison, but now, it touched him so deeply he thought he might start crying himself. He coughed and pointed at his father. "There was no frost fire."

"I carried the black acorn with me for some time, time enough for quite a bit of Her poison to rub off on me," he said.

"Are you okay?" Konowa asked.

Jurwan brought a hand up to his cheek as if to stroke some whiskers, but then brushed some hair from his eyes. "As water is in rain or mud."

"I'll take that as close enough," Konowa said. He motioned to the sea around them. "Is this you? Are you the one driving us?"

For an answer, Jurwan walked toward the area where the main mast used to be. Konowa followed.

"It's the deep forest that calls us home. I am merely helping to guide us by the safest path. The Wolf Oaks are powerful, but they have little concept of travel. They would pull us straight across the land to Her mountain, so I am gently steering us to a more advantageous route."

"The river," Konowa said.

"Yes. I thought it the wiser course. It will take a little longer, but we will arrive in one piece."

"I didn't know they could do that," Konowa said, realizing just how much of his own culture he was ignorant of.

"There's much they can do, but little they've done, until now. They sense the danger."

"About bloody time," Konowa said. "Any chance they've got some other tricks up their sleeves, er, trunks, we might use?" he asked half-jokingly.

Jurwan sat down on the deck and faced the wind. He closed his eyes and placed his hands in his lap. "I will ask."

Konowa stared openmouthed at his father for a moment then decided he'd leave him to it. "Tell them . . . thanks," he said.

"They say you're welcome," Jurwan said. Konowa looked closely and saw the tiniest smirk on his father's face. He shook his head and left his father to commune with nature as he walked back toward his cabin. A flapping noise caught his attention and he turned in time to duck as Wobbly launched himself into the wind just over Konowa's head. The pelican strained to get airborne, its huge wings flapping madly as it careened off some rigging and took a dangerous turn over the railing and down toward the water. Konowa ran over to the side and peered down, almost throwing up in the process. The sight of the rushing water made his knees buckle. He looked up and saw Wobbly slowly gaining height and heading due north before he started to tack east and kept turning until he flew right back over the *Black Spike* heading south. Konowa watched him until he disappeared from sight, said a silent wish for good luck for the bird, and walked to his cabin. He found the assembled group dispiritingly small, but he trusted every one of them with his life and that made up for a lot.

As he looked at each person in the room, he realized they were more than fellow soldiers and travelers. This really was his family. It was an odd thought, and far too sentimental for what they were about to face and what he would ask of them, but it was the truth.

He opened up the map and gave a corner each to Corporal Feylan and Corporal Vulhber to hold. The big man smiled and Konowa nodded back. He let out a breath and took off his shako, tossing it to Color Sergeant Aguom, who deftly caught it and tucked it under his arm. Konowa turned to the map and pointed to the Greater Kantanna River.

"This time tomorrow, we'll be at the foot of Her mountain. So, here's what I'm thinking . . ."

Konowa slept little as the *Black Spike* churned its way through the Xephril Straits. He doubted he'd ever become used to the unnatural speed and the constant protest of wood and sail from the ship, but that wasn't what made his sleep fitful. Nor was it the sound of soldiers and sailors hammering, sawing, and shouting as they worked to transform the *Black Spike* for what would most likely be a one-way trip up the river. It was, as it so often was, a bloody dream.

The scene remained unchanged. There was the birthing meadow, the Shadow Monarch's Silver Wolf Oak, and a figure that he thought was Her, but now knew was himself. And as before, he held an ax in his hands. A voice told him repeatedly to do it, to swing the ax. He tried to make sense of what it really meant. The figure kneeling by the Wolf Oak turned, and this time it was the Shadow Monarch.

"Now I understand," he said, hefting the ax in preparation to kill Her. He paused. She looked old and frail. A frightened little elf. *Damn it!* The ax started to fall to his side, but then the voice started up again, louder, more insistent. He shook his head. *It was a trick.* She might be old, but she wasn't as she appeared before him. She was the Shadow Monarch, and Her power was untold. This was a test. If he couldn't swing the ax in his dream, how the hell could he do it when the time came? He gritted his teeth and swung with all his might, taking the Shadow Monarch's head clean off.

Konowa woke in a sweat. He sat up and brushed the hair from his face, noticing that his hands were trembling. He should have felt relief, or accomplishment, or even righteous joy at killing Her, even if in a dream, but nothing about it felt right. His conversation with Rallie on her wagon came back to him, but what would compassion get him when he faced Her?

A knock on his cabin door brought him welcome relief from his thoughts.

"Yes?"

"Begging the colonel's pardon, but the captain wanted you to know we've changed course and are now heading due north up the Kantanna River."

"Excellent!" Konowa shouted. He got out of bed,

realizing he'd fallen asleep while still fully dressed, grabbed his saber and shako, and went outside.

The deck of the *Black Spike* was transformed. Gone were the clean, smooth lines of a sailing ship. It looked more like a floating castle now, all bulk and angles. Oak planking from belowdecks had been braced along the railings, backed up with slugs of pig iron from the ship's ballast, and then sandwiched in with barrels filled with everything from salted pork to what appeared to be beer and rum. The effect was to create a thick, protective wall for those on deck. More impressive were the additional cannons winched up from below to be placed on the bow. It would have been suicidal to sail like that in open waters, but under their current propulsion and within the confines of a river it was a risk they'd decided to take. They were ridiculously top heavy, but woe be to whoever came close enough to try and tip them over.

RSM Arkhorn walked past barking orders to a group of sailors trailing him in various states of fear and awe. When he spied Konowa he winked and shooed the sailors on their way. "Not the brightest of lads, but they're learning."

Konowa smiled and began to walk along the deck as Yimt described the modifications. They stopped at a gap and Konowa ventured out to the railing and looked over the side.

"You've put chunks of oak planks over several of the cannon mouths," he said, stepping back again quickly as his stomach started to churn.

Yimt greeted his observation with a smile that didn't bode well for any creatures coming too close the *Black Spike*. Konowa briefly wondered how many had perished with Yimt's pewter-colored teeth the last image in their eyes? *Better them than him.*

"Noticed that, did you, sir? Well, it's a bit nasty I'll admit, but can't say as the buggers don't deserve it and then some. If you look real close, I had the boys score the wood to help it splinter easier, and a few of the planks have a little extra surprise in them."

He sounded so proud that Konowa had no choice but to go back to the railing and look over the side again. "Are those nails?" He peered a little closer and saw a piece of chain dangling. He followed it and saw it attached to several more planks further down the ship. "Are you sure you wouldn't be better employed in weapons manufacture instead of as a barrister?" Konowa asked, stepping away from the railing again.

"Same basic principles apply really," Yimt said. "You got to hit the buggers hard with everything you got before they hit you."

"I'm not sure that's *exactly* how it works," he said, then left the rest of his thought hanging as he spied Yimt's old squad a few yards away. He walked over to the newly minted Corporal Vulhber and shook the man's hand, congratulating him on his promotion. Privates Scolly and Zwitty stood nearby. Konowa's first thought was they'd already dipped into the rum. "Someone has to explain this to me."

Corporal Vulhber looked at him and smiled. "Colonel. Well, it was the RSM's idea and we figured why not." The look on Zwitty's face suggested he'd figured differently, but he kept his mouth shut.

"You appear to be dressed as trees," Konowa said. And not just trees, but *sarka har*. Each soldier had the metallic-impregnated bark of a *sarka har*, no doubt from all the pieces that had fallen on deck when they'd been ripped free back at Tel Martuk, wrapped around his arms, legs, and torso like a knight's armor. Twine and strips of sailcloth that appeared to have been darkened with pitch held everything in place.

"They don't have ribs like a dwarf," Yimt said, knocking his knuckles against his chest. "After my recent experience, I got to thinking it'd be just the thing for the lad going into battle. If we had more time I think I could come up with some kind of helmet, too."

Konowa walked over and rapped his knuckles against Vulhber's bark plate. Small sparks flew. "It is tough," he said, standing back. Garbed as they were in black bark over their dirty and worn green uniforms and black caernas, they could probably pass as *sarka har* from a distance. He turned to Yimt with an idea.

"My thinking exactly, sir," Yimt said, anticipating him. "I've got the rest of the regiment kitting out the same way. Going to add some branches on top when we're closer. Doubt it'll fool them for long, but if it buys us a few more seconds, that might just be all we need."

Konowa grinned. The fire inside had been smoldering for a while, but as he looked at the black-clad warriors before him the first flames began to grow.

The Iron Elves were coming home.

***

Visyna stood near the bow of the *Ormandy*, ignoring the freezing spray that flew up every time the bow dipped down into another wave. She'd tried sleeping, but every time she began to drift off the horrors of the last few days

came rushing at her. She wondered how soldiers like Konowa and Yimt withstood the assault on their unconscious
mind. To lose friends, to kill the enemy, to forever walk
into danger knowing—absolutely knowing—that not everyone would walk back out again had to take its toll.

She hunched her shoulders, grateful for the tunic
loaned to her by one of the soldiers on board the ship.
I'm even starting to hear things, she realized, imagining the
erratic flapping of Wobbly somewhere in the night. A
moment later, a white blur drew her attention off the
starboard bow. *It is Wobbly!* She ran to the railing to
watch his arrival. He seemed to be going faster than was
safe, much too fast to make a landing. He skimmed over
the main mast, did a slow banking turn, and started
heading northwest, back the way he came.

"Wait, you didn't deliver your message!" she shouted
after the pelican. She brought her hands up to weave,
hoping perhaps to use the wind to guide him back this
way, when a new sound reached her ears. It was more
wings flapping. She turned and saw a massive bird of
prey swoop down from the sky, its beak glinting like
polished steel.

"Dandy!" she cried, marveling as the bird flared its
wings and came in for a pinpoint landing on the railing
just ten feet from her. He tucked in his wings and
squatted down on the railing, but with each blast of sea
spray he got up again and fluttered his feathers in
annoyance.

"I'm guessing Rallie sent you," Visyna said, inching
a little closer to Dandy. "But why?"

For an answer, Dandy hopped off the railing and
began walking across the deck. His claws gouged huge
splinters out of the wood as he did so.

"Here! We can't have your bloody bird tearing up the deck," a sailor said, running across the main deck to stand in front of Dandy.

Dandy turned his head so that a single, golden eye stared at the sailor. Visyna said nothing.

"It'll be a deuce of a job for the ship's carpenter to repair," the sailor said, his voice quavering as he tried to look around Dandy at Visyna.

"Are you the ship's carpenter?" Visyna asked.

"No," the sailor said, backing up a few paces. Dandy followed him.

"Then I wouldn't worry about it," she said, following after the bird.

The sailor seemed to think about that for a few seconds and then promptly turned and ran. Dandy didn't give chase, but moved toward the canvas-wrapped body of Chayii laid out on the deck. He lowered his head and using his beak, gently pulled Chayii's body underneath so that it rested by his claws. He raised his head and looked at Visyna. His right claw was open and extended toward her.

She realized it was an invitation.

"You're here to take us to Konowa, aren't you?" she said.

Dandy ruffled his feathers as another wall of spray pelted the deck.

"You're leaving us," Prince Tykkin said, walking along the deck and coming to a stop a few yards away.

"It appears I am," Visyna said. She started to move toward the bird, then paused and looked back at the Prince. "I am sorry for your loss. For what it's worth, I think you have it in you to be an excellent ruler. In the short time I've known you . . ." She realized she couldn't finish the sentence as it would sound too patronizing. The Prince finished it for her.

"I've grown. Yes, well, I suppose it was inevitable," he said, offering her a wry smile. "I had some very good examples to learn from." He bowed toward her.

"May your reign be a long and peaceful one," Visyna said.

"And may the winds of fortune favor you and the Iron Elves in the coming battle." He nodded and turned to walk away, then stopped and turned back. "And for what it's worth, tell that elf of yours that if I'd had my choice, I would have been there at his side."

Visyna smiled. "He knows that already, but I'll remind him."

"Off you go then," the future king said, giving her a quick salute.

Visyna returned it and turned to Dandy. "Okay, how do we do this?"

Elation and terror fought for dominance as she realized she would soon rejoin Konowa. She'd hoped a miracle would happen, and it had, but now she wished she'd put a little more thought into the details.

Dandy's claw snatched her up and his wings extended. He crouched low, then pushed straight up, his other claw scooping up Chayii as he did so. He pumped his wings a few times and Visyna buried her head in his feathers as they cleared the mast and vaulted into the sky.

She didn't scream, but not because she didn't want to.

THIRTY-SIX

P enny for your thoughts."

Konowa smiled and motioned to a spot beside him where he was staring out through the oak planks at the passing forest lining the river. The smoke from Rallie's cigar arrived a second before she did. He pointed at the trees.

"Wolf Oaks, but these are small ones, still young, maybe a few hundred years at most. The deeper we go, the older they get," he said. Pride had crept into his voice, which surprised him. He hadn't been back to the Hyntaland in years, mostly because there was so little here he wanted to remember. Now, however, his homecoming felt long overdue. He shivered. It was growing colder the further north they traveled. The ship continued at a far faster rate than should have been possible, but it navigated smoothly down the center of the river as if on a rail. He took a quick glance at his father. Jurwan remained seated near the main mast position, deep in a trance. Whatever his father was doing was working.

Dawn colored the sky a deep purple. He took that as a good omen.

"Glad to see it's not red," Rallie said.

"Will she get here in time?"

Rallie puffed on her cigar before answering. "It's in other hands, or feathers, at this point. Have you thought about what you're going to do when you confront Her?"

Konowa had tried very hard not to. "I'll do what needs to be done. This has to end, Rallie, it has to. She was a scourge before, but with the return of the Stars she's become a monster. If She isn't stopped now I see no hope for anyone, or anything."

Rallie said nothing, continuing to smoke her cigar and watch the passing trees. Finally, she turned and looked at him. "Do what needs to be done, just don't assume you know what that is yet."

"With all due respect, you're starting to sound a lot like my father with all the cryptic advice. Is there some school that older, wise advisors attend where they learn how to say something without actually saying it?"

Rallie laughed. "Now that's a school I'd like to attend. I think, however, you've got the shoe on the wrong foot. Wouldn't it be better to ask why young people are always so eager to know everything now? There's a joy in patience that quick gratification doesn't offer."

"In a few hours it'll all be moot," Konowa said. "If there are any last revelations you'd like to share, now's the time. Like maybe who you are, and the Stars?"

Rallie smiled and turned back to watching the trees. "Excellent questions. Very pertinent, too. I can see why you'd want to know."

Konowa waited. "Well?"

"There are many ancient myths about the creation of

the heavens and stars. Some think they are the eyes of gods peering down on us. Others think they are huge diamonds floating in the ether. There's even a legend that at least some of the stars, like those that fell, were in fact bundles of natural energy long ago gathered up and flung into the heavens for safekeeping. And that one day, when that natural energy was needed, they would return."

Konowa had the eerie sensation of standing on the edge of a thundering waterfall. One misstep and he'd go over and he'd never be seen again. Still, he decided to step a little closer to the abyss.

"Interesting. How do you suppose all that energy was put in the sky in the first place? Sounds like some powerful magic would be required to do something like that, if that's what happened . . ."

"No doubt," Rallie said. The end of her cigar was glowing like a white-hot brand.

"But if that is what happened, it happened—as you say—a very long time ago." Konowa could feel the heat coming off the end of her cigar.

Rallie pulled the cigar out of her mouth and studied the glowing tip. It lit up her face, throwing her many wrinkles into stark contrast. "Tell me, Colonel, what would you find more disturbing? The knowledge that I have some information that might be of use to you and I don't impart it, believing that to do so might create more problems than it solves, or, that I actually don't have any more information to give. That I'm just a little old lady a tad wise beyond her years, with a keen mind, a quick quill, and a mind that's not always focused on the here and now?"

"Both?" Konowa answered, only half in jest. "But if I have to choose, and it sounds like I do, I'd rather believe in the former. In fact, I do. You probably have so many secrets you don't even know them all yourself . . . if that makes sense."

Rallie stuck the cigar back in her mouth. "You, my dear elf, are smarter than you look."

"Thanks?" Konowa said.

"Time, I think, to get my quill and paper," Rallie said, stepping away from the railing.

Konowa looked into the distance. A gray smudge discolored the horizon to the north. "The mountains."

"I'm curious, Colonel," Rallie said, starting to turn away then stopping. "The aid of the Wolf Oaks in getting us here this fast has been spectacular. Do you know if your father has given any thought to how we stop?"

Konowa watched her walk away, a trail of blue smoke in her wake. He looked out at the passing trees. They were whipping by. Faster.

The *Black Spike* was picking up speed.

Konowa tore away from the railing and ran over to his father. He didn't bother waiting and simply grabbed Jurwan by the shoulder and shook him. "Father! This isn't a carriage. We don't have brakes."

Jurwan opened his eyes and blinked. "This is a concept that, unfortunately, the Wolf Oaks are not familiar with. They only know that the Shadow Monarch represents danger, and they seek all aid in fighting Her."

Konowa ran to the bow and looked forward. The land sloped upward into a short range of hills before the mountains themselves. He knew the river wound its way through them, but he doubted the draft would be deep enough for a ship this size. He'd always expected they would disembark at the base of the mountain and climb from there.

Captain Ervod appeared at his side. "Colonel, I don't have control of my own ship! If we hit a rock now we'll be destroyed."

"Don't you have things you do when you want to slow down? Throw your anchors."

Captain Ervod stepped back a pace. "At this speed? We'd probably rip the line right off."

"If you have a better idea I'm all ears," Konowa said.

Captain Ervod seemed to consider his options. "Fine. Tell your men to brace themselves. This is not going to be gentle."

"All right, laddies," Yimt said, standing a few paces away and obviously within earshot, "start thinking soft thoughts. Find a sack of something and put it in front of you. Don't be standing out in the open where you can go flying. Get low, grab on to something, and stay there."

Konowa waved his acknowledgment at Yimt and sprinted back toward his father. "Anything?"

Jurwan looked at him and pursed his lips. "Trying to commune with a forest of agitated Wolf Oaks is not . . . easy. Your mother was much better at this than I."

"Well, she's not here anymore, is she!" Konowa shouted, immediately regretting it. He knelt down in front of his father and placed his hand on his arm. "Father, tell them . . . tell them to think in terms of late fall as their sap starts to thicken and slow."

Jurwan looked at him with obvious surprise on his face. "The Wolf Oaks were mistaken in not choosing you, my son. You understand better than they know."

Konowa stood up. "Just tell them. Hurry." He turned and sprinted back to the bow. The hill range was easily visible now in the growing light. As were the first signs of chop in the water. Rapids. And that meant rocks.

"Anchors away!"

Konowa wedged himself between bales of gun cotton and closed his eyes. He heard the anchors splash into the water and a moment later the port anchor hit bottom, yawing the ship toward the left bank. A moment after that, the starboard anchor dug in, yanking the *Black Spike* back toward the right bank.

Something snapped and went rolling across the deck to crash into something else. Konowa didn't bother turning around to look. He lifted his head and opened his eyes to see up ahead. They were still going too fast, but at least they were keeping dead center.

"Captain! Get everyone topside now!" Konowa shouted, hoping he'd been heard.

The *Black Spike* hit its first rock. The entire ship juddered. There was a horrible screeching noise from far below as the ship passed by the rock on the port side. It felt like a nail being scraped down his spine. When it was passed the ship picked up speed again, but not quite as much as before. Perhaps the anchors and his father were having an effect.

"We're taking on water!"

Or that.

Konowa wasn't too worried about drowning in a river with land in sight on either side, but he hoped they wouldn't have to get wet if it could be helped. The ship took several more hits, jostling one way then the other as it continued moving upstream. Its speed had definitely slowed, but nowhere near anything Konowa considered safe. He saw a large hill pass by on their starboard and had a moment of vertigo as the ship climbed past it.

"After this, I walk everywhere," he muttered.

He also realized they'd passed through the Deep Forest of the Hyntaland and were now moving into Her realm. The temperature seemed to drop as soon as he thought it, or perhaps he just finally noticed. Though the sun was now well up in the sky, it was a gray, muddy day. Thick clouds boiled above suggesting rain or snow. Konowa felt the first drop on his neck and cursed. Naturally, it would be sleet.

"Not nearly as fast as *The Flying Elf,* but much more exhilarating," Major Alstonfar said, crawling up to lay beside Konowa at the bow.

"I hadn't noticed," Konowa lied, wishing he had Captain Ervod here. Now there was a man who knew this wasn't supposed to be fun. "Are the men ready?"

"And raring to go," Pimmer said, then held up a finger in question. "Is that appropriate military parlance? Would you prefer more formal reports?"

"Major, raring to go is music to my ears. And what about you? Not your first dance, but you've never officially led before."

It took a moment for Pimmer to get the pun. "Ah, very droll, sir. Well, yes, I must admit to a certain trepidation, but—"

The *Black Spike* leaped into the air as it bounced off a series of small rocks and slammed into a massive one. Timbers from below the waterline cartwheeled past the ship.

"—I look forward to having the opportunity to prove myself in battle and want to thank you again for the belief you've shown in me by giving me this chance."

Konowa looked at the man. "You do know we're sinking, right?"

"I imagine we have been for some time. Makes things that much more exciting, really. Will we sink before we get there? Will we get a chance to fire the *Black Spike*'s guns or will we all have to swim for it? Miss Synjyn will no doubt find ways to make it sound even more dramatic."

Great swaths of white water ahead told Konowa they were about to get their answer. Her mountain loomed above them now. Konowa risked a look back and shuddered. They had to be halfway up it already. He'd felt a certain degree of safety on the ship as they traversed Her realm, but looking back it appeared as if they were hanging off a cliff. He was ready to jump now when the ship slowed and the bow drove between two large rocks and came to a surprisingly gentle stop.

"That wasn't so bad at all," Pimmer said, a hint of disappointment in his voice.

Konowa wanted to agree, but he was busy trying to throw up. The sound of rushing water battering the bow didn't help. The icy spray was coating everything. They'd be a solid block of ice inside an hour. They'd have to get off the ship now.

"Arkhorn will be disappointed we didn't get a chance to try out his handiwork," Konowa said, standing up.

The first black arrow missed him by a few inches. The second by less than an inch. He was facedown on the deck before the third arrow had a chance.

THIRTY-SEVEN

They're in the trees!"

Black arrows zipped through the rigging of the *Black Spike* and lodged with loud thunks into the decking. Others twanged as they bounced off the extra planking. The yammering howl of rakkes broke out all around them. Other, stranger cries added to the clamor.

"RSM, you have the guns!" Konowa shouted. He crawled forward and poked his head up and around a barrel of what he suspected were pickles. *Sarka har* dotted the rocks. There was little purchase for them here on the mountainside, but great snakes of roots connected one to another, helping to anchor them in place. Rakkes streamed toward the ship from both sides of the river, coming to the riverbanks and throwing rocks in their frustration. Further back, Konowa spotted the dark, flitting figures of Her dark, twisted elves. "There but for my parents," he said, making a mental note to thank his father when all this was over.

He was starting to wonder what happened to Yimt

when he heard the dwarf's voice rise above the din. "This is for Ally! Fire!"

The *Black Spike* didn't disintegrate, not entirely. The combined fire of over sixty cannons shook what was left of the ship to its core. Massive oak ribs snapped like twigs. Whole sections of deck collapsed and the aft mast split all the way to the top before toppling over.

The effect on the riverbanks for two hundred yards deep, however, was total obliteration. A gale of death swept over the rocks, scouring everything on it like a million scythes. Elves, rakkes, and *sarka har* simply vanished in a pulverized mist of bone, flesh, and blood. Konowa tried to stand, but for a moment his legs wouldn't cooperate. The ringing in his ears was so loud it merged into one long wail. When he finally regained some balance he stood, coughing in the thick cloud of smoke now choking the *Black Spike*. When the smoke finally dissipated Konowa simply stared. Even the rocks bore the scars of the *Black Spike*'s cannonade. Everything was cracked and gouged.

"I would have liked a few more cannon, but overall I'd say that worked," Yimt said, walking up to the bow. "You think Ally saw that?"

Konowa looked down at the dwarf. "Saw it, felt it, and most definitely heard it."

Yimt beamed, his metal teeth gleaming. "Aye, that's what I think, too."

Corporal Feylan came running to the bow. "Colonel! We're starting to drift."

It took Konowa a moment to understand what that meant. And then it hit home. "Get everyone off now. We got our free ride, but this is the end of the line. The *Black Spike* is going back down the mountain."

Gangplanks were hurriedly thrown over the starboard

side, which was now less than two yards from the river-bank. Some men jumped, but most waited their turn and traversed the planking to land on the shore. Konowa watched the procession, aware the ship was drifting backward faster and faster. The end of the gangplank was scraping against the rocks.

"I'm sorry about your ship," Konowa said, addressing Captain Ervod.

"She served us well. I'll—"

The *Black Spike* lurched and began listing heavily to starboard, cutting off the captain's eulogy. The man stumbled and fell down the gangplank to land at the river's edge where waiting sailors fished him out. Konowa ran onto the gangplank and was soon tumbling himself the last yard to land in a heap on the rocks. He looked back and saw with horror that his father was still on the ship. The older elf was standing in front of the shimmering image of his *ryk faur*.

"Father! Get off the ship!"

Jurwan reached out a hand and patted the bark, then turned and slowly walked across the deck and down the gangplank as if his life wasn't in mortal danger. A shadow flitted above Konowa and he looked up to see Tyul leap gracefully from the tree to land casually on the rocks as light as a, well, leaf. The image of the Wolf Oak flickered and then was gone.

A moment later, the *Black Spike* turned onto its side, its remaining masts splintering on the rocks as it was carried away by the river. Cannons rolled across the deck and splashed into the water, and then the ship shuddered and broke apart.

"A sad end to a brave girl," Rallie said, scribbling in her papers.

Konowa could only nod in agreement. He picked himself up and brushed off the knees of his trousers. A soldier handed him his shako, which he jammed onto his head. Looking around, the sailors were all grouped together looking forlorn and lost. They were, however, armed. RSM Arkhorn had apparently seen to everything.

"Captain," Konowa said, "this wasn't part of the plan, although I suppose it was always the likelihood. I don't feel right about leaving you here, but if you come with us . . ."

Captain Ervod shook his head. "We'd only slow you down and be in your way. And I have wounded. We'll get ourselves sorted and set up a defense here as best we can. Depending on what happens up there, you'll have a place to fall back to."

Konowa smiled. If they needed a place to fall back to, they wouldn't need it because they'd be dead. "Be well," Konowa said, saluting.

Captain Ervod returned it. "May a fair wind favor you."

The flapping of wings brought everyone's heads up. Konowa broke out into a huge grin.

"They just did."

A huge falcon the size of a horse landed on the rocks near the group. It laid its cargo on the ground before hopping awkwardly over to Rallie, who cooed and petted it. Konowa ran to Visyna and held her, ignoring the frost fire. She awoke yelling and he reluctantly let go only to be bowled over by Jir. Konowa could only offer him a couple of playful swipes before he stood up and motioned for Jir to back off.

The area grew quiet as Jurwan walked over to the

body of Chayii. Konowa followed, and knelt down beside his father. "I am sorry. I feel like if I had—"

Jurwan held up his hand. "She was proud of you. Always. She may not have agreed with the path you chose, or that I helped put you on, but she never once doubted the good in you. Know that. Cherish that."

Konowa realized he did. "We must go, Father. She'll know we're here."

Jurwan stood and faced him. "Yes, you must go. I, however, will stay here with your mother."

Konowa opened his mouth to object and then understood. "You climbed Her mountain once. Best you stay here and help the sailors. It's my turn now."

Jurwan nodded. He reached out and placed his hand over Konowa's heart, the palm of his hand resting against the black acorn.

"When all this is done, you may wish to plant this."

Konowa gently removed his father's hand. "It's evil. Look what it did to you. Imagine what it could do as a tree."

Jurwan nodded. "Perhaps, but perhaps its proximity to your heart all this time has changed it more than it has changed you."

"I have to go now, Father," Konowa said, stepping back. He motioned with his hand and knew RSM Arkhorn would get the troops moving. "Stay here, stay safe, and know . . . know that I love you."

"Good luck, my son," Jurwan said.

Konowa looked at him one more time, then turned and headed up the mountain, slowing his pace so that Visyna could match his stride. Rallie came up behind them and fell into step. Konowa felt comfort, surrounded as he was, but he knew his place was at the front.

He spoke to the two women. "Whatever happens, She is mine to deal with." It wasn't a question.

"Konowa—" Visyna started to say, but he just stared her down.

"She is mine." He turned to look at Rallie.

"As you wish. I've only ever been along for the ride," she said.

Konowa watched her a moment longer then turned back to the path leading up the mountain. He guessed it would take until just before nightfall for them to reach the top, but he planned to sprint ahead long before then. He couldn't explain it, but the dream was clear. It all came down to him.

"Major Alstonfar, let's pick up the pace. The *Black Spike* did a good job of scaring off anything within a couple of miles of here, so let's make good time while we can."

Orders were passed along from soldier to soldier, which didn't take long as they numbered a little over five dozen. Color Sergeant Aguom ordered the unfurling of the regimental and Queen's Colors. The two cloth symbols were raised and snapped and rippled in the wind. Konowa took a moment to watch them, feeling a sense of pride and honor. His heart beat faster to see them in the air. He looked around at his men. They were a sight. Clad in black bark with tree branches sticking from their shakos they looked more like the monsters they were about to do battle with than Calahr's finest.

His chest swelled at the sight of them. They weren't his elves. Those soldiers were gone, lost a long time ago. He'd never had a chance to say he was sorry, to try and make them understand why he did what he did, and why, if he had the chance to do it all again, he would do the same damn thing. All this time he'd spent searching for them, believing that finding them would set everything right, only to realize that he'd had his Iron Elves with him the whole time. This ragtag collection of misfits were his regiment. RSM Arkhorn, quite possibly the best and worst soldier to ever wear sigger green. He sought out the soldiers he knew best, looking each in the eye, perhaps for the very last time. Color Sergeant Aguom, Corporals Vulhber and Feylan, Scolly and even Zwitty. He found his eyes searching for soldiers no longer there. RSM Lorian, Privates Meri and Kester and Teeter and the religious farmer, Inkermon, and above all, Private Renwar. He could still see the slender boy looking far too young to be carrying a musket, and how he changed before his eyes into something Konowa doubted he'd ever fully understand.

He caught himself daydreaming and stomped his boot on the ground. It was time. He motioned to Major Alstonfar and the order went out.

The Iron Elves shouldered their muskets, and marched forward, and into battle.

THIRTY-EIGHT

They'd climbed almost two hours without a sign of any living creature except the sporadic carcasses of *sarka har*. They were all dead, or dying.

"What killed them?" Konowa asked, walking off the trail to get a closer look at one. It didn't look like it had been attacked, more that it had just wilted and died.

"The natural order is so polluted here, and there is nothing of value for them to feed on," Visyna said, her voice quavering.

Konowa was worried about her. She appeared weak and ill. He felt it in the ground himself, but it only fueled his desire to get to the top. "Perhaps you should—"

Visyna glared at him and he closed his mouth.

"I am going with you all the way. If you even think of suggesting otherwise the Shadow Monarch will be the least of your worries."

Konowa smiled in spite of the situation. "As you wish."

The snap of a single musket broke the unnatural quiet.

"Rakkes!"

The beasts poured out of the rocks like ants from a nest. "Steady! It's nothing we haven't seen before," Yimt shouted, moving quickly between the soldiers and forming them into a double line as the first row knelt and prepared to fire.

Konowa judged that he was close enough to make his run now, but something gave him pause. The rakkes coming at them were not like those of even a few hours ago. These seemed disoriented, and weak. The first volley of musket fire crashed into them, knocking down thirty and sending an equal number backward where they shrieked and beat their chests, but gave little indication of charging again.

Soldiers cheered, but Konowa didn't trust it. This wasn't right. First the dead *sarka har*, and now less than maniacal rakkes.

"Archers!"

The sky darkened as hundreds of arrows arced toward them. Konowa's sense of suspicion had been right. He went to grab Visyna to push her to safety, but Rallie stepped into his path and knocked him off balance. The arrows reached their apogee and began to fall straight toward them.

A sudden wind gust tore along the path blowing most of the arrows astray. The few that fell either hit the stony ground or bounced off the *sarka har* bark the soldiers wore as armor. Konowa looked to Visyna. She swayed where she stood, but she was weaving. Rallie had her quill poised above a sheaf of papers.

"Visyna!"

"We can hold them off," she said, bravely smiling at him.

Konowa would have returned it, but the clicking sound of hundreds of pins on rock made him blanch. Dozens of korwirds were scrambling through the rakkes and charging at the Iron Elves. Konowa shivered at the look of the things. They clattered over the rock like armored snakes on hundreds of pointy twigs. Each was easily five feet long and possessed a pair of clacking pincers at its head. He'd never seen one before, but Yimt had gone into great detail about them so that there was no mistaking the nasty-looking things crawling toward them.

"Fire!"

Musket shot spewed out of barrels and raced across fifty yards to tear into rakke and korwird alike, blasting them apart in a mess of blood and chitinous plating. More arrows launched skyward and Visyna called up another wind, though not as strong as the last one. A soldier screamed and went down, his hands pressed over his hip where a black arrow had lodged, blood spurting between his fingers.

The scratch of Rallie's quill across paper set a hum on the air, and more black arrows went wide of the mark. Konowa cursed. They were pinned down to the spot. They could hold off Her creatures, but there was no way to move forward. Dusk was already tinting the sky, elongating shadows on the ground.

"Colonel," Major Alstonfar said, jogging up to crouch beside Konowa. He was sweating and breathing heavy, but he sounded calm and in control. "The men are doing a superlative job, but at this rate of fire they'll expend their ammunition in the next half hour. I've ordered them to wait until they have a clear shot, but that will only buy us a little more time."

Konowa reached out and patted the man on the shoulder, taking his hand back quickly as frost fire began to burn on Pimmer's uniform. To his credit, Pimmer simply brushed the fire out with his hand. A rumbling roar came from somewhere up the mountain. Whatever it was, it was coming this way. "Tell the men to fix bayonets."

"What is it?" Pimmer asked.

"No idea, but it won't be pleasant," Konowa answered, sprinting away to check on Rallie and Visyna. The women had taken up station behind a large boulder and were continuing to aid the regiment. Visyna was leaning against the rock, her hands trembling as she weaved. Rallie was crouched down by her side, a large sheaf of paper resting on a thigh as her quill flew across the page. "Do you know what's coming?"

Both women shook their heads, too busy to speak as they concentrated on their magic. The hairs on Konowa's arms stood up and a trickle of cold sweat raced down his spine. He turned and ran back toward the line, growing all the more frustrated that he had no good plan about what to do next. Were this any other battle, he'd order a tactical withdrawal to a more defensible location, but that wasn't an option, not here, not when he was so close.

The rumbling grew louder. Konowa unsheathed his saber, the frost fire sparkling along the blade at once.

"Steady now," Yimt ordered, moving behind the line and offering encouragement to the troops. His drukar was clenched in his right fist, and like Konowa's saber, sparked with black frost.

A long, guttural scream was answered by a dozen more, and a pack of misshapen dyre wolves bounded from among the *sarka har* and raced toward the Iron Elves. Each wolf was easily the size of Jir, but where the bengar was sleek muscle, fluid movement, and controlled violence, these creatures were starvation thin and ran with a stilted, drunklike gait. A sickly yellow foam drooled from their muzzles filled with serrated teeth and black pus oozed from their milky white eyes.

Before the order to fire could be given, Tyul sprang up from the rocks and moved in front of the firing line and began loosing arrows at the wolves. Four went down in a matter of seconds, but not even the elf's lightning-fast reflexes could take them all before they reached the line.

"Tyul! Get the hell out of there!" Konowa shouted, running forward.

Tyul never turned, but continued to fire arrow after arrow as the wolves bore down on him. When the creatures were only a few yards away the twang of many bowstrings reached Konowa's ears. Arrows whistled past his head, between the Iron Elves, and struck the wolves in mid-jump. The bodies fell and slid along the ground and stopped just inches from where Tyul stood.

Konowa turned. Elves of the Long Watch emerged from the shadows, their bows still active as they engaged Her elves and the rakkes and korwirds. Jurwan walked among them, still as serene as if he were out for a walk on a warm, summer day.

"Father?" Konowa shouted.

"The elves of the Long Watch may not listen to the advice of another elf," Jurwan said, "but when their own Wolf Oaks saw the rightness of aiding you, they felt compelled to help."

More rakkes appeared among the trees, their gibbering calls growing in intensity. Konowa knew he had to act now.

"Tell them thanks!" he shouted, and turn and ran back to the line. "Major, fix bayonets and on my order, wheel right and clear that line of trees. The elves will cover you. Once you've secured that find cover and keep them busy."

Pimmer nodded. "And you, Colonel?"

"Just see that it's done."

Pimmer saluted and passed along the order to Yimt.

A volley of Long Watch arrows cleared the woods for twenty yards. The Iron Elves stood up and charged, their bayonets ablaze with frost fire. Any rakke or korwird in their path was stabbed to death. The few remaining dark elves stepped forward to plug the gap, but those not killed by the Long Watch fell to the blade of Tyul. The elf slid between tree and elf, slashing and stabbing with an economy of movement and absolute precision. Konowa could have watched him all day, but already a new pack of dyre wolves was racing through the *sarka har* and more rakkes were massing.

Konowa ran past the soldiers. He spied Yimt and slowed. "I'll be back," Konowa shouted over his shoulder, running up the path. He looked down at his saber as he ran. Stygian black frost crackled along the length of the blade.

A black blur preceded him up the path and took a rakke by the throat, shaking the beast so hard the head ripped off. Jir dropped the body and launched himself at the next beast, swiping his claws at its thighs and quickly pouncing on its chest when the creature screamed and fell. A moment later there was a snap and the screaming stopped.

Konowa leaped over Jir and kept running. It was his turn now.

He wasn't sure how many rakkes and dark elves and other creatures crossed his path. He slashed and stabbed as he ran, ignoring the arrows that flew past his head and the claws that tried to rip his face. The frost fire arced out from him like lightning, striking creatures five and ten yards away from him. Soon, he had no need to swing his saber at all. As the sun dipped below the mountain and darkness settled in, he followed the path by the light of his own black flame.

He was well into the thorny thicket of Her forest at the very peak of the mountain before he realized it. He'd expected a ferocious response, but the *sarka har* here could only flail in mad desperation. He pushed his way through, destroying the blood trees with sturdy swipes of his saber. Instead of feeling emboldened, he grew increasingly cautious. It was a trick, it had to be. The Shadow Monarch was too powerful. Her forest and Her creatures couldn't be dying, because if they were dying . . . Rallie might be right.

He paused, breathing in the cold air. He watched his breath mist in front of him. *It doesn't matter! You came here to end this. End this!*

Konowa stood up straight and gripped the pommel of his saber so hard that black flame shot twenty feet in the air from the end of it. He slashed through the last ring of trees and emerged on the rocky summit where the Shadow Monarch knelt by Her Silver Wolf Oak.

The power here was caustic. The acorn against his chest flared, driving needles of cold deep into his heart.

He coughed, breathing in the mix of cold, toxic magic permeating the surrounding rocks. The ground beneath his feet groaned. Large fissures crisscrossed the summit from which moans and screams echoed from the far depths. Konowa moved carefully around them, staying well away from the edges. He could make out claw marks where rakkes and other creatures had emerged.

The Shadow Monarch turned to look at him as he approached, and like the dream, a small, scared, elderly elf woman stared up at him.

"My child," she said, reaching out Her hands to him. Her voice grated on his ears. It was high and shaky, far from the commanding voice he'd often heard in his dreams.

Konowa stopped and looked around the space. Even here the *sarka har* looked sick. He studied the Silver Wolf Oak and felt revulsion at what he saw. What should have been a tall, straight tree was instead a gnarled, twisted mess of branches sloughing off their bark. Its metallic leaves were either wilting or already fallen, and black ichor oozed from hundreds of cracks in its wood. It was dying!

He knew She couldn't stop him. Neither could the Silver Wolf Oak. All he had to do was walk forward the last few paces and strike. Yet he couldn't bring himself to do it. Not yet.

"Why?" he asked, swinging his saber around to encompass everything. "Why? Why do this?" He wanted to laugh. He wanted to cry. "Why any of this?"

The Shadow Monarch began to babble. Konowa waited, expecting a trap. Tears were running down the old elf's face as She gently tried to piece back together the dying Silver Wolf Oak.

"She doesn't have any answers," Rallie said, stepping into the clearing. "She never did. Her mind is all but gone. It has been for a long time."

Konowa spun, the acorn against his heart burning cold. "You? Rallie?" His world was spinning. *No, she couldn't be.*

"All this time, and you really thought She was the power behind all of this?" Rallie asked.

It felt as if someone had pushed him off a cliff. His muscles grew weak and he felt dizzy. Rallie pulled a cigar from her robe and placed it between her teeth, then brought out a tinderbox and lit it.

"I don't understand," Konowa said, trying to keep his wits. He could hear the slithering and creaking of branches all around him. Something was happening. He knew he was missing a piece to the puzzle, but what?

"No? I'm not surprised," Rallie said. Her cigar hadn't lit so she tried the tinderbox again. Sparks flashed, but the cigar would not catch flame.

Konowa blinked. In all the time he'd known Rallie, he'd never seen her use a tinderbox. "You witch." His strength returned in a rush. "I may not be the brightest candle, but I know a forgery when I see one." He raised his saber and took a step toward the Shadow Monarch. She still knelt by the tree, keening softly now and rocking back and forth.

"Finish Her, Konowa, and this will be over," Visyna said, appearing out of the trees to stand beside Rallie. Again the acorn flared and Konowa cried out in pain. He dropped to one knee.

"You aren't Visyna," he said through gritted teeth. "Your parlor tricks won't work on me."

"Then kill Her and be done with this," Yimt said,

emerging from the right. Konowa fell to both knees as the pain pierced through to his back. "Kill Her, and set me free."

Branches began moving around Konowa. He forced himself to his feet. He ignored Yimt and turned his attention to the Silver Wolf Oak. "You said *me*."

"Kill Her, Konowa, kill Her," the Duke of Rakestraw said, stepping out of the trees just a few feet away from him. His long red locks fluttered about his face, and he held his long sword, Wolf's Tooth, in his hands, but the cold pain squeezing Konowa's chest told him what he already knew. That wasn't his friend. Tears filled Konowa's eyes, but turned to ice as they froze on his cheeks.

"You . . . said . . . me." He took a step forward, then another and pointed toward the Shadow Monarch. "You called to Her all those centuries ago."

Jurwan approached with his hands outstretched. "It is really me, my son. You must focus. Kill Her, and this will be done."

Konowa laughed, though it felt as if his ribs were breaking. Cold seeped into every joint. He ignored the images of his friends and family and looked past the Shadow Monarch, and directly at the Silver Wolf Oak. "This wasn't about Her. It was about you. Kaman Rahl made the same mistake She made. You're the real power here, not Her."

In answer, the avatars of those he loved began to close around him. Konowa held his saber in front of him, coaxing the frost fire to a shimmering black furnace. He heard the grinding of wood on wood. The figures around him shuddered, and he saw through the facades to the twisted mess of ichor and wood forming the structure on which the illusions projected.

His mother appeared in the circle surrounding him. Her sad eyes found his. She reached out her hands. "Kill Her, my son. Kill Her and set me free."

The cold now was so intense Konowa was having difficulty breathing. His entire body was shaking so hard it took all his strength to hold on to his saber. He watched with horror as the frost fire on the blade began to sputter.

"You must do this," Chayii said, moving closer as the ring tightened.

Konowa shook his head and swung his saber around him like a drunk. He almost toppled over, but caught his footing in time. "No! I won't. I want to know why. Why mark us? Why seek us out?"

The sound of branches moving grew in volume. The circle opened leaving Konowa no route except straight forward. The group of people he knew closed to within arm's reach, but Konowa could no longer lift his own. The frost fire on his saber went out. Tears of frustration streamed down his face and froze. "I want . . . an answer!"

A branch reached out and circled around his right wrist. Frost fire burned at the spot, searing his skin. The branch tightened, and pointed his saber at the Shadow Monarch. It pulled him forward.

Konowa dug in his heels leaving a trail of black flame in his wake. "Why?"

Chayii moved to his side. "Kill Her my son, kill Her."

Konowa wrenched his arm until his shoulder joint burned and lights began to flash behind his eyes. "Tell. Me. Why!" He pulled his arm and broke free of the branch. More snaked toward him. Frost fire burst again along his blade and he began slashing wildly at any that came close, setting them afire. The Shadow Monarch cringed, throwing Her hands over Her head.

Chayii moved toward him, but he held his saber in front of him and kept her at bay. "My son, this can all be over. She killed so many you love. She killed me. Kill Her, and the oath is broken."

A new cold washed over Konowa's body. The shades of the dead Iron Elves appeared, taking their place beside him. The circle of avatars surrounding Konowa moved back. RSM Lorian on Zwindarra. One-eyed Meri. Private Teeter. And Private Renwar. They said nothing, but there was no need. They and he were one. Their pain was his. Their need was his need.

"Break the oath. Set them free," Chayii said.

Konowa stepped forward again. "No."

Waves of anguish washed over Konowa as the shades writhed. He was prepared for battle, but this was something else. Life after life cut far too short flashed through his mind. Husbands that would never return to their wives. Sons who would never see their parents, and fathers who would never hold their children. The sorrow left him breathless. He sobbed until he thought he'd pass out.

"Why?" he screamed, staggering another step forward.

The image that was Chayii shattered, and in its place he saw the Silver Wolf Oak as it saw itself, as it wanted to be. It stood tall and proud, a towering, monstrous example of a Wolf Oak, its leafy crown a sky-blotting collection of glittering Stars. "This is why," a new voice emanating from the Shadow Monarch said. "I was destined for more! I am more, and I will be, once She is gone."

Konowa roared. "You're a tree! You're a damn, bloody tree! Why? Why all of this? If you hate Her, kill Her yourself. Why mark me?" he asked, pointing to his ruined ear. "Why mark any of us?"

"You wonder why I marked you? Why I marked the others? She is dying. She was always going to die. Do you know what happens to a Silver Wolf Oak when its *ryk faur* dies?"

A light of understanding dawned in Konowa. "You die, too. Not right away, but you wither and die. The bond has its price." Konowa understood better now why Tyul was the way he was. "If you kill Her, you kill yourself."

"And so I need a new bond, a new life to take Her place. The acorn your father gave you was my gift. She did my bidding as Her own. But now I need more. Her strength bleeds away. I need a strong elf, one not enraptured by the natural world as all these other elves are. As She was. And so I sought to set some of you apart in the hopes that one day I would find one strong enough to bond with and create a new world."

The acorn against Konowa's heart cracked. He felt the first tendril of what was inside pierce his skin and start to worm its way into his flesh.

"I created you, my child, and now we will be one."

Konowa screamed and reached for his chest. He ripped his tunic exposing his flesh. He grabbed the acorn and pulled, but he couldn't remove it. The saber fell from his right hand. Everything was going dark. More branches snaked around him.

He looked to the shades for help, but they were trapped in a shimmering wall of frost fire. He was alone.

A branch wrapped itself around his right wrist while another reached to the ground for his saber.

The saber wasn't there. Konowa forced his head up. The Shadow Monarch stood next to the Silver Wolf Oak, his saber in Her hands.

"I cannot kill you, my love, my life," She said, the tears streaming down Her face. "I saved you, I gave you life." Her voice was broken with sobs. The love and agony in it made Konowa hurt.

The branches of the Silver Wolf Oak shook and thrashed in an attempt to get to the Shadow Monarch, but they were so interwoven now around Konowa they could not reach Her. She moved forward until She stood beside the tree's twisted trunk. Her sobs grew louder as She sunk to Her knees beside it.

Branches snapped as the *sarka har* flailed around them. The entire mountain began to tremble. Konowa stumbled as the rock heaved beneath him. The air turned so cold he could no longer breathe. His vision grayed at the edge.

"You have to!" Konowa choked. He struggled to move forward, but the cold and the shaking ground made it impossible.

The Shadow Monarch turned to look at him. "No, I can't. I won't. But if I cannot be with my love in this life, I will be with it in the next." She turned the saber so that the point was facing Her chest, and then She fell forward.

The mountain shuddered. Rocks cracked and blew apart as the Silver Wolf Oak's roots ripped through the deep, climbing back to the surface to ensnare Konowa in their grasp. The first roots broke free and wrapped themselves around his ankle, but they were too late.

The summit exploded in a shower of black, crystal flame. The Shadow Monarch's body vanished in a gale of frost fire. The flame ignited the ichor dripping from the Silver Wolf Oak and set it ablaze. It flamed at once, burning so dark the night appeared as day. Konowa burned, too, only now, he had no protection from the frost fire. He stumbled blindly through the flame, struggling to find a way out. He tripped and fell, landing hard on a rock. He struggled to stay conscious as the black flames roared skyward, consuming everything on the mountain peak. He knew if he stayed here, he would die.

The pain tried to keep him pinned to the ground, but the fire inside made him roll. He climbed to his feet, still reeling. He couldn't see. Everything was aflame. *Sarka har* shrieked as they burned. The Silver Wolf Oak's branches thrashed and tore itself apart in its funeral pyre of ugly, black flame.

A wave of cold air suddenly surrounded him. He looked up. The shades of the dead stood beside him again, shielding him from the raging fire. Private Renwar stepped forth. His shadowy form solidified for a moment, revealing the young lad Konowa had first met. They locked eyes. Alwyn smiled, and saluted. The other shades followed suit. Lorian. Meri. His men. His brothers.

Konowa struggled to stand upright and returned their salute, the tears streaming freely down his face. It wasn't the salute that made him cry. It was seeing their smiles.

The oath was broken.

"Thank you," Alwyn said, and was gone.

Konowa blinked. He was alone on the mountaintop.

The fire still burned. He flung his body off the rock, tumbling and sliding until he could no longer feel the icy flames. He came to rest in the crook of two rocks. The mountain was shaking beneath him. Rocks split and fractured as chasms dug too long and too deep collapsed. Debris began falling past him. The irony that he would survive his encounter on the mountaintop only to be killed by a falling rock put a grin on his face.

He waited for the fateful blow, but none came. The mountain stopped shaking. He sat up, clutching his chest. When he brought his hand away and looked, the black stain on his chest was still there, but already he could feel warmth spreading through his body. He ripped the black acorn stuck to his chest, and this time it came away. As he held it in his hands he felt the coldness leave it. He thought about what his father said, about how its contact with him would have changed it.

He took in a tentative breath, waiting for a stab of pain to black him out, but beyond a level of overall agony he had become accustomed to, he felt pretty damn good. He gingerly climbed to his feet and looked up. The black flames had gone out. He looked around. There were no signs of *sarka har* anywhere. He clenched his fists. Nothing. No frost fire.

He climbed back up to the mountaintop. A thick, black ash floated in the air, coating everything. Nothing else remained to show the Shadow Monarch and Her forest had ever been there. The rock where the Silver Wolf Oak had grown had been scoured clean by the frost fire. Konowa kicked his boot through the black ash until he heard a familiar clink. He bent down and picked up his saber. He hefted it in his hands and made a couple of practice swipes in the air. He spun around, expecting something to be standing behind him, but he was alone.

Konowa sheathed his saber. There wasn't even an echo. He wanted to feel something more, but after all this time, the feeling that overwhelmed all others was that for the first time in his life, he could see himself being happy.

It was a scary thought. He shivered, and decided it was time to get back. He took one last look around and started to set off back down the mountain, but paused.

He opened his hand and looked at the acorn. Could his father be right? Was this a chance for things to be different? After everything, maybe he could find a way to bond with nature. Gently, he knelt down and placed the acorn on the ground. He stood back up and looked at it. A light breeze drifted through the clearing, tousling his hair across his face. For a long time he stared at the acorn, waiting. Then he raised his boot and slammed his heel down on the acorn with all his might. The acorn splintered into several pieces. He lifted his boot and brought it down again and again and again until there was nothing left.

"Bloody trees," he muttered, turning and never looking back.

"I'll leave out the parts where I screamed," he said to himself as he began composing his story for the others. The rest of it, he decided, he'd tell more or less as it happened.

More or less.

Konowa smiled.

It felt . . . good.

THIRTY-NINE

Konowa walked along a path among the trees, occasionally reaching out a hand to brush against the bark as he went. Autumn was in the air. He still wore his uniform, although it no longer conformed to any regulations. His trousers were neatly patched with pieces of Hasshugeb robe, and his jacket no longer carried epaulettes or shiny buttons, the latter having long been replaced by polished pieces of wood from a few shards of the *Black Spike*. He reached up and scratched his head, still not used to not having a shako there. He rolled his shoulders, feeling the weight of the musket on its sling. His right hand rested on the pommel of his saber with a light but firm grip.

The wind chased fallen leaves before him like a covey of startled quail. It had been three months since the battle on the mountaintop. Three months and he still kept a wary eye on the trees around him. Better safe than sorry. He paused and took in a breath.

"Okay," he said to himself, closing his eyes, "I can do this."

He stretched out his arms, palms up, and listened to the forest. It was alive with the sounds of birds and beasts and all manner of insects and other living creatures. The distant voices of the Wolf Oaks were there, too, but if they were talking to him, he couldn't understand a word they were saying.

A squirrel scampered down a trunk nearby and paused to look at him. Konowa raised an eyebrow at it. "Father?"

The squirrel bushed its tail and darted back up the tree.

"Guess not." He tried again, straining to hear more than the usual buzz of noise. He closed his eyes and concentrated. *C'mon, something talk to me.*

"You look like a juggler who's lost his balls."

Konowa opened his eyes. Yimt stood a few feet up ahead on the path. His teeth gleamed as he smiled. He was dressed in soft brown and green leathers, and carried a custom-tailored long bow on his back. His trusty drukar hung at his side off his old Calahrian uniform's belt.

"The forest and I remain, unsurprisingly, not on speaking terms."

"Just as well," Yimt said, stepping forward as he shoved a wad of crute between his teeth. He offered some to Konowa, who politely shook his head. "Brigadier generals that hear trees don't stay brigadiers for long."

Konowa snorted, and fell in step with the dwarf as they started walking back down the path. In the distance just visible through the trees, a small cottage and a neatly domed pile of rocks with a small wooden door sat by a river in a lush, green meadow. "I told you, I'm not taking the commission. Marshal Ruwl got me once, but not again. The Iron Elves are in good hands with Pimmer."

"What about the message from Miss Synjyn, and the King? They all seem rather keen to have you back under arms," Yimt said. His voice was filled with mirth at Konowa's discomfort. "The Shadow Monarch and Her forces might be gone, but the Empire is far from stable. And you *are* the hero. I read all about it in the *Imperial Weekly Herald*," Yimt said, flourishing a scroll of paper.

Konowa made a face. "They can send Rakestraw's cavalry out looking for me for all I care. I am officially retired. I'm back where I belong, in a forest . . . among the trees . . ." Konowa stopped walking and took the scroll from Yimt and unfurled it. A very lifelike sketch of several members of the regiment graced the top of the page along with the official citations commending their acts of bravery. Fifty-two had survived. It hurt to read that, but Konowa was grateful that many had come through. For a very long time he feared the number would be zero.

He easily recognized Corporal Vulhber, RSM Aguom, Private Scolly Erinmoss, and a beaming Major Pimrald Alstonfar. They formed the core of the fully reconstituted Iron Elves, and Konowa couldn't be happier about that. He ignored his own sketch and grinned when he saw Yimt's. Rallie had somehow managed to capture the glint of his metal teeth and mischievous twinkle in his eyes. Even newly minted Ensign Feylan of the Imperial Calahrian Navy was depicted. At this rate the lad would have his own ship in a couple more years.

Konowa's joy dimmed as he scanned down to the

posthumous awards. The list was long, much too long. Rallie had drawn the deceased with grace and humor, capturing them at their best, their eyes bright and their smiles genuine and strong, but it still hollowed Konowa out to look at them.

He let the scroll roll up and handed it back to Yimt.

"What about you? Don't you have a wife and family missing you? You're a free dwarf. Why not go home and open your law firm? I'm sure there are guilty men in jail right now for no other reason than you're out here and not in a courtroom working your particular brand of magic."

Yimt looked down at the ground for a moment before looking up into Konowa's eyes. "I had to make sure you were okay. I . . . we lost a lot of good lads. I couldn't stand to lose anymore."

Konowa reached out and rested a hand on his friend's shoulder. "Yimt, look at me. For the first time in my life, I can honestly say I'm happy."

A rustling in the trees cut off his next words. Both elf and dwarf turned. Konowa's hand slid to the pommel of his saber while Yimt drew out his drukar. The sound grew louder as it moved closer. Konowa crouched, tensing his muscles. A moment later, Jir bounded out of the low brush covered in burrs. A moment after that the smell hit them. He looked at both of them, wagging his stubby tail.

"*Yirka umno*, Jir! I told you, stay away from skunks!" Konowa turned to Yimt. "Whose turn is it to wash him?"

Yimt was already several yards down the path. "Sorry, can't hear you. See you at dinner!"

Konowa shouted a curse and reluctantly started

walking toward the river, motioning for Jir to follow. "Do you think you'll ever learn?"

"Do you?" Visyna asked.

Konowa looked up to see her coming up the path to meet them. "Yimt tells me you let Jir get in trouble again."

Konowa smiled. Visyna looked . . . perfect. Her long brown hair gleamed in the sun and her almond-shaped eyes flashed with joy.

"Me? You give me too much credit. I was just going for a walk." He closed the distance between them and took her in his arms. He shooed Jir away with his boot and the bengar loped off after the dwarf. "Yimt asked me about the offer to rejoin the army again."

Visyna tensed in his arms. "What did you say?"

He squeezed her tight. She felt perfect, too. "I told him I was happy, and that I was back where I belong."

Visyna frowned. "But you hate the forest."

Konowa leaned down and whispered in her ear. "Forest, what forest? All I see is you."

She reached up and wrapped an arm around his neck, pulling his face to hers. The touch of her lips on his was warm and soft. They pulled away slowly, and then started walking back down the path hand in hand.

"No sparks," Konowa said, licking his lips.

Visyna playfully jabbed him in the ribs and as he bent over she wrapped an arm around his neck and pulled him to the ground. "I'll show you sparks," she said.

Konowa held her tight and did indeed feel sparks. Twice.

If the forest had anything to say, Konowa couldn't hear it.

He finally realized, he didn't have to.

GLOSSARY

Arr An aromatic, if bitter, bean grown in hot climates that when dried and then boiled in water creates a drink that awakens and revives.

Bayonet Typically a ten-inch piece of steel shaped like a dagger and attached to the end of a musket. Used primarily for close-in fighting as a stabbing weapon.

Bengar A large, carnivorous predator weighing up to eight hundred pounds and usually sporting black fur with dull red stripes, large fangs, and a short tail. The full extent of their range is unknown. One male of the species, Jir, has been adopted as mascot of the Iron Elves.

Black powder Also known as gunpowder, it is a mixture of coal, sulfur, and saltpeter that when ignited by a spark creates an explosive reaction. Used in muskets and cannons.

Blood Oath Oath taken by the Iron Elves pledging loyalty to the regiment. Due to Major Konowa Swift Dragon's possession of an obsidian acorn from the Shadow Monarch's Silver Wolf Oak at the time of the oath, all the soldiers are now bonded to the regiment and increasingly under Her sway, in death and beyond.

Brindo A rare deer species native to Elfkyna known for its floppy ears and distinctive dull black hide of interlocking plates.

Caerna Traditional Hyntaland elf garb of cloth worn around the waist and reaching to the knee. Soldiers in the Iron Elves wear caernas though the officers do not, as they are often mounted on horses.

Cannon A large length of metal tube with a smooth bore that fires projectiles such as iron cannon balls over long distances. Gunpowder is used as the explosive force. Typically made of brass for smaller sizes and iron for larger ones.

Carronade A very large, short-barreled cannon capable of firing a heavy projectile over short distances.

Colors Every regiment in the Calahrian Imperial Army carries two large flags known as the Colors into battle. Usually made of cotton with fine wool stitching, one flag bears the Queen's royal cypher while the other the regimental crest.

Crute Rock spice chewed by dwarves. The powder is rich in mineral ores and has the side effect of turning the user's teeth metallic in color.

Darkly Departed The nickname given to the shades of the dead of the Iron Elves.

Dïova gruss Elvish, meaning a lost one, referring to an elf that has bonded with a Silver Wolf Oak and been overwhelmed by the purity of its magical powers.

Drakarri Name for drake spawn that legend suggests were the offspring of the mating between the wizard Kaman Rhal and a she-drake (dragon). The creatures walk on four legs, have large jaws filled with sharp teeth, and spit pure white fire.

Drukar A heavy, angular blade favored by many dwarves over the battle-ax for its ease of use and durability in battle.

Faeraug Also known as dog spiders, these eight-legged creatures attack their prey with a pair of curving pincers at the front of their heads.

Halberd A long pole of perhaps eight feet or more, often topped with a metal spear point and/or ax blade. Carried by NCOs as an easy way to identify them on the field of battle.

Housewife Small cloth or leather pouch containing such items as a needle and thread and used by soldiers to mend their uniforms.

Jewel of the Desert Name of the Star believed to be returning to the Hasshugeb Expanse. Also known as the Blue Star.

Korwird A long and thin multi-legged creature with needle-sharp teeth much like a centipede, except korwirds can grow more than twenty feet in length. Previously thought extinct.

Linstock A wooden staff that holds a length of lit cord used to ignite the gunpowder in a cannon.

Maiden Works Dwarf metal foundry specializing in weapons manufacture, especially the drukar.

Muraphant Standing more than fifteen feet tall, with huge ears, a long trunk, and a pair of curving tusks of black ivory, the animal is used in Elfkyna to carry supplies.

Musket A muzzle-loading, smooth-bore firearm that fires lead balls by way of a gunpowder charge placed at the base of the barrel by a ramrod.

Puttee A long strip of cloth used to wrap around a soldier's leg from the ankle to below the knee.

Rakke A large, bipedal carnivore growing up to eight feet tall and known for its ferocity and willingness to attack any living thing. Once thought to have been hunted to extinction, its return is credited to the magic of the Shadow Monarch.

Ramrod A thin metal rod used to press a lead ball and powder charge down the barrel of a musket.

Red Star Also known as the Star of the East and the Star of Sillra, this Star of Knowledge and Power returned to Elfkyna during the Battle for Luuguth Jor.

Regiment The standard military unit of the Calahrian Imperial Army comprising several hundred men armed with muskets and usually led by an officer holding the rank of colonel.

Rok har Elvish for tree's blood, meaning tree sap. As prepared by the elves of the Long Watch, the liquid acts to give the drinker renewed vitality.

Ryk faur/faurre Elvish for bond brother/sister, referring to the magical bond that is created between an elf and a Wolf Oak.

Saber A long, curved sword used primarily by the cavalry.

Sarka har Elvish for blood tree, one of the sapling offspring of the Shadow Monarch's Silver Wolf Oak. These trees thrive on the blood of the living.

Shabraque A covering placed over a saddle to protect from wear. This covering is typically colored and embroidered to signify the regiment the rider belongs to.

Shako A tall, cylindrical hat with a leather peak worn by soldiers in the Calahrian Imperial Army. It is typically adorned with a metal badge, plumage, or other devices to identify a particular regiment.

Shatterbow Double-barreled crossbow that fires explosive darts. This is Sergeant Yimt Arkhorn's main weapon.

Siggers Nickname given to soldiers in the Calahrian Army derived from the silver-green color of their uniform jackets.

Sreex A bird with large, leathery wings and a whiskered muzzle instead of a beak. It was once thought to be extinct.

Wolf Oak Ancient tree species able to channel the natural power of the world. They were brought to a state of sentience by the first elves, and since then form a magical bond with elves. Silver Wolf Oaks are rare and channel the purest energy. Elves bonding with Silver Wolf Oaks typically are unable to cope with the energy and become *diöva gruss* as they lose themselves in the natural order of the world.